F   Robson, Lucia St.
ROB   Clair
                                    55252
         Fearless

$24.45

F   Robson, Lucia St.   55252
ROB   Clair

         Fearless

$24.45

DATE	BORROWER'S NAME	

FEARLESS

A NOVEL OF
SARAH BOWMAN

FEARLESS

A NOVEL OF SARAH BOWMAN

Lucia St. Clair Robson

BALLANTINE BOOKS

The Ballantine Publishing Group

New York

A Ballantine Book
The Ballantine Publishing Group

Copyright © 1998 by Lucia St. Clair Robson

http://www.randomhouse.com

Library of Congress Cataloging-in-Publication Data
Robson, Lucia St. Clair.
Fearless : a novel of Sarah Bowman / Lucia St. Clair Robson.
        p.   cm.
ISBN 0-345-39771-1 (alk. paper)
1. Bowman, Sarah, d. 1866—Fiction. I. Title.
PS3568.O3185F4 1998
813'.54—dc21   98-5396
                                                      CIP

Text design by Ruth Kolbert

Manufactured in the United States of America

First Edition: July 1998

10   9   8   7   6   5   4   3   2   1

This book is dedicated to
the two most important men in my life:

ROBERT McCOMBS ROBSON,
who taught me to do my best to do right
June 9, 1916–January 26, 1997

And

BRIAN CHARLES DALEY,
who made every day a holiday
and every meal a feast
December 22, 1947–February 11, 1996

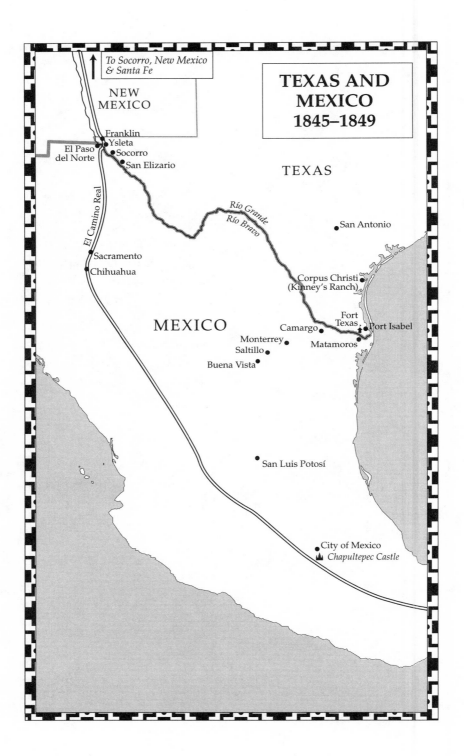

To Socorro, New Mexico
& Santa Fe

NEW
MEXICO

**TEXAS AND
MEXICO
1845–1849**

Franklin
Ysleta
El Paso
del Norte
Socorro
San Elizario

TEXAS

Río Grande
Río Bravo

San Antonio

El Camino Real

Sacramento
Chihuahua

Corpus Christi
(Kinney's Ranch)

MEXICO

Fort
Texas
Camargo
Port Isabel
Monterrey
Saltillo
Matamoros
Buena Vista

San Luis Potosí

City of Mexico
Chapultepec Castle

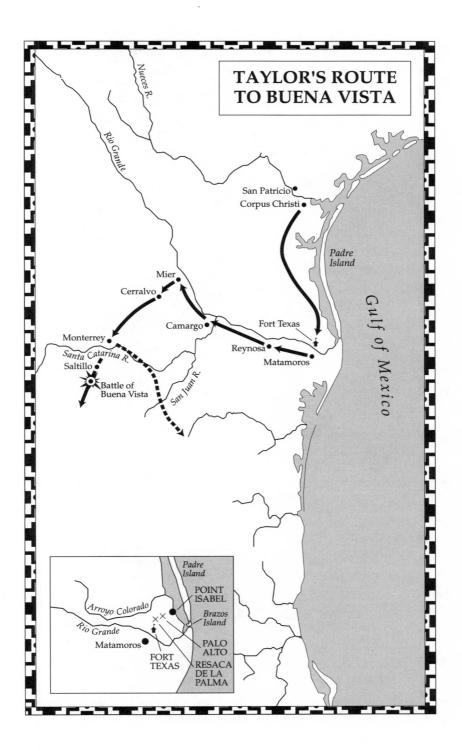

TAYLOR'S ROUTE
TO BUENA VISTA

Nueces R.

Rio Grande

San Patricio
Corpus Christi

Padre Island

Gulf of Mexico

Mier
Cerralvo
Camargo
Fort Texas
Monterrey
Reynosa
Santa Catarina R.
Saltillo
Matamoros
Battle of
Buena Vista
San Juan R.

Padre
Island
POINT
ISABEL
Arroyo Colorado
Brazos
Island
Rio Grande
PALO
ALTO
Matamoros
RESACA
DE LA
PALMA
FORT
TEXAS

ACKNOWLEDGMENTS

I'm indebted to many people who offered assistance along the way while I researched the Mexican War and Sarah's life.

Karen Snyder Roberts of the Arizona Historical Society knows as much about Sarah Borginnis Bowman as anyone, and generously shared her knowledge. Don Zuris, head curator, and Martha Lynn Hill, registrar, of the Corpus Christi Museum of Science and History, found valuable information on Zachary Taylor's army at Corpus Christi. Aaron Mahr of the National Park Service in Brownsville took me on a tour of the site of Fort Texas and made the siege there come alive. Sr. Keno at the Stillman House in Brownsville also keeps the lamp of history burning.

I want to thank Ronda Bazemore and her cohorts for showing me around the Quartermaster Museum at Yuma Crossing, Yuma, Arizona. They gave me a glimpse into what life was like in the place where Sarah spent her last years.

Jose Guzman, monument manager of the Fort Selden State Monument in Radium Springs, New Mexico, and Elva Melendrez, a ranger there, also had valuable information to pass on to me, and I thank them.

Charley Eckhardt, writer, historian, and Texan (not necessarily in that order), gave me the first, best leads on Sarah, with his copy of Brian Sandwich's monograph, *The Great Western*, (El Paso: University of Texas Press). Thanks for getting me started and keeping me going, Charley. Jeanne Williams, friend and historical novelist, also encouraged and informed me. Thanks to Darlyne Morales, friend and guide in San Antonio, and sage on things Texas. Bill Morales performed a reprise of services rendered for my first book, *Ride the Wind*. He loaned me a car to carry me on a meandering course along the Rio Grande border, and he shared his knowledge of military history, tradition, and tactics. Carl Regan trusted me with his collection of books on Mexico and the Mexican War. Judge Steve M. King of Fort Worth and Mike Tabor of Dallas sent pertinent information.

Tracey Voorhees of Annapolis infected me with her enthusiasm for horses, and Linda Stanier of the Rose Farm Horse Center gave me insights into their remarkable abilities and personalities. Joe Bohr, Michael Gear, and Eric Smith know about guns and tried to keep me straight on the subject, but any errors that appear are mine entirely. Jerry Arp has an impressive grasp of the geology, flora, and fauna of south Texas and northern Mexico and was an immense help in that area.

Vivian Waters went with me in search of Sarah's bones at the Presidio in San Francisco. Without her I probably wouldn't have found them.

I want to thank Pamela Dean Strickler, formerly of Ballantine Books, for buying the idea of a novel about Sarah's life, and for encouraging me to do it.

I owe special thanks to Jim Luceno for a task he recently completed that has nothing to do with this book, and everything to do with it. My love to Myra DiBlasio, who arrived when we needed her. Also, my affectionate gratitude to the many friends who pulled me through, especially Keith Murphy and Tom Harner.

So beware of those boarding-school lasses
And never by beauty be led;
The girl who all others surpasses
Is one who can work for her bread.

IRISH FOLK SONG

Prologue

Roaming the adobe-hard plain with his dog, his dusty sheep, the artful coyotes, and drifting hawks for company, the Mexican had witnessed strange sights. On lightning-spiked nights he had seen balls of pale green incandescence pulse in the thorny branches of the mesquite trees. He had dodged lanky funnels of wind that whirled and skipped across the ground, each with a soul trapped and moaning in its center. So he hunkered in the shade of a scraggly mesquite tree and waited for the shimmering apparition that approached from the north, wagging its tail of dust. Even at this distance he could tell the traveler was too big to be Mexican and too burdened to be a Comanche.

"*Tejano,*" the shepherd murmured. He crossed himself and waited for whatever mischief the Texans would visit on him this time.

So many thieving *tejanos* had passed by on their way to the gulf coast that he had only this remnant of his flock left to steal. He supposed the stranger might kill him, but his death, as well as his life, was in the capable if capricious hands of God. Only a capricious God could have created Texans, though some of the shepherd's compatriots claimed they were the work of the devil.

As the silhouette neared, it separated into a horse and rider and a mule carrying a small foothill of cargo. The mule veered from side to side, jerking his lead rope taut to snatch at sweet blades of mesquite grass. That was to be expected of a mule, whether he belonged to a Texan or a Mexican. Something was odd about the rider's profile though. The shepherd squinted into the late-summer glare.

¡Dios mio! He crossed himself again.

Even though the woman was sitting, the shepherd could see that she was taller than most Texans. She rode astride the old Mexican saddle, her spacious skirt hiked to the thighs of legs that looked, to him, long enough to span a river. Her hips undulated in rhythm with the big sorrel mare's easy walk. Her thin cotton shirtwaist, soaked with perspiration, required nothing of the imagination as to how generous God had been in the creation of her. She had tied her cayenne-colored mane back under the crownless brim of a battered felt hat. Errant tendrils stuck up from the center of the brim like dark flames from a chimney.

The shepherd had never seen a *colorada*, a redheaded woman, before. He had no notion of whether she was a beauty or not, but he suspected she was. And she was bounteous by any definition. God was surely good from time to time.

She stuck the stocking she was knitting into a sack slung from the saddle skirt and reined the mare to a halt. If she had dismounted she would have stood chin and collarbone above the shepherd. She wiped her face with a bandana, rearranging the coating of red dust there.

"*Hola.*" When she smiled, her teeth flashed white and even.

"*Buenos días, Señora.*" He removed his hat and held it to his chest. He might not recognize beauty in an anglo face, but he knew kindness when he saw it. Her wide, supple mouth, full lips, and startling green eyes were stamped with it.

The shepherd tried not to stare at her legs, but her bare thighs hugged the sorrel's sides at eye level, and they were magnificent. A man could find considerable shelter between them. And considerable comfort, too, he supposed.

He also decided he'd rather not look into the glittering green pools of her eyes, which he was fairly sure were amused by him, and by life in general, for that matter. In any case, his line of sight to her face was obstructed by those breasts, suitable companions for the thighs. The shepherd tried not to stare at them. He tried not to stare at the angled shadow where her thighs converged under her skirt. He studied his dog thoughtfully and waited for her to move on.

"Are General Zachary Taylor's men bivouacked anywhere in this vicinity?" she asked, though nothing but cactus, creosote bush, and small islands of mesquites interrupted the horizon that encircled them.

"*No hablo inglés, Señora,*" he said softly.

"Soldiers. *Soldados.*" Her voice was surprisingly melodic. It carried a husky undertone that stirred a furtive desire in him.

"*¡Soldados! Ay, soldados.*" A rueful smile broke through the thickets of his black mustache and eyebrows. He pointed his chin toward the southern quadrant of the horizon. "*Bastante soldados.*"

"How far?"

He shrugged again, mystified by the rigidity and harsh edges of English.

The woman looked at the shepherd's brush shelter, the blackened remains of his fire, the flat stone that he would have used to bake tortillas if the meal sack hadn't been empty. She reached into another sack hanging next to the big iron skillet slung from a hook on the saddle skirt.

"Looks like you've got no more'n mouse manure in your larder, *Señor.*" She leaned down to hand him a piece of dried beef, the size and resilience of a shoe sole, and a packet wrapped in cornhusks and tied with straw.

"*Muchas gracias.*" He smiled at her, his tobacco-stained teeth golden in his brown face.

He retrieved the goatskin water bag dangling in the mesquite tree and handed it up to her. She held the opening away from her, squeezed the bag, and squirted a stream of water into her mouth without losing a drop. To waste another's water out here was more than discourtesy.

"*Gracias, Señor.*" She nodded and kicked the mare into motion. The jerk of the lead line yanked the mule away from the rooster's-foot grass and hauled him forward. He protested loudly.

She rode away singing. The shepherd unwrapped the packet of husks and ate the square of corn bread inside. For the rest of the morning he chewed on the jerked beef and watched her diminish against the sun-bleached indigo of the sky. She dropped from sight now and then behind a gentle rise, as though the hard ground had devoured her. Or she disappeared into a copse of mesquite, only to reappear smaller on the other side. By early afternoon she had vanished completely.

Men Taken In and Done For

WHAT APPEARED TO BE STACKS OF DRIFTWOOD ON
the horizon turned into something like houses when Sarah
and her little caravan got close enough to see them clearly. A few
dozen of them leaned this way and that along a narrow, unpaved
street, though most slanted away from the prevailing gulf wind.
Fringes of tula grass hung over the eaves of the sagging roofs. The
builders had set the crooked mesquite trunks vertically in the
ground, then woven them together with osiers to form the walls.
Large gaps in the wickerwork revealed that the houses contained
nothing much inside.

In the center of the village stood a small adobe church surrounded by a mud brick wall several feet thick. It looked like the
fortress that it was, providing physical protection as well as spiritual.
Comanche raiders regularly plundered the Mexican villages of
southern Texas, and Sarah had felt the fear, as smothering as the
dust, when she passed through them.

Still singing softly to herself, she rode her big mare down the
street, through the pigs and the chickens and the barking dogs. A
muted chiming from the mule's load accompanied her. A pint-sized
tin mug had worked loose there and was pinging against the carapace of the upturned iron washtub.

Children, dark-eyed as doves, gathered in the doorways or
peered around the corners of the mesquite fences. She grinned at

them and gave a small wave of her hand close to the saddle horn, as though the greeting were their little secret. The women sat in their dooryards, grinding corn in their stone *metates* or patting out tortillas. They watched Sarah with sideways looks.

Sarah stopped at the largest garden next to several old fruit trees. Bean vines shinned up the cornstalks. Dense swags of hairy leaves and firm yellow squashes draped the picket fence of mesquite limbs. A young woman moved among the corn plants, only her head and shoulders visible. She, too, watched Sarah from the corner of her eye.

Sarah checked and tightened the lines that held her goods on the mule's back. She had done the packing herself, and obviously had experience at it. She circled the mule, tugging at the folding cot, the washtub, and the satchels to test the knots. Then she walked to the fence and looked over it at four portly, earthen pots. They wore plaited-straw harnesses, and their rounded bottoms forced them to lean against each other as though exhausted from the heat.

"Trade you for those jugs, miss."

The woman stopped with the tips of her slender fingers just touching the ear of corn she had been about to pick. She turned to look at Sarah. She had a delicate face, dark and smooth as polished walnut. Her eyes were the shape and color of watermelon seeds and they slanted slightly upward under curved black brows. She had the strong, arched nose of Indian ancestry and plum-dark lips, their curves and planes sharply defined. She reminded Sarah of Eve in the garden, for this was the sort of garden Sarah imagined when the subject of Eden came up. When she looked at Sarah, her eyes gave the impression that her soul was much older than her body, that she had seen Eden and still mourned its loss.

Sarah pointed to the pots and pulled a flowered bandana from a carpetbag behind her to offer in payment. The woman held up ten fingers.

"Ten!" Sarah affected outrage. She dangled the bandana from the top two corners and flapped it to show the size of it. It was as big as an apron. "I made these specially, *Señora.*"

The ten fingers never wavered, and Sarah could see that she wasn't dealing with some simple peasant.

"Three then." Sarah displayed the appropriate number.

The woman folded down four fingers to change her demand to

six. Sarah added two to her count. The woman nodded. She carried the pots through the gate while Sarah rifled the carpetbag in search of more bandanas. She had to untie the fifth one from the ring on the saddle skirt and empty things out of it to complete the number.

The young woman helped Sarah lash the pots on top of the mule's load, padding them with a length of calico and a pair of long flannel drawers. She walked to the mare and ran a hand down the arched neck under the fall of the white mane. The mare did a little two-step and shook her head.

"*Alazana,*" the woman said.

"Alice Ann?"

"*Alazana.*" She stroked the mare's bright, reddish-brown coat. "*Alazana.*"

"I reckon you mean that sorrel color." Sarah patted the mare's flank. "Alice Ann."

"*Sí. Alazana.*" The woman smiled, shy and sensuous and ingenuous and shrewd. She picked several chile peppers and put them in the center of a cornhusk. She folded the edges over and gave them to Sarah.

"*Para suerte, Señora.*"

"*Gracias.*" Sarah nodded to the other women who were staring openly at her now. She gave a brilliant, green-eyed smile to the children who tittered and jostled one another. "Move on, Alice Ann." She flicked the reins and started off down the street.

Only a half dozen or so men lounged about. They eyed her from under their straw hats. They would be the enemy in the war that was brewing with Mexico, and Sarah studied them with an oblique stare. They were small and lean as weathered cedar, with dark faces, hooded eyes, and the strong, arched noses of Mayan stock. Long black mustaches curtained their mouths. Their leather leggings flared below the knee. Even in the heat most of them wore cotton blankets with holes for their heads. The blankets hid their hands and the guns and knives they undoubtedly carried. Their obsidian eyes harbored a lot of larceny and no remorse.

Sarah was unfamiliar with Mexicans, but she had grown up on the Tennessee frontier and she knew farmers and herders. These were not farmers. Nor were they herders, in spite of the hundreds of horses and mules cropping the grass for miles around. She assumed they dealt in contraband, trading stolen Mexican livestock for American tobacco, whiskey, and unbleached domestic cloth. Sarah had heard that such business was brisk at Kinney's trading post where the Nueces River emptied into the gulf. Ships could carry the Mexican goods away from there without the inconvenience of customs officers or tariffs.

The mare minced along while Sarah made her regal progress through the village. She kept one hand on the butt of the old horseman's pistol stuck into the waist of her skirt and tethered to a cord around her neck. The men were treacherous, no doubt, but she figured not as treacherous as some she would encounter at Kinney's ranch. Sarah knew what sort she could expect to find there. They would be the same riffraff that trailed the army wherever it went.

A little treachery couldn't subdue her high spirits anyway. She would be seeing General Zachary Taylor's boys again. Her heart beat lighter at the prospect. Sarah hadn't much use for civilian men, but she liked soldiers of all sorts. She was especially partial to the dragoons of the Second Battalion, a unit of mounted riflemen formed to fight the Seminoles. She was more than partial to one Sergeant Jack Borginnis, her husband.

Jack was tall and solid and fearless. He had a broad chest, long, strong legs, and a mischievous twinkle in his big brown eyes. He possessed a quality not found in many men: he was at ease with a woman who could look him straight in the eye. Sarah's heart jigged at the thought of him.

She wished the steamboat *Dayton* had not left New Orleans without her. The army's heavy artillery and Jack and his broken leg had been aboard it. If she had had to do it again, though, she wouldn't have acted differently. The young laundress had had no one to help her when her child came due. Sarah had stayed with her, sure she could still board the boat before it steamed away. But the baby breeched and the mother screamed and struggled for hours before she began to bleed. So much blood.

Sarah had served as an army laundress for seven years, through some of the grimmest campaigns of the Florida war. She was used to blood, but she had wept at the sight of the stillborn child and the young woman's life flowing out of her. Sarah had sent for a priest to administer last rites, and she gave him money to bury them both.

Through the sweltering heat of August she had run to the dock and found the *Dayton*'s slip empty. The dragoons had started overland a week before, so she'd set out alone to follow them. She took the stagecoach along the old Spanish road to Nacogdoches, where she caught a ride with a freight caravan. In San Antonio she'd spent the last of her savings on the mare and the mule, the cot, the washtub, and other necessities. She had traveled the six hundred miles as fast as she could, but she'd been more than a month on the road. Now she was here. Jack and the others must have arrived long ago. He would be worried about her, she knew that. He would have set up their tent and would be waiting for her. She grinned at the thought of how the two of them would rattle those tent poles tonight.

When she spotted the wagon and riders, she pulled the hem of her skirt down to the tops of her boots, then veered to intercept them. The soldiers had piled the wagon high with mesquite limbs. They were tired and scratched, their white canvas fatigue dusters filthy and torn from the thorns. Sarah smiled to herself. Plenty of washing and mending for a laundress here.

Sarah ignored their gape-mouthed stares. She was used to those. Her height startled men and her magnanimous breasts usually struck them speechless. She had observed that men as a species had an abiding interest in a woman's breasts.

"Are you boys with Taylor?" Sarah's husky drawl was a blend of Irish whiskey, Tennessee bourbon, and the Missouri brew known as tangle-foot. Not even someone experienced in dialects could have sorted out her origins.

"Yes, ma'm." The corporal recovered first, which was why he was corporal.

"Do you know when the *Dayton* arrived?" Sarah asked.

"It hasn't, ma'm. They had to turn back to New Orleans for repairs. Old Zach says they should be here any day, though."

Sarah stiffened, disappointment tangling with apprehension in the pit of her stomach. She knew when she first saw the steamer at the New Orleans dock that the leaky old wreck wasn't sound.

Well, Jack Borginnis had come through scrapes with snake-filled swamps and Seminole bullets, alligators, panthers, and diseases of more varieties and horrors than she would have thought possible. He was indestructible. He said her love kept him safe. It always had.

"Do you know where a lady could find lodging at Kinney's ranch?"

The corporal blushed and tried to cover it by wiping his face with his bandana. "Not many ladies there, ma'm, but you could try Delfinius Burch's place."

"I thank you."

The sun was setting when she rode to the edge of the bluff at the southern rim of Texas. While the mule and the mare grazed, she sat looking out over the broad white crescent of the beach called Corpus Christi and the water glittering like quicksilver beyond. She let her right foot dangle free of the stirrup and bent her left leg in front of her, the inside of her knee hooked around the pommel. General Taylor always sat this way on his horse, and she understood why. It eased the aches that weeks in the saddle created. She flapped her skirt to stir the air underneath it and turned her face into the breeze blowing off the gulf.

A sloop and a yawl rode at anchor beyond the sandbar while a fleet of skiffs and barges ferried goods and troops ashore. Some of the soldiers frolicked in the surf as they waded ashore, finding relief from the heat. Others swarmed over the sand like an anthill that had been kicked. They were sorting and carrying off the mountains of baggage strewn up and down the beach. Sarah smiled as she watched Taylor's army wrestle order from pandemonium. It was a wonder to behold, and she never tired of seeing it. She gave them a salute and turned the mare toward Kinney's ranch.

The population of Colonel Kinney's trading post had multiplied tenfold from the original hundred or so inhabitants. The palisade was barely visible beyond the sprawl of tents and lean-tos and hastily erected shacks, most of which advertised themselves as saloons. It seemed as though everyone who wasn't hammering was playing cards. Sarah steered the mare into the smell of manure and new-sawn wood.

"Looky at this sorrel-top." The man approached spraddle-legged and ripe with menace. "She's a frockful, ain't she?" Others abandoned their tasks to watch. "I reckon I'll be your first customer, ma'm."

"I'm not in that business, sir."

"Then I'll surely be your first customer." His laugh sounded like a dry axle churning through deep sand.

Sarah regarded him fondly. He would do just fine. He was a great hairy brute, almost as tall as she was. He wore a chimney-pot hat, a mangy wool vest, and Indian leggings. He liked attention and he was attracting an audience. Yes, he would do just fine.

He made a grab for the mare's bridle as Sarah unhooked the iron skillet. It weighed twenty pounds but she regularly hefted sodden wool uniforms that weighed more. She swung the skillet with one hand. It clanged when it hit the side of his head, unseating the chimney-pot hat. Sarah thought of it as a tocsin for the unschooled. He fell as abruptly as a sack of nails dropped from a height.

She balanced the frying pan on her knee. "Do any of you gallants know where Mister Delfinius Burch has pitched camp?"

"He operates a doggery called the Annexation, over beyond the farrier's." A lathy individual pointed down the street.

Sarah hooked the skillet back on its ring and guided the mare, sidestepping in distaste at the tumult, into the throng of wagons and horses and men. It was almost dark when she approached the saloon known as the Annexation. Lengths of cotton domestic had been nailed over a wooden frame to form the walls. The lanterns inside glowed through them, giving them the look of a scrim for an amateur theatrical.

Sarah rode the mare through the hanging pair of oxhides that served as a door and led the mule after her. No one gave her more than a glance. Along the wall men lay sleeping on the dirt floor. On a small platform at the far end of the room, a partridge-shaped woman sang to a listless fiddle. Her lusty rendition of "You Never Miss Your Sainted Mother Till She's Dead and Gone to Heaven" skirmished with the whir and snap of cards being shuffled and dealt. A short, round man stood behind the counter of rough-sawn boards set on barrels. He was leaning on his elbows and surveying the card players seated on kegs around the tables.

"Mister Burch?"

He glanced up, then pushed himself hastily erect. "We don't allow jackasses in here, miss."

" 'Tis the jackasses out there that concern me." Sarah dismounted, doing a heel-and-toe to avoid the puddles of tobacco juice. "I hear you let rooms to ladies."

"You'll have to take the animals outside." Burch refused to allow even the prospect of profit to distract him. "There's a livery stable down the way."

"The mule carries the means of my enterprise, Mister Burch. Were I to let it out of my sight it would be picked cleaner than a corncob in a chicken yard." Sarah smiled. She had discovered that if the contrast of her radiant smile with her size didn't always charm people, at least it confused them.

"Show me the room," she said. "And you will be shut of the three of us."

→ ←

Sarah lay on the length of canvas nailed across a folding wooden frame. Each of the cot's legs stood in a pan of water to prevent six-legged creatures from joining her, a ploy she had learned in the Florida war. She had dragged the establishment's stinking cornhusk ticking and its fleas, lice, and bedbugs outside and left it under the crudely lettered sign that read "Men Taken In and Done for."

Now Sarah's cargo filled the tiny space. A muslin screen separated her cubicle from the one next to it. Sarah guessed this had been an army hospital tent, probably sold to Burch by some enterprising quartermaster sergeant. Burch had divided it into a dozen tiny cells, six on a side with a narrow hallway down the middle. From the energetic rustlings of her neighbors' cornshuck mattresses, Sarah surmised the business in which Burch's women boarders engaged.

Exhausted and dusty she lay fully dressed, staring up at the moon glowing through the top of the tent. She figured she was as far from her parents' cabin outside of Grinder's Stand, Tennessee, as she had ever been, but probably not as far as she was going to get. She wondered, briefly, what her mother and father and her three younger brothers and two sisters were doing. She'd had no word of them for five years, nor had she sent any. If she could have written a letter, they couldn't have read it, nor could anyone else in that mountain cove.

She listened to the shouts and laughter and oaths, the night music of any settlement like this. A man with a rushlight poked his head through the curtain that served as a door. Sarah reached down, selected a rock from the pile of them she had gathered, and heaved it. It bounced off his forehead and he backed out, cursing.

She closed her eyes, put her palms together under her chin, and murmured the same psalm she recited every night, just as her father had done for as long as she could remember.

> *Whither shall I go from thy spirit?*
> *Or whither shall I flee from thy presence?*
> *If I ascend up into heaven, thou art there,*
> *If I make my bed in hell, behold, thou art there:*
> *If I take the wings of the morning, and dwell*
> *   in the uttermost parts of the sea;*
> *Even there shall thy hand lead me.*

When she finished she made the sign of the cross.

She was floating into sleep when she heard the distant sound of "Taps" from the army's encampment. It arrived so faint it could have been imagined, or dreamed, wispy as an old memory. The melody reminded Sarah of funerals, of the bodies of the soldiers she had watched lowered into watery graves after the battle of Okeechobee that terrible Christmas almost four years ago. The memory brought tears to her eyes.

The bugle's song sounded so sweet, so familiar. The army was near. Sarah was home.

Blown All to Atoms

THE AIR OVER CORPUS CHRISTI BAY RATTLED WITH
neighing and lowing, braying and shouting and hammering.
Army carpenters were throwing together storage depots, black-
smiths' shops, and sheds for the wheelwrights to repair wagons and
gun carriages. Hundreds of vehicles and artillery carriages filled the
wagon yard.

Behind the baggage stacked on the white sand beach, the five precise rectangles of the regiments' bivouac areas followed the arc of the
shoreline for a mile or more. The surveyors were still laying down
their stakes and lines while chaos unreeled in their wake. Men
shouted and waved their arms at each other as hundreds of tents rose
in absolutely straight ranks, like dragons' teeth sown in the sand.

Between the tents and the bluff lay a large garden. To the rear of
that sprawled the picket lines for the horses and mules. As she rode
past them, Sarah heard a string of New York City oaths muttered in
a thick Irish brogue. She looked for the source.

The soldier was short and lean, with eyes the color of dark blue
smoke and a complexion that had no doubt started out pale, but had
been browned by long exposure to the sun. A new slouch hat
shaded the upper half of his slender face and a thick black mustache
hung in a shaggy valance over the lower half. Only dragoons were
allowed to cultivate mustaches, and they flaunted them.

Sarah reined in the sorrel and draped her long leg over the pommel to watch him shovel manure. Even in a pet Murphy seemed to appreciate the view. He gave her a sideways look and a wink.

"I see you drew pilot duty, Murphy."

"Aye." He regarded the odorous heap glumly and scratched the dark stubble on his chin. "Pile it here, pile it there." He didn't seem to find the old joke amusing. "I know more about horseflesh than any blighted West Point idler, yet they use me like a bloody navvy."

Sarah was accustomed to James Murphy's moods. Sobriety put him out of sorts.

He used the sleeve of his once-white canvas duster to mop at the sweat rolling down his flushed face and into his collar. He grinned as he turned to survey her properly from top to toe. When he smiled, Sarah remembered why all colors and configurations of the female gender from New York to Florida to New Orleans fell under his spell. The women of Texas and Mexico were in for a treat. Or a treatment.

"It's a sight you are for sore eyes, Western," he said.

"You're still full of blarney, Murphy." But she was pleased to hear her nickname again. No one had called her the Great Western in six weeks. When the dragoons named her that, they used as inspiration the largest steamship afloat. The *Great Western* was a sleek, powerful craft, and the first to make the transatlantic crossing. She was the talk of the country.

"I wager we'll whip a few Mexicans before it's over." Murphy seemed content to lean on his shovel, admire Sarah as others might a work of art, and chat the morning away.

"Rumor in San Antonio says that the Mexicans have attacked Old Zach's little army, whipped it, and knocked it into a cocked hat," Sarah said.

"Rumor will always outrun truth, even on a muddy track." Murphy had lost his corporal's stripes somewhere on the trip here. He must have been drinking to excess again, or brawling, or seducing some lieutenant's wife. Or he'd taken one of his unofficial holidays.

Sarah surveyed the holes in the knees of his filthy duster. "You look a sight."

"We've felt the want of your domestic skills, Western."

"No one ever accused you of fastidiousness, James." She shook her head at the hopelessness of reforming him. "Fetch me three dozen feed sacks and I'll mend your uniforms as well as wash them."

"Ye'll be bivouackin' in Sudsville then?"

"I'm fixin' to enter my name on the ration roll now." She nodded toward the tents billowing in the sea wind while men strove to subdue them with poles, ropes, and imprecations. "That would be where the Second's pitched, would it not?"

" 'Twould."

"And have they all arrived?"

"Aye. Rode in two weeks ago." He grinned at her. "The ailing, including a certain Sergeant Borginnis, were to sail later. But then I suppose you know that. I'd've thought you'd be with him."

"I missed the boat." Sarah touched her sagging hat brim in a mock salute. She kicked the mare's sides and moved on past the corrals and the garden.

The sprouts of beans and carrots and radishes stood crisp and green in spite of the heat. Sarah recognized Lieutenant Lincoln's handiwork. It was a New Englander's garden, austere and orderly, and not like the ones Sarah was used to in Tennessee. Northerners cajoled plants to grow. Southerners fought to keep the pole beans and pumpkin vines from running riot and smothering the babes in their cradles.

Sarah guided the mare among the enlisted men's tents and the patter of wooden mallets on pegs. She ignored the whistles and catcalls, but she nodded to the men she recognized. She saw a lot of new faces. The dragoons' mounted drills would be entertaining until the recruits learned to stay atop their horses.

"Western, how many Comanch did you scalp along the way?" The man rested on his ax, a tumble of split logs around him.

"I saw nary a one of the tanned banditti, Fletcher." She looked past him to a private struggling to untangle a tent's ridgepole from the ropes and cotton cloth. "Re-enlisted, did you, Martin, after all your oaths to the contrary?"

"Aye, Western. I came to see the elephant."

She chuckled. In the United States, P. T. Barnum's elephant was all the rage. People traveled hundreds of miles to see the animal. He had come to represent any new and surprising phenomenon.

As Sarah rode along the line of larger tents in Officers' Row, she heard Colonel David Twiggs long before she saw him.

"Goddamn son of a bitch!"

The last tent quaked and leaped on its guylines as though a whirlwind danced inside. The men, silent and attentive now, gathered at a safe distance. Whapping noises and the shrill of ripping fabric filled the air along with Twiggs's oaths.

Sarah raised one eyebrow. "I would say the Tiger's on a tear."

The men laughed, and she flicked the reins to move the sorrel into the outer perimeter of Twiggs's wrath. Twiggs emerged from the tent and slashed at it again with his sword. He had the shoulders of a well-worked ox and the cloth split easily. By now it hung from the ridgepole in tatters. Nearby, Lieutenant George Lincoln waited for him to wind down.

"That Judas, Jesup, sent us tents of domestic, transparent as gauze and rotten besides," Twiggs bellowed. "Now that he sits his fat backside in Washington City, he has forgotten conditions in the field. I would expect as much of the man." He rounded on Lincoln. "Lieutenant, post a requisition for tents of canvas duck."

"Yes, sir."

"Good morning, Colonel." Sarah nodded. "Lieutenant Lincoln."

"Good morning, Mrs. Borginnis." Lincoln doffed his cap and gave her a crisp bow.

His summer uniform dazzled white in the sunshine. On him the regulation forage cap, which sat like a fat blue muffin on most heads, looked dashing. He was long and bony, with big knees and elbows that seemed capable of bending either way, but he also had the air of a man perfectly at ease kissing a lady's hand.

"Western!" Twiggs's misshapen lump of a head seemed to sit directly on those massive shoulders. His round face was red as a chile pepper against his shock of white hair and beard. His pale blue eyes bulged. "I thought you had taken ship on the *Dayton* with your husband."

"Saint Peter moved about on the water, Colonel, but I do not."

Twiggs threw back his head and laughed, as enthusiastic in merriment as he was in rage. "Ah, Western, we've missed your wit and your fair form." Then he scowled. "The government hired the *Dayton* at $130 a day. At best it's a foundering scow not worth scuttling. More of Jesup's idiocy, no doubt." Twiggs turned to Lincoln. "Lieutenant, add Mrs. Borginnis to the list. Company B as always, Western?"

"Of course."

Twiggs took off his cap and wiped his brow. "You'll receive one ration a day as usual, though with Thomas Jesup in charge of supplies we may all starve." He jabbed at the ruins of the tent with his sword. "If we don't drown first in these miserable rags."

"The same Thomas Jesup who captured Osceola under a flag of truce, sir?"

"The very same. Not content with bringing mere shame upon the army, he must contrive its ruin as well."

"Will you remain with the laundresses or lodge at Colonel Kinney's ranch?" Lieutenant Lincoln asked.

"Sergeant Borginnis and I shall reside in Sudsville." Sarah glanced at the low bluff and Kinney's settlement. It looked harmless enough from this distance. "I would guess that all the thieves, cutthroats, and murderers of Texas have assembled there."

"All the thieves, cutthroats, and murderers of Texas and the United States," Twiggs barked. "Though the local variety is hardier."

"Three more men didn't answer roll this morning, sir." Lincoln must have figured he might as well give Twiggs the news now rather than set him off again later.

"Damn me!" Twiggs nodded in Sarah's direction, a perfunctory apology for his language. "Have we done nothing more than provide meals and transport for every man who wants to go westering?"

The shriek of a steam whistle distracted them from the subject of desertions.

Lieutenant Lincoln put his hand to the short bill of his cap to extend its meager shade, and stared into the glare of sunlight on water. "It looks as though you have preceded your husband by less than twenty-four hours, Mrs. Borginnis."

Twiggs lumbered off to harry his other officers and entertain the enlisted men in the process. Sarah dismounted and tethered the mare to the tent pole. She walked with Lincoln to the water's edge.

As she watched the ship grow larger, she imagined the feel of Jack in the dark, his hard, scarred body, silky with perspiration, sliding against hers. She smiled in anticipation.

"They're throwing up too much steam," Lieutenant Lincoln said.

Sarah watched the sparks and the dense plume of vapor rise from the *Dayton*'s stacks and swirl into the wind. Perspiration soaked her blouse and ran in rivulets between her breasts, while a cold stone of dread hardened in her chest.

When fire erupted on the boiler deck, it did so silently. The bodies that hurtled into the air seemed to frolic there, spinning and tumbling upward. For an instant Sarah thought it was a trick of the light or the heat. Then a low report rolled ashore.

"Dear Jesus." Sarah waded into the water, as though she could reach the ship and pull Jack Borginnis to safety.

The explosion in the first boiler launched the second one. The big iron cylinder arced through the air, hit the water, and detonated with a crash like thunder. Steam rose over the bubbling water. Sarah now heard the hissing and the screams. Flaming debris and chunks of white-hot metal rained on the men clinging to pieces of wreckage.

Paralyzed by horror, Sarah stood with the warm waters of the bay lapping around her legs. She roused herself like a wet dog shaking and waded toward the soldiers shoving the first rowboat off the beach and into the gentle surf. She was unaware that she was calling Jack's name, over and over again.

→ ←

Sarah knelt beside the man and searched for Jack Borginnis in the charred and melted flesh that used to be a face. He had Jack's big body and knobby-knuckled hands. Sarah lifted away the torn shirt and studied his chest. He had no puckered scar where a Seminole arrow had imbedded itself just above Jack's heart. Jack had carried the arrowhead with him as a good luck piece.

Sarah stood up and tied a rag over her mouth and nose to filter the stench of roasted flesh. Flies buzzed around her. The air inside of the hospital tent felt as hot as an oven. The screams and groans and pleas for water filled Sarah's head. The cries buffeted her heart, but she preferred them to silence. When a man fell silent, it meant he had died, though for many here death would be a mercy.

As the twilight deepened she moved among the scalded and mutilated bodies, careful to keep from stepping on an outstretched hand or foot. She stopped beside each one and offered a drink of water from the bucket she carried. She peered into each face, many of them charred beyond recognition. Jack was not here.

Sarah stood too fast. She swayed and squeezed her eyes shut to scatter the swarming worms of light. She looked back across the dispensary. The orderly had lit the lanterns hanging from the tent poles. In the light and shadows they threw, the tent's dirt floor seemed to writhe with dark snakes.

An old man in a soiled blue linen coat and jeans trousers and a torn straw hat stopped to speak to one of the doctors. The coat fit him like a blanket thrown over a fence pole. Its pockets bulged with the articles he had stuffed into them. He moved toward Sarah, his stiff-legged shamble pushing a compact little paunch ahead of him.

"The scene confounds one's powers of description, does it not, Western?" Zachary Taylor raised his voice to be heard over the moans and the screams.

"It does, General." Sarah kept her voice calm. Every soldier's wife knew that the possibility of death was as constant a companion for her man as his musket and boots. Sarah would not shame Jack's memory by crying openly when the possibility became fact.

"I thought we had seen the worst at Okeechobee, but this beggars it." Taylor took off his hat and released a damp mass of gray hair to curl about his ears and forehead. "Have you found your husband among these poor souls?"

"No, sir. I hoped the men might yet discover him in the water or . . ." Sarah stopped, knowing how little chance she had of finding Jack alive.

"The boat was blown all to atoms. Sergeant Borginnis isn't among the deceased we've identified. I suppose some may never be found."

"Where are the remains?" Shock numbed Sarah, her mind protecting her from the unbearable.

"In the armory. We shall have to bury them promptly. In this heat . . ." Taylor didn't have to finish.

"I'll go there after I leave here."

"To die so miserable a death from the carelessness of others." Taylor shook his big head mournfully. "Please accept my most heartfelt condolences."

"Thank you, sir."

The creases and folds of Taylor's weathered face formed a map of the sorrows and triumphs he'd experienced. Sarah knew his face well. She had been close by when some of those sorrows and triumphs had left their marks there. She figured this would add more of the former.

Now she would have creases of her own, the tracks of loss and grief. And guilt. How could she have let him go without her, to spend the last six weeks of his life apart from her, to die alone? Maybe if she had sailed with him, this wouldn't have happened. In any case she would have died with him, which was far preferable to living without him.

From the distance came the call of the bugler blowing "Retreat." The men were assembling for the evening dress parade. The soldiers would bury their dead and move on, following their duty, or maybe being pursued by it.

Sarah walked to the beach and stood where the small waves lapped the sand. She stared into the fading glow of the sun that had set. The sky looked as though a boat still burned just beyond the horizon. Now that no one was there to see them, she let tears burn their way down her cheeks.

She had always dreaded the thought that death would take him before it took her. She had spent the past eight years trying not to think about it. Now she wondered how she could possibly live without him.

She raised a hand to her hat brim and saluted. "May you rest in peace, Jack Borginnis," she whispered.

3

Poking a Rattlesnake

FTER THE EVENING DRESS PARADE LIEUTENANT
George Lincoln left the well-ordered bivouac along the
shore. He set out for a jaunt into what Sarah always called "the sulks
and the suds." He rode his big white gelding to Sudsville, the laundresses' camp in a grove of cottonwoods along a stream that emptied into the Nueces River.

The lean-tos and wagons and tents straggled about the landscape
as though a whirlwind had deposited them there. Women shouted
at the children, who shouted at each other. Unprincipled-looking
mongrels barked at everyone. Tatters of smoke rose from the
evening fires to weave into a blue-gray gauze that got caught in
the trees. Wet laundry shrouded the bushes and hung from low
branches.

The women had just returned from rinsing the clean clothes at
the river, and their wet dresses still clung to them. Not many of
them had seen the age of twenty-five for some time. From behind
tangles of hair they stared at Lincoln with a boldness he found dis-
concerting as his big gelding splashed through puddles of soapy water. The camp followers' settlement stirred melancholy in George
Lincoln, especially at twilight. The women called their children
then, and the packs of youngsters jostled and divided and scattered
for whatever makeshift shelter served as home. The husbands returned—sergeants, most of them. They sat at the cooking fires with

their blue coats unbuttoned and polished their carbines and blacked their cartridge boxes and played with their little ones.

The children made Lincoln the saddest. When he left, his own child was starting to make an impression under his young wife's apron. He had spent that last night lying with his hand cupped over the mound of her belly, marveling at the life inside.

Captain Lincoln had spent thirty-two years on earth. He had a high span of a nose and a salt-and-pepper mustache that drooped over his upper lip. His short blue jacket was tailored to fit his narrow waist. His white pantaloons gleamed spotless, which was little short of a miracle. In the pocket inside his jacket he carried volume one of John Stephen's *Incidents of Travel in Yucatan*. He pulled the brim of his shako further down over his thick black brows and pale blue eyes.

He kept the gelding on a steady course through the shoals of sun-browned, straw-haired urchins. A little specimen skittered at a crouch under the horse's belly. As the child charged out the other side, Lincoln leaned down and grabbed him by the twine that kept his feed-sack breeches from falling around his sparrow ankles. The boy continued to run in place, kicking sand against Lincoln's stirrup and marring the polish on his boot.

Lincoln lifted him off the ground. "Are you a man of the Second?"

"Yes, sir." Still suspended by his pantaloons, the boy saluted.

"Tell me where to find Mrs. Borginnis, trooper, and you'll have a penny." He set him down.

"Yonder she comes, sir."

Sarah waved her cudgel at Lincoln as she led the mule in his direction. The mule was a knife-hipped individual with ears that operated like semaphores, signaling his thoughts with their twitches and angles. He wore an expression that was part mad alchemist, part snake oil salesman, and part Christian martyr. Sarah had piled the wash high on his back.

George Lincoln had known Sarah for seven years. He had recruited her husband in 1838 and added her name to the laundress list at Jefferson barracks in Missouri when the army was mustering men for the Florida campaign. They had endured misery in the swamps together. Still, her stature, combined with the unexpected harmony of her unruly mass of dark red hair, her resolute jaw, and laughing green eyes, startled him every time he saw her. He had asked her once if the attention she received from men bothered her. She had laughed. "God saw fit to give me this carcass through no merit on my part. It's nothing to take on airs about."

Sarah broke into Lincoln's thoughts. "Won't you set a spell, Lieutenant? I'll roust the embers and brew you some coffee."

"Your coffee would be a treat indeed." Lincoln spoke with a pinched Massachusetts accent that Sarah had likened to watery soup when she first heard it. "New Englanders have a miserly kind of conversation," she had said. "As if they're loath to expend energy on the syllables." She had leaned forward, as though to let him in on a secret. Her green eyes had twinkled. "Southerners, now, they know how to stretch words to their fullest length, and fill in the spaces on the meager ones. Southern talk is like baked possum stuffed with corn bread and pecans. Ain't much meat on a possum's bones, but we make the most of it."

Sarah scratched the gelding's ears affectionately. "Well, Gator, you're sleek as a tallow candle. The lieutenant's treating you kindly, I see."

The horse whickered and nudged her shoulder with his muzzle. The mule, however, swung his head low, like a cobra preparing to strike. He drew his lips over his long yellow teeth, a look of malicious abandon in his walleyes. Before Lincoln could call a warning, Sarah backhanded him with the cudgel. It landed hard on his nose. Looking aggrieved, he sidled off to the end of his lead and grumbled.

"He gets jealous," Sarah said. "Ain't that just like a man?" She looked over at him. "Still, he's a Kentucky fox-trotter, out of Henry Clay's Mammoth Warrior himself. Don't stand near him in a thunderstorm, though. His eyes attract lightning." She looked so solemn he couldn't tell if she was tweaking him or not. He never could.

Lincoln knew Sarah had loved Jack Borginnis. Anyone with a thimbleful of sense could see that the two of them belonged together. With an oblique glance he looked for the glitter of tears, but he could detect none.

She beckoned Lincoln toward her camp and what looked like a heap of brush and laundry. She had roofed the mesquite corner poles and crosspieces of her shelter with the brush. She had tied sacking to the frame to filter the sand that the wind insinuated into every crevice. When a gust lifted the feed-sack door, Lincoln glimpsed a piece of canvas for a floor, goods heaped to the eaves, and the corner of a cot with the leg sitting in a pan of water.

She had built a tripod over the stone-lined circle of embers and lashed a table of sticks between two cottonwoods. She had almost completed a two-foot-deep trench nearby, encompassing a piece of ground about ten by fifteen feet. It looked like the foundation for a house of mesquite pickets.

With her hat brim, Sarah thrashed the sand off an upturned wooden bucket to serve as a seat for Lincoln. She went to one of the earthen jars that dangled in its wet feed-sack-and-straw sling from the branch of a mesquite tree. She poured water into a dented tin cup and offered it to him. The water was surprisingly cool.

While more water heated in the kettle, Sarah threw the wash over the roof of her lean-to and the nearby bushes. The smell of damp wool called up in Lincoln a sodden recollection of long marches in the rain.

"Your blouses and trousers have not dried yet, Lieutenant. Jake and I will deliver them in the morning." Sarah nodded toward the mule, who glared balefully at Lincoln from his picket. Two or three feet of snake dangled from his mouth. It shortened inch by inch as Jake chewed thoughtfully on it. The sorrel mare whinnied in panic and danced to the far end of her picket line at the sight of it.

"Is that a rattlesnake?" Lincoln asked.

Sarah glanced over at the mule. "It is. He relishes them, he does."

"Perhaps I could beg the loan of him sometime. I found two of the devils in my bed."

"It would be my pleasure. And Jake's. He's about cleaned them out around here." She took a snake's rattles from her pocket and gave them a shake. The dry whir set the hair to stirring on the nape of Lieutenant Lincoln's neck. He had learned to fear that sound in the Florida swamps and pine barrens. Jake's head came up expectantly, though. The mare squealed and shuddered and fishtailed.

"I awoke to find the rest of this fellow lying on my chest," Sarah said. "I had to lie still until His Snakeship decamped. Twelve buttons on this beauty. I'm keeping it for luck."

"Mrs. Borginnis, I came to express my condolences." Lincoln

reluctantly broached one of the reasons for his visit. He knew Sarah had known all along why he had come. Expressing condolences was a duty he always dreaded. "I've had little time, what with the burials, identifying the remains, writing reports and letters to the kin."

"Death requires a lot of paper and ink, doesn't it?"

"Indeed." Lincoln knew she was jesting to make his task easier and he was grateful. "Sergeant Borginnis was a fine soldier."

"I thank you, Lieutenant."

A girl no more than seven or eight arrived to occupy the silence that followed. A much smaller child rode on her hip and another trailed her like a gosling. All three had hair the color and texture of corn silk, if the corn had weathered a dust storm in a high wind. The youngest two were naked. The oldest wore a shift of calico, faded to an ashen gray.

The two little ones sat on a log and stared intently at the kettle while their sister helped Sarah shuck corn. She tilted her head slightly to stare slant-eyed up at Lincoln. Her eyes narrowed to sapphire slits behind the bleached fringes of her lashes. She had the wary expression of a creature who'd had adults spring traps on her before and intended not to be caught again if she could help it. Her teeth were too large, so that when she closed her lips over them her mouth formed a pucker. Usually her lips were slightly open, giving the lower half of her face a look of wonderment that was at odds with the watchfulness in her eyes.

"This is Nancy Skinner, Lieutenant, and her sisters, Caroline and Fanny." Sarah threw Lincoln a look over the children's heads. Lincoln knew the look. It meant that their mother was most likely entertaining some soldier and had sent them out until she finished.

Sarah didn't sit down. She didn't slow down. She took grain to the mule and mare and split kindling, one-handed, for the fire. She raised a storm of flour around her arms and elbows as she mixed dough and pummeled it on a board. Her hands blurred chopping a slab of beef and several carrots and potatoes into chunks and tossing them into the kettle. She put the dough into the iron Dutch oven, set it in the coals, and shoveled more embers onto the concave lid.

As she moved swiftly from one chore to another, Lincoln admired the grace and rhythm that made the work look effortless. Lincoln had attended a ballet once in Boston. Sarah's movements reminded him of that performance. He was struck again by how absolutely at ease in the world she seemed.

"General Taylor will be sending a fatigue detail to build houses for the laundresses." He waved his tall hat at Sarah's foundation trench. "Though I see you've wasted no time waiting for help."

"The generals were in such an all-fired rush to get here that I knew we would spend a lot of time waiting."

"Mexico will not relinquish its claim to Texas. We shall certainly have to take it from them, no doubt sooner than later."

"And have a grand jubilee in the halls of Montezuma." Sarah grinned. "The Texans will get their chance to have at Santa Anna again. That rascal owns more lives than old Sam-Jones-be-damned, don't he?"

Lincoln laughed at the memory of the wily Seminole leader who had outfoxed the army again and again. As far as any of them knew, the old man called Sam Jones was still toasting his withered knees at a campfire in the swamp that covered the lower half of Florida.

When Lincoln took off his hat, he exposed curls that were already showing strands of gray. He blamed the gray on Sam Jones and Osceola and the other Seminoles. Perched on the bucket, he rested his elbows on his knees and turned his shako in his hands. He broached the second subject that had brought him here. "I suppose you've heard the complaints about the cook?"

"I heard he used all the baking hops to brew beer."

"And deuced poor beer at that." Lincoln paused. "Six of us officers have decided to mess together. We thought you'd be just the one to cook for us. Each man will pay five dollars a month, from which you will buy supplies."

"I reckon I could."

"I'll send a detail tomorrow to start on your quarters. The brigade will supply the materials. We'll have you hutted by next week." The prospect of a woman's cooking cheered him. "The hunting here is the best I've seen. We can bring fish and quail and venison, thereby saving you the expense of beef and pork and adding to your profit. You know how to prepare game, don't you?"

"I can cook anything that walks, crawls, flies, digs, or swims, including rattlesnake, turtle, and alligator."

"It's done then, is it?"

"Done." On her way to stir the stew, she leaned over and offered her flour-whitened palm. Lincoln shook it, impressed by the strength of such a slender hand.

The lights of cookfires glowed in the darkness. Somewhere in the settlement a baby cried. The sound made Lincoln want to weep himself, with the longing to see his wife and the babe who would be born in his absence.

He would have liked to visit for a while, to enjoy in relative solitude the coffee and the stew and the evening breeze. He wanted to hear the soft cadences of a woman's voice, even though he knew he and Sarah would most likely fall to reminiscing about the Seminole campaigns, which was what he would do with the other officers. But to linger with a newly widowed woman, even to attempt the impossible task of comforting her in her grief, wouldn't be seemly.

Lincoln swung into the saddle. Sarah and the three children, a paradigm of domesticity under the soaring canopy of a star-bright sky, waved to him.

"Lieutenant," Sarah called softly after him.

He reined Gator around. "Yes."

"I thank you."

He touched the brim of his shako, then cantered away.

→ ←

Sarah rode the mule along the trail that followed the crest of the bluff. Nancy Skinner perched behind her between two wicker baskets tied on either side of the animal's haunches. The Mexican settlement had seemed alien and sinister when Sarah passed through a week ago. Now, compared with the havoc around Kinny's trading post, it looked tranquil and familiar and homey. Sarah noticed things she hadn't before.

Fruit trees shaded the houses, and beehive-shaped ovens of hardened clay sat behind some of them. Irrigation ditches carried water from the muddy stream to the gardens. Chickens scratched in the dust. Sarah found the woman among the bean vines and chile plants and the tall corn where she had first seen her. She stopped the mule at the fence and ventured one of the few Spanish phrases she knew.

"Buenos dios."

The woman flashed small, even white teeth in an amused smile.

"You just said 'Good God,' " Nancy murmured in Sarah's ear.

"Then I'll stick with my first plan and have you translate," Sarah muttered.

Sarah dismounted and tied the mule to one of the fence pickets. Nancy jumped down and shook the dust from her skirt.

Sarah was mindful of the unspoken courtesy of gates. One didn't enter them until one had introduced oneself. "Tell her my name and that I'm pleased to make her acquaintance."

The child obliged. She had been in Texas only a few weeks more than Sarah, but she ran with the children of a Mexican laundress.

"Her name is Cruz," Nancy reported. "She says she's at your service and God's."

Sarah pushed open the gate. Nancy followed her in and closed it behind them.

The woman was so lovely, so serene there among the foliage. She was the perfect shade of brown. Half the human species was darker than she and half lighter. She couldn't be more than eighteen years old.

"Nancy, tell her the frock is right pretty."

"*La Señora dice que su falda es linda,*" Nancy Skinner said.

"*Gracias.*" Cruz smiled again.

She had sewn the skirt out of four of the kerchiefs Sarah had traded her for the earthen jugs. Each quadrant was a different color and pattern. Over it she wore a white cotton tunic belted with a red sash.

Nancy interpreted as Sarah bargained for vegetables and eggs. Faces, young and old, appeared at the top of the fence to watch. Others peered through the openings between the palings. Sarah helped Cruz pick the beans and squash and chiles while Nancy crawled into the brush-covered henhouse and retrieved eggs from the indignant setters. They carried the wicker baskets and sacks to the ancient table under the trees behind the house. They sorted and packed the produce there while Cruz's neighbors watched.

Cruz added handfuls of fruit, the size and shape of quail eggs, from the tree overhead. Their golden skin was as downy as a young mouse. "*Un regalito para suerte.*"

"She says they're a present for luck." Nancy sneezed and brushed the dried chicken dressing off her hands and onto her skirt. "They're called *chabanaco.* In English they're apricots, I think."

"Gracias, Señorita."

Everyone jumped at the shout from inside the house. *"¡Carajo! ¡Maldito sea!"*

"He's cursing." Nancy kept on dutifully with her interpreting.

The women and children scattered, and terror flashed in Cruz's eyes. She stuffed the last of the corn into a sack and shouldered it. Sarah picked up the market baskets, one under each arm. Cruz propelled her through the garden with shoves to the small of her back.

They found the man beating Jake with a piece of firewood. The mule had nibbled the knot loose from the fence post and had grazed the thatch on that corner of the house as far up as he could reach. He stretched his neck for one last mouthful before he trotted out of reach. He stood chewing contemplatively as though none of it was his affair.

The man whirled, ready to take on the mule's owner. He wore the usual cotton poncho and flared leather chaps over baggy white trousers. His lidded eyes were bleary with sleep or drink, and they reminded Sarah of the rattlesnakes Jake enjoyed. The creases of a straw mat were still impressed on a cheek pitted with smallpox scars. His coarse black hair had been pressed flat on one side of his head. His features looked like lumps of terra-cotta clay pressed to the disk of his face. Sarah half expected to see a potter's thumbprint in his nose. His murky eyes were lifeless even in rage. A long scar dented his nose and trailed across his cheek to his ear.

He looked up at Sarah, an act that required him to tilt his head back. He spat a string of insults in Spanish, thought better of attacking so formidable a foe, and turned on Cruz instead. He brandished the club, and she raised an arm to deflect the blow. Sarah stepped in and caught it with one hand. The two of them struggled silently for it.

"Nancy, apologize to the esteemed gentleman and tell him that I shall recompense him for damages on the next payday." She stared him in the eye until he looked away. Both of them still gripped the club, arms and fingers taut, but sweat began to bead on his forehead. "And tell him that because he chased my mule away, I shall need his wife to help me carry the produce home."

"I don't know how to say all that, Mrs. Borginnis." Nancy had taken refuge behind Sarah's skirts.

So Sarah gave him a warning look instead. She wrenched the club from his hands and heaved it in a high arc that ended on the roof of the house.

With her pistol cocked she directed Nancy and Cruz to pick up the goods. She looked over her shoulder as she walked away. Not only had she made the man mad, she had humiliated him. She had poked a rattlesnake with her finger.

But at least Cruz was safe for the time being. Maybe he was one of those who ignited easily and burned fast, though he looked like the sort who operated most efficiently at a slow smolder. All the way back to camp, with sly innocence in his backward glances, Jake stayed just out of reach, as Sarah knew he would.

A Garboil of Gamblers

>─┼─◄◄>─•─◯─•─◄◄◄►─┼─◄

WITH HIS HAND ON SARAH'S WAIST, JACK BORGINNIS guided her through the circling flight of a waltz. Even at arm's length, they were connected by the sensuality of moving as one, beguiled by the chance to be alone in a room full of people. They had danced out of reach of the laws of gravity and the rules of decorum. The music swelled, the room whirled, and Sarah knew she could be happy doing this forever. Then a bugle call shattered the violins' melody.

Each company had at least one bugler, and all of them blew "Reveille" with varying skill and timing up and down the beach. Sarah lay with her eyes closed, trying to reconcile her dream with the cornshuck mattress and the brass serenade. She put a hand out to touch Jack and felt only the rumpled cotton coverlet. A fist of dread formed in her chest. Something was wrong. Then she remembered that something was indeed terribly wrong. Jack was gone and she couldn't even find his remains to bury them. She gasped with the grief that drove her breath away. The dread squeezing her heart turned into an ache so intense she pressed her hand against it to try to ease it. Each day she had awakened the same way.

In searching for something to distract her, she remembered that this was payday, the first since she had arrived three months ago. The first for most of the soldiers in six months. She heard the birds squabbling in the cottonwoods. The morning had started while she waltzed. If she didn't hurry, the gamblers and whiskey sellers would separate the soldiers from their money before she could collect what they owed her.

She pushed open the shutter of packing-crate wood, leaned out, and shouted for Nancy Skinner. When she opened her trunk, the layer of sand that had blown through the chinks in the walls slid off it. She shook more sand out of the apparatus she pulled from the trunk's bottom. It contained stiffened muslin and whalebone struts with enough cotton cording and tin clews to rig a catboat.

The officers' wives would be waiting in a flock for their husbands at the end of the pay line. They would bestow honeyed greetings and condescending smiles like papal benedictions on Sarah and the other laundresses. With the crowns of their bonnets hardly reaching her chin, they would manage to look down on her. But when they did, they would see her looking her best.

She lowered the corset over her head, straightening the calf-length white linen chemise under it. She was untangling the lacings when Nancy opened the door. Her baby sister, stolid and goggle-eyed, bounced on her hip.

"Good day to you, Mrs. Borginnis."

"No time to chat, child." Sarah slid the corset around so the lacings were at her back. "Tighten the harness on this rig." She reached up and grasped the beam where the canvas ceiling had fallen away.

Nancy set the baby on the floor and pulled the crisscrossed laces from the bottom up, straightening them in their eyelets. Sarah saw her glance dubiously at the roof.

"It'll hold. I told the boys to build it to withstand a Texas norther and a corset lacing."

Nancy wrapped the ends of the cords around her hands. She planted her bare foot in the small of Sarah's back and heaved while Sarah sucked in her breath. In the ensuing tussle her grip on the beam shook loose a shower of dirt, several beetles, and a scorpion from the thatch. The results were worth it, although Sarah had no mirror big enough to see them. She always turned heads, but today she would stop men in midstride. What mattered to Sarah was that she would be fashionable when she encountered the officers' wives.

She tied the cords of her padded bustle around her narrow waist and centered it at the small of her back so that it formed a semicir-

cular curve from hip to hip. She snatched her linen shirtwaist from
the stub of a twig on one of the vertical posts forming the wall of
the house. She buttoned it to the hollow of her throat and pulled
her best skirt over her head. She drew on her only pair of stockings
and garters and found her good leather pumps in the trunk. This was
not a day for sensible footwear.

She reached for the pistol hanging on another peg along with the
cartridge belt and shot pouch. It was the standard 1836 model issued to all the soldiers. The barrel flowed in an elegant arc into the
butt. The lock mechanism was case-hardened in a mottled blue-
green, the barrel polished steel. She laid her fingers along the black
walnut stock. Jack's hand had gripped that stock, and she tried to
feel his presence in it, some connection with his spirit.

She left the pistol on the peg even though on payday trouble was
as likely to appear as the army's paymaster. If someone didn't shoot
someone else before sunset, she'd be surprised. But she couldn't be
fashionable and armed too.

She shook her hair free of the braid she wore to bed, until it stood
out in a cinnamon-colored cloud around her face. She raked her fingers through it, gathered it off her shoulders, and pinned it up. The
curls spilled over the wooden combs.

She went to the water keg and splashed her face and arms, then
she scrubbed her teeth with a chewed willow stick. The water
wagon had delivered the water only yesterday, but already it tasted
bad. She would have to cadge more vinegar to make it drinkable.
Sarah gulped the last of the cold coffee, bitter and gritty with sand.
She grabbed a stale piece of corn bread from a covered tin pot, and
she noticed the hungry look in the children's eyes.

"Take the rest of the pone, Nancy, and divide it with Fanny and
Caroline."

With her sunbonnet under her arm, she hurried outside and into a
perfect November morning, sunlit and cooled by a salty gulf breeze.
A kite dipped its wings in salute overhead.

Sarah forked hay to the mule and the mustang. She shooed
Nancy and her sister outside and was putting the padlock on the
door when she saw Cruz walking toward her. Cruz wore straw sandals, a skirt of unbleached muslin, a white cotton chemise belted
with the red sash, and a fringed cotton shawl draped over her head.

Sarah had learned from Nancy that Cruz's evil-tempered husband was Antonio Águila.

"*Buenos días, Señora Borgeenis.*"

"*Buenos días, Señora Águila.*"

Cruz held out a gourd filled with hens' eggs packed in straw.

"Thank you kindly." When Sarah took the eggs, she noticed the purple ring around Cruz's eye. Her lip was cut and swollen. A bruise covered her cheek. Cruz dropped her chin and pulled her shawl lower over her forehead.

"Oh, Lord," Sarah muttered. "I haven't time for this today." But even as she said it, she was unlocking the door.

She rushed back inside and emptied a handful of tobacco into a square of sacking. She twisted the ends and tied them in a knot. She gave the packet to Cruz, who thanked her and turned to go. Sarah held her arm.

"Nancy, tell the *Señora* I need her to help me cook. She can start today."

Nancy relayed the message and translated Cruz's answer. "She says she has to take the tobacco to her husband. Pronto."

"Tell her I'll send one of the boys with it."

"She says her man will not allow it," Nancy reported.

"I'll persuade him later." Sarah wanted to scream with impatience. She knew she had to extract her pay from the soldiers of Company B before the faro and monte men, the thimbleriggers, grifters, and whiskey sellers got to them. Not to mention the fancy women from Delfinius Burch's place.

"Nancy!" Bertha Skinner's voice shrilled above Sudsville's morning racket. Nancy hustled off, the young child bouncing on her hip.

Sarah pondered what to do. After getting her wages she could accompany Cruz back to the village, pay her husband for the damage Jake had done to his roof a couple months ago, and give him her extra-potent evil eye. But what should she do with the poor woman in the meantime? The frayed hem of Cruz's skirt revealed her slender ankles and far too much of her shapely calves. The neckline of her loose chemise hung below the first gentle swells of her breasts. If she leaned forward, a bystander would have a clear view of the rest of them. And a charming view it would be, no doubt.

Cruz would cause a stir among soldiers anytime, but on payday she would incite pandemonium. With a sigh Sarah pulled her inside the house.

→ ←

The mare galloped wild-eyed down the line of tents with Sarah mounted sidesaddle and Cruz perched sideways in front of her and clinging to the mare's mane. Sarah had shrouded Cruz like an Arab in her other chemise and a shawl pinned to cover her from her throat to her hips.

When Sarah looked toward the encampment, she detected a collective stir. Three thousand soldiers were converging on the paymaster's table. A thousand or more of the riffraff from Kinney's ranch were headed there too. The bluff was alive with them. A regular garboil of gamblers, she thought. Not to mention floaters, men released from jail somewhere else on the condition that they leave town.

"¡Ay, Dios!" Cruz cried when Sarah reined hard to the left and charged the sorrel into a knot of vexatious-looking civilians in rusty black claw-hammer coats and side-by-side trousers.

They scrambled out of her way, swearing and shaking their fists. Sarah grinned back at them. Carrion crows and circuit preachers favored black garb and so did gamblers, as though to give an air of sanctity to their sinning.

The restless line of soldiers stretched down the beach, past the bakery and around the commissary tent beyond. They all craned to see the small leather sacks piled on the boards laid across two barrels. Each pouch had "U.S." stenciled on it.

The men of Company B, Second Dragoons, were nearing the table. Lieutenant Lincoln was removing one white glove to sign the receipt for his pay when Sarah reined the mare to a halt in a spray of sand and crushed shells. Cruz slid down and Sarah tethered the mare among the other horses. She led Cruz past the officers' wives flocked under their parasols. Less than a score of them had accompanied their husbands to an impending war that the newspapers predicted would end in a massacre of the small U.S. force.

"A good day to you, ladies." Sarah nodded and received reserved murmurs in return. She noticed the rise of eyebrows at the sight of Cruz. She was used to their disdain, but her face grew hot when she realized that some of them assumed Cruz was a whore, and Sarah her procuress. She wanted to stand nose to nose with them, though that would require leaning down into the quagmire of their morality, and set them straight.

Instead, she led Cruz to where the laundresses waited at the far end of the paymaster's table. Beyond them milled the grocers, tailors, barbers, gamblers, a few women in evening attire, and anyone else to whom a soldier might owe money. The sutlers had set up shop under arbors and awnings. Their prices were exorbitant, but business would be brisk. A private only earned seven dollars a month, so the competition to relieve him of it was fierce. Old Zach had forbidden whiskey sales, but Sarah knew the merchants had thrown blankets over kegs of Forty Rod, liquor that would bring a man to his knees in that distance.

"Will I see you here next payday, Mrs. Borginnis, now that you'll be preparing breakfast as well as dinner?" Lieutenant Lincoln handed her the silver dollar and change he owed her for his laundry.

"I shall take in wash for some of the gentlemen." Sarah didn't mention that she had contracted the work out to women in Cruz's village.

"The boys will be happy to hear it." He gave her his lopsided grin before he moved on. "As the bard said, 'Apparel oft proclaims the man.'"

Private James Murphy had just reached the table when a marginal member of the human race elbowed him aside. The interloper smelled like warm snake entrails. His beard resembled a stand of chaparral, thorns and all. His greasy, fringed buckskin shirt and trousers and wide-brimmed Mexican hat marked him as one of Jack Hays's Texas Rangers. Like a fair number of them, he didn't hold with standing in line.

"Here now, what d'ye think ye're about?" Murphy stepped in front of him.

"Make way, you inconsiderable Irish whiffet." The accent was British and patrician, and it sounded odd coming from such a source.

Murphy leaped on him and the two of them rolled in the sand, punching and gouging, while the rest of Company B hooted and cawed. Murphy had his teeth in the man's ear when Lieutenant

Lincoln waded into the fists and elbows, grabbed Murphy by the collar, jerked him upright, and flung him aside.

"That'll be enough, Jones." Lincoln glared at the Englishman, who picked up his hat and grumbled off. "Public brawling will earn you more time in the guardhouse, Private Murphy," Lincoln said. "You know where to report."

"Aye, sir." Murphy brushed off the sand and straightened his clothes. He swatted his hat against his leg to knock the dust from it.

In honor of payday and the convivial ladies of the brawling settlement now known as Corpus Christi, James Murphy had cleaned himself up. He hardly looked possessed of almost every vice to which a man could lay claim. Fine black curls tumbled around his face. Locks dangled to the dark eyebrows that angled like two inverted vees on the sharp ridge of bone over his gray-blue eyes. Without his usual stubble of beard Sarah could see the dimple on his chin and a patch of pink through the tan on each cheek.

His uniform fit his slender body, a feat almost impossible for taller men. The army's suppliers skimped on the cloth in the uniforms. Soldiers snatched up the few larger sizes so they could have them altered to fit. Most men were left with wrists and ankles poking out of the sleeves and legs, but not James Murphy.

"You owe me a dollar, Private Murphy," Sarah said.

But he stared past her, his mouth slightly ajar. She turned to see what had transfixed him. Cruz was staring back at him.

"Oh, Lord." Sarah took the silver coins from his hand and separated out her dollar. "Move on, man." She pressed the rest into his palm, closed his fingers around them, and gave him a shove that sent him stumbling backward. Then she turned on Cruz, who followed him with her eyes. "Have no truck with James Murphy, Mrs. Águila. He will make a shipwreck of your affections before you cross the bar." She knew as she said it that the advice was useless, even if Cruz had understood the English.

Not by Bread Alone

><del>—</del>I<del>—</del>◄◆►<del>—</del>◄◆►<del>—</del>◯<del>—</del>◄◆►<del>—</del>◄◆►<del>—</del>I<del>—</del>◄

THE SUN HOVERED ABOVE THE WESTERN HORIZON
when Sarah sauntered through the sprawl of the encampment. Singing and shouting and laughter gave the place a festive air. Payday had that effect. Through the open flaps of the same flimsy wall tents that Twiggs had raged about, she could see men sitting amid their weapons, trunks, blankets, clothes, and rucksacks. Some played cards or read novels rubbed almost illegible by the many hands through which they had passed. Others wrote letters, using sections of barrel heads for desks. The tents contained men of all sizes and dispositions and Sarah felt, at this moment, immensely fond of every one of them. Walking among them, watching them all unaware, she knew she could never be this happy anywhere else.

She carried some of her cherry cobbler fresh from baking in the Dutch oven. She intended to use it as an excuse to pass the time of day with General Taylor, though she knew Old Zach didn't require excuses for that. She found him where she expected to, sitting on a camp stool in front of his tent. Men of all ranks and stations stood around or perched on bales of hay and sacks of corn. In his straw hat, flannel shirt, faded blue-checked gingham coat, and jeans trousers, his white hair in disarray, he looked, as always, like an old farmer relaxing after a hard day behind the plow.

Then Sarah noticed the two men who sat on the edge of camp chairs and shared a pipe of tobacco with him. They wore moccasins, breechclouts, and buckskin leggings. The tails of their ruffled calico shirts hung below faded, sweat-stained army tunics. Egret plumes dangled languidly from the folds of their turbans. One had a rumpled-looking face dark as strong coffee, and cinnamon-colored eyes as remote as the African continent that had produced his ancestors.

The other was an Indian, tall and thin and taut like a tent line in a high wind. He had an imperious set to his chin and an abiding insolence in his black eyes. He wore a necklace of teeth, alligator by the look of them. A silver crescent dangled from each ear.

"If it ain't the devil in feathers," Sarah muttered.

"Western!" Taylor beckoned to her. "Look who has appeared, like Odysseus after his travels. You remember Wild Cat, don't you," he nodded toward the Indian, "and John Horse?"

"Yes, sir, I do." Sarah remembered them all right.

She remembered Wild Cat's laughter floating across the snake-infested water and sawgrass surrounding Lake Okeechobee. It wasn't fear that whuttered in her belly at the sight of them, but memories of horror, rage, grief, and, worst of all, humiliation.

She remembered searching for bodies in the stinking black swamp. She remembered hauling the wounded out through the tall grass, each blade edged with saw teeth. Hardly able to breathe for the stench of putrefaction, she had helped load the casualties onto the makeshift litters. She remembered the starved horses collapsing under the weight of the dead and wounded.

Taylor smiled fondly at his two old enemies, as though they were wayward but favored nephews. "Wild Cat has been telling me of his strategems at the Battle of Okeechobee."

I imagine he has, Sarah thought. Wild Cat lacked modesty as well as tact.

"Remember that young buck we captured before the battle?"

"Yes, sir."

"Wild Cat says Alligator left him behind for us to interrogate. He feared we wouldn't be able to locate his position if left on our own hook." Taylor seemed amused by Alligator's low opinion of his intelligence-gathering capabilities. "And a brilliant position it was, too. Never in thirty-eight years of campaigning have I encountered a more difficult assault."

Wild Cat stood abruptly, signaling that the visit had ended. John

Horse rose too and waited to the left and a little behind his friend. Taylor creaked erect, his knees and ankles popping. Wild Cat pumped the general's hand, talking rapid-fire in his own language all the while. John Horse interpreted, and Sarah was as disoriented by him as she had been when she first saw him at treaty talks in St. Augustine five years ago. The only Negroes she had ever known were slaves. John Horse was most definitely not a slave.

"Wild Cat says he's happy to see you well, General Taylor," John Horse concluded. "He says you are a great leader, with strong medicine. Under the clan arbors they still talk of your bravery and cunning. Also, Apee-aka sends his regards."

"Apee-aka. Sam-Jones-be-damned." Taylor chuckled. "Is he in Texas?"

"No." Even John Horse allowed himself the trace of a smile at the thought of Apee-aka. "He still hunts and fishes in the waters of Paha-okee. The place you call the Everglades."

"I would relish an afternoon's conversation with that old weasel." Taylor nodded to Wild Cat. "Tell Wild Cat we could use his services and yours too, John, as scouts."

Wild Cat grinned. "Comanche plenty good enemy," he said. "Mexican . . ." He shrugged. "Not so good." He picked up his rifle and saluted smartly. He and John Horse mounted their ponies and kicked them into a gallop, throwing up sand and leaping tent lines.

"Imagine, Western . . ." Taylor watched them go. "They rode from San Antonio to pay their respects. Gave me a pang of nostalgia to see them."

"The sight of them gave me a pang too, sir, but in a place you'd not find hardly any nostalgia at all."

She handed him the tin of warm cobbler. He lowered himself onto his stool and dipped a finger into the sweet syrup. He smiled his thanks before handing it to his cook. He retrieved the sword he had been polishing.

"Wild Cat is a bit of a show, but Alligator . . ." Taylor shook his head. "As a tactician, Alligator is worth every Indian I ever met and most of the white men too."

Sarah knew that. They all did. Lieutenant Lincoln had named his horse Halpatter, Alligator, in honor of him.

"What brings them to Texas?" she asked.

"The government exiled them here. They took Wild Cat when he came under a flag of truce to visit his wife and daughter. Jesup was holding the women and children prisoner—hostages, really." He shook his head at the disgrace of it.

"Jesup's paid for it, sir. I can't say as he's thought highly of anywhere."

"I suppose you're right."

Sarah put two fingers to the brim of her bonnet in a farewell salute and left Taylor and the officers refighting the Battle of Okee-chobee. She walked through a gathering darkness spangled with the campfires of soldiers roasting the delicacies they had bought that day. She intended to cajole extra flour and beans from the quarter-master sergeant, which wouldn't be an easy task. He had served in the 1814 war against the Creek Indians and in Black Hawk's War in 1832, as well as the recent campaign against the Seminole and Mi-cosukee. He was at least fifty now, tough as kiln-dried oak and wily as a wood rat.

Even if he were inclined to be generous, the army wouldn't allow it. The same authority in Washington City that allocated $130 a day to charter the dilapidated steamboat that killed Jack Borginnis and a dozen others demanded a written accounting of six cents for every empty feed sack.

In the commissary tent she found only a sullen and sober corporal and two equally morose privates. They were playing "old sledge" as though the fate of nations dangled on the outcome. They sat crosslegged on the floor with the cards laid out on a blanket among the barrels of flour, cornmeal, rice, beans, and sugar they were guarding.

"Sergeant's over yonder." The corporal gestured toward the bak-ery tent.

Sarah found the quartermaster sergeant bare-armed and floured to his shoulders as he wrestled with a mass of dough the size of a water spaniel. Other lumps shrouded in sacking sat rising on a massive table that could have accommodated a set of the Virginia reel. She didn't have to ask where the bakers were. In their enthusiasm to prove that man does not live by bread alone, army bakers often converted their bread-making ingredients to a liquid form. They had an eager market for their wares today and were probably out celebrating.

The sergeant's shiny scalp reflected the lantern's light. His procurement duties required him to make distant forays in search of beef cattle. He shaved his head, he said, to discourage Comanches from barbering him with a flencing knife. He looked up from his dough and nodded. He hadn't become any more loquacious in the week since Sarah had last seen him. That he seemed oblivious to her intrigued her. She was used to every sort of reaction except being ignored.

"Good evening, Sergeant Kelly." She perched on the corner of the table and watched him work. He had served as a cook in the Florida campaign, and he knew his way around a kitchen.

She enjoyed the sight of his biceps, thick as ship's hawsers, tensing and flexing. His scarred fingers dug into the soft dough. They squeezed it, flattened it, and folded it. With his fingertips he scooped flour from a big wooden bowl, sprinkled it over the mass, and repeated the process. The sight of someone so masculine doing a task so delicate started something to kneading deep in Sarah too.

The feeling startled her. Jack, she thought, what would you have me do?

She knew the answer. They had spoken of it only once, before the Battle of Okeechobee. Scouts had arrived with their report of the terrain. Everyone knew a lot of men would die crossing it. "Sarah, my girl," he had said, "when my time is up, you must continue to march. You're too fine a woman to retire from the field. It would be an affront to the God who created you." Sarah had put a finger to his lips to silence him. "You will live forever, Jack Borginnis." She had kissed him to make the prospect sweeter.

Now she remembered the ache in her chest each morning and the intensity of the grief that assailed her at random during the day. She thought of the craving for the touch of a man that threatened to overwhelm her at times. She knew Jack had liked Sergeant Will Kelly. More than that, he had admired him.

She hitched closer to the sergeant. "You haven't baked since Florida, have you, Will?"

He made a noise that sounded as though he were clearing his throat, but Sarah recognized it as a reply of sorts. A sly sideways glance accompanied it. The look was far more eloquent, and it told her that he hadn't been oblivious to her at all.

He did have the devil's own eyes; golden as a hot flame. Why had she never noticed before?

"In that heat you'd turn around and the batch would've risen." Sarah couldn't take her eyes off his fingers, strong and flexile and proficient.

She slid along the edge of the table until she'd arrived next to him. When she leaned over and licked a smudge of flour from the corner of his mouth, she surprised herself as much as him. She took his hands and pressed them to her breasts. With a low moan he began to caress and knead them while she pulled his face close and nipped his lower lip with her teeth.

The two of them toppled onto the table and across the dough. He moved on top of her and between the legs she wrapped around his waist. Pushing her skirt ahead of him as he went, he slid a hand up her thigh. She sighed a welcome when his fingers arrived. In their enthusiasm they overturned the big wooden bowl, but they hardly noticed the flour that drifted over them like fragrant snow.

6

If the Devil Were a Tenor

>━┼━◀▶━━●━━◀▶━┼━◀

THE LAUNDRESSES' CHILDREN SWARMED OVER THE VE-
hicles in the wagon yard, quarreling for seats from which to
watch the artillery learn maneuvers. For drama and mayhem, Hart
and Wells' troupe of thespians in Corpus Christi couldn't compete,
though the young officers accused them of murdering both tragedy
and comedy on a nightly basis. Twenty or more of the artillery carriages with their brass cannons and horse teams formed a ragged
line across the plain.

Nancy Skinner sneaked to a carriage abandoned at the edge of
the field. A missing wheel gave it the look of a genuflecting peni-
tent. She climbed the spokes of the remaining wheel to perch at the
apex where she could have the best view of the dashing Captain
Ringgold.

Sam Ringgold sat straight as a rifle barrel on his big thorough-
bred, Davey Branch, and surveyed the dejected ranks of new troops.
Bad water had afflicted most of them with the flux. They would
desert the line in ones and twos and groups to relieve themselves on
the bare plain, unavoidably in view of everyone.

"You, soldier." Ringgold pointed his crop at one of the few
healthy-looking individuals. "You'll do as a driver. Put on the spurs,
take the whip, and mount up."

"I can't ride, sir."

"You'll soon learn."

Looking convinced that fractures, dislocations, and death would be his lot, the soldier clambered aboard the rear left horse harnessed to the last carriage in line. Cruz Águila's husband and his associates had only recently delivered the horses. The animals looked as confused as the drivers and the crews who clung to their high seats on the limbers, the vehicles to which the cannons were attached.

At the sound of the bugle some of the horses reared and kicked until they managed to leap the traces. The rest of the cannons lurched forward in a clangor of trace chains and oaths, with Sam Ringgold and Davey Branch paralleling them at a gallop. The battery careened across the field in a mob so out of control that some of the children put their hands over their eyes and peeked through the slits between their fingers.

The riders on the rear horses dropped the reins and clung to the necks of their mounts, leaving the six-horse teams to veer to the left and the right. Some dashed straight for the line of men who squatted with their trousers about their ankles. The children shrieked with delight as the soldiers scattered, bare-arsed, or tripped on their fallen pantaloons and rolled into the cactus.

Teams collided and went down in roiling heaps of legs and hooves and chains. Their riders leaped clear while the crews scrambled to unhook the traces, haul the horses to their feet, rehitch them, and jump back aboard the limbers. With whips flailing and cursing creatively, the drivers set out again after the battery that by now had advanced half a mile.

A big piebald broke away from the melee. He thundered past the armory and bore down on the officers' privies as though the rider clinging to his mane had an urgent need to use them. James Murphy heard him coming and peered around the corner of the long privy shed. His three friends, all of them Irish, continued to stare at their cards.

"Would he be meaning to use the gentlemen's jakes?" the one named Riley asked.

"I think not," Murphy said.

"Praise God for that. 'Twould not do for an enlisted arse to sully the boards where an officer has shat."

The horse swerved at the last moment and his rider took wing.

He landed in the sewage that had overflowed the latrine boxes and seeped outside. He picked himself up and retrieved his black felt hat, new moments before, but looking old now. Swearing, he limped away.

Murphy rolled tobacco into a cornhusk, Mexican style, and lit it with the saltpeter-soaked cannon fuse smoldering in a can. He took a drink of white mule from the jug and passed it to his tentmate, a copper-haired, freckle-sown gnome named Seamus Hooligan. Some alchemist had brewed the whiskey less than a week ago at the ever-expanding settlement of Corpus Christi. The potion sparkled clear as spring rain, and it burned a path to Murphy's vitals.

It was the first he had had since payday. By the time the authorities had released Murphy from the guardhouse for brawling, the woman he loved had disappeared. The Great Western refused to tell him where she lived or even divulge her name. Murphy had consoled himself with most of a gallon of white mule. He had ended the day naked atop the farrier's shed shouting that he would fly to Mexico and whip ten thousand of the dirty little axle-greasers himself. The officer of the day awarded him latrine duty for his patriotism. For a fortnight he would be shoveling sand into the privies, scrubbing the seats, and igniting a handful of gunpowder in each hole to roast the cockroaches and rats and scorch the snakes that dined on them.

The sergeant major assigned him latrine fatigue so often Murphy usually held his card games here. He had a proficiency at Spanish monte and one other advantage. He knew all the subtle markings on the deck that Seamus thought was his. Murphy had left it lying near a cookfire months ago. Someone picked it up, of course, and he had been following its progress through the camp, joining games and beating the bank wherever it appeared. Now Seamus had come into possession of it, unaware that its original owner shared his tent.

Murphy had spread his blanket in the tall grass on a dune, above the ordure that saturated the lower ground. The sergeant rarely checked the rear of the shed. Officers never wandered back here.

"They caught Shawnessy." Murphy made the sign of the cross when he picked up his cards. "They found him in bed with Burch's one-armed whore."

"Were I to desert, 'twould be for no whore," Seamus said.

"And what would ye be desertin' for, Seamus darling, when they treat us so kindly here?" Twenty-eight-year-old Sean O'Raghailligh, John Riley, was tall and broad-shouldered, red-faced, homely, and vivid.

"Land." Seamus waved an arm toward the northwest and the low green rollers of grass that fled toward the horizon.

The others grunted in agreement. They all hungered for land, and they had seen what lay beyond the Nueces River. Thousands of bison and deer and mustangs grazed the plain there. Islands of fine timber grew as though planted on a gentleman's estate. The Texans claimed that pumpkin vines bolted from the ground at an inch a minute, and a man with a measuring tape had no need of a clock.

"They've promised us our acreage when the war's over," Murphy said.

"Aye, and the rivers will run with whiskey and pigs will be after asking us if we desire bacon or ham." Riley wore the artillery's wide stripes of red worsted tape sewn down the legs of his sky-blue trousers. He should have been drilling with Sam Ringgold's men, but his thumbs were still swollen and purple and too sore to handle the reins. A lieutenant had ordered him hung by them for failing to salute smartly enough.

" 'Tis no different here than in the old country," Seamus grumbled. "We Irish are still cleaning up gentlemen's shit."

"But they made us horse soldiers." Murphy had been training with his own mount, a high-spirited, compact black he had named Duke. Duke encouraged him to think army life would change for him.

"The dragoon officers would be needing servants, now wouldn't they," Riley said. "And so they've mustered a few of us as strikers."

One in every four soldiers in the United States Army came from Ireland, and more than half those who answered roll call were foreign-born. The assignment of most of them to the infantry and the army's failure to promote them rankled.

Murphy came alert as a spaniel, though, when he saw Sarah's mule loaded with mesquite limbs. The figure that led the animal along wore a shawl over her head, but Murphy recognized her. Love and Kinney's white mule whiskey sent his brain into a spin and his tenderest part into a thrumming salute.

He stood and stretched. "I'll be finishing the jakes, lads, then we can play till 'colors.' "

He picked up the slow match and rolled the keg of powder to the front of the shed. Behind him he could hear Seamus singing, " 'Did you ever hear of Captain Wattle? He was all for love, and a little for the bottle.' "

Instead of putting a small amount of powder in each hole, James poured the contents into the middle opening. He blew on the end of the cord until it glowed and tossed it in. Then he sprinted for cover.

The explosion tore the roof off and knocked the men behind the shed several feet. Flames poured out the door. Soldiers headed on the run toward the blaze.

While the fire occupied everyone, Murphy pelted between the rows of storage sheds and dodged among the horse pickets. As he approached Cruz and the mule from behind, doubts waylaid him. Murphy was unfamiliar with doubts, and he stopped abruptly in confusion.

He took off his hat and tried to slick back his unruly hair. He tucked his errant shirttail into his trousers and tugged at the waist of his white canvas fatigue jacket. He was suddenly distracted by the certainty that he reeked of the privy. He sniffed his sleeves and searched his clothes for soil that might have landed on him in the attack on the latrine. Then he took a deep breath, hurried after her, and discovered that he could think of nothing to say.

He had never been at a loss for words before. On the trip to Corpus Christi, he had wooed Mexican maidens without the bother of speaking their language. Now both his wit and his tongue failed him. His face grew hot. He held his hat to his chest and crunched the brim like a schoolboy called on to recite.

He cleared his throat and Crux turned, startled. He stared into her eyes, the softest, gentlest, loveliest eyes, fringed with such long black lashes, and he thought he would melt with yearning. Murphy stood transfixed by the sorrow in them. They ordered him to go. They begged him to stay.

She gave him a hint of a smile, with her mouth only. *"Dios le dé un buen día, su merced,"* she said.

Murphy recognized the familiar greeting: May God give you a good day, your honor. It soothed the uproar in his soul like angel song.

"And a good day to ye, too, miss." He blurted it out and cursed himself for an oaf.

She tried to edge around him, but desperation recruited some of his old snap. "I'm Murphy." He tapped his finger on his chest. "James Murphy. And what would your name be?"

"Cruz." She laid a slender brown hand on her throat, over the wooden cross that hung there. Murphy wished he could be that hand, that crucifix, for just a moment. He ached to lay his palm there and feel the flutter of her heart's beat.

"May I court ye then, Miss Cruz?"

She shook her head and backed away from him, pulling the mule's lead to position him between them.

"I would ne'er hurt ye, lass." He put out a hand to reassure her and saw the fear start up in her eyes.

"No."

It was an unequivocal rejection in his language and hers. Two letters. The slightest puff of wind. A light tap of the tip of a tongue against the roof of a mouth. A hammer blow to Murphy's heart.

"Why not?"

"No." Cruz turned and hurried away, dragging the mule after her.

"Why not?" He called again.

"*Peligroso. Muy peligroso.*"

He stood without moving, until she disappeared among the tents and windbreaks of thorny brush.

Peligroso. It was one of the few Spanish words he knew. It meant "dangerous."

→ ←

The clouds hung low like sodden gray laundry. Thunder muttered far out over the bay. Gusts toyed with Sarah's skirts as she hurried from the tents and sheds that formed Quartermaster Sergeant Will Kelly's empire. Her mouth twitched in a smile. Sergeant Kelly was tough as Spanish beef and not much for oratory, but he could love her till her toes curled. In fact, he had just done so.

He had also agreed to exchange a barrel of surplus flour and a dozen cans of peaches for her officers' excess beef rations. So many men brought in wild game that beef was a glut and not much use in barter. Sarah had disposed of it in the past by selling it at Corpus Christi, but only the sergeant had been able to procure tinned peaches.

Sarah was passing the wagonwright's shop when Murphy stepped into her path. He looked more wild-eyed than usual. Sarah regarded him warily.

"Western, I'm beggin' ye to help me."

"Stay away from her, Murphy."

"I love her."

"You love every woman you see."

"I swear I shall not harm her. I would sooner tear my heart out and feed it to the crows." He looked about to do it, too.

"You harm everything you touch, Murphy. It's not a meanness in you, you just can't help it."

He dropped to his knees in the sand and clasped his hands in supplication. "For the dear love of God, put in a kind word for me, else I die of longing."

"Get up, man." She hauled him to his feet as though he were an empty pair of pantaloons on sagging galluses. "Unless they hang men for longing, you'll not die of it, for you will end dancing on a rope, I'll wager." She started to walk away, and he followed her.

"I thought I knew love, Western, but I didn't. Real love kicks like a mule. It shakes you to your cleats like a temblor."

"I'll shake you till your teeth come loose if you come skulking about anywhere near her." Sarah strode off without looking back.

When she reached the brush arbor that sheltered her kitchen, Cruz was unloading the last of the mesquite. If Murphy's suit preoccupied her, no hint of it penetrated her calm. She finished stacking the wood near the stone-lined hearth and tripod outside the arbor.

Cruz's husband and his men had gone on what they called a trading expedition, but Sarah knew it was horse thievery, pure and simple. Cruz said he might be gone for two months or more. While he was away, she had come to work for Sarah.

Cruz dipped water from the barrel and added it to a basin of cornmeal. She patted the dough into tortillas and set them on a piece of cast-iron boiler plate over the mesquite coals. The iron was part of the wreckage from the explosion aboard the *Dayton*, and it gave

Sarah a sad tug in her chest every time she looked at it. She wasn't surprised to see Nancy Skinner helping Cruz prepare the evening meal. Sam Ringgold had joined the officers' mess, and the child usually appeared wherever he was.

Sarah's mess has grown to include a dozen lieutenants and captains. The original members lounged on campaign chairs under the nearby fly of Lieutenant Lincoln's tent. The newer ones sat on the bench under the arbor, but out of Sarah and Cruz's path from the fireplace to the worktable of stacked packing crates. The Texas Ranger, Bravo Jones, lounged among them. The tar on his filthy shirt indicated that his former occupation had been teamster.

Jones was English by birth, and an aristocratic birth at that, but Texan by necessity. No one asked him, however, what peccadillo had impelled him to cross the ocean and muddy his trouser hems in the Sabine River separating Louisiana from Texas. Rumor had it that he came home to find his wife in a situation that reduced him to the position of "also-ran." He had been tarred by other conjecture, too, as well as the thick black pitch he used to lubricate the wagon's axles.

His wide mouth and small teeth looked capable of biting the head off a chicken. His greasy hair, glossy as the carapace of a carrion beetle, was slicked back over his flaring ears. His eyes had all the hue and joy of ashes. He looked out of place among the elegant young West Pointers.

Usually the officers would be discussing Spinoza or practicing Spanish or debating theories of fluid offensives and the influence of terrain on tactics. The dragoons would be reminding the artillery that General Taylor referred to them as drones. The artillery would opine that the dragoons sat their horses like so many clothespins. In any case, the conversation would get as hot as Cruz's cuisine. But today Jones was talking about an armed expedition by Texans into Mexico three years earlier. Three hundred and fifty men bent on conquest had never returned from it.

Everyone listened. Jones had been where they were going, and in spite of bullets, lances, machetes, disease, starvation, thirst, exposure in the worst desert on the continent, Santa Anna's deadly lottery, and a firing squad, he had lived to brag about it. Some men, Sarah thought, are too ornery to do anyone the favor of dying.

"Your experience proves," Lincoln said, "the stupidity of sending twelve hundred men to make war on a nation of eight million inhabitants."

Sarah ladled out the hunks of bison boiling in the kettle, piled them into a basin, and handed them to Cruz. She moved the pot of bean soup with onions and venison to the center of the coals. The distant thunder rumbled louder now. Sarah caught Cruz's eye and glanced up at the bloated gray underbelly of clouds. Cruz nodded.

She shredded the cooked meat and tossed in chopped chiles by the fistful. Sarah covered Cruz's small hand with her big one and shook her head. Cruz extracted some of the chiles. Sarah shook her head again and Cruz picked out more. Cruz looked to heaven, as though asking God how he could have created men with such timid palates. She pressed cornmeal dough onto each wet cornhusk and placed a small portion of the meat and chile mixture on top of it. She folded the husks over to make packets, tied each one closed with straw, and set them to steam in the Dutch oven.

"I thank you, Western," Sam Ringgold said. "Mrs. Águila is overly generous with the peppers."

"Here's to that." George Lincoln lifted his glass of brandy in salute. "I've felt ablaze from those little devils."

"Maybe you were the fellow who set the jakes afire this morning." Ringgold lowered his voice enough to give the appearance of sparing feminine ears an indelicate subject, but not enough to exclude Sarah from the conversation. He knew Sarah could hold her own in any conversation, indelicate or otherwise.

Bravo Jones reached out to bar Cruz on her return from the kettle. "I'll show you my chile pepper, Señorita. It's guaranteed hot stuff."

With a flick of her wrist and unerring aim Sarah rapped his knuckles with her iron ladle. He yelped like a kicked dog.

She didn't shake the ladle at him. She held it level, pointing it at his nose while he tried to suck the pain from his hand.

"Do not ever touch anyone in my employ." She kept her voice low and calm, but even Jones knew that fury contained was more dangerous than fury vented. "Do not ever speak to them with disrespect."

He opened his mouth, glanced around, and saw that conversation had stopped and the men were watching him, amusement plain on their faces. He closed his mouth and turned away to light his pipe, shielding it from the rising wind.

Ringgold turned to a lieutenant sitting on the bench, the heavy lids of his eyes half-closed as he waited out the effects of too much brandy the night before. In his misery he had a good deal of company among the other officers, but that wasn't much consolation.

"Ulysses," Ringgold spoke loudly, maybe on purpose, and Ulysses Grant winced and squinted as though trying to minimize the pain behind his eyes. "You were superb as Desdemona Thursday night. Lucky for us Longstreet was too portly for the part. You put on quite a leg show. You should consider a career in acting."

Grant sighed, apparently decided a reply took too much effort, and went back to watching the thunderclouds charge across the bay toward them.

"The white sand beach, the tower of iron-gray clouds over the gulf, lightning unraveling at the horizon, they put me in mind of Florida." Lincoln turned his face into the wind.

"The thunderclouds looked like God's anvils there," Sarah said. "And what sparks He struck on 'em."

"Bolts that brought you upright," Lincoln added. "It was like being inside a cannon."

"We're in for some right smart weather." Jones smiled pityingly at Florida's teapot tempests. "A norther, I would guess. A Texas norther will freeze whiskey so you can carry it around in your pocket and bite off a chunk when you're thirsty."

As though to prove him right, the light faded, turning dark as late dusk. A thunderclap roared much closer than before. When the echo rolled away, Sarah heard Murphy singing in Gaelic. Its title meant "Thou Fair Pulse of My Heart." Sarah knew the song. The Irish soldiers sang it around their fires at night. Its melancholy strains often haunted the darkness, with the murmur of the surf substituting for a piper's drone.

Now Murphy stood with his hat held over his heart. Great ragged strands of lightning played along the horizon behind him. The rascal could sing, Sarah had to admit that.

"Pay him no mind, Mrs. Águila." But Sarah saw the glitter of tears in Cruz's eyes. "If the devil were a tenor," Sarah muttered. "His name would be James Murphy."

"What is that bog donkey braying about?" Jones asked.

The thunder detonated in reports that resonated in Sarah's skull and left her ears ringing.

A wind raced toward them, setting the tents to snapping in its path. Several collapsed. One ripped from its moorings and flapped away before the occupants could run out and hang on the lines. Brush flew off the arbor roof and away from the windbreaks.

The wind pushed against two men, soldiers of the guard, as they arrived at a trot. They flanked Murphy and pinioned his arms as though trying to anchor themselves and him too. Murphy continued to sing while the first huge drops hit him like a hatful of gravel.

"For what is he arrested, men?" Lincoln asked.

"He burned down the privy, sir." The guards touched the brims of their forage caps in salute. If the hats hadn't been strapped under the men's chins, they would have taken flight.

"He'll be safe in the guardhouse till Christmas." Sarah sighed in relief. Cruz was a fine helper. Sarah didn't relish love complicating things.

"The Irish are only good for arson," Jones grumbled.

"Your own Baron Macaulay disagrees with you," Lincoln said. "He describes Ireland as an inexhaustible nursery of the finest soldiers."

"A nursery of knavery and sedition."

Murphy was still singing as the guards hauled him away. He looked back over his shoulder in such a show of despair that Sarah almost pitied him.

The next crash of thunder seemed to explode the clouds, emptying them of torrents of rain that blew sideways into the arbor. Hailstones the size of pullet eggs tore through the brush roof.

Cruz began to sob. Sarah put an arm around her, felt her shiver.

"We'll be all right."

Cruz shook her head. She raised one hand, palm up, to the turbulent heavens and laid the other on her breast. "*La culpa es mía,*" she said.

"You think this is your fault?" Sarah wasn't sure if Cruz meant the storm or Murphy's arrest, and she didn't know how to ask her.

"*Sí. La culpa es mía.*"

A Plug of Whiskey

S ERGEANT WILL KELLY WAS HELPING SARAH CELEBRATE
Christmas in the warmest place in camp, her bed. She ran a
hand across the dark fuzz covering his skull. It looked like a carding
comb and felt like one too.

"Happy Christmas, old girl." He lifted her chemise and burrowed
his head between the pale bolsters of her breasts. He pulled back
the waist of her footed, red wool drawers and blew "Reveille" into
her navel. The hot explosions of his breath and the rasp of his scalp
and chin stubble sent her into a storm of laughter.

She twisted and plunged to dislodge him while the pine box
frame creaked on its stout legs. The struggle carried the two of them
over the edge. They landed in a knot of blankets in the thick layer
of straw spread over the canvas and the grain sacks on the cold
ground.

They rolled close enough to the iron stove for the sergeant to
snake a hand and arm from the bundle and feed it a few more sticks
of mesquite. Still laughing and wound in the covers, he and Sarah
hitched and humped onto the bed. They put the sergeant's blue
wool tunic and greatcoat and most of Sarah's clothes back on top of
the heap and pulled the blankets over their heads. They lay entwined in the musky fog under the heavy mound of covers, and
pressed closer together to avoid winter seeping in around the edges.

Sarah ran her fingers along the shiny welt parting the curly gray fur on the sergeant's chest. It was one of many in the map of scars that showed what he had risked for his country. Conversation would have been difficult even if he had been inclined to it. The cotton-wood branches thrashed and creaked outside. The wind shrieked like a steam whistle. Sarah and the sergeant had weighted the roof with rocks and lashed it down with guylines. They had banked sand and brush and broken shells as high as the window sills, but the house swayed and vibrated anyway. The sacking nailed to the walls bellied in the gusts blowing through cracks in the mud chinking.

As she lay in the cocoon of their shared warmth, Sarah worried about the soldiers huddled in their rotten tents on the exposed beach. The tenting was so thin the dew passed through it. By now most of the tents were probably headed for the Yucatán anyway, flapping out over the gulf like so many petrels in a rush. She wished she could wrap her arms around all the men of Company B to warm them, to cheer them this Christmas Eve.

Between the storm outside and the fusillade of the sergeant's snores in her ear, it was a wonder Sarah heard the pounding on her door. She put her red-clad feet into her boots, wrapped a blanket around her shoulders, and shuffled across the room.

She opened the door a crack and the wind hit her like an icy cataract. Nancy Skinner slipped in and hurried to stand almost close enough to the stove to ignite the cast-off dragoon's tunic she wore as a coat.

"Mama's having the pains," she said.

With a sigh, Sarah pulled on an army-issue knit undershirt over her chemise. She took her wool skirt from the heap covering the sergeant, floated it down over her head, and tied the drawstring at her waist. She put on the sergeant's tunic and her late husband's old greatcoat.

"Don't set yourself alight, child." She draped a blanket over Nancy's meager shoulders. Holding the greatcoat tight around her, she went out into the night, sliding on the frozen ground and bend-ing into needles of ice driven slantwise by the wind.

She found Nancy's sisters shivering on the cornhusk mattress. The youngest wailed dispiritedly. Bertha Skinner sat on the dirt floor, propped against the chest that held the family's few posses-sions. She wore every article of clothing she owned. Her legs sprawled in front of her, her hands clutched the taut hillock of her belly. She was as drunk as Sarah expected she would be, her red-rimmed eyes sorrowfully regarding some interior disaster. Empty brown bottles were the hut's only decoration this Christmas. Snow sifted through the cracks on the palings of the walls. It added to the drift that inched toward the worn soles of Mrs. Skinner's shoes.

Sarah hauled Mrs. Skinner to her feet and led her in a waddling stagger to the bed. She laid her on her back and covered her with the two thin blankets. She picked up the two little ones, gathered them to her chest, and wrapped the coat as far around them as it would go.

"I'll return for you, Mrs. Skinner."

She groped through the dark settlement and left the girls in Nancy's care. She was headed out again when she heard Jake complaining about his accommodations under the bare branches of the cottonwood. Snow lay between Jake's and the mare's ears and along the ridges of their backs.

The mare whickered and nuzzled Sarah, looking for the cactus fruits she fed her. Sarah warned Jake as she opened the door and led them inside. "I expect no thanks from you, but if you eat anything in my house, I shall turn you out and the devil take you."

When she returned carrying Bertha Skinner, she found the mule and the sorrel taking up half the single room, but their body heat was a blessing. Nancy had fed her sisters the last of the tortillas and the venison stew. The sergeant sat on the only stool and stared at the stove's iron door as though he could see the flames inside. He would have been far more at ease with a Seminole war party than a pocketful of female children. The younger girls sensed it, of course. They stationed themselves one at each of his knees and stared up at him without blinking.

Sarah kicked the straw into a thick pile on the floor and laid Bertha on it. Nancy was familiar with the procedure. She used the iron bar hanging near the water keg to break the ice on it. She filled the kettle and put it on the stove to heat.

The sergeant looked alarmed. "Is she about to . . . ?"

"That she is." Sarah took off his tunic and handed it to him along with his hat.

He threw on his greatcoat and was out the door before he had finished buttoning it.

Bertha Skinner was too drunk to help Sarah with the delivery, but she didn't feel much pain either. With the girls and Jake watching, Sarah eased another daughter into the world and jolted life into her with a swat on her backside. She cut the cord and tied it. She washed the infant in warm water, wrapped her in a shift, and gave her to Bertha, who was somewhat sobered by the experience.

While Nancy threw the bloody straw into the stove, Sarah added whiskey to a mug of hot water. They all climbed into bed with Bertha and the infant, and Sarah passed the mug around to warm them.

"I reckon the first Christmas was like this." Sarah watched the new child nurse at Bertha's breast. "So cold in that stable."

"Tell us the story of it," Nancy begged. And Sarah did.

When she finished, she realized the wind had quieted while she talked. Bertha began singing in German. *Stille Nacht.*

Sarah and Nancy joined her in English. "Silent night, holy night."

As Sarah lay under the heap of children smelling like a nest of puppies, she remembered past Christmases.

I have had worse, she thought.

→ ←

With his three filthy blankets wrapped around him, James Murphy left the guardhouse late in the afternoon of Christmas Eve. He wore the same clothes he had had on when he was locked up three weeks earlier. A covering of clouds the color of tarnished lead had lowered and darkened the sky considerably. A raw wind scattered the chaparral brush men had piled up as windbreaks. James had to dance to avoid their thorny branches as they blew past. From the distant cemetery he heard the mournful cadence of a drum marching someone else to his last rest.

He had heard the funeral drums constantly through the log walls of the guardhouse. It had been accompanied by explosions of thunder, flares of lightning, and rain that poured through the holes in the guardhouse roof, collected three feet deep in the tents, and turned the beach into a morass that had now frozen. More green turtles lay washed up on the beach. A few hungry men were collecting them,

but so many turtles had frozen in the past week that most of the soldiers were as sick of them as they were sick from them.

Snow began to fall, blurring the tents that James counted as he
made his way down the line of them. His teeth chattered, and he
shook like a wet dog inside his caped greatcoat. He stepped over
the tangle of stormlashing, ropes stretched up taut from pegs at the
corners of the tents and crossed over the roof ridges. When he came
to the fourteenth one, he ducked and entered.

Seamus was the only one there, but James wasn't surprised to
see the belongings of four neighbors piled inside. Their own tent
had blown away. A dirty, trampled square of ground marked its
launch site.

The coals had gone cold in the fire pit in the frozen ground.
Wood for cooking had to be hauled from farther and farther away,
and few could spare it for heat. James's breath hung in the same
cloud of vapor here as outside.

"Jamie, me darlin', welcome home." Seamus peered from the swad-
dling of blankets, scraps of canvas, rags, and a cowhide on the cot.
His voice, usually booming, barely carried across the tent. His
breath formed ice crystals on the wool of the blanket. He was pale
as tallow under his freckles, though that was hard to tell with the
red beard covering his face.

"You must be sick as a whipped dog to miss the officers' Christmas
Eve cakes and nog." James rapped a small keg of water with the
butt of his pistol. It was ice to the bottom. "Or are you after dodging
stable detail?"

"Me bowels are runnin' like a sluice, Jamie." Seamus nodded to
the leather bucket by the bed. The contents were also, mercifully,
frozen. "Me belly feels like a threshing machine's at work in the
lower end of it."

James rummaged through his chest for his only flannel shirt and
trousers and a cracked piece of mirror. He glumly surveyed his
grimy, bearded face. "Would you be warming a skin of water under
the covers?" he asked. "I must wash and shave."

"Nay. I have only a plug of whiskey in me pocket."

The old jest about the ability of a Texas norther to freeze alcohol
no longer seemed funny. "I'll wash in the whiskey then."

Seamus drew back in horror. "Ye've gone mad."

"The hounds of love are hallooing, Seamus. My heart's on a steeplechase." James peeled off the uniform and the guardhouse filth that stained it. He put on the flannel shirt over his wool drawers and undershirt.

Seamus looked at him dolefully. "I would rather be disordered in the bowels than brought low by passion for a woman. Everything women rub against begets grief."

"I've known you to rub against a woman or two." James grinned. "I'm going to find her, Seamus. I'll give her a kiss as loud as a whip crack and convince her to be mine."

"God go with ye, then." Seamus knew of Cruz's husband's reputation, and he knew James had heard about him, too. "But I'll not be giving precious whiskey to a man to spruce up for his own slaughtering."

James rubbed his teeth with his finger and spat into the sand. "I'll wash in the horse trough. They've kept it thawed." He put on his greatcoat, aware, suddenly, of how shabby it was.

"This arrived for you." Seamus extended a crumpled paper from under the covers. "The seal froze and cracked and fell off," he said apologetically.

James unfolded the letter. It had evidently passed through many hands. It was dated three months earlier. His father had written only a few lines. He read them twice.

"You know what it says, then?" he asked.

"Aye. Your father says a fog rolled in just before harvest and withered the potatoes." Seamus shivered and pulled the blankets higher under his nose. "They speak of famine throughout the country, and they want you to send them your pay."

When James read the last line again, he could almost see the faces of his eight younger brothers and sisters on the page. *Don't let us die with the hunger.*

Seamus tried to cheer him. "Duke was well when I fed him this morning. Riley's gray froze stiff as a carpenter's bench. He won't be able to skin him till springtime."

James grunted, but worry over his horse added urgency to his preparations. Propping the mirror on an upended crate, he squatted down and shook out the last drops of cinnamon oil from the small jar. He rubbed it into his scalp, spit on his broken comb, and tugged it through the tangles of his hair. Combing his mustache was less trouble. He set his wide-brimmed hat lightly on his head to dis-arrange his hair as little as possible.

His blankets were all that had kept him from freezing in the un-heated pit of the guardhouse. He draped them over Seamus.

"It's grateful I am to you evermore, Jamie lad."

"Happy Christmas, Seamus." James touched the brim of his hat and hurried out.

→ ←

The plain reached away so endlessly in all directions that even in the gloom of the storm James had the odd feeling there wouldn't be enough night to fill it. When darkness did arrive, it came suddenly, as if a black kettle had been turned upside down over him. One minute he could make out the silhouette of a few trees on the hori-zon and the next he couldn't see his little gelding's sleek black neck and ears. The wind shoved at him as though trying to turn him back. Ice pellets mixed with snow stung his face and hands.

Approaching Cruz's village, he could see scores of fires burning there. He thought fear would suck the breath from him. Maybe some of the soldiers, drunk on Christmas liquor, had made good on their threats to burn out the Mexicans. Maybe the Comanches had ridden through like death on horseback. James kicked the black into a canter and leaned lower so the horse's head would shield him from the wind.

He slowed to a walk as he entered the main street and saw that the flames were confined to small bonfires in front of the houses or contained in shallow earthenware bowls on the flat roofs. They hissed when the snowflakes fell into them. Like welcoming beacons they flickered in rows. Soft light also glowed through the cracks in the closed shutters, but no one stirred outside. The snow lay un-marked by footprints.

James rode to the stone well in the central square and looked around at the silent houses. Now that he was here, he realized he had no plan to find Cruz. He couldn't go knocking on every door asking for her. He considered shouting her name and then challeng-ing Águila when he appeared.

Instead, he walked Duke to the small adobe church, its earth-colored walls stained with night. Snow blew against the rounded corner of it and sprayed outward. James dismounted, led the horse to the church, and tied him to the railing outside.

Several candles on the altar provided the only light. They illuminated the carved oak beams and wide swirls in the thick plaster of the walls. Standing in the doorway, James crossed himself. As his eyes adjusted to the darkness, statues of the saints solidified in the black oblongs of their niches. They were as familiar to James as his family back in Ireland.

The smell of hot wax and dust and incense roused an ache for the comfort and certainty of the ancient faith. The altar stood as a silent, solid link with the God from whom he'd felt estranged since leaving home.

He saw a solitary figure kneeling on the earthen floor to one side of the altar. A black shawl covered her face and hung past her waist, but he knew she was Cruz. He walked closer and whispered the words he had practiced in the guardhouse while around him the drunks had raved and wept and pleaded with their demons, and men had made sexual accommodations with each other in dark corners, though not always voluntarily.

"*Señorita Cruz, mi cielo. Te adoro.*"

She jumped as though scalded. "Why do you come here?" She had learned some English from Sarah in the past months, and she spoke with a Mexican version of a Tennessee drawl.

"I came to ask you to live with me."

Cruz stood and took his arm. She led him behind the altar and out the small rear door. She retrieved the horse, then guided them between the shuttered houses to her own. She bolted the door, though it hardly seemed sturdy enough to keep out anyone who wanted to come in.

She knelt and blew life into the embers in the clay stove and added a few peeled sticks. The flame guttered in the cold draft, but by its feeble light James could see most of the house's single room. Its earth floor was neatly swept. Forked sticks and crosspieces supported two rough planks for a table. The other furniture consisted of a small bench, some earthenware pots, and a few faded striped cotton blankets on the floor. It hardly seemed the estate of a thief of Antonio Águila's renown.

James touched the grip of his pistol for reassurance. He felt a brief and irrational fear that the woman he loved had led him here to be killed. He peered into the shadows that clung to the walls, reared up in the corners, and hovered among the beams of peeled logs.

"Where is your husband?"

She nodded toward the south. "He goes to find mules for the *yanqui* army." She crossed her arms over her chest and buried her hands in the shawl to warm them.

They stared into each other's eyes, the cold forgotten. Cruz swayed toward him, as though drawn by the force of his desire or impelled by her own.

With her eyes closed she murmured the litany that Sarah had repeated so often Cruz had memorized it. "Way-stern says you are a prime sample of human folly."

"You can't believe half of what the Great Western says." He put his arms around her and held her against him, inhaling the aroma of mesquite smoke and candle wax in her hair.

He tilted her face up and kissed her. Motioning for her to stay where she was, he hurried outside and came back with his saddle blanket. He laid it next to the stove and took off his greatcoat to use as a cover. He couldn't bear to touch the blankets she had shared with another man. The thought of her brute of a husband taking her here in this room set the blood to ringing in James's ears.

Cruz put her arms around his neck and drew him down to lie next to her. She draped her shawl over them both. James kissed her throat, feeling with his lips the vibrations as she moaned. Lost in the warmth and the softness of her, the smoky fragrance, the silken bonds of her hair, he forgot every other woman he had known. He forgot her husband. He forgot the cold.

He forgot the time. The church bell startled him awake hours later.

"*Medianoche*," Cruz said.

"Midnight?"

"*Sí*." She stirred, sighed, nuzzled against his chest. "We should go give thanks to *La Virgen*. And say 'welcome' to the baby Jesus." She was silent awhile, reluctant to leave the haven of his arms. " '*Duermete, niño lindo*,' " she sang softly. It was an old song. The sigh of her breath stirred the hair at the opening of James's shirt.

Sleep, beautiful child in the arms of love.
The pangs of my sorrow have flown like the dove.
A la ru, a la me, a la ru, a la ru, a la me.

James rested on one elbow and looked into her face, one half shrouded in shadow, the other glowing like brown satin in the stove's light. "Then you will leave your husband and come with me?"

She trailed the tip of her finger along the square angle of his jaw and circled the slight bulge of his chin. "He is not my husband."

"Why do you live with him?"

"He say he will go to my village in the south . . ." She struggled to find the words in English. "He say he will hurt my little sister there if I do not."

"We can fetch her."

"No, we cannot." Tears welled up in Cruz's dark eyes. "She fall with the pox. Today a mule driver tells me they bury her three days ago. Tonight I pray for her soul."

Together they joined the others walking across the bare plaza. James wanted to sneak away with Cruz, but he knew she was right about not trying to hide him. James came from a village no bigger than this one and even poorer. A person might think he had done something in secret in a place such as this, but that was almost never so. Everyone knew about a sinner's fall before he landed.

As he walked with the silent congregation, James thought of his family's windowless mud dugout gouged into a wind-scoured hill. He remembered his father and mother trying to feed nine children on the potatoes they could grow in a quarter of an acre. And now the potato crop had failed.

"Why do you light these?" He gestured to the small fires outside the houses.

"They are *luminarias*. They light the road for the three kings to find the baby Jesus." Cruz pronounced it Hay-soos, a much gentler word than the harsh-sounding "Jesus," profaned so often by the soldiers.

Pine torches and candles filled the little church for the *novena*. People sang softly and sweetly in Spanish. James listened with tears streaming down his cheeks.

8

Half Dandy, Half Devil

>━━┼━◄)━━◉━━(►━┼━◄

THE SUN WAS SINKING THROUGH A GAUDY OCEAN OF gold and crimson clouds. It was an awesome spectacle, but one Cruz had seen most days of her life and she didn't notice it. She sat crosslegged on the edge of a blanket spread under a cottonwood tree, her back to a breeze that carried a welcome spring warmth in late February. A cornhusk cigarette clung with a delicate tenacity to her full bottom lip. The rising smoke brushed past her cheeks and eyelashes and caught in the dark, heavy drifts of her hair.

"Dice!" The suggestion scandalized Cruz. She looked severely across the stack of silver dollars to the man who made it and recited James's favorite poem. " 'I've told you once, I've told you twice. There're sinners in hell for shooting dice.' "

Half a dozen men sat around the blanket and ten more squatted or stood behind them. They were almost as interested in the game as in catching a glimpse of the soft swells of her breasts when she leaned over the cards and the neck of her blouse gaped.

The pasteboard rectangles blurred in her hands as she shuffled them. The sound of cards being shuffled always entranced Cruz, resonated in her bones. They whirred like a curved fingernail drawn across the ivory vanes of a noble lady's fan. It was a noise both delicate and powerful and seductive. When Cruz held a deck of monte cards, she felt as though she held her fate too. She could control not only her own destiny, but men's as well. She disdained cheating, but she knew that if she wanted to she could slide a card from the center of the deck or from the bottom. None of these soldiers would have eyes keen enough to catch her doing it even if they had been watching her hands, which few of them were.

She cut the cards, then held the pack face downward, drew off the two bottom cards, and laid them side by side on the blanket face-up. From the top she drew two more and put them facedown while the men placed their bets on them. When they finished she turned the pack faceup to expose the "gate," the bottom card. This one was the queen, and it matched none of those turned up. She shrugged, smiled, leaned over, and raked the men's bets toward her with slender fingers. The soldiers seemed to consider the view worth the loss.

She felt a burst of warm air in her ear. Duke's loud whiffle tickled deep inside her nose and throat. She shoved his velvety muzzle away, but he snuffled about in her hair as though in search of thistles to eat. His black coat glowed with the brushings James gave him three times a day, and he looked quite content with himself.

The horse had a way of cat-footing up behind Cruz and grabbing her by the sleeve or dropping his head and wrapping his tongue around her ankle. She knew James had probably sent him this time. The light was fading into dusk. James must have finished his latest attempt to teach the recruits to break the wild Mexican mules to harness. Cruz felt light-headed at the thought of him.

"Cruz." She heard his voice as clearly in her head as if he were standing next to her. She heard him often that way, his thoughts reaching her across the distance between them. He was waiting for her in the tent they shared in Sudsville.

"I go, estee-med *Señores*." Cruz spoke English with a gentle lilt, and a generosity of syllables, adding them where they didn't exist before. James said she didn't speak the language, but caressed it into being. He often asked her questions just to hear her speak the answers.

She slid the battered stack of forty cards into a leather case and slipped it down the front of her blouse to the accompaniment of a collective sigh from the men. She had more chits, silver coins, brass buttons, and packets of tobacco piled in front of her than the rest of her victims combined. She gathered them into a shawl and knotted it to form a satchel.

She smiled sweetly. "I throw monte here tomorrow, if you desire to win back what you leave with me today." She stood and smoothed her skirt.

"You might be here, Sinoreeta, but we won't." The speaker had just arrived at a trot and out of breath. "We're barnosing this *fandango*." He did the usual soldier's damage to the Spanish language, but Cruz had learned to interpret. *Fandango* meant a ball or dance. "*Vamos*," let's go, had become the all-purpose "barnose."

The other men turned to stare at him.

"Tomorrow the Second Dragoons and the Third Artillery prepare to march for the Rio Grande."

"Another rumor," someone grumbled.

In an effort to keep the army from leaving, the citizens of Corpus Christi propagated plenty of rumors. Three weeks ago they whispered that two thousand Mexicans were on their way to attack. A few days later the number had grown to twenty thousand. Two days after that they said a Mexican army of sixty thousand to a hundred thousand had been ordered to retake Texas. While the men discussed this latest news, Duke caught the corner of the blanket in his teeth and jerked it, tumbling the men's winnings into the sand. Cursing, they scrambled to recover them.

"*Medio pavo, medio diablo.*" Cruz shrugged angelically. "The horse is half dandy, half devil."

She took the blanket from him and threw it over his back. He butted her lightly between her shoulder blades as she walked away, her brows furrowed in thought. When Antonio Águila returned from his horse-thieving expedition, he would come looking for her. She would be glad to put miles between herself and his village and his pack of cutthroats.

On the other hand, the American army surrounded her here. On the march they would be scattered, prey to the sort of raid at which Águila and his men excelled. No matter where she went, he would track her. Of that she was certain.

→ ←

The sun wouldn't rise for another hour, but shadowy figures moved through the pale light of the laundresses' settlement. Crying children and barking dogs competed with the rackety roosters. Under

the cottonwood tree Sarah peeled the rough linen shirt away from
Seamus's back. He winced when the dried blood stuck to it. The
wounds from the whip pained him so much he didn't even leer at
Sarah or try to proposition her, as was his ever-optimistic wont.

"Why'd you not go 'round to the medical tent?" Sarah smeared an
ointment on the grid of lacerations that covered him from shoulders
to waist.

"I'll not be having them touch me, the dogs."

"I would say they have touched you already. What crime earned
your stripes this time?"

"No crime at all. I swear by the Holy Trinity." He crossed himself
solemnly.

Cruz heaved a thin mattress pallet onto the back of Sarah's new
wagon. *"Borracho."* She nodded at Seamus.

"Were you drunk on guard duty again?" Sarah asked.

"Partaking of whiskey is no crime."

Sarah tore a clean feed sack into strips, wrapped them around
Seamus's bony torso, and tied them in place. Seamus gingerly pulled
on a uniform blouse and his tunic.

Sarah glanced toward the encampment. It seethed with activity
now that the sun was about to appear over the horizon. The indignant brays of three thousand draft and pack mules and the swearing
of their drivers drowned out the other hubbub.

"Ye wouldn't be havin' any of the heavenly juice about, would ye,
Western?"

"Use your head, man." Sarah pointed toward the camp. "Return to
your company before you're sentenced to another lashing." She
shook her head at the obdurate folly of humanity as he ambled
away, rocking from side to side in his horseman's gait.

Jake and the new mule, Buck, stood snubbed to the cottonwood.
With growing suspicion Jake had watched Sarah and Cruz pack the
wagon. Now, when Sarah reached for his halter, he bobbed his head
and sidled away, pushing against Buck. Sarah jerked his head down
and rubbed the rest of the ointment into the raw flesh where the
new harness had rubbed away the hair and skin during Jake's tumul-
tuous training as a dray animal.

Wagons were scarce, and Sarah was proud of the rig she had
bought from the grocer in Corpus Christi. It was solidly joined and

well-ironed for all its light weight. She hopped onto the small back step and climbed over the tailgate. She wedged her feet between the water cask and the sacks of cornmeal and reached for the bundle of canvas and tent poles that Cruz heaved up to her. Sarah pulled it aboard and tied it on top of the load.

She and Cruz pulled the canvas cover across the willow hoops arcing above the load. They had just finished securing it when Bertha and her girls appeared. Nancy carried the baby on her thin hip, and Bertha wore her usual look of befuddlement, as though she had no idea why things were not going well for her.

"The master sergeant says there's no room in the baggage train for us."

"I told you to ask him about it yesterday, Mrs. Skinner."

"I was busy with the children. And the packing."

"Then you'd best go by steamer with the infantry."

"No, missus. After that terrible time I will not set foot to a boat again."

Sarah had heard about Bertha's dreadful voyage in the belly of the tub that brought her and the other hapless colonists to Texas from Germany. Sarah disliked boats herself and she understood Bertha's hatred of them.

"Have you readied everything?" she asked.

"All ready."

Sarah knew Bertha would almost certainly not have everything ready, but Sarah didn't usually bother herself with recriminations and in Bertha's case they would do no good anyway. Most of the Germans Sarah had met, and there were many in the army, had a sense of order. Bertha, however, lacked it.

"As soon as Jake and Buck are harnessed, I'll stop at your place and you can load your possibles. Nancy, Fanny, catch the chickens whilst we hitch the mules. We're late as it is."

Sarah wanted to stamp her foot with impatience. An army setting out on the march was a spectacle like none other and she wouldn't miss it if the clouds parted and the archangel Gabriel called her to judgment.

When Sarah finished harnessing the other mule, Jake backed to the end of his short lead and planted his feet. He rolled up his eyeballs, big as quail's eggs, and laid his ears against his head slick as a gambler with a fistful of pomade in his hair. He folded his leathery lips back over the ivory pickets of his teeth.

"Damn you for a devil, Jake."

He brayed a retort.

Sarah wrestled him into place next to Buck while Cruz saddled and bridled the mare. She managed to get the harness on him by putting a feed sack over his head, sliding the gear over it, then cutting it away. With a look of wary triumph she collected her whip, climbed onto the wheel hub, and settled herself on the high seat. Cruz mounted the mare. Jake sat down in the traces. Sarah climbed back down.

She poured some corn into a basin and Jake's ears swiveled at the sound of dried kernels hitting tin. She held the basin aloft and rattled it as she went by his harness mate. Jake stood up, intensely interested.

Sarah handed the basin to Cruz. "Keep ahead of us and I'll try to hold him in." She barely had time to scramble onto the seat and grab the lines before Jake took off after Cruz, the mare, and the corn.

They galloped the hundred yards to where Bertha and her brood waited in the litter of their dooryard. The wagon wheel grazed the corner of the hovel and it canted, then collapsed. Sarah added Bertha's things to the load while Jake devoured the corn with far more crunching and chomping than the few paltry kernels merited. Either the bribe sufficed or he had decided that he wanted to add to the general excitement in camp. He set off promptly at the flick of Sarah's whip.

The three older girls and the chickens perched atop the load. Bertha and the baby sat next to Sarah on the seat. Sarah steered Jake and Buck to a low dune with a good view of the line of march and braked. Nancy stood behind her, her knees pressing into Sarah's back.

"¡Madre de Dios!" Cruz crossed herself as she stared at the milling sea of horses and men.

"Didn't I tell you?" Sarah folded her arms and smiled.

Like spilled water flowing back into a jug, order began to coalesce from the confusion. Companies formed, each distinguished by the color of the horses: one of grays, another sorrels, a third bays, a fourth blacks. Four hundred soldiers stood waiting by their mounts.

Colonel Twiggs, trailed by his orderly, bugler, and staff, rode to the
head of the line. Colonel William Worth, irate that Taylor had ap-
pointed Twiggs commander instead of him, pouted in the back-
ground. The sight tickled Sarah. She had seen enough of Worth's
arrogance in the Florida war.

The buglers blew "Prepare to Mount." The men took the reins in
their left hands and put their left feet in the stirrups. At the single
note signaling "mount" they swung as one into the saddles. Sunlight
glinted on their buttons and the heavy Prussian sabers slung from
their belts. Plumes and guidons fluttered in the sea breeze. Twiggs
raised his hand, then dropped it. The long blue column, four men
abreast, moved out. As they rode, they sang the tune from the
Florida campaign that had become their signature.

> Then cheer, boys, cheer for the girls afar,
> We'll all go home at the close of the war;
> And sadly tanned by the southern sun,
> We'll spin long yarns of the deeds we've done.

Cruz stood in the stirrups and craned to see. The rumble of
hooves shook the ground, rattled the wagon, and vibrated Sarah's
bones outward from where she made contact with the wagon seat.
The men posted by, each one erect and solemn and achingly handsome in his high-collared dark blue tunic, tight light blue kersey
trousers, and tall black boots.

In 1837, a House military committee referred to the West Point
graduates as "novelists and magazine writers, effete, arrogant dabblers
in art, French and drawing." But the young officers' rigorous discipline and incessant drill had created an army on this desolate stretch
of beach. Now their men only had to prove they could fight.

By all that's holy, Sarah thought, I would take any one of them,
though I knew him for the orneriest cur in creation when afoot and
wearing mufti. She smiled at them, enjoying the tide of affection
that rose in her.

"Murphy!" Cruz waved.

James rode at the front of Company B, behind Lieutenant Lincoln. He hadn't had a drink of whiskey since Christmas. He said living with Cruz was intoxication enough. The new corporal's stripes

gleamed white on their red field against his dark blue sleeve. He sat straight and easy in the army's much-cursed new saddle. He was polished, buffed, scrubbed, and pressed, and every inch a soldier. Even Sarah had to admit it.

James had combed Duke's long mane and tail and brushed him until he gleamed like black satin. He had oiled his saddle and polished the brass fittings. Cruz had made thick tassels of red yarn to hang on his bridle along with small hawk bells. Duke held his tail high. He shook his head so that his mane flared and settled in waves along his neck and withers.

He made a sudden, mincing sidestep, a caracole, by way of salute. James turned his head toward Cruz, touched his fingers to his hat brim, then looked straight ahead again. Duke continued his high-stepping prance. Cruz flicked the reins and urged the mare forward, flanking James and Duke.

After the dragoons passed, Captain Samuel Ringgold approached on Davey Branch. The column of artillery carriages lumbered behind him, the polished brass cannons gleaming in the sun. The teams pulled with a precision no one but Ringgold himself would have thought possible a few months ago. The drivers sat their mounts as though born to the saddle. The crews standing on the carriages saluted Twiggs smartly as they passed him. Sarah's sergeant, transferred from quartermaster to artillery, rode with them. Sarah had sewn the artilleryman's crimson tape down the legs of his trousers.

Nancy Skinner waved to Ringgold, and he turned his head ever so slightly to wink at her. She jumped down from the wagon and, hiking her skirts up, ran alongside the first caisson. The sergeant and John Riley grabbed her outstretched hands and swung her up to sit atop the cannon's barrel. If Ringgold saw them do it, he pretended he hadn't. With her pale hair blowing in the wind, grinning like the Queen of Sheba, she rode off with them.

The three hundred supply and ammunition wagons followed in a storm of oaths and braying from the teamsters and the mules. The baggage wagons overflowed with laundresses and their children, and after them plodded the herds of cattle. Sarah covered her nose and mouth with a bandana, but the cloud of dust they stirred up set her to coughing.

Most of the population of Corpus Christi, including the theater troupe and a company of mountebanks, would follow the infantry later. Those who were leaving now converged behind the cattle herds. Children and animals spilled from the white canvas covers of the baggage wagons. Dogs snarled and fought among the wheels. Teams collided and their harnesses tangled while their inexperienced drivers lashed their whips and swore.

Among the carts and shays, a milk wagon or two, and the light vehicles called ambulances rolled a score of the massive local oxcarts. They rode on wheels made of solid oak disks six feet in diameter. The wheels were never truly round, which made for an interesting ride. Their Mexican owners walked alongside with brushes and buckets of lard to grease the axles, but the carts squealed like hogs being dragged along by their tails.

The poorest folk, setting out barefoot on the two-hundred-mile journey, brought up the rear. They carried their pots and kettles and clothing in baskets on their backs. Others pushed barrows among the steaming piles of ox, mule, cattle, dog, and horse dung. Sarah flicked the reins and cracked the whip and nosed Jake and Buck in at the head of the swarm. She sang her sergeant's favorite romantic ditty as she rode along.

> *Here's to women, then to liquor.*
> *There's nothin' swimmin' can be slicker.*

➤❮

Cruz woke with a start next to James. With eyes wide in the darkness she stared at the pale ceiling of the tent. Her heart pounded. She didn't know what noise had wakened her but she strained to hear the footsteps. She knew what they would sound like, heavy and erratic. In Antonio Águila's village she had cowered under the old striped cotton blanket many a night, waiting for him to return from drinking with his friends. She would lie there, trembling, knowing he would arrive drunk and angry that fate had not delivered the wealth and prominence he thought he deserved.

James stirred and turned. Still asleep, he put his arm across Cruz's chest. Sweat soaked through the cotton shift that served her as nightgown and blouse. Her skin prickled under the weight of his arm, but she lay quiet so as not to wake him.

The sudden blast of the bugle in the darkness knotted her stomach and jerked her upright, struggling to catch her breath. James groaned, sat up, and fumbled for his boots in the dark.

"Shake them, *mi amor*," Cruz murmured.

Often when the bugle jolted James from his heedless and lead-heavy sleep, he forgot that scorpions, tarantulas, stinging ants, and lizards took shelter overnight in unoccupied shoes, trousers, and helmets. Rattlesnakes were more sociable. They preferred to share the blankets with their owners.

James and Cruz dressed in the dark. Cruz ignited a straw from the embers in the tin box and lit the lantern. James sat on the ground, and she knelt in front of him. With the old razor and a small basin of water she scraped off as much of his stubble as she could. When she finished, James kissed her.

He looped his galluses around her back and pulled her to him. "I reckon we'll see Mexico today."

Cruz didn't remind him that according to the Mexicans' reckoning, the Americans had been in Mexico for the past three days, ever since they crossed the Nueces River. When an army was on the march, enemy claims of sovereignty had little weight. She only murmured, "They say Matamoros is very beautiful."

"Not so beautiful as you." He kissed her again, and she laughed when his long mustache tickled her lips and cheeks.

He fastened his galluses while he walked and she followed him out, admiring the way his sky-blue flannel trousers hugged his slender hips and haunches. She tucked in the errant tail of his blouse poking from under his tunic at the back. She leaned against him, fitting her cheek into the solid hollow of his back and shoulder blade. The unrelenting, hardpan-and-yucca-flats heat had already dampened the flannel. He turned, holding his arms out so she could see the whole package, and he flashed her a quizzical grin.

She folded her arms across her stomach and pretended to frown. Finally she held her thumbs up, a gesture of approval she had learned from Sarah. James exacted a toll of one last kiss and joined the other men hurrying through the darkness for inspection. From there they would go to the horse pickets to feed and curry their animals. Cruz picked her way through the scattered equipment to Sarah's tent.

Jake stood tied to a stake pounded into the ground nearby. He had cropped the sparse grass in a circle whose diameter equaled the length of his tether. The tail of another rattler, his breakfast, slipped up out of sight between his teeth. When Sarah's mare saw it she squealed and shuddered and crowhopped at the end of her lead. The sergeant was just leaving, and he gave Cruz a nod. He had the look of a satisfied soldier, happiest when he had the memory of heated sex behind him and the prospect of cold carnage in front of him.

Nancy Skinner was already gathering mesquite limbs for the fire. She smiled at Cruz. By the time the bugle sounded "Stable Call" and the dragoons headed for the horse pickets, Cruz had ground the green coffee beans and toasted them and put the water on to simmer. Nancy had pulled the corn cakes from the ashes where they'd baked all night. Sarah was frying hunks of beef in her two huge skillets. She set aside some for James and Seamus and the sergeant.

Over the months Cruz and Sarah had fallen into the routine of a friendship so comfortable and essential it didn't need definition. Cruz shared the pleasure Sarah said she got from cooking for her boys when they'd just emerged from their blankets and the abandon of sleep. Cruz liked this time, when those around her were still drowsy, subdued, but sharing the intimacy of the fire's light in a dark world, and stirring with a sense of purpose. At this hour the day hung unblemished by whatever was to come.

And Cruz felt safer with Sarah than with anyone else, even safer than with James. To protect her, James would fight Águila, maybe kill him, maybe be killed by him. But Sarah, Sarah was a force of nature. Águila might as well attack the wind or the flood or a mountain avalanche.

The first wisps of dawn's light were dusting the horizon when Lieutenant Lincoln and the other officers drifted into the cookfire's smoke for their breakfast. They had just come from stable duty, and they wore about them the rich aroma of horses.

They knew they would reach the Rio Grande today and that the Mexican army most likely would greet them there. They had anticipated that for months and they should have been jubilant. They were subdued, though, enervated by the heat that would only

worsen when the sun rose. They ate standing, spearing the blackened strips of meat with their knives. They washed down the crumbly
ash cakes with coffee, passing around Sarah's three mugs. Then they
hurried off to supervise preparations for the day's march. It would be
a long one and a hot one, and death might wait for some of them at
the end of it.

The Spirit of the Times

>—{—◆)—◆—⊖—◆—(◆—{—◄

ENERATIONS OF TRADERS AND HERDERS, INDIANS,
outlaws, and smugglers had used the old road that snaked
south to the Rio Grande and beyond. Hooves and wheels and feet
had worn it below the level of the parched land around it. Taylor's
little army plodded along it, through thorny masses of chaparral and
yucca that lined the trail in a wall fifteen feet high. The thorns
reached out to rip clothing and hides and the cotton duck wagon
covers. The shrill of cicadas was deafening and unrelenting. The
path narrowed until the column had to go from four abreast to two.
It stretched for miles. A cloud of umber dust enveloped the dragoons, the artillery limbers, the livestock and supply wagons, and
the civilians who followed them. By now, a week after leaving the
encampment, they all looked as though they were made of the same
earth that formed the hills.

Sarah could hardly see the sun through the pall, but it blazed like
an overstoked furnace. The ponds had shrunk to caked rings of
brine, and the number of springs dwindled. As Sarah walked beside
her wagon, her tongue felt like a club swathed in lint. She wiped the
sweat from her eyes, pulled her hat brim further down, and adjusted
the bandana higher on her nose. Squinting into the brown haze, she
could barely see the high rumps of her own two mules.

From inside the cover of the wagon Nancy coughed and so did

the Mexican women and children perched in every cranny of Sarah's goods. The stones and thorns and the scorching sand had long since worn away the straw sandals, the rags, and scraps of leather tied around their feet. Sarah had loaded them aboard as she found them limping along or fallen by the wayside. She had dumped some of her belongings and gotten out and walked to spare the mules her weight. She had found a place for Bertha and the three younger girls in one of the baggage wagons, but she didn't know how long Jake and Buck could pull the load.

Swaddled in her cotton shawl, Cruz rode Alice Ann, Sarah's sorrel mare. She wore a pair of discarded uniform trousers, mostly patches, cut down to fit her. She carried Sarah's old musket in a boot slung next to her leg. The shot bag and powder horn straps crisscrossed between her breasts. She leaned over and handed Sarah a wooden canteen.

"This is the last of it." Sarah passed it back to Nancy, who shared the water with the other children. Whenever Sarah opened her mouth to speak, dust filled it in spite of the bandana. "D'you think we shall come to a spring soon?"

"No." Cruz went back to staring into the clay-colored weeds interwoven with mats of prickly pear and briars sporting steel-colored thorns as long as her little finger.

"Are you looking for Águila in there?"

"Yes."

"That shrubbery is so solid, thirty-two-pound shot would bounce off it."

"He and his men know how to hide in the chaparral."

"I shouldn't be surprised. That's what I would expect of a snake." Sarah coughed, swallowed dust, gagged, and recovered. "We don't need you here. Ride with James."

Cruz's dark eyes came alight above the edge of her shawl. She saluted Sarah, kicked the mare's sides with her bare heels, and set out at a trot.

A shout rose from the rear. Fearing that Águila had found them, Sarah drew her pistol, set it at half cock, and peered back along the trail. She couldn't see anything in the swirling fog of dust, but the shouts turned into cheers and the cheers grew louder. A figure appeared, and Sarah could tell by the slumped profile of the rider and the hammer head of the horse that it was Zachary Taylor on Old Whitey.

Sarah pulled up at the road's edge, and Taylor reined Whitey in as he came abreast of her. The sun had burned his face the color of raw tenderloin and cracked the skin of his lips. Behind him a pair of mules pulled his pride, a springless Jersey wagon that would jolt cream into butter in a mile of road much better than this. Taylor's old blue war chest bounced around the wagon's bed.

"Are you and yours faring well, Western?"

"I favor this over swamps and sawgrass any day, General."

"The infantry's half a day's march behind me. They might not agree with you." Taylor peered into the dust ahead. "I take it the resistance predicted by the rabble at Corpus Christi has not materialized?"

"Nary a whiff of it." Sarah grinned. "And the supply train?"

"The boats arrived at Port Isabel a few hours before we did. The Seminole taught us the importance of the supply line, didn't they?"

"That they did, sir."

He touched the frayed brim of his straw hat and smiled. "A good day to you, Western."

"And to you, sir."

Sarah watched him until the brown haze swallowed him. She had met a lot of generals, but Old Rough and Ready Taylor was the only one who would stop to pass the time of day and discuss logistics with a woman.

→ ←

Sarah thought the terrain couldn't get any worse, but the next day's march proved her wrong. Her wagon had made hardly any headway since the last foul-smelling slough. It came to a stop, the wheels sunk halfway to the hubs in the sand. The mules leaned into the traces as though that were all that was holding them upright.

From the wagon seat Sarah gazed out at the blackened scenery, flat as a tabletop and burned over, probably by the Mexicans to destroy the grazing. Soot covered man and animal alike. It mixed with her sweat in a gritty coating.

With the butt of her whip Sarah rattled the first hoop supporting the wagon's canvas cover. "Lead the mules, Nancy."

She tied off the reins, climbed down from the wagon, and sank to the ankles in the hot sand. Jake and Buck stood with their lower lips almost brushing the ground. Jake mustered the energy to swing his head around and look accusingly at her.

"When I holler," she told Nancy, "heave on the mules' harnesses."

Sarah slogged to the rear of the rig and the sand flowed over the tops of her boots, scorching her feet and ankles. Most of Sarah's passengers, young and old, jumped down and stationed themselves at every wheel.

"Do you need help?" The corporal and the men assigned flanking duty among the camp followers watched from their horses.

"I reckon we can manage. There're others need you more."

Sarah adjusted her bustle and hitched her skirts up, tucking them under her belt. She lay a folded feed sack between her shoulder and the searing heat of the metal rim.

"Heave!" Sarah braced her hands on the spoke and pushed on the wheel until the veins bulged in her temples and points of light scintillated before her eyes like sparks from a steamboat's stack.

She pushed until she thought she would faint, then she pushed some more. A comet of pain seared a trail behind her eyes. The wagon swayed and she eased up, then she shoved, backed off, and shoved again, increasing the rocking motion each time. The wheels began to creep forward, axles shrieking, the rims slicing through the sand until they reached harder ground. Sarah stood up and wiped the sweat from her eyes.

"I've heard stories about the Great Western, but still I'd've wagered you couldn't do it." The man's voice was unseasonably jolly.

Sarah turned to regard him as he stood under an umbrella next to his little Indian pony. He regarded her back with the look of stunned admiration that she'd grown used to.

The crown of his black silk stovepipe was just tall enough to tickle Sarah's nose. Its narrow brim didn't cast much shade. In spite of it and the umbrella, the sun had already burned his face as red and shiny as a freshly skinned rabbit. A tight pair of linen pantaloons encased his stout legs like sausages. Both his trousers and his short linen coat had begun white, but had turned the color of dust overlaid with soot. Gaiters showed above the sand that covered his shoes.

"My name is Lewis Leonidas Allen." Beaming, he extended his hand. It was plump and moist and soft, but the grip was unexpectedly strong. The spectacle of her at close range so stunned him he forgot to let go of her hand. She disengaged him.

He tried not to stare but was only partially successful. Her sweat-soaked blouse clung to her. Amusement glinted in her emerald eyes in spite of the mired wagon, the exhausted mules, and the pitiful condition of her passengers and rig.

"I'm with *The Spirit of the Times*," he finally said.

"If your shoulder ain't to a wheel, Mister Allen, you ain't with the spirit of these times a-tall."

"*The Spirit of the Times* is a newspaper, my good woman, informing the great city of Philadelphia. I'm a journalist, determined to march with our brave gallants into the fray and relay their tales of glory to a breathless nation."

Sarah looked around at the travel-worn women and children and their mired and rickety conveyances. "We're frayed, and that's a fact."

"Actually, I've ventured amongst you fair damsels in search of a quiet haven to transcribe my notes."

"Old Zach ordered you out from underfoot, did he? Sent you back here among the bandbox and bundle, the ragtag and bobtail." Sarah climbed onto the wagon and cracked the whip. Allen chased his pony in a tight circle at the end of the reins before finally hauling him in like a large fish. He clambered aboard and rode alongside.

"Not a bit of it." He opened a leatherbound memorandum book. "On the trip here I had a most marvelous interview with Old Rough and Ready himself." He read aloud from his notes, gesturing grandly with his free hand. "The general says, 'We shall gaily enter the halls of the Montezumas and throw our wearied limbs upon a couch of down 'neath a canopy of pure gold studded with sapphires and diamonds.' "

"Old Zach never said any such." Sarah laughed. "That would be his adjutant, Perfect Bliss. Bill Bliss is Death and a stud of pale horses on rhetoric."

Allen shuffled through the book. "Ah yes. My error. That was Lieutenant William Wallace Smith Bliss."

"What did Old Zach himself say?"

"Um . . . Something about it being time for those dithering buffoons in Washington to—to . . ."

" '. . . to shit or quit the privy'?"

"I believe those were his words exactly."

"Way-stern," Cruz called softly. She pointed with her chin to the army's dust cloud ahead. It had changed shape, the compact tail expanding to either side. The column had stopped.

Everyone had been anticipating a battle since the night before when James Murphy and a platoon had returned from scouting. He had reported Mexican irregulars camped on the far bank of the fast-running stream called Arroyo Colorado.

"*Rancheros,* maybe," Cruz said.

"What are *rancheros?*" Allen held his pen poised above the notebook.

"Some say they are brave men who fight for their motherland, Mexico. Some say they are *banditos.*" Cruz swiveled in the saddle, surveying the desolate plain. "I say," she murmured in Spanish and too low for anyone but Sarah to hear, "that they are the devil's own spawn."

"I'll have a look-see." Sarah waved her hand for Cruz to dismount and took her place in the saddle.

She passed through the ragged mob of civilians who'd arrived in the infantry's dust. She circled the cattle and caught up with the weary foot soldiers. The column had halted and three thousand men crowded next to the three hundred supply wagons. Some squatted to take advantage of the slender stripes of late-morning shade the wagons provided. Others dug pits in the sand, stretched canvas on stakes over them, and collapsed inside. Most of them had removed their shoes and were lamenting their burned and bloody feet.

Sarah found her sergeant and his men extricating their six-pounder's carriage from the sand. The limbers that weren't stuck had deployed in a wide semicircle behind the dragoons. Their crews were cleaning the cannons, trying to get the grit out of the breeches.

The sergeant stared at something behind Sarah and she turned to look. Lewis Leonidas Allen had followed her on his pony. He was trying to balance the ink pot between his legs on the Mexican saddle so he could write in his memorandum book.

"Pay him no mind," Sarah said. "He's a Philadelphia scribbler." She squinted at the shimmering band of heat that distorted everything under it. "What's happening?"

"Greasers."

Sarah grinned. "The ball's about to start then, is it?"

The sergeant waxed eloquent at the prospect. "Maybe."

Sarah rode among the dragoons who hunkered in the shade of their horses. They waved and shouted to her as she passed and promised her a souvenir from the first Mexican they killed. She rode to the edge of the bluff and pulled up next to Zachary Taylor, who sat with one leg hooked around Whitey's pommel. She and Taylor looked down at the river twenty feet below. The engineers were hacking at the face of the bank, grading a gentler slope for the men and horses, wagons and artillery carriages. Details of soldiers were cutting mesquite trees to lash into rafts for the crossing.

A hundred yards away, on the other side of the river, mounted Mexicans galloped back and forth among the thorny thickets of mesquite and prickly pear. No one could tell how many there were, but their bugles blatted for a mile up and down the river. Sarah studied them, looking for Águila.

"They're raisin' dust, ain't they, General?"

"I would say so."

"How far to the Rio Grande and Matamoros from here?"

"About thirty miles." When Taylor pushed his straw hat farther back on his head, more of it broke off from the brim and drifted to join the other bits on the shoulders of his old linen duster. He gazed beyond the engineers and the stream, a hundred yards wide, and the agitated enemy on the other side. "Why would anyone want this godforsaken country, Western? A man couldn't grow whiskers here."

"Not to hear the Texans tell it. They say if a farmer plants Texas ground with corn and takes first-rate care of it, he'll harvest a hundred bushels to the acre. If he takes middlin' care of it, he'll get seventy-five. And if he don't plant at all, he'll get fifty."

Taylor chuckled and Sarah returned to the business at hand. Let Zachary Taylor get on to weather and farming and he would discuss them all day, even in a rain of artillery shells.

"General, when will we—"

"'General . . .'" Colonel William Worth galloped up on his big bay, forcing Sarah to move out of the way or be run down. "I've told Twiggs that I'm in charge of the crossing, but he takes too much upon himself." He yanked so hard on the reins that he jerked his horse's head up sharply. The harsh breaking bit had already slashed the animal's mouth. He stood with chest heaving, foam speckling his wet coat.

"Western . . ." Taylor turned so Worth couldn't see him roll his eyes toward heaven.

"Of course, General." She nodded to him, ignored Worth, and walked the big mare away so the two men could talk.

→ ←

Four companies of dragoons, Lieutenant Lincoln and the Second Dragoons in front, stood in formation next to their mounts at the head of the gentle slope the engineers had hacked in the river bank. The horses were as restless as their riders. They whickered and danced in place. Sam Ringgold's battery of six-pounders formed a wide semicircle behind them, ready to lay down covering fire. The artillery's horses, still in harness and with their drivers in the saddles, faced the rear ready to wheel and reposition the carriages.

The infantry had deployed into a mesquite grove to wait in whatever shade they could find. The band was tuning up under a striped marquee. A few acrobats and a juggler from Corpus Christi had arrived with the infantry and were practicing their routines. The women and children fidgeted at the periphery, craning to see. Sarah stood with the mare on the river bluff and fretted.

The afternoon shadows crawled farther along the baked earth. For an hour Worth and Twiggs argued with each other, Worth insisting that his temporary rank of general qualified him to lead the charge. The Mexican irregulars galloped about in the chaparral on the other side of the river. They had bugles and men who could almost play them and they were active and noisy. One individual, resplendent in wide hat, bright serape, and gold braid down the outside seams of his flared leather pants, rode to the water's edge. He stood in the stirrups and cupped his hands at his mouth to amplify his words.

Sarah couldn't hear him over the bugles, but she knew he was threatening or insulting or both. She would have guessed he was Águila, but at this distance she couldn't be sure. Her chest tightened and her stomach churned with anticipation. What must it be like for the men who had waited so many dreary months for a battle? Why was there always so much waiting in war?

"Damn you for an ass, Worth," she muttered.

She kicked the mare into a canter and rode through the lane left between Lincoln's B Company and Company A. She pulled up in front of the three officers, gave a crisp salute, and shouted so even the infantrymen and the acrobats could hear her.

"If you'll give me a strong pair of trousers, General Taylor, I will wade that river and whip every scoundrel who dares show himself."

The dragoons cheered and the infantry and artillery took it up. Taylor smiled, and nodded at Lieutenant Lincoln.

Lincoln didn't wait for the bugler, who had chosen that moment to go relieve himself. "Prepare to mount," he shouted. "Mount!"

The dragoons swung into the saddle in a peal of metal and creak of saddle leather. Lincoln raised the tip of his sword toward the cloudless sky.

"At the ready." He lowered it until it pointed at the far shore. "Forward," and the column moved out, the horses' hooves sinking in the moist sand.

Sarah put her hand to her heart and felt it thumping. She waited for the Mexican guns to sound and lay down a winnowing scythe of lead. In perfect order the dragoons rode into the water while General Worth, swearing and waving his sword, galloped to the head of the column, sending spray over everyone in his path. The water reached neck-deep on the horses in the middle of the stream. When the first dripping rank scrambled up the opposite bank without a shot fired, the band struck up "Yankee Doodle." The irregulars had vanished.

The men began unloading supply wagons so they could detach the beds and use them as pontoons. An engineer rode across with one end of a stout picket rope. He tied it to a tree on the other side, and the men pulled it taut so they could fasten the wagon beds to it for the infantry to cross. Sarah studied the swift current and the

near embankment, already churned to a slough by the dragoons'
horses.

"Lordy," she muttered. "Getting the wagons across will be a trick."
But she knew the engineers could do it. If God needed a miracle accomplished where terrain was concerned, He had but to call on the
engineers.

Bucking Authority

JAKE LURCHED OUT OF THE RIO GRANDE, DRENCHING Sarah as he went. The day had turned hotter than she would have imagined in March, and the tepid spray felt cool on her skin. She finished filling the water buckets, hung them on a pole, and slung it over her shoulders. She ignored the stares of the Mexican water sellers and wood cutters at the edge of the river and followed the mules up the embankment. When Jake reached the top, he sank to his knees and rolled over. He squirmed in the dust and the mesquite grass and pea vine, flailing his hooves at the sky. He brayed loudly enough to drown out the infernal morning bellowing of the doves occupying the orange, lemon, peach, and fig trees in the abandoned garden nearby.

Sarah regarded Jake ruefully as she passed. "Some folks are easy to please."

He regained his feet with a fusillade of grunting and made a half-hearted grab for her hat as he followed her back to the maze of tents and arbors and lean-tos of mesquite brush that the civilians had erected. Sarah stopped to watch Lewis Allen wrestle a big black contrivance. As best she could tell, he was fighting it off with a bellows.

"What in creation is that, scribbler, a hot air balloon?"

"*Caoutchouc,* my dear Western. A great advance in comfort and hygiene." Allen paused to wipe the sweat out of his eyes.

"Cow-chuck, you say?" Sarah watched him pump the bellows. The apparatus gradually assumed the shape of a squat little boat with plump, cylindrical sides.

"Vulcanized india rubber." He patted the beast affectionately on a taut flank. It gave off a strong odor of must in the heat. "I bought a pontoon from those the army was disposing of after the Florida war. I had it modified as a bathing tub."

"I heard of those rubber bridges," Sarah said. "The army'd given up on them by the time we got there. The Seminoles learned right quick to shoot holes in them. They sank the whole enterprise."

A short brown man approached bent almost double under the water jug on his back. He had the same generosity of nose and noble slant between chin and brow that Cruz did. He wore a loose white shirt that reached halfway down his thin thighs, and nothing much else that Sarah could see. He emptied the jug into the tub.

"Diez." Allen held up ten fingers. "Ten more."

"Sí, Señor." He hoisted the jug into the agave cord harness on his back and set off at a trot.

"Such nobility of features." Allen watched him go. "He looks descended from the Caesars, does he not?"

"He has more respectability in his appearance than one would expect from a man lacking pantaloons." Sarah saluted Allen and moved on to her own tent. At least the rubber bathing contraption distracted him from the questions he rained down on her and everyone else who happened upon him.

The sergeant sat on a rock cleaning his musketoon with vinegar. He had let his hair grow back. It was soaked with sweat and stuck out all over his head like thread-fine steel wire. George Lincoln stood with one of Cruz's shawls draped across his bare shoulders and bony chest. Cruz had spread his shirt on a barrel lid and was spraying starch and water across it from her mouth. She laid a piece of sacking over the shirt. With a folded towel she picked a hot brick from the embers and used it to iron.

Sarah inhaled the smell of starch and clean, hot linen. They always put her in mind of civility and comfort. She ladled water into the earthen pots she had bartered from Cruz so many months ago, and hung them from the branch of a fig tree so the faint breeze from the river would cool them. She caught the sergeant's attention and nodded toward Allen, who was hanging blankets to screen his rubber tub.

The sergeant's eyes narrowed ever so slightly as he calculated. "A day and two bits," he said finally.

" 'Tattoo' and a dollar."

" 'Tattoo' and a dollar for what, Mrs. Borginnis?" Lieutenant Lincoln asked.

"I'm betting the scribbler's contraption will get punctured by the time they blow 'Taps.' "

Lincoln listened to the splashing and singing coming from behind the blankets. "I'll put a dollar on tomorrow, by 'Reveille.' "

Bertha Skinner ran shrieking from her tent. Nancy grabbed the mesquite limb she kept handy and sprinted inside. She came out holding the club high with both hands so the rattler draped over it wouldn't drag on the ground.

"Supper." She grinned. Jake lurched toward her.

"Bring it here before that fool mule gets it," Sarah said.

"You mustn't eat that foul creature." Bertha gyrated like a blond dust devil, shaking her clothes, front and back, in case more spiders had crept in after the two she found while dressing. She kicked at the log before she sat gingerly on it. She gathered her skirts tightly around her, and her pale blue eyes never stopped surveying the ground around her for poisonous creatures. "A snake brought evil into the garden."

"If God didn't intend us to eat them, he wouldn't have made them taste like spring chicken." Sarah flensed the rattler, gutted it, chopped it into pieces, and tossed them into the pot of beans simmering on the fire.

She picked up the ax next and set a chunk of oak on end. Both the sergeant and Lincoln took it as a signal to leave. Lincoln collected the shirt that Cruz handed him. She had mended the thorn tears so neatly they could hardly be found. Lincoln ducked behind Sarah's tent to lower his suspenders, pull on his shirt, and tuck it into his trousers. Then he joined the sergeant and they both hitched their galluses onto their shoulders as they walked away.

Sarah grinned after them. Then she split the log with one blow and set up another one.

"Nothing discomforts a man more'n seeing a woman chop wood," she confided to Nancy and Cruz. "A Southerner, now, he'll go hunt up a son of Africa to do the job forthwith. Even an enlisted man would rather not see it, but they've chopped too much wood in their career to offer to help." She worked with a smooth rhythm, the halves of the logs falling away from the blade. "You want your oak like your men, straight, with no knots in their character. Fine-grained and hot-burning; not green nor so seasoned they turn hard on you."

She had just finished enough for the morning's fire when a covey of trumpets struck up a tune from across the river. Nancy snatched a blanket from the tent, shook a scorpion and two hairy spiders the size of her fist out of it, and rounded up her sisters. Even Bertha brightened and joined the crowd hurrying toward the river.

All along the bank soldiers and civilians spread blankets and sat on them. Mexican women and children circulated among them with trays of sweet bread, tamales, strange fruits, and the flat pads of the prickly pear cactus, scraped clean of thorns. They sold hand-rolled cigarettes, cotton shawls, straw hats, and the balls of resin called chicle that they chewed constantly.

The succulent grass, the fragrance of the acacia blossoms, the shiny, dark green canopy of the ebony trees, and the chuckling of the river reminded Sarah of a park, but one more beautiful than the few she had seen in her life. The desert to the east had hardly seemed worth defending, but she wasn't surprised that General Ampudia was sending daily letters of protest about the Americans' presence here.

Sarah joined Cruz and James, Nancy and the other Skinners, and set the basket of food in the middle of the blanket. Cruz passed around the tortillas and the bowl of beans and fatback. The citizens of Matamoros had put on their best clothes and thronged the shore to stare at the Americans on the other side. The musicians there had just started a lively tune and people were dancing, the women's bright skirts twirling out around them like poppy petals. They laughed and beckoned to the Americans to swim over to them.

The town of Matamoros sat like a jewel on a low bluff against the sunset sky. Gardens and orchards surrounded the white adobe houses. The delicate cathedral spire rose above the tile roofs. Fields of cotton and cane, elegant haciendas, and groves of ebony trees fringed the city. As the sun dropped toward the horizon, the billows of clouds framing the town turned from pink to magenta. The light painted the plastered walls a lighter tint of the same color.

"Have you ever seen such a town, Cruz?" Sarah asked.

"No." Cruz shook her head without taking her eyes from it.

"Until now, Corpus Christi was the biggest human menagerie she'd ever seen." James took Cruz's hand and held it to his lips. "I plan to show her New Orleans when the war is over."

"The war doesn't look likely to start," Sarah said.

When the Mexicans stopped playing, the army's band started. They played on after nightfall, and Cruz and James and the others waltzed on a carpet of grass lit by the glow of a moon filtered through golden clouds of acacia blossoms. Even Sarah's sergeant steered her through the dance with surprising grace.

➜ ⬅

Hundreds of soldiers, stripped to the waist and glistening with sweat, swarmed around the six-sided earthworks rising on a bluff across the Rio Grande from Matamoros. Lieutenant Joseph Mansfield's plans called for walls ten feet high and fifteen feet thick at the base. James and Seamus worked at the bottom of the twenty-foot-wide, eight-foot-deep trench being dug around the fortification. James hacked at the clay with a pick. Seamus shoveled the loosened dirt into the buckets that were heaved up on ropes and carried to the construction site.

"May the devil take a liking to engineers." Seamus laid his head back to look up, although from here he couldn't see Lieutenant Mansfield roaming the works with his surveyor's tripods and cylindrical map cases. "This is not worth the thimbleful of whiskey they give us. Even a fool knows that a gill of whiskey is like six inches of cord wood."

James stopped to retie the strips of cloth Cruz had wrapped around his bloody hands when she brought him tortillas and beans and spicy shreds of beef at the noon break.

"Stop loafing, you son of an Irish bitch."

James tilted his head back to look up at the boot soles and blue-clad knees of Lieutenant Casey. He saluted the boots. "I was but adjusting the bandages, sir."

"I'll have you bucked if I catch you malingering again."

"Yes, sir."

When the boots disappeared, John Riley's face appeared at the rim of the trench. "They're back." He called to them softly so the men farther down the trench wouldn't hear him.

The four other Irishmen nearby dropped their picks and shovels and rushed the ladder. James held out his hands, palms up, fingers intertwined. Seamus stepped onto it and James heaved him up to Riley, who pulled him over the top. Seamus extended a hand to James, but he waved it away.

"Are ye daft, man?" Seamus continued to hold the hand out to him. "Ye cannot spurn such a gift from God."

"God has given me the most beautiful woman in creation. I'll not risk my stripes for something I have no need of."

"May He bless ye for a simpleton then." Seamus shouted it as he pelted after the others.

James continued digging alone, though to tell the truth he would have liked to go with them. For splendor and bedazzlement the view would be like nothing he had ever seen before arriving here, nor was likely to again after the army left Mexico. Each afternoon a crowd of women, as brown and buxom as any naiads of Greek myth, gathered on the other side of the river. With no embarrassment whatsoever they stripped off their clothes and splashed naked into the water. They called out to the spellbound soldiers as they frolicked, blew them kisses, and invited them to join them. The lure was so invidious that Taylor had issued orders to shoot any man who attempted to swim across.

James could never explain to Seamus what it meant to love a woman to the marrow of his bones. To have her become so completely a part of him, flesh, blood, and breath, that death was preferable to life without her. But in a way Seamus was right. To pass up the chance to witness the scene occurring on the river right then seemed the basest ingratitude to a benevolent God.

➜ ←

When James and the ten men of the guard reported to Lieutenant Casey, he wasn't surprised to see John Riley, Seamus, and the other four who had sneaked away to the river the day before. The fact that he himself wasn't standing with them as he had so often in the past disoriented him.

Casey, his hands clasped behind his back and twitching his riding crop, turned to James. "Corporal, have you the tent poles and rope?"

"Yes, sir."

"And you'll be knowin' the best place to plant that pole, now wouldn't you, Lieutenant darlin'," Riley said.

"Damn you, you goddamned hound." Casey's face turned so red James could imagine it bursting and showering them with teeth. "Strip, you damned son of a bitch. Strip, goddamn you, and I'll whip you within an inch of your life and that inch too." He spun on his heel to face James. "Corporal, flog the villain while I count fifty."

"I cannot do that, sir." James kept his voice calm, respectful even. But a tight writhing in his gut and a ringing in his head told him he was in for another run of bad luck.

He stood rigid while Casey tried to rip off his corporal's chevrons, but Cruz had sewn them on well. "Buck him and gag him with the others," the lieutenant shouted.

"I've done nothing to deserve that, sir."

"I'll have none of your insolence, you damned son of an Irish bitch. I shall be damned glad when the Mexicans kill all of you. Talk back to me and I'll have you flogged as well as bucked, goddamn you."

Without being aware of it, James brought his carbine up. He felt a chill in his bones. He saw the lieutenant through the red haze of rage that he thought love had exorcised. He was no longer free to play the devil-may-care, but he would not allow anyone to whip him. Not ever.

"Flog me and I will kill you for it." His voice was calm, but as he spoke he began planning an escape into Mexico with Cruz.

"Damn you!" But the lieutenant stepped back from him. "Seize the rogue and buck him with the others."

Riley had stripped to the waist. While two men tied his hands high around the trunk of an ebony tree, James and the other five sat in a row with their feet drawn up in front of them, their arms held out at their sides, elbows bent. Two of the guards ran the tent pole under their knees and over their elbows, then tied their wrists tightly in front of them. When the guards finished, James and the others looked like so many chunks of meat on a skewer.

Casey jammed a large tent peg horizontally into James's mouth and tied it in place. The gag forced his mouth so far open that a searing pain started at the corners of his mouth and spread through his face and behind his eyes.

Colonel Worth sauntered past and stopped to watch. James had a fleeting hope that he would put an end to this, but when he saw the look on his face, he gave it up. As always, Worth looked strong and fit, pressed and shined and every inch the soldier, except that his mouth was set in something very like a pout. He was in one of his snits, and a good flogging would no doubt suit him.

Casey pointed his quirt to one of the guards. "You, take up the whip."

"I cannot, sir."

"Then you too shall be bucked."

Five more refused, and Casey turned to the sixth, a hulking, moonfaced fellow with an unkempt mustache and shaggy brown hair like bison fur hanging over his collar. He wore a baffled stare that had all the appearances of being permanent, as though an order to straighten his belt buckle would require a great deal of study.

"Davis, what say you?"

Davis turned an apologetic glance to the guards who were now sitting, knees up, waiting for their own tent pole. He slowly took off his belt and jacket.

"Damn you for a cur, Davis," one of the guards said. The others elaborated on the theme.

The lash landed with a gut-wrenching thud and Riley screamed. Davis was unskilled but strong. He rained the blows down as though he could hurry through it and end Riley's pain sooner. In his haste the lash sometimes curled around Riley's abdomen to lay open a trench there. Riley was screaming for the Virgin Mary and all the saints to save him when Colonel Twiggs happened by, puffing from the heat. His wild wisps of hair poking from under his hat were startling white in contrast with his red face.

"That's enough, Davis," he said.

"The hell it is." Worth pulled himself up in his high black boots.

Twiggs ignored him. "Cut him down, boys."

"This is the last straw." Worth shook his fist, purple with rage. "I am the ranking officer. I will suffer no more of this ignominy. I shall tender my resignation immediately."

He stormed away, and Twiggs pointed his quirt at James. "Take the gag from that man's mouth, but leave them all bucked for the rest of the afternoon."

James smiled his thanks when a guard removed the tent peg and he could work his jaw back into order.

Saved by the Tiger, he thought.

1 1

Rattled

J AKE FRISKED THROUGH THE MESQUITE GRASS, THE
poppies, indigo, and paintbrush. He found the pea vine so irresistible Sarah tussled with him to keep him from turning the foray
for supplies into a leisurely breakfast. Cruz rode the mare who
seemed in less of a pique than usual. She had come into season and
she pranced along with her tail an arched and streaming pennant.

An April wind carried the faint chime of Matamoros's Sunday
bells from across the river. Doves raised the usual din in the pale
green lace of the mesquite trees. A pair of hummingbirds circled
Sarah's head, maybe mistaking the red tendrils spilling from the center of the crownless hat brim for a bouquet of flowers.

Sarah took her knitting out of the bag hanging from the saddle
tree. "You're sure this is the way Ortiz said to go?"

"I think so," Cruz said.

"No matter. A day like this, we don't need an excuse for a jaunt."

Sarah sighted the house as she was tying off the stocking. She
stuck the wooden knitting needles through the holes in her hat
brim, like the quills of moth-eaten feathers.

As they approached the hovel, Sarah began to take on misgivings.
Holes gaped where the mud plaster had fallen away from the lattice-
work of the walls. The remnants of the roof thatch hung in tatters.
All that remained of a garden were dusty bean vines clinging to the

fragments of a fence. A few bony chickens wandered the hardpan of the dooryard as though in search of better accommodations.

"I see no squash nor corn nor cattle, not for trade nor domestic consumption neither."

They tied Jake and Alice Ann to a fence paling, though the act was merely a suggestion to Jake that he stay put. It would hardly slow him down if he decided to bolt. Cruz took her musketoon from the boot. Sarah cocked her pistol. The house had no door and they peered through the warped opening.

"*Buenos días,*" Cruz called out. Ribbons of sunlight illuminated small patches of a bare dirt floor. As their eyes grew accustomed to the gloom, they saw a few rags clinging to the bones of a human skeleton. The rats that had been gnawing the bones scattered into the shadows crouched along the walls. "*Dios mio.*" Cruz crossed herself and backed out, bumping into Sarah.

"We've been bamboozled." Sarah wasn't surprised to see the trio of riders approaching at a saunter.

She knew she and Cruz wouldn't get far if they bolted. Águila rode a stallion, of course, and the other two were mounted on big geldings, the pick of their plunder probably. They could easily outrun Jake and Alice Ann. She could shoot Águila and do the world a favor, but she wouldn't have time to reload before the other two killed her and Cruz. She doubted that Cruz had the stomach yet to kill a man with the musketoon. She hadn't even thought to raise it to a firing position.

Sarah untied the mare and handed the reins to Cruz. "You got your pig-sticker?"

"Yes." Cruz patted the fold of her skirt that hid the slit in it and the knife strapped to her thigh underneath. Sarah had taught her that trick and Águila wouldn't likely know about it, although with so many Mexicans in the Americans' camp to inform on their doings, there was no telling what he knew. The wood seller, Ortiz, had sent them into this trap after all.

"Cut the lariat when I say 'bacon.' Then let go the mare and cut Águila's cinch if you can." It was a lot to ask.

"*Sí.*" Cruz waited calmly, one hand holding the reins at the mare's mouth, the other her short musket, muzzle pointed toward the ground.

Sarah palmed the snake rattle she always carried in her pocket for luck. She knew her plan didn't amount to much, but she did have two advantages. Men like Águila always rode stallions. Already Águila's horse smelled the mare's fecundity ripening the warm breeze. He whickered and sidestepped and tossed his head. Sarah could also count on Águila's sort to underestimate her and Cruz because they were women.

The three slowed their horses to a walk, and the two henchmen uncoiled their ropes. They both wore the silly leers of men planning to take by force a pleasure they could never obtain otherwise. They assessed the abundance of Sarah's breasts and the inviting curve of her hips. She could see them measuring with their eyes the considerable distance between those hips and the ground and imagining the length of the legs under her skirts.

"¡Qué mujer!" one of them murmured.

If they have rape in mind, Sarah thought, so much the worse for them. A man's most cherished piece was easier to spike when his pants were down. A drunken soldier had tried to have his way with Sarah in Florida and he had regretted it. He had limped for days and had suffered ridicule besides. After that the other men took their hats off when they spoke to Sarah, and they limited their admiration to surreptitious looks. Sarah had not told Jack Borginnis of the matter, knowing he would kill the fool and spike his own career in the process.

Sarah stood still while the lariats arced with a faint whistle toward her and Cruz. The rope settled over her head, pinning her arms at her sides. The man at the other end pulled her close enough for her to see the smudge of whiskers on his undershot jaw. The second man pinioned Cruz and she dropped her musketoon. He handed the end of his line to Águila, who pulled Cruz close.

"Yanqui puta, vas a sufrir," he said.

Yankee whore, you're going to suffer. Sarah concentrated on the Spanish. Their lives depended on her knowing what the men said. Cruz just stared at Águila's saddle girth as though he didn't exist.

Águila tied the end of the rope to his saddle horn, keeping the line taut. Sarah realized he intended to drag her to her death, but if Cruz knew it she gave no indication. Sarah's captor flicked the rope so it hit her chin, the harsh fibers leaving a livid red mark. He pulled it tight again, backing his horse to keep it that way.

"*¿Y ella?*" he asked. What about her?

Sarah rubbed the sleek coils of the snake rattle with her finger. She saw everything with a preternatural clarity, the eagles engraved in the tarnished silver conchos on their flared leather pants. The mud crusted on their boots. The eight-inch rowels on their spurs.

"*Mátala.*" Águila said it casually. Kill her. He added, in Spanish, "Fuck her after she's dead if you want."

"Bacon!" As Sarah gave the signal, she shook the snake rattle and everyone around her exploded into motion. Jake broke the fence post where it had rotted at the ground. With it leaping and clattering behind him, he charged the horses in search of the rattlesnake and a morning snack. The whir sent the mare into her usual wild-eyed, squealing panic. She leaped sideways, lighting six feet away in a trembling squat, her ears scissoring back and forth. The stallion reared and plunged trying to get at her.

While Águila fought to control him, Cruz cut the noose around her chest. Dodging the stallion's hooves, she slipped the blade under the saddle girth and sawed through it. The mare sped away, the stallion after her. In less than a hundred feet the saddle slid off, dumping Águila with his spurs tangled in the stirrup straps. The stallion and the mare continued their course toward the horizon, dragging Águila along with them.

Sarah swiveled abruptly, yanking her man from his pitching mount. She pushed her elbows outward, loosening the noose, and ducked out of it. She kicked the fallen rider in the back of the head. His hat absorbed some of the blow, but he went limp. Sarah grabbed the reins of his horse.

While she held him, Cruz hiked up her skirts, vaulted into the saddle, and pulled his carbine from its boot. When the third man tried to run Sarah down, Cruz rode up behind him. Holding the gun barrel in both hands, she knocked him senseless with the walnut stock. Sarah caught his leg, yanked him to the ground, and swung into the saddle. The one Sarah had kicked regained consciousness, got his feet sorted out, and made a teetering lunge for her. She yanked the knitting needle from her hat brim and stabbed it through his hand. He fell back with a scream. As she rode past Cruz's fallen musketoon, she unhooked her far foot from the stirrup, leaned down from the saddle as the Texas Rangers had taught her to do at Corpus Christi, and scooped it up.

"Jake, fetch your sorry carcass along," she shouted as she and Cruz galloped for the Rio Grande.

Jake kicked and brayed after them, the fence post clunking behind him. The conscious henchman recovered the pistol that had fallen from Águila's holster, loaded it and fired, but Cruz smiled as she laid her cheek against the sliding muscles of the horse's neck and the bullet whined past. She was safe within the Great Western's charmed fortification.

"Way-stern," she called out. "Do not tell Murphy."

"If you say so." Sarah set her mind to inventing an explanation for these two horses and the elaborate Spanish tack. And she knew she could not sleep easy until Águila was well and truly dead.

→ ←

The line of sentries, posted every hundred yards, stretched for two miles along the river. James had drawn the last spot downstream, beyond the horse pickets and the wagon yard and cattle herds. He and his two companions had spent the dark predawn hours sharing a tin of brandied cherries Sarah had given him and lying about their military exploits. Their flintlocks leaned against the backside of a big live oak, and they lounged against the front.

James listened to the sonorous call of the cathedral bells and watched the first rays of the sun strike fire from the ripples in the river. On the Mexican side, upstream, across from the main encampment, the usual crowd began to gather to watch the soldiers. James recognized many of them by now. Judging by the angle of the sun, he only had a few minutes left of this watch. To pass the time, he wondered who the Mexicans were, what their lives were like, how they earned their livings.

When he saw Seamus Hooligan and John Riley pushing through the tangled brush, he assumed they were going for water. He started to wave and hail them, to remind them they should get their water upstream—but the two men carried rucksacks, not buckets, and they didn't stop at the shoreline. Without taking off their civilian clothes or shoes, they waded as far as their waists, sank to their necks, and began swimming.

"Halt!" James scrambled through the bushes along the shore. "Riley, General Taylor gave orders to shoot."

"Jamie, lad." Riley turned onto his back and kept on stroking. "I am seized with the desire to go to church."

The next sentry in line heard the commotion and ran toward him. "Shoot, Murphy."

James primed and loaded his piece with trembling fingers. He rested the stock into the hollow of his shoulder, aimed just to the left of Riley's ear, and fired. The bullet kicked up a spray. James took Riley's hat off with the next shot and creased Seamus's foot with the third, but they didn't turn back.

When the other sentry opened fire, Seamus and Riley sank beneath the surface and reappeared among the reeds on the other side. They clambered up the bluff with people at the top reaching out their hands to help them. Seamus was limping.

So, Seamus, he thought, you're going for the three hundred twenty acres and the women.

James watched them disappear into the greenery without a backward glance. Then he heard a shout farther upstream, and more shots. He saw another man in the water, paddling like a spaniel. He was headed for the beautiful women and the land and lieutenant's rank and pay the Mexicans had promised in fliers that had mysteriously appeared in camp. A bullet hit him and he sank beneath the surface.

"I wager they won't be the last." The man who was to relieve James sauntered up with two other sentries.

"Lieutenant Blake's nigger Moses took a swim last night," the second man said. "Made it to the other side, too, with Blake's humidor of Cuban cigars and a bottle of brandy. Blake's fit to be tied."

"Can't blame a slave for running." James ran a hand over Duke's sleek withers.

"They brought Colonel Cross's body in this morning. Bare to the buff. The greasers took his horse and everything on him, including a gold tooth." The replacement put down his carbine and unbuttoned the top of his jacket. "They went and killed the best quartermaster officer in the army. Damned shame."

"What happened?" James asked.

"On the way here I met a Mex who said some fellow named

Águila killed him. Roped him like a steer and stove his skull in with a pistol butt for the fun of it. He and his gang of cutthroats are calling themselves government troops."

In spite of the heat, intensifying now that the sun had risen, James's blood felt cold in his veins. He took a running start and leaped onto Duke's bare back. He gathered the reins, collected his piece from where it stood against the tree, and galloped to Sarah's camp. He found Jake and the mare grazing there, but his own tent stood empty nearby. He rode to the artillery battery positioned behind sandbags at the loop of the river in front of the fort's massive earthworks. He found Sarah's sergeant inspecting the breech on the eight-pounder he fondly referred to as Old Blue. The other pieces hunched under their canvas covers, their muzzles projecting as though sniffing the wind.

"Have you seen Western or Cruz?"

The sergeant shook his head without taking his eyes from his work.

"Did you know Águila killed Colonel Cross?"

"Son of a bitch." The sergeant glanced up in a rare show of curiosity.

"He and his men are operating as a company of irregulars on this side of the river."

"The supply line."

"What?" All James could think of was the danger to Cruz.

"They'll attack the wagons and pack trains between here and Port Isabel."

James didn't stay to discuss it. He searched Sudsville, but no one had seen Sarah or Cruz. Even Lewis Allen didn't know where they were, and he had his nose in everyone's affairs. Allen seemed miffed that Sarah had eluded him because he had taken to trailing her. Her stories made good copy and better fiction, and she and her kettles and skillet usually occupied the center of a group of young West Point officers full of book-learning, philosophy, opinions, and gossip.

Nancy Skinner was rubbing a brass cannon barrel to a high shine, probably in hopes that Sam Ringgold would flash her one of his brilliant smiles or spare her a few words, or, if she was especially fortunate, pat her on the shoulder. She was almost twelve now and adding inches to her height faster than she could gracefully incorporate the new real estate. She had become all knobs and angles under her unruly sheaf of pale hair. Insect bites covered her big feet and skinny ankles. She couldn't give James any information either.

He had ransacked the army's camp and was heading for one of the paths through the chaparral behind it when he saw Sarah and Cruz approaching. He raced to them and reined to a sliding stop that sat Duke back on his hocks. He pulled Cruz from her horse to his and sat her astride in front of him. He wound his hand in her hair and turned her head so he could cover her face, neck, and throat with kisses. Then, with his arms encircling her and his cheek resting on the top of her head, he rode back to their tent. He was so distracted he didn't notice the two strange horses. And he didn't mention the fact that Antonio Águila was marauding in the area. He figured there was no point in alarming her.

➔ ◀

When Sarah raised her hand to push a damp lock of hair out of her eyes, she realized it was shaking, a delayed reaction to her *fandango* with death. She picketed the Mexican's big gray gelding to graze with Jake and Alice Ann and went in search of her sergeant.

She found him at the cannon and handed him a packet of corn pone and bacon, the rations she and Cruz had not eaten in the excitement that morning. He took them, and then he surprised her by reaching out and brushing his fingertips along the red scrape on her jaw where the Mexican's rope had dragged across it. She knew how improbable such a gesture was and she felt a current of affection for him.

She smiled sheepishly. "Águila's little prank."

The sergeant sat in the shade of the cannon and peeled away the cornhusks to reveal the pone and bacon inside. "Have a care, old girl," he said.

"I shall." Sarah settled down to share the shade with him, and the pone and a comfortable silence.

She sat with her shoulder barely touching his and she thought how lucky she was. She had found another man who recognized the spirit inside her, and made no fuss about the package in which it came.

12

Cold Iron

DUKE REFUSED TO BE LEFT OUT OF ANY TENDER FARE-
wells. When James took Cruz in his arms, Duke laid his
muzzle on his shoulder, inches from Cruz's face. He snorted, his
breath fluttering the wisps of hair at her temples. Cruz pushed him
away, but Duke muttered and began tugging James's trouser leg with
his teeth. Cruz and James laughed and gave it up.

With Duke following they walked among the stacks of crates and
sacks and barrels, two weeks' worth of supplies that the men of the
Seventh Infantry were carrying into the big earthen redoubt. The
soldiers had packed their tents, leaving the trampled campsite
strewn with litter that Mexican women and children were already
picking through.

The army created the usual pandemonium as it prepared to march
to Port Isabel to protect the supply lines. The men of Sam Ringgold's Flying Artillery chivvied their cannon carriages and ammunition caissons into line. The teamsters cracked their whips and swore
at the mules, who gave as good as they got in the way of insults.
The dragoons and their horses dashed here and there.

"The road is dangerous," Cruz said. "Arista's army is very big." But
Antonio Águila and his roving band worried her more than General
Arista's entire force. They had been plundering travelers and strag-
glers. They had attacked a company of Texas Rangers on a scout
and killed ten of them.

"Only Arista's lancers are worth their salt. The rest are half-starved wretches who'll run away faster'n flour through a sifter at the first shot." What James wanted to say was that if he had known he would be leaving Cruz behind in Fort Texas, he would have dug the trench deeper and built the walls higher and thicker. Cruz had just told him that she carried his child inside her and that intensified his anxiety.

The bugles signaled "Prepare to Mount." James kissed Cruz, then he swung into the saddle. In a great clanking and rattling, squalling of axles, braying, shouting, swearing, singing, and laughing, the army and its three hundred empty supply wagons lurched forward.

Cruz ran to join Sarah and the Skinner girls. They all hoisted their skirts and toiled up the packed earth slope to the parapet where the sergeant stood with the eighteen-pounder. From there they could see the line of march toward the coast, as well as the looped ribbon of the river, the Mexicans' artillery batteries along it, and the trees and rooftops of Matamoros. Nancy stood on the parapet wall, the wind whipping her skirt around her thin legs, and fixed on the artillery and Sam Ringgold. She swiveled to watch them when they moved forward.

As the dragoons passed below, a trio of drummers slackened the heads of their big drums. The Irish in the Second began one of their own songs. Sarah's knowledge of Gaelic was limited to the lullabies her mother had sung to her and her brothers, but she understood these words in her bones and in her soul. The drums' deep, measured throbbing and the men's wild harmonies told of ancient wars and recent ones, of death and sorrow, courage and loss.

No one, she thought, could sing of war like the Irish. They had known so much of it. She turned to look across the Rio Grande. The Mexicans had sandbagged emplacements for their nine-pounders so near the shore she imagined she could converse with the crews. Beyond the batteries the Mexican soldiers knelt. Priests in black cassocks walked among them, sprinkling them and the cannons with water from the pails their acolytes carried.

"What's afoot, Cruz?"

"They ask God's benediction."

Sarah didn't say what she was thinking, that if the Mexicans thought God was on their side, they were mistaken. But the sight of the vestments made her uneasy. They recalled the makeshift Catholicism to which her parents held a fierce loyalty, even though they had no church where a priest could say mass, if a priest could be found within five hundred miles.

She looked north to the ravines that gouged the land and the thick chaparral that surrounded the fort. The bend in the river almost formed a circle, and if the Mexicans could take possession of the single road out, they would have the meager force here bottled in.

She moved to the sergeant's side and nodded to the wild country around them. "Lots of places for Arista to hide his army."

The sergeant shifted the cigar stub to the other side of his mouth. "Yep."

➤ ⭠

A heavy shroud of dust, of blue sulfurous smoke, and the stench of exploding gunpowder made breathing a misery. Sarah's throat ached and her mouth was so dry her tongue stuck to her lips when she tired to moisten them. Her ears had been ringing since the bombardment started at five in the morning, as it had every morning for the past four days.

A Mexican cannonball the size of a large orange whistled overhead. Lewis Allen scuttled behind the cast-iron sheet Sarah had propped up on two posts by the fire to reflect the heat onto her baking bread. Sarah pushed the wads of cottonwood fluff deeper into her ears and went on stirring the beans simmering in the kettle.

The shot hit the last standing mesquite tree and snapped it off halfway up the trunk. Allen crawled into the open again. He waited until the roar of the Americans' six-pounders and the eighteen-pounder on the parapet died away before speaking. He was hoarse from shouting for days over the din of artillery.

"D'you think the hostiles shall run out of ammunition soon?"

"Men might want for bread and clothing, but they can always find ammunition." She paused. "And liquor," she added. With a long wooden paddle Sarah shoveled loaves of bread onto the wide plank that served as a tray. "They're finding the range."

With the baby balanced on her hip, Nancy ran to where the

spent ball lay. She kicked dirt on it to cool it, and began pushing it
with her bare foot.

"Child, leave it and get over here close to the wall," Sarah
shouted. "I told you it's a nine-pounder. It won't fit our guns."

"We can drop it on them if they try to scale the walls." Nancy
added it to the pyramid she had collected and stacked near the ramp
to the parapet.

Another projectile arced over the wall and Sarah saw that it
wasn't solid roundshot. She pulled Nancy and the baby to the
ground and shielded them with her body while the baby screamed.
The shell exploded, sending fragments of jagged metal whistling in
all directions. One of them ripped through the Skinners' tent, setting the dry canvas afire. Bertha ran out shrieking, her other two
daughters clinging to her skirts.

She beat at her pale hair, as though afraid it had caught fire too.
She sobbed and pleaded. "Make it stop. Make it stop."

"Come along now, Mrs. Skinner. Let's join the others." Sarah
herded them all to a sandbagged bombproof for the dozen or so officers' wives.

The space was crowded already, and a few glared at the intruders,
but the others pressed closer together to make room. One tried to
soothe Bertha and another held the screaming baby.

Cruz returned from the parapet with the empty bucket that had
held the watery brew of toasted barley that served as coffee. She
bent over, gagged, retched, and wiped her face on her skirt. When
she arrived, she reached for the tray, but Sarah took it from her and
set it down.

She poured water from a jug onto the corner of a towel and rinsed
Cruz's face. "Go sit with the others. It's the only shade left."

"I can help you."

"Murphy would shoot me if I let anything happen to you and the
baby, and I wouldn't blame him for doing it."

Sarah walked her to the officers' wives' sanctuary. She ignored the
looks from some of them, obviously indignant at having a Mexican
in their midst. "My dear friend is feeling poorly," Sarah said. "I know
you'll want to do what's Christian."

Sarah left them to sort it out and went to get her tray of bread.

She found Lewis Allen there. "Pick up that pail of water and the ladle, scribbler. We're taking refreshment to Major Brown's Cotton Balers."

"I was about to transcribe my notes." He held up his ink pot and quills and the stub of a pencil he had cadged from Lieutenant Lincoln. "And I do not fancy a lump of lead scattering my brains and the knowledge I have stowed there all these years."

" 'Ay me . . .' " Sarah recited Lieutenant Lincoln's favorite poem. " 'What perils do environ the man who meddles with cold iron.' "

With a sigh Allen stowed his ink and pencil and memorandum book in the tent he shared with an ailing drover. He picked up the heavy bucket. "Why do they call the Seventh Infantry Cotton Balers?"

"You're just topped off with questions, aren't you?"

"It's my job."

Sarah nodded to a wiry little man of sixty or so squatting among the wounded in the torn hospital tent. "Major Brown there and the Seventh put up a right smart scrap from behind cotton bales at the Battle of New Orleans." She glanced back at Allen. "You gonna write that in your memorandum book too?"

"It's all grist for my mill, Western."

"Well, I'd hate to have to make shortbread of your grist. From what I've heard of it, it's mostly dust and rat scat."

With the pail bumping against his short legs, Allen followed her across ground pitted and harrowed by the Mexican artillery. Shredded tents, trees, and dead animals lay strewn about. Two infantrymen were butchering a mule killed in the last bombardment. Those who weren't wounded or shoring up the defenses, manning the guns, or standing guard lay against the wall, trying to sleep.

Sarah had almost reached them when a shell exploded nearby. A fragment hit her tray and shattered it, then passed through her hat. Her fingers tingled from the impact, but she salvaged what bread she could. She brushed the dirt from it and dropped it into the pocket she made of her skirt front.

"This must be what hell is like, Western." Allen was so busy scanning overhead for the arrival of more shot he almost fell over the rotting leg of a horse.

"No, sir." Sarah was emphatic. "You ain't experienced hell till you've summered in Florida."

➜ ←

Sarah and her sergeant sat with their arms touching and their backs against the wheel of the eighteen-pounder's carriage. The cannon was of iron, not brass. It had taken six yoke of oxen, a block and tackle, and a large portion of the Seventh Infantry to get it up here and it felt solid and unmovable against their shoulder blades. A warm breeze blew some of the stench of gunpowder and rotting horseflesh the other way. The full moon hung like a lantern above the western horizon. Sarah cherished the night and the respite from the heavy rain of death. But even in the silence she heard a ringing in her ears that was hard to distinguish from the shrill of the cicadas.

Being left behind had put the sergeant in a foul humor. He said Taylor and the rest of the army would have to fight its way back from the coast and he would miss the fun. Sarah didn't doubt that he was right. He could always sniff a scuffle.

Now he was listening for the noises of a force sneaking up under cover of night. And probably hoping for one. Sarah heard rustlings in the dense thickets, but they were the traffic of animals hurrying to their secret destinations while the rest of the world was supposed to be asleep. An owl hooted and a fox barked. A panther's scream sent a cold ripple of dread up Sarah's spine.

"Puts me in mind of Florida," she said softly.

The sergeant continued to stare through the darkness toward the east and the coast, but he lifted his chin, inflated his cheeks, and loosed a rumble of boisterous grunts from deep in his chest. Sarah remembered that sound booming over the black waters of the swamp and she chuckled.

"I never reckoned I'd pine for 'gators," she said.

"Is all well here, Sergeant?" Major Brown ambled toward them with his hands in his pockets. He had left his hat behind and the breeze ruffled his white hair until it stood out around his head like a disheveled halo.

The sergeant stood and saluted. "It is, sir."

"You should be in your blankets, Major Brown," Sarah chided. "You've not slept two hours together since this *fandango* began."

"Nor have you, I would wager." He smiled and turned to the sergeant. "General Taylor sent for volunteers from the States."

"How many, sir?"

"Five thousand." The major tipped his absent hat to Sarah and returned the sergeant's salute. Humming "Onward, Christian Soldiers," he strolled away along the ramparts, inspecting the damage the Mexican shot had done to the earthen parapet.

"May the saints preserve us. Five thousand." Sarah had seen state militias in full riot in Florida. "They'll get drunk and rile up the countryside and steal the wash from the line and the lint from our navels."

"They won't *get* drunk, my girl, they'll arrive tighter'n wax. And they won't sober up for Judgment Day. Five thousand of them." The number made the sergeant glummer than Sarah had ever seen him.

She understood why the news deepened his gloom. If Arista's army attacked the Americans and their supply wagons on the road between here and the coast, it likely would be the first and last battle the regulars would fight without unruly militiamen getting in their way. And the sergeant would have no part in it.

"We'll have to do something to put you in a better mood." Sarah leaned against the cannon and pulled him to her.

The rasp of the rough canvas of his trousers on her bare thighs sent a tingle up her spine. She arched her back along the curve of the barrel and gave a sigh of pleasure. With her face toward the stars and her arms lying along the cold iron of the barrel above her head, she closed her eyes and moved her hips to meet the thrusts that took him deeper into her. One last great shuddering spasm and he fell against her, panting.

They stood a few moments in silence, savoring the warmth and pressure of each other's body until a rustling came from outside the wall.

The sergeant raised his head and listened. "I smell Texan." He kissed her. Then he buttoned his trousers and pulled up his galluses. "Not one of the riper ones, though. This one's bathed in the last few years."

He cocked his pistol and leveled it into the darkness of the ditch below the wall. He called down softly. "I hear tell General Sam Houston is the finest, bravest human being ever to spring from a woman's mill."

"Shee-yut," came a voice from the ditch. "All that opium-smoking, corset-wearing bag of breeze knows how to do is retreat."

When the sergeant winked at Sarah in the starlight, it was like the moon going down over the badlands. " 'Tis a Texan all right." He threw a knotted rope over the side and it tautened as the man shinned up it.

When he had climbed close enough Sarah recognized him. "Welcome to Fort Texas, Cap'n Walker."

Sam Walker wasn't a big man, and Sarah grabbed his arm with both hands and hauled him the rest of the way. She deposited him on his feet as easily as if he'd been a half-filled bucket of well water.

"Why'd you not enter by the back gate?"

"The Mes-kin irregulars've pitched at the crossroads back there, and they're moving artillery in."

"I'll wager John Riley's with them," Sarah said. "He trained with Ringgold and he helped build this redoubt. He'll know how best to position the Mexican guns for a crossfire."

"Well, it does appear they're planning a dustup." Walker used his hat to brush the dirt off his plaid flannel trousers.

He was slender and sandy-haired with a face quite forgettable in a crowd. But he had fought in the Seminole War. He had ranged through Texas and into Mexico for six years and been a prisoner of Santa Anna for two. His men would follow him anywhere. He was almost the only Texan with some notion of military discipline, though he didn't go so far as to wear a uniform or salute anyone. Taylor seemed to like him the better for it and had given him a commission as a captain of dragoons. He was also one of the few who could get through enemy lines to come here.

"I'm to speak to Major Brown, have a look around out there," he nodded toward the dark tangle of mesquite, prickly pear, and black thorn, "then carry a report of your condition to General Taylor."

"I'll take you to the major." From the slight wrinkling around the sergeant's eyes Sarah knew he was pleased at the opportunity to ask about the chances of a battle with Arista's main forces. Before he went he succumbed to an avalanche of affection and gave Sarah a pat on the bottom.

She stood on the ramparts awhile longer, looking across the river to the sleeping town. A rooster crowed. Sarah wondered if John Riley and Seamus Hooligan slept in one of those demure, whitewashed houses, and if they were among the Mexican artillery crews firing at her day after day.

A Game of Long Taw

THE GLOWING RED TIP OF CRUZ'S *CIGARRILLO* BOBBED
into view in the predawn darkness, followed by the ghostly
cloud of her white blouse. When she came into the cookfire's light,
she set down the chicken she carried and the basket of dried apricots and tortillas, still warm in their wrapping of plantain leaves.
One end of the cord that Cruz had used to lower the basket over
the fort's parapet was tied to the handle. The other was knotted
around the chicken's leg.

"*Señora* Juarez say the *generales* and *políticos* are fighting in the capital. Maybe Paredes president now."

Cruz and Sarah spoke a mix of Spanish and English, although
when they were alone together Spanish had begun to predominate.

"The foxes quarreling in the henhouse again?"

"*Sí.*"

"When Old Zach wins this war, he won't know who to make
peace with."

Before the break of each day the local farmers gathered in the
ditch at the base of the side wall. The news that Cruz brought back
from her bargaining with them was more important than their produce. Sarah knew she had already stopped at the hospital bombproof,
where Major Brown was recovering from a shot in his leg. She had
told Brown what she had learned. Sarah also knew that Brown

would discount most of it as fabrications, though *Señora* Juarez's stories usually proved reliable.

"What did *Señora* Juarez say about yesterday's battle down toward the coast?" During lulls in the artillery barrage they had heard the sound of distant gunfire. Cruz had spent the day with her hands twisted in her skirt, anxiety sharp in her eyes.

"*El Viejo* won." Cruz always referred to Zachary Taylor as *El Viejo*, the Old Man. "The *Señora* says Arista's men very tired. Very hungry. But they will fight again today."

"*El Viejo*'ll whip 'em today, too."

"They carry men over the river." Cruz pointed upstream. "From Matamoros."

"I reckon they mean to fling themselves at us like dogs on a gut wagon."

If the Mexicans were ferrying across in numbers, Sarah knew they would probably try to breach the walls today. The knowledge rested heavy in the pit of her stomach, but she was strangely at peace with it. She welcomed the dawn light, lolling now like a glowing snake of mist along the eastern parapet.

Let them come, she thought. Let it begin, let it finish.

When the bugler hit his first note, she didn't even resent him, though she couldn't help but blame him for the daily inconvenience of artillery shot. His cheeky rendition of "Reveille" opened the ball this morning, too. A cannon coughed in the distance and the artillerymen on the north bastion yelled "Old Scratch" so the fort's inhabitants would know from which emplacement the shot was coming. Then their piece boomed in answer. The men of the Seventh ran from the rags of their tents. Some began filling sacks with sand. Others, muskets in hand, headed for the sloped causeways to the diamond-shaped bastions at the six corners of the ramparts.

Sarah rolled up her sleeves, fitted the bucket handles in the notches she'd carved on a tent pole, and hoisted it to her shoulders. She walked up the nearest slope to the north bastion and the sleek eight-pounder that hawked and spat, bellowed, smoked, and rocked back with a self-satisfied air on the long wooden trail of its carriage. She ladled out drinking water for the six men of the crew who were stripped to the waist and already glistening with sweat. Then she headed for the next gun in the circuit she intended to follow the rest of the day.

By the time she reached the sergeant's eighteen-pounder, a pall of smoke hung over it. Burning powder had blackened the crew's faces and striped their sweaty chests. She didn't try to talk to them. Even if they hadn't stuffed tow into their ears, their skulls would ring too loudly to hear her well. The sergeant leaned on his seven-foot-long ram and waited until the others had drunk before he dipped the ladle into the bucket.

"Heads up!" The loader squatted and threw his arms over his head.

The shell burst like a desert poppy opening next to one of the men. His blood sprayed those nearest him. Glowing iron fragments caromed outward, and Sarah's sergeant tilted with a look of annoyance and fell to his knees. He clutched his thigh and drops of blood formed garnet-colored necklaces along the clefts between his fingers.

"Men down," Sarah shouted to the compound below.

The sergeant nodded to the gunner. "Corporal Simms, you're the one."

Sarah bent to help him up, but he put the ram into her hand instead. She shook her head and looked for a man to give it to. "I have to see you to the hospital, Will."

"No one else to do it, and you know the game of long taw as well as anyone, Sarah." He winked and pretended to shoot a marble. He unbuckled the wide leather shoulder strap that held his sword at his left side and handed it to her.

He put an arm across Sarah's shoulders and she helped him limp to a shaded section of the wall. She eased him down so he sat with his back to it, then she strapped on the sword and settled it on her hip. She tucked her skirt up under her belt, bringing the hem halfway to her knees.

Two orderlies sprinted toward the bastion, weaving in and out of the lines of men on the ramp. Sarah wasn't surprised to see Lewis Allen following them. She had told him more than once that he had a keener interest in death and festering than the average maggot. He always reminded her that his boss paid him to report the glories of war and eulogize the fallen. And besides, lists of the names of dead heroes sold a lot of newspapers.

The orderlies helped the sergeant down the ramp. Sarah caught hold of the dead man's remaining foot and dragged the left half of him off to one side for the men to retrieve on their return trip. He should provide enough death and mangling in one messy package to suit the scribbler. Before she left him she bowed her head, closed her eyes, made the sign of the cross, and murmured a verse from Psalm 31. "Into Thy hands I commend my spirit: Thou hast redeemed me, O Lord God of truth."

When she opened her eyes, she saw that the men of the crew had removed their hats and stood with heads bowed. She didn't say aloud another verse from that same Psalm, but she thought it. "I am forgotten as a dead man out of mind: I am like a broken vessel."

The gunner beckoned her to take her place. He looked rattled by his new command.

"We're still short a man," Sarah reminded him.

Lewis Allen arrived out of breath, sweat staining his grimy linen shirt and trousers.

"Here's a hero for you, scribbler." Sarah nodded toward the remains. Allen paled under his sunburn. Sarah prodded him with her ramrod to get his attention. "You must prick for us."

"Prick?"

"Whilst I ram the barrel, you cover the touchhole so sparks don't fly out. When I pack the charge and ball, you fill the touchhole from the priming flask. We're out of fuses, so we'll have to use powder to set it off."

"It's not my job, Western." Allen would have run, except that Sarah held a fistful of his sweaty shirt.

"This ain't a job, scribbler, it's a duty."

"I'll prick, Western." The powder monkey was a slat of a boy with a Massachusetts twang that reminded her of Lieutenant Lincoln. "He c'n fetch the powder."

"Hellfire." The gunner looked frantically around him. "The thumbstall."

"What are we looking for?" Allen watched, bewildered, as they clawed through the bloody debris of metal fragments and drifts of tow used to pack the ammunition in the caissons.

"Here it is." Sarah held up the dead prick's hand, sheared at the wrist. The orderlies who had carried away his remains had missed it.

She removed the horsehair-stuffed leather thimble still strapped in place on the thumb and wrapped the hand in a rag to bury with him later. She wiped the thumbstall on her skirt before she gave it to the powder monkey. Allen looked as though he would very much like to send his breakfast over the parapet. He swayed and blinked in the sunlight as he listened, dazed and intent, to the gunner's shouted instructions.

Sarah pulled two tufts of tow from the ammunition caisson and pushed them into her ears. She gave two more to Allen. While the loader ran the iron corkscrew of his worm down the bore to dislodge old shreds of cloth, Allen went to the half-empty caisson and brought back a powder charge packed in a cotton sack. The new prick used his leather-encased thumb to cover the touchhole while Sarah dipped the swab end of her rammer in a keg of water and reamed the bore with it. She tapped the bore with the heavy wooden end to alert the loader, who dropped the powder charge and ball into the muzzle. Then she shoved the wooden plug into the barrel and pushed hard, packing the load against the breech.

The gunner squinted through the sights on the breech and muzzle, lining up the brush-covered sandbags of the Mexicans' emplacement on the other side of the river. When he had adjusted for windage and elevation, he shouted, "Ready!"

While the loader applied the smoldering slow match to the trail of powder, Sarah assumed her position at the carriage wheels. She leaned away from the gun and opened her mouth to reduce the effect of the concussion. She had stood close to many a cannon in full throat, but she never got used to the swell of sound that battered her skull and left her dizzy and confused. When the piece had settled back on its trail, she prepared to do it all again.

Cruz and Nancy brought water, but they had hardly moved out of sight when Sarah's mouth turned dry as dust. The acrid smoke stifled every breath. Sand flying from a cannonball's impact on the parapet coated her. Before long the sodden mop on the end of her ram hissed and gave off steam when she pushed it into the barrel. Under the coating of gunpowder, burns reddened her hands and face. Sparks ignited her skirt, leaving black-rimmed holes when she swatted them out. The cannon gave off so much heat that the weather little mattered. But as the day grew hotter, the drying pool of blood produced a sweetish odor that mixed with the stench of burning sulfur and nitrates, and ammonia from where the men relieved themselves against the parapet.

The crew performed a sort of ballet in the midst of it, moving in rhythm with each other, forward and back, breaking cadence only when the enemy's shot forced them to dodge. Even Lewis Allen trotted smartly back and forth from the caisson to the cannon and held the powder and shot ready at the instant the loader turned to take it. Aside from the gunner's hoarse shouts of "Ready!" no one spoke. Sarah's arms hung as stiff and heavy in their sockets as the ramrod itself. Nothing existed but the roar and smoke and searing heat.

Around midafternoon a large section of the nearby wall slid into the ditch. The Mexican guns stopped firing. The crew stood stunned in the ringing silence. Sarah surveyed the chunk of daylight where the parapet had been.

Her voice echoed in her skull as though she were shouting into a well. "I think they mean to join us for supper." She hauled her pistol out from the waist of her skirt. She primed and loaded it from the powder flask and bullet pouch hanging at her side. She smiled at the men, her teeth brilliantly white in her blackened face. "Shall we serve them up some hot lead, boys?"

➔ ←

Sarah washed the soot and sand from her face and pressed a lint dressing to her cheek. The gash underneath it throbbed in time to the beating of her heart as she knelt next to her sergeant's pallet. After all these hours the harried physician had been unable to do more than put a hasty bandage on his torn thigh. Sarah removed the dressing from the ragged wound, and with her free hand and a pair of tobacco tongs she picked bits of bone from it. While she worked she positioned her body so it shaded him from the late afternoon rays that slanted under the torn awning. His face was haggard and stiff with pain.

"You look sad as a hound dog with the janders, Will."

"Life's a hard bargain, Sarah."

"Doc says you'll be back in business in a month or three. But as for pleasure, I reckon tonight's time enough." Sarah grinned at him and the long cut on her cheek began to bleed again.

"Did you get a field commission for that nick?"

"Had a brush with a Mex major and his boys." Sarah felt vaguely ashamed of her pride in the saber wound. "We sent the boys scampering back the way they came."

"And the major?"

"He made the return feet first." She raised her head and listened as the shelling began again from the Mexicans' batteries. "I'll leave the saber in the tent for you."

"Glad it was of use." His eyes narrowed in the spasm that usually served him as a smile, though it could have been a tic of pain. "You've killed a man, my girl, and been bloodied in the doing of it." He said it so softly she moved closer and bent over him.

"I only did what I had to."

"That's soldierin' to a T, ain't it?" His smile expanded to include a twitch at the corners of his mouth.

A shovel-shaped metal fragment keened like a hawk as it ripped through the awning and tore Sarah's sleeve. It sank almost to the trailing edge into Will's neck. For a few long heartbeats Sarah could only stare at it.

It had severed both his windpipe and his jugular vein. If she extracted it, she could never stop the bleeding; but he would choke to death in any case. Pulling the shrapnel out would speed him on his way.

"I will miss you, Will." She kissed him on the forehead. Then with shaking hands she grasped the thin edge and tugged it gently.

When it came free, the blood spurted like a fountain, pouring over the tattoo of the alligator on his chest. He looked up at her, his breath rasping and bubbling in its efforts to reach his lungs. She realized this was the first time she had seen sadness in his eyes.

His mouth moved, and though no words sounded she could tell from the shapes his lips made what he was saying. "Good-bye, Sarah."

"I know you aren't a church-going man, Will, but I reckon you'd want me to say this anyway." Still looking into his amber-colored eyes she recited the prayer she had heard so often in the past six years. " 'I am the resurrection and the life, saith the Lord. He that believeth in me, though he were dead, yet shall he live: and whosoever liveth and believeth in me, shall never die.' " And she made the sign of the cross and gave him a last kiss to send him on his way.

They hadn't time for an elaborate funeral inside the low picket fence of the small cemetery next to the oxen's corral. Sarah and Cruz and the Skinners gathered with the artillery crews to pay their respects to the sergeant while shells and solid shot continued to fall. Major Brown had finished the short ceremony and Sarah and the others were walking away when an exploding shell hit the shallow grave. It blasted the loose sand away and jolted Will's canvas-wrapped body half out of it.

Sarah returned to the grave and smiled sadly. "Will, I believe you misunderstand the notion of resurrection."

→ ←

Muffled artillery fire popped miles to the northeast where gray smoke smudged the horizon. Out in the vast bewilderment of mesquite and blackthorn Taylor's army battled Arista's, but no one in Fort Texas knew what was happening, much less who was winning. Everyone able to walk or be carried stood on the banquette at the rear wall and watched hundreds of Mexicans pelt past beyond musket range. Most of them wore the dirty canvas coats and faded, frayed blue trousers of conscriptees, although officers' brilliant blue tailed coats with crimson cuffs and turnbacks flashed among them.

Nancy sat astride the eighteen-pounder. Cruz and Caroline Skinner stood on a caisson.

"Do they mean to attack again?" Nancy asked.

They all dreaded that. The artillery crews had fired the last of the canister and shot and the infantry had almost no ammunition left. Sarah wore Will Kelly's saber and she meant to use it if the enemy swarmed over the walls.

"No." Sarah peered through the sergeant's dented brass spyglass. "Looks like they're barnosing the *fandango*."

From around the bend upriver, two scows bumbled into view. Even at this distance Sarah could see that the ferryboats' decks seethed with humanity.

"¿Qué pasa, Way-stern?"

Sarah passed Cruz the glass. The scene on the ferries elated her, but it wasn't one she wanted to describe to Cruz.

The two boats floated rudderless on the current. Conscriptees and officers alike tossed aside their old Brown Bess muskets and waded out to the ferries. They pulled the boats aground on a sand-bank and fought with those already aboard. A company of cavalry, their plumed shakos atilt, splashed into the river. They urged their mounts onto the boats and the last ones shoved them away from the shoal. They pushed the occupants into the fast-flowing water. When a priest held up his crucifix in an attempt to restore order, a cavalryman put the point of his lance to his chest, forcing him over the side.

Sarah couldn't tell what Cruz thought of such a humiliating scene among her countrymen. When she handed back the glass she wore what Sarah called her monte gaze, neutral and unreadable. Without a word she left the rampart.

➔ ←

The fifes and drums struck up "Yankee Doodle" when the Second Dragoons got within earshot of the fort. Zachary Taylor rode at the head of the ragged column and his Jersey wagon, loaded with wounded, trundled along behind him. Sarah ran with the rest of the fort's garrison to greet them. When the two sections of the army re-united, Sarah could not have said which looked dirtier and wearier and bloodier. Some men of the Second Dragoons rode slumped along their mounts' necks with their arms dangling. Some limped on foot, having left their horses dead on the battlefield.

Calling James's name, Cruz darted among the dragoons. Nancy ran in search of the artillery and Sam Ringgold. Sarah looked for George Lincoln's big white gelding. When she saw him, she maneu-vered through the press of people and animals and vehicles to walk beside him.

"Made captain, I see."

"I'd rather I were still a lieutenant and the owner of these bars were alive." Lincoln had the look that Sarah recognized. It was the stare of a man whose legs had carried him away from the field of death, but whose mind and heart and soul still wandered there among the smoke and the corpses.

"How did the Mexicans fight?"

"Well. Very well indeed." Lincoln drew a deep breath, as though surprised his lungs still functioned, his heart still beat, his blood still ebbed and flowed in his veins. "The artillery sowed terrible carnage among them. They fell in heaps with the ghastliest wounds, yet still could glare defiance at the enemy as they expired. We found one poor fellow who'd lain wounded all night. He asked for *agua*, water, and Twiggs exclaimed, 'Men, give this poor lad something to drink.' In an instant the whole company offered him their canteens."

"How did the artillery perform?"

"My God, Western . . ." Lincoln brightened and forgot his abhorrence of using the Lord's name frivolously. "They were brilliant. Sam Ringgold has given us the gift of ubiquity when it comes to artillery. His pieces flashed from one line of engagement to another. They turned on a dime and their crews had them positioned in minutes. I've never seen the like. Even Taylor was impressed."

"Nancy will be proud of Captain Ringgold."

"Major. He was breveted a major." Lincoln's eyes went remote again.

"He's dead, isn't he?"

"The Mexicans concentrated their fire on the artillery, of course. A shot tore the flesh off Sam's left leg, passed through his horse, and took off the right one, both above the knees. He bled to death."

"Western," Twiggs roared, "we need help with the wounded."

"Yes, sir."

As she walked next to George Lincoln, Sarah put a hand on his knee and he covered it with his own for several heartbeats. It was their way of consoling each other. It was their way of saluting a comrade whose laugh they wouldn't hear again at the evening cook-fire. Then she turned away and climbed onto the running board of a baggage wagon.

She looked over the sideboard at the wounded piled inside. They were all Mexican, and much quieter than an equal number of American wounded would be. Only low groans escaped them, instead of the screaming Sarah was used to. They were small men, not much over five feet, and they looked so very young. They had the dark faces of Indians, the poorest of the poor. Sarah could see the swollen bellies and brittle hair, the preternaturally bright eyes that marked malnutrition.

"Never mind these." James joined her on the running board. "We're taking them directly over the river to be cared for by their own." Then he jumped down and trotted toward the next wagon.

"Did Cruz find you?" Sarah shouted.

"Yes."

Sarah lifted the men gently from the wagon beds, carried them to the awning next to the hospital bombproof, and laid them in lines on the ground there. She and Cruz worked until sundown cleaning wounds, bandaging, soothing. Finally she stood up in the fading light.

"Where's Nancy?" she asked.

Cruz shrugged. George Lincoln passed by and Sarah intercepted him.

"Have you seen Nancy Skinner?"

"No. Some of the artillerymen said she begged a horse of them. Do you think she went to Port Isabel to find Sam Ringgold?"

"She would do that." Sarah turned one way, then the other, biting on the side of her finger in distress. So many wounded lay untended. She couldn't leave them. "Trying to talk sense to her is like whistling jigs to a milestone."

"I'll fetch her."

"I'd be forever obliged."

Lincoln put a finger to the brim of his hat and swung onto his big white gelding.

→ ←

Lincoln found Nancy at dawn, huddled on the freshly turned mound of earth inside the fence made of captured guns and bayonets. The weapons had been sawed off to produce a neat slope from the head to the foot of Ringgold's grave. An ordnance captain had designed it and it stood out like a shrine among the rude palings and unsodded graves of the others.

He knelt next to her and put his arms around her. She fell sobbing against his chest.

" 'Dulce et decorum est pro patria mori,' " he murmured. Then he translated. " 'It is sweet and fitting to die for one's country.' "

Outfoxing the Tiger

S ARAH DUCKED TO CLEAR THE LOW LINTEL AND CRUZ followed her inside. A tiny Mexican woman stayed in the doorway, her ancient black shawl shading her face. Sarah suspected she didn't want to be trapped in a closed space with such a large and unpredictable flame-haired creature. Cruz had already reported the stories swirling through Matamoros—that with her pistol and saber Sarah had single-handedly fought off the attack on Fort Texas. That her beauty could strike men mute. That she could lift a loaded wagon with one hand. That she would shoot a man as soon as look at him.

Sarah opened the shutters and looked out into a dusty garden shaded by orange and apricot trees and surrounded by a crumbling adobe wall. A domed clay bake-oven squatted in one corner. In another, a tumbledown shed of mesquite limbs leaned against the wall. It contained a privy, a big selling point.

The scent of orange blossoms drifted through the window and wandered into the far corners. From the warren of alleys and shabby single-story houses around her, Sarah heard dogs barking, a *burro* braying, the contented cackle of chickens. The more enterprising neighbors had trooped to the plain beyond the huts of mesquite wood that straggled outward from neighborhoods with slightly more substantial houses like this one. They were offering their labor and hawking food, water, cigars, firewood, striped cotton blankets, and the evil-smelling brew they called *pulque* to the troops setting up their tents there.

Dust motes danced in a morning sunbeam. The floor was packed earth, the walls limed. Sarah swept her hand through the cobwebs curtaining the corner near the ceiling. She didn't have to reach far. The soot-blackened poles that served as rafters were only two feet above her head. She would have to get Cruz to show her how to make the best use of the clay stove that rose like a mesa in the center of the room.

She peered through the interior doorway into a cubicle barely long enough for her cot. She wondered how rife the fleas were.

She turned to Cruz. "How much would she be wanting? I'd pay by the week."

"She say three *pesos*, but that is too much."

Sarah nodded at the woman who inclined her head gravely in return. "Tell her we have a deal." She retrieved the coins from the sack in the pocket of her skirt.

The woman accepted them, then took her hand and bowed so low over it Sarah wondered if she intended to kiss it. "May God bless you, *Señora* Western."

"And you, *Señora* Lopez."

Sarah's new landlady shuffled out into the sunlight, and Cruz smiled. "Come see my new house, Western."

"Don't get too attached to it, *mi hija*, we'll be moving on soon." Sarah had heard older Mexican women call younger ones "my daughter" so often the words came automatically to her.

They didn't have far to walk. The house that *Señora* Lopez had rented to Cruz backed up against the rear wall of Sarah's garden. As she followed Cruz through the alley and around the corner of the wall, she did feel motherly. She knew that since their escape from Antonio Águila, Cruz considered her an invincible protector. She seemed content to let Sarah worry about Águila now.

Sarah leaned a forearm against Cruz's lintel and ducked her head to see under it. The single room was smaller and in poorer repair than Sarah's, but it boasted shutters that closed and adobe walls two feet thick to keep out the heat and the wind. It was the grandest Cruz had ever called home. She had already put flowers in an old cracker tin on the plank shelf pegged into the wall. She had laid out the army issue bed ticking and covered it with striped cotton blankets from the local market. James's army chest sat in the center of the room with the single tin plate neatly laid out and the spoon next to it.

"It's right nice, Cruz." She felt a pang of longing though. She missed Jack. She missed Will Kelly. "I'd best go foraging before the Tiger picks the town clean. Old Zach's put him in charge of procurement."

"¿El Tigre?"

"Colonel Davey Twiggs. The Bengal Tiger is a one-man plague of locusts."

"I go with you, so the people they don't cheat you."

"No. You stay and set things to your liking." Sarah started to leave but turned back. "I'll be in need of some bettys, so if any likely looking women apply for work, tell them I'll talk to them this afternoon."

"Bettys?"

"Maids. Servants. We call them bettys."

"Why?"

Sarah shrugged. "It's a common name among the servant class, I suppose."

Sarah paused in the doorway feeling the coolness of the interior against her sweat-damp back. She gazed out at her new neighborhood. This quiet suburb in an alien country didn't seem all that strange to her. It reminded her of St. Augustine. The Second Dragoons had bivouacked there before slogging toward their disastrous rendezvous with Wild Cat, John Horse, Alligator, the indomitable old Sam Jones, and a swampful of their warriors.

Here on the outskirts of Matamoros, fruit trees and fenced patches of corn and beans and plantains separated the adobe buildings, most of which looked like larger versions of the clay stove in Sarah's garden. She found something soothing in the look of the houses, raised as they were from the earth around them, molded by bare brown hands rather than sawed and hammered and planed into being. She nodded to her new neighbors and bid them a cheerful good morning in Spanish. When they realized she would not shoot them or bewitch them, they smiled shyly and called her friend and wished God's blessings on her.

She found her team and rig in the small pasture she had rented

earlier from *Señora* Lopez. In fact, she was beginning to think that
out-at-elbows *Señora* Lopez owned most of Matamoros. Jake was
cadging dried apricots and *cigarrillos* from the boys who clambered
over the wagon. He was devouring them both with equal relish and
he objected noisily when he saw the harness in Sarah's hand.

While she hitched the mules, the boys surrounded her, all
promising to work themselves into an early grave for her. She had
heard the list of services before—polish boots, carry water, feed and
curry the mules, guard the wagon, sweep, scrub, dig, haul, garden,
plunder, and pander.

One of them stood back from the swarm. The tatters of a white
shirt fluttered about him. His white breeches ended in shreds at the
scuffed knobs of his knees. His thin legs and feet were bare.

He looked her straight in the eye and winked, slowly and with
great gravity, as though he had the answer to life's deepest mysteries
and were willing to share them with her alone. A doe-eyed flimflam-
mer and a grifter in the bud. Charmed in spite of the certainty that
he would do his best to swindle her, she nodded to him. He pushed
his way through the crowd and gazed up at her, as though assessing
the best way to reach a nest of omelets in the top branches of a very
tall tree.

"What do you have?" she asked.

He held up his hand next to the large brown ear poking from his
rick of stiff black hair and opened and closed it, beckoning her to
bend down. *"Un tesoro,"* he murmured.

"A treasure, eh?" She gave him a baleful stare as she collected the
reins and her whip and climbed into the wagon. She slapped the
seat beside her. *"Vamos."*

He took a cornhusk *cigarrillo* out of the pouch hanging on a cord
strung diagonally across his chest. He lit it from another boy's, and
with a triumphant grin at his inferiors, he appeared so suddenly next
to her it seemed likely he had flown there.

He tapped his bony chest. "Hanibal."

He began a galloping and largely unintelligible commentary. The
cigarrillo bobbed and circled in his mouth as he used his chin to
point out Matamoros's scenic and social wonders. When the cigarette had burned almost away he produced a packet of husks from
somewhere in the remnants of his clothes. He took a pinch of to-

bacco from the pouch, rolled another one, and lit it with the last embers of the first.

Sarah stopped next to one of the hundreds of water sellers who roamed Matamoros's streets. A huge pottery jug rode on his back, suspended by a leather strap attached around his head. Another jug hung in front to balance it.

Sarah pointed back the way she had just come. "*Mi casa,*" she said. "*Mañana.*"

"*Sí, Señora.*"

She didn't know her address, but she knew that didn't matter. By tomorrow everyone within a mile radius could tell the man where she lived.

The dusty lanes turned to cobblestone-paved streets and the buildings loomed larger, closer together, substantial as continents. Their massive oak doors rose eight feet tall. Their walls were painted in blues and yellows and greens. Their owners would not likely have chickens for sale or pigs either.

The boy pointed out the turns until Sarah had no idea how to get back to where she now lived. Toward the center of the city the lanes narrowed and twisted and the houses stood shoulder to shoulder. People here, with more to lose to an occupying army, had disappeared. As Jake and Buck ambled down the empty streets, the clatter of their hooves echoed off the canyon of cut stone and brick. No one leaned on the delicate wrought-iron filigree that enclosed the second-floor balconies. The shutters were closed behind the bars that spanned the windows from top to bottom.

"Where's this treasure, sprat?" Sarah raked him with a sideways glance.

He pointed to a passage next to an unpainted stone building with a small door and no balconies or windows.

"The rig won't fit." This might be a trap, but she didn't care. She already had one saber scar and she didn't mind risking another.

The boy took two of the empty sacks, jumped to the ground, and held up a finger, commanding her to wait. He jogged around the back of the building and returned just about the time Sarah decided he meant to abandon her here. With a conjurer's flourish he held up one of the sacks. She took it and peeked inside. It bulged with fat cigars, redolent and smug in their taut leaf jackets.

"La guardia se fue." The boy pantomimed the warehouse's guard running off. He spread his arms toward the building and rotated them, including it all, from side to side and floor to rafters. *"Tabaco y cigarros bastante."*

Sarah frowned. "I don't abide thievery."

"No, no, *Señora.*" He agitated his finger indignantly. *"Son del gobierno y el gobierno es ladrón."*

Sarah laughed. The smokes and their makings belonged to the government, he said. And the government was a thief. Well, that was as true a statement as had ever been made.

He stowed the sacks under the seat, crossed his arms over his chest, and used his chin to point straight ahead. Several more turns and the street opened out into a large plaza bordered by china trees. A market was in noisy progress there. The troupe of mountebanks that had preyed on the soldiers in Corpus Christi had already set up business in the center of the plaza. Its members were industriously selling the elixir of branch water, wood alcohol, pepper, and coloring that they claimed increased male potency and female fertility.

Sarah wasn't surprised to see that Colonel David Twiggs, the Bengal Tiger, had already arrived with a dozen supply wagons and a detail of dragoons. In spite of the bushy white side-whiskers, round face, and knob of a nose that earned him his nickname, he looked more like a red-faced walrus than a tiger. His shadow could have shaded any three Mexicans, and they eyed him warily, as though they expected him to go suddenly amok and crash through their flimsy stands. He trotted his big roan in Sarah's direction. Hanibal slipped over the side of the wagon.

"Good morning, Colonel." Sarah was as wary as the Mexicans. David Twiggs was entertaining from a distance in about the same way a volcano was.

He had a very unhappy looking man in tow on a liver-colored jennet. Sarah recognized him as the *alcalde,* the mayor of Matamoros. He and the other city officials, all dressed in radiant, starched white, had welcomed General Taylor at the Mexicans' fort on the river two days ago. General Arista had decamped with his army, leaving the citizens to deal with the Americans. The mayor still wore his white suit, but it was rumpled now. His expression was equally rumpled, but Sarah didn't feel sorry for him. She had already learned that the folk of Matamoros considered him the biggest thief in public office, and he had stiff competition for the title.

"Good day to you, Western," Twiggs shouted. "The mayor here has been most helpful." He waved at the wagons loaded with crates, sacks, barrels, and fresh lumber, and the mayor seemed to shrink a little more inside his suit.

Sarah knew the man could hardly be blamed for disclosing the whereabouts of anything of value the government might have hoarded. No one could stop the Tiger.

Twiggs held up a round tin. "I've just found oysters. A case of them. The last in the city, I do believe."

Sarah took a cigar from the sack under the seat and handed it to him. "Then I reckon you found these, too."

"By Jupiter, just the thing!"

The mayor looked as though he were about to cry. Giving up weapons and ammunition was one thing, tobacco quite another.

"Colonel!" A dragoon held Hanibal up by his middle while he kicked and squirmed. "I caught him pilfering the corn and beans in our wagons, sir."

"Damn." Twiggs's ruddy complexion deepened to a hue that hardly seemed possible in a human being. His nostrils flared, his cheeks expanded, his eyes bulged, and his white whiskers seemed electrified with rage. Sarah had seen his act often, but it always impressed her.

"It's a misunderstanding, Colonel," Sarah said. "I told him I intended to purchase supplies. He must have thought I was buying them from you and went to get them for me."

"Abiding theft abets it." Twiggs glared at the boy as the dragoon rode up with him still dangling and kicking. Twiggs could terrify even this urchin, who didn't strike Sarah as easily terrified.

"He's been a help to me, Colonel. Let him go and I'll give you a dozen cheroots."

"One doesn't buy justice, Western."

"The blame lies with my lack of the lingo."

Twiggs didn't hesitate long. "Let the felon go." He reached for the cigars Sarah held out to him and the dragoon dropped Hanibal.

The boy scrambled up beside Sarah. He knew a protector when

he saw one, and this one had saved him from being boiled for a red-faced *yanqui's* supper. Twiggs started off.

"Colonel, I'd be willing to give you the rest of these cigars for the case of oysters." Sarah held out the sack with a show of reluctance.

"Half the case."

Sarah pulled a cigar from the sack and passed it under her nose, inhaling with a blissful expression. "These are *cincos*," she said. "Cost you five cents apiece if you can find them, which you can't. I'll trade you three-quarters of the oysters for them."

"You drive a hard bargain." But Twiggs looked pleased with himself as he made the exchange.

When he had ridden away, Sarah grabbed the boy before he could slide down again. Holding him with one hand she patted his trousers, fore and aft, with the other. Underneath she found more cornmeal and beans in another satchel around his waist.

"You are a slippery salamander." But she knew what he had been thinking. He had helped himself to the spoils of two governments, his own and the enemy's. "You didn't believe I was fixin' to pay you for your time, did you?"

She handed him the food and a peso and grinned. "Let's go get more of them cigars, before the Tiger figures out where they came from."

He guided her back to the warehouse and disappeared around the corner of the building while she kept watch in front. She didn't hold with stealing, but outmaneuvering David Twiggs at procurement wasn't theft, it was triumph. Hanibal returned with five full sacks and gave a cigar each to Jake and Buck. When they reached the market again he clambered down.

He raised a hand in salute. *"Hasta luego, Señora."* He stopped to buy a roll of warm tortillas and beans heaped on a plantain leaf. Then he ran across the plaza, opened the heavy oaken door of a stone building, and slipped inside.

The morning was wasting and Sarah needed to do her marketing, but curiosity drew her after him. She tied the team to a post and opened the door. She couldn't see into the darkness inside, but she heard a loud buzzing of flies and voices pleading in Spanish. The stench hit her in the face, stung her eyes, forced its way into her nostrils and down her throat. She gagged and backed out. She put her kerchief over her nose and mouth, opened the door again, and allowed it to close behind her. She took shallow breaths while she waited for her eyes to adjust to the gloom. Scores of bodies paved the floor.

A girl of sixteen or seventeen waved the flies from a boy about the same age. An older woman baked tortillas on a flat rock propped up next to a small fire while several children sat by a man Sarah assumed was their father. Next to him lay a corpse. She saw Hanibal in a far corner, rolling beans into a tortilla and feeding it to a gaunt individual.

A voice speaking in English startled Sarah.

"Those are the ones mowed down by your artillery." The speaker appeared from the shadows. He had rolled up the full sleeves of his bloodied white linen shirt. He wore the short leather jacket and tight, laced trousers of a member of Mexico's upper class. "As you can see, canister and grape reduce the human body to its elements. Like turning a loaf of bread back into dough. Over there you have those merely struck down by bullets. A neater bunch."

"Sarah Borginnis." Sarah offered her hand, then pulled it back when the man brought his hands from behind his back and she noticed that he held a bloody saw and a gangrenous leg cut off below the knee. "I can help you here."

"Gerald Malloy. Physician. Originally from Hoboken, New Jersey, and resident of this fair city for eight years." He held up the leg. "This reminds me of the old story of the soldier who brought an enemy's leg back from the field of battle and displayed it proudly as proof of his bravery. 'Why didn't you cut off his head?' the other fellow asked. 'Why, bless me, someone had already done it.'" He tossed the leg onto a waist-high heap of limbs, raising a cloud of the flies that crawled over it. "I have not had to amputate any heads, however."

Sarah realized she had found the Mexicans wounded in the battle Taylor's army had just fought. Among them were probably the men she had seen in the baggage wagon before they were sent here. General Arista had abandoned them.

"I'll send for some bandages." She rolled up her sleeves, tore a strip from the hem of her dress, and began binding up the nearest wound.

A Snake in the Garden

>———I—‹•›—•—‹›—•—‹›—I—‹

A STEADY RAIN DISPELLED SOME OF THE JUNE HEAT.
Sarah's new servants had rigged several awnings and two
marquee tents in the center of the garden. The big marquees were
the first of their kind the locals had seen. The canvas rose in fits and
starts all morning, with shouting and gesticulating and pleas for the
assistance of God and the Virgin and most of the saints. The officers, tired of waiting, pitched in to roll up the sides. They filed inside while Sarah's employees were carrying out the stools and laying
the boards on trestles to serve as tables. Besides three men, Sarah
had hired two neighborhood women to cook and two more to help
Nancy ferry meals and rum and brandy punch. Those two now circulated with trays of cigars, and soon a dense cloud of aromatic
smoke mixed with the damp summer air under the tents.

Cruz was already at work under an awning beneath the apricot
tree in the far corner of the garden. She stood barefoot at the small
table, and wore a gambler's green eye shade in spite of the cloudy
day. James had given it to her and she said it brought her luck. Most
of the men hunched around Cruz's monte table called themselves
journalists. More of them arrived daily.

Cruz had on James's second-best linen shirt and a pair of his uniform trousers. Wearing parts of his uniform was against regulations,
but she looked so charming no one said anything. She had mended

the shirt and scrubbed it until it was a blinding white, then pressed it. The trousers almost fit her waist now that the child inside her made its presence noticeable.

George Lincoln sat near the end of a long table under the open tent. His elbows rested on the table boards and his long legs projected his perfectly polished boots out the other side. He read aloud from a newspaper that had arrived so recently it hadn't passed through more than five or six pairs of hands.

> During the whole of the bombardment, the wife of one of the soldiers remained at Fort Brown, and though the shot and shells were constantly flying on every side, she disdained to seek shelter in the bombproofs, but labored the whole time cooking and taking care of the soldiers without the least regard for her own safety. Her bravery was the admiration of all who were in the fort, and she has thus acquired the name of "The Great Western."

"Did you write that, Allen?" Lincoln asked.

Lewis Allen bowed in acknowledgment.

"Not a mention of Western at the cannon." Captain Braxton Bragg had taken over the Third Artillery after Sam Ringgold's death. He lounged on an upturned keg with his back to the end of the table. His elbows were propped behind him on the boards and his legs splayed in front of him. One of his feet rested on a small box where Hanibal hunkered, vigorously rubbing his left boot with tallow and lamp black.

Allen shrugged. "Our readers prefer to read about more womanly feats."

"That reminds me." Bragg beckoned Sarah closer. He reached into his haversack and took out an army issue cap with the gold trim of the artillery. "The men want you to have this." He placed it on Sarah's head then held up his glass in salute. "To the Great Western, the heroine of Fort Texas."

"Here, here!" Everyone stood and raised a toast. "To the Great Western."

"Long may she wave." Lincoln kissed her on the cheek.

"I don't have Lieutenant Bliss's way with words, so I'll just say 'Thank you kindly.' " Sarah curtsied and returned to supervising the cooks and the maids in the kitchen arbor.

"For pure rhetoric no one can hold a candle to Bill Bliss," Lincoln said. "Remember the lieutenant who swam across the river and was taken by the Mexicans?"

"He claimed he intended to look for a missing officer," Bragg added.

"In fact, he had become enamored of a damsel on the other side. In his report of the affair Bill Bliss said the lieutenant was 'laboring under mental alienation at the time.' "

" 'Mental alienation.' " That elicited catcalls.

"Only Perfect Bliss would describe a man determined to dip his wick as suffering from 'mental alienation.' " Bragg dropped his polished boot from Hanibal's box and replaced it with the scuffed one.

"This country puts me in mind of Don Quixote." Lincoln gestured with his cigar to the two dark-eyed women carrying food from the kitchen. "Wineskins, balconies, a profusion of flowers, enchanting *dulcineas*."

"Here's to the *dulcineas!*" Bragg lifted his glass again.

Bragg and Lincoln had to shout above the patter of rain on the canvas overhead and the hubbub inside. So many officers crowded Sarah's garden that she had had to set up more trestles and boards to accommodate them. The men ate platters of fried hominy grits and chicken gravy, boiled beef, and biscuits baked in the domed oven. They talked and argued, drank, smoked, and sang while the local folk circulated among them, delivering laundry and selling souvenirs. In spite of the steady rain, more people filed in and out of the house with firewood, water and charcoal, produce, chickens, and the occasional goat or pig. Two trumpets, a guitar, and a *guitarrón* struck up a frantic waltz under an overhanging eave on the other side of the wall.

A row of dragoons' horses stood tethered in the street with their heads over the wall, watching the activity. A small army of boys brushed their flanks and withers, combed their manes and tails, blacked their hooves, and oiled the saddles under a nearby arbor. Other people, young and old, held banana leaves or cotton blankets over their heads and stood on tiptoe to peer over the wall, too. They seemed vastly entertained by the goings-on inside.

With a tray held above her head Concepción steered around the bootblack boys and the officers' orderlies and black servants. She pushed through the clouds of cigar smoke that the men were replenishing faster than the river breeze could dissipate them. She stepped over legs and swerved to avoid the stacked muskets, scattered haversacks, and the swords leaning against the tables. She had come-hither eyes and a beguiling smile. She wore a white skirt and a long white blouse gathered by a red, yellow, and blue–striped belt around a waist so small it enticed hands to circle it. She jumped, though, when Sarah shouted. Even the musicians fell suddenly and deafeningly silent.

"Welcome, General! Come in and set a spell."

Sarah strode so vigorously toward the gate she snapped the hem of her skirt like a canvas sail luffing in a brisk wind. She only slowed down to grab the muddy hems of Bravo Jones's flannel trousers. She yanked his boots from the table top with such force she flipped him heels over head off his stool and into the mud. Captain Lincoln hurried along behind her. He had been promoted to Taylor's staff and he was anxious to please.

Tenting a blanket over her head with one arm, she held Whitey's bridle while Zachary Taylor dismounted, his knees cracking audibly in the silence. Rain dripped from the drooping brim of his wide Mexican *sombrero*. He wore a coat of no particular cut or color and a pair of denim trousers that had defied all of Sarah's attempts to scrub the stains out of them. The edges of the pockets had frayed from the rubbing of his hands. Sweat soaked the checked kerchief knotted at his neck, but he took it off and wiped his flushed face.

It looked as though half the population of Matamoros had splashed along after Taylor and his entourage. They stood under more banana leaves in a rain that was finally abating. Sarah could hear murmurs of *"El Viejo"* and *"El Sastre,"* the Tailor, and even *"El Desastre,"* the Disaster. A woman pushed to the front and presented him with a wailing newborn.

"I think she plans to name the sprout after you, sir," Sarah said. "And she asks your blessing."

Taylor looked at Lincoln. "George, you've had your nose in that Spanish grammar for a year now. Tell her I do not hold with naming babies, buildings, or boats after men still alive. Nor coon hounds either."

While Lincoln struggled to summon up the words for the sentiment, Sarah waved at a man mending Jake's harness under the nearby arbor. "Juan, take the general's horse to the pasture and see to him."

Juan was shorter than the average Mexican, with wide shoulders, long arms, and big hands. His skin hung on him as though it had once contained a lot more meat. Large pouches sagged under pain-hazed eyes. His neatly cropped black hair stood out from his head in the shape of the bowl used to trim it. He had a strong nose and wide, full mouth, deeply etched. He bore an unmistakable resemblance to Hanibal. He looked hardly strong enough to stand and his hands trembled, but he saluted Taylor smartly before he led Whitey away.

"General, you know I'm not one to ask favors." Sarah included him under the blanket she was using as an umbrella although as usual Taylor seemed oblivious to the weather.

"There's none to whom I'd rather grant one."

Sarah nodded at the Mexican's back. "That fellow is by all accounts the best *arriero* ever born."

"He's a muleteer? He looks unsteady on his feet."

"He took a dose of our grape in the brisket. I found him among the wounded that Arista abandoned."

"Another of your hapless chicks, Western?"

"You're in need of *arrieros*, sir."

"I am that. Twiggs has purchased a mob of the most intractable mules I've ever seen." He turned to Lieutenant Bliss, who was trying to look starched in spite of being soaked to the skin. "Bill, take the man's name." Taylor held Sarah's arm as though on a promenade and steered her toward the gate.

The musicians had been conferring, and now struck up a skull-rattling approximation of "Yankee Doodle."

"His name's Juan Duran," Sarah shouted. "And I'm much obliged." She put her fingers in her mouth and whistled so shrilly she got the musicians' attention. The serenade softened enough to make conversation possible.

"I have decided that the mountain must come to Mohammed, Western." When Taylor smiled at her, his nose, mouth, and red-rimmed blue eyes sank deeper into the webbed entrenchment of wrinkles that surrounded them. He glanced over his shoulder at his adjutant, Lieutenant William Wallace "Perfect" Bliss, and the slender, dark-haired captain who followed him. "Western holds my officers hostage to indulgence." He winked at her. "Besides, if I am to know what's going on, I have to ask her. News loiters here before it reaches my tent, just as some of my men do."

Sarah looked at the dark-haired newcomer with Taylor and bobbed in a curtsy. He had that effect on women.

"Western, this is Captain Jefferson Davis, First Mississippi Rifles."

"Pleased to meet you, Captain Davis."

"Likewise, ma'm." Jeff Davis swept off his shako, took her hand, bowed over it, and lit the gray day with the smile that had wooed and won Zachary Taylor's daughter.

"And is this the famous newfangled rifle?" she asked.

"It is." Davis handed it to Sarah, who held it up to study the percussion system. "Accurate to six hundred yards."

"Damned unreliable." With a wave of his hand Taylor dismissed the rifle as a passing fancy. "Flintlocks have been tested in all sorts of conditions. We can always keep flints on hand, but a little rain'll ruin those percussive caps."

Sarah had a multitude of questions she wanted to ask about the weapon, but this was not the time. "I take it the First Mississippi Rifles have arrived," she said instead.

"And glad they are to be here." In spite of his West Point education, Jefferson Davis spoke with a soft drawl. There were two sorts of southern accents, one hard on the ears, the other soft and cultured. Jeff's called up visions of colonnaded mansions, sloping green lawns, and drawing rooms arustle with pale women in taffeta gowns. His was the accent of gallantry and honor above all, and perhaps more pride than was useful. "Camped on that wind-scoured isle of Brazos," he added, "I swallowed so much sand that a shoal formed in my vitals. Food and drink go aground on it."

"We have something here that will wash it away."

"I pray 'tis so, else I'm a gone sucker, as the boys from Arkansas are fond of saying." Again the melting smile, warm and intimate and wry.

"Jeff's troops are civilized enough," Taylor grumbled, "but each day more steamboats arrive at the coast and spit out volunteers who are little more than a rout of savages. They're perfectly ignorant of discipline. And their officers are a drunken lot."

"They tell me the guardhouse at Brazos is stuffed tighter'n a Christmas goose with them," Sarah said.

"Alas, too many remain free to molest the citizenry."

The men had stood and saluted when Taylor entered the garden, and he waved them back to their seats. Sarah led him to the breeziest table where the top of the marquee brushed the spreading branches of an old avocado tree. The journalists abandoned their hopes of winning back their losses from Cruz and rummaged in their haversacks for pens, ink, memorandum books, pencils, and sketch pads. They rushed Taylor, the writers shouting questions, the artists demanding that he lift his grizzled chin, put his hand in his vest, and stare Napoleon-like toward imminent victory.

"Shoo." Sarah flapped her apron at them, as though they were gulls on the scrap heap. "You've no more breeding than a pack of Rackensackers."

They retreated to sketch and eavesdrop from a distance. Lewis Allen stayed, though. He had learned to coast in Sarah's lee and behave well enough to avoid the others' fate. He had confessed to her that after the war he planned to retire from the distractions of society and write the great novel that fermented within him. But now, with pen and memorandum book discreetly out of sight, he ventured a question.

"Rackensackers?"

"That's what the regulars call the Arkansas Volunteers," Lincoln said, "for reasons obvious to anyone who has the misfortune to encounter them. They've been wreaking havoc for miles around their bivouac on Brazos Island."

Sarah unfolded a camp chair and Taylor settled into it with a sigh. His trousers rode up and his shapeless gray socks sagged low, exposing bulging calves and remarkably thin ankles. Nancy brought him his favorite drink, a mug of cool water from the Rio Grande. When he finished it, he pulled his hat down over his eyes and appeared to nap. The discussions of politics and tactics and the battles with

Arista's forces at Palo Alto and Resaca de la Palma regained momentum around him. The men of Walker's company of Texans and three companies of Second Dragoons had just returned from a scouting mission, trailing Arista's retreating army. Bravo Jones was recounting it.

"I tell you, the road was littered with dead greasers." Jones started to put his boots back on the table, caught Sarah's look, and thought better of it. "Broken muskets, spiked guns, baggage, those miserable damn shoes of theirs, rotting mules and horses. Fattest, happiest damn buzzards I ever saw."

"Poor devils," Lincoln said.

"Poor devils, my arse. I'd've been pleased to see the whole army laid out and bloating like bladders in the sunshine."

"For the most part they're conscripts, ground down by taxes, subject to the caprices of every military upstart, deprived of all their freedoms," Lincoln added.

"Annexation is the means to bring them liberty," Braxton Bragg broke in.

"Manifest destiny," Allen added.

"Manifest destiny?" Lincoln asked.

"A term current in the States these days. It describes our nation's divine mandate to occupy the length and breadth of the continent."

"It was never intended that a country this rich should remain in the hands of such an ignorant and degenerate people," Bliss said. "The Anglo-American race will rule her when we're done. By our superior mental and physical abilities we will turn this into a land of milk and honey."

"I came to kill greasers for what they did to my mates in '42," Jones said. "What do we want of Mexico anyway? It ain't worth a damn. And if we get it, we're sure to have Mexicans thrown into the bargain, and a damned lot of them, too. They're almost as black as my niggers and a sight more treacherous."

"If Arista's army is as badly routed as you say," Jeff Davis said, "I wonder that we aren't chasing them. We could deliver the death blow and go home."

"You resigned your commission before the Florida conflict, Jeff." The hat over Taylor's face muffled his voice.

"Yes, sir."

Sarah felt a little pity for Davis, but he should have learned by now that his father-in-law heard everything that went on around him.

"With all that West Point poppycock about fluid offensives and logistical science, didn't they teach you cadets not to outpace your lines of supply?"

"Yes, sir, they did."

"If you'd fought in the Florida quagmire, you'd not have forgotten the lesson. Horses so starved they ate their own bridles. Men forced to wear winter wools in weather hotter than this. And why? Because we couldn't protect the supply ships and the hostiles sank them in the rivers."

Davis's jaw went white where it angled up toward his ears. He turned away and stared at a large noisy bird in the apricot tree. The silence that followed was a chilly one. Sarah knew why. Everyone had heard the story.

Zachary Taylor never mentioned his daughter in Davis's presence, but her memory bound the two men together and it held them irremediably apart. After only weeks of marriage both she and Jeff had fallen ill with malarial fever. She hadn't recovered.

It hadn't been Davis's fault, of course. Everyone knew that. But he had married her despite her father's protests, and he had resigned his commission because Taylor hated the idea of his daughter being a soldier's wife. Now her bones lay in a box in a swampy cemetery outside of New Orleans.

Nancy arrived with a tray of glasses and a bottle of whiskey, locally brewed. She had rolled up the sleeves of her patched and faded brown cotton shirt, but the shoulder seams hung halfway to her elbows. The tails almost reached the hem of the skirt. The shirt had been found in the laundry of a deceased soldier who would no longer need it, since, as Sarah observed, this particular soldier was probably now in a place even hotter than the present one.

Nancy put the tray down and with the back of her brown hand wiped a damp strand off her forehead. Cruz had combed the tangles from her pale, fine hair and plaited it into a single braid that hung past her shoulder blades, but wisps always eluded capture.

She had learned her patter from Sarah. "Try this. It'll make a tadpole entertain designs on a whale."

"Thank you, Nancy." Perfect Bliss took charge, pouring the drinks and passing them around. The silence between Taylor and Davis was especially uncomfortable for him. He was courting Taylor's seventeen-year-old daughter, Margaret, via letters, and the general was no happier about it than he'd been with Davis.

As Sarah moved among the men, one of them beckoned her aside.

"What can I do for you, Lieutenant?"

He leaned close and spoke in a low voice. "I was wondering how much . . ." He paused and blushed and stammered. "How much for the—for the, um, pleasure of the young lady's company?" He nodded toward Concepción.

Sarah started to correct his error, to tell him she ran a respectable enterprise. Then she saw Concepción slide him a smoldering glance and purse her full mouth ever so slightly, as though blowing him a kiss. Sarah knew in an instant of clarity that she could either supervise this particular service or lose every one of her bettys to such as the lieutenant—and worse.

My mother didn't raise any fools, she thought. What she said was, "I would need her here during the day."

"Certainly." He shuffled his boot. "I have engaged a little house where she can stay at night. I'm quite taken with her and will treat her well."

"I know you will, Lieutenant." Sarah crossed her arms over her chest and gave him The Look. The Look assured consequences for promises not kept. "We can discuss the fee after I've spoken with her."

"I'm much obliged." He touched the brim of his cap, clicked his heels smartly, and strode away.

Sarah intercepted Concepción on her next trip to the kitchen and explained the situation in Spanish as best she could.

"*¿Cómo no?*" Concepción shrugged the round, brown shoulders that the low neck of her blouse left bare. "Why not? I would do it anyway. To be paid is a good thing."

When Sarah returned to the garden, she found a newcomer, one even less welcome than Bravo Jones.

"Good day, Colonel Worth." She put two fingers to the brim of her new artillery cap, more to bring it to his attention than to salute him.

Worth abhorred the misappropriation of military equipment. He also hated being addressed by his actual rank rather than his brevet rank of general. He hated that even more, she was sure, now that his old rival, Davey Twiggs, had been promoted to brigadier general after the battle at Palo Alto and Resaca de la Palma. Rumor had it that Worth's new motto was "A grade or a grave."

He nodded curtly and went back to his conversation with Taylor. Sarah walked to Cruz's table, empty now of players, and drew a stool close to her.

"Looks like we got a snake in the garden." She spoke in Spanish. Worth had never bothered to learn even the rudiments of the language.

"I thought he had resigned."

"He did. He left Old Zach and the boys in the lurch and now he's back. Most like he'll find a way to take credit for winning Palo Alto and Resaca de la Palma, though he was most notable for his absence."

William Worth didn't stay long, but while he was there he managed to lower the high spirits considerably. As he left, Sarah agreed with Braxton Bragg's muttered assessment of him. There were few officers who required more from the private soldier or who would put themselves to less inconvenience for them.

Three Things That Can't Be Ruled

I N THE DIM LIGHT JUST BEFORE DAWN, THE LOADED
hammock bounced and swayed and emitted laughter. Arms and
legs appeared above the rim then disappeared again into its bulging
pouch. Inside it Cruz and James had romped into such a sweaty,
naked tangle they could hardly have said which limbs belonged to
whom. When they sorted themselves out, they lay spooned with
her on top of him and his arms around her. Their bottoms hung at
the nadir of the hammock's sag, their heads and bodies inclined upward at one end and their legs entwined along the farther slope.

James kissed her neck and ear and laid his palms on the warm,
bare swell of her belly. They swung that way in silence while the
neighborhood dogs barked at the morning water carrier passing in
the street outside, then at the charcoal seller.

"I felt him kick."

"He kicks like a mule." Cruz put her hands over his. "I think he'll
be mule-headed, like his father."

They extricated themselves and James helped her out of the skittish hammock. Still naked, she laid straw on the banked embers in
the stove, blew them into flames, and lit the lantern with one. While
he put on his trousers and the socks she had knitted him, she emptied her cloth sack onto the wall shelf. She sorted through the silver
dimes and *pesos*, several crumpled bits of paper with "IOU" written

on them in various hands, and a gold collar button that until the afternoon before had belonged to a reporter for the *Cleveland Gazette*.

James leaned over to study the pile in the lantern's flicker. "Looks like five dollars' worth to me." He kissed her as he tucked in his shirt. "We're well on our way to buying that farm in Texas when this dustup's done."

He picked up the tack and kissed her once more at the door. With the saddle and bridle, blanket and fleece slung over his shoulder he walked through the quiet streets. The rim of the sun was just clearing the horizon when he met Sarah on the mare at Company B's horse pickets. He breathed in the animals' familiar odor, a heady mix of musk and damp loam. Their coats shone with last night's brushing. They turned their heads with a deliberate grace to watch them approach, as though they knew the full measure of their magnificence. All except Duke.

He had chewed through his tether, probably in pique at being left here instead of going home with James. He led James on a chase, keeping just out of reach and ignoring the succulent thistles James waved at him.

"The world looks like it's been polished with spit and a chamois, don't it?" Sarah called out cheerfully.

James grunted as he dodged the horses and ducked under the picket lines. Finally he fed the thistles to Lincoln's big white gelding. He made much of Gator as he pretended to untie him, crooning to him about the ride they were going to take. Duke trotted over, muttering, and butted James in the back. James grabbed his halter and tied him to a mesquite. He threw a clean corn sack over his back, then the blanket and saddle.

"He's being recalcitrant today, is he?" Sarah asked.

"Sure'n you should have been present when they tried to break him to saddle." James kneed Duke in the belly to deflate the air he always sucked in so the girth would be loose.

"They say he tucked his nose between his hind feet," Sarah said. "He rose like a hot air balloon with the wind rushing out of it and lit twenty feet away. Half killed three men."

James laughed and arranged the sheep's fleece over the saddle. "He took off running, stretched out like a string with the poor sod's arms around his neck and his flat feet flapping out on each side of Duke's tail."

From the Arkansas Volunteers' camp under the rosewood trees on the other side of the river came a long, piercing whoop. Howling and yipping and yodeling amplified it. The militia's packs of mongrels joined in, keening as though their hearts would break. Disgruntled birds rose in a dark and noisy cloud from the trees above them.

"Texas reveille," Sarah said.

As though on cue, the Texas Rangers who had invented the wake-up call joined in from farther upriver. After a chorus of Comanche yells that chilled the blood and silenced the infernal bellowing of the doves in the chaparral, they launched under full steam into their morning anthem with bugle and drum accompaniment.

> There's a Yellow Rose in Texas that I am gwine to see,
> Nobody else could miss her, not half as much as me.

Sarah was glad she'd left Jake behind, since he always joined in. She saluted the Yellow Rose, the beautiful mulatto slave, Emily, who had distracted Santa Anna in his tent at San Jacinto and allowed the Texans to win the day. Sarah had to admit that the Texans knew about gratitude. They would have elevated her to sainthood if they could have.

Sarah and James urged their horses into a trot upriver. As a finale the volunteers would begin firing their guns for the sport of it. They generally aimed at the far bank, which made loitering there perilous. The two of them rode east, following the loops of the river until they saw a lot of smoke rising above the trees.

Sarah stood in her stirrups. "Looks to be Juan's village."

"Likely the work of the Rackensackers." James crossed himself in anticipation of disaster. "Or else the Third Illinois."

"Ringgold's Avengers?"

"Aye. I hear they went on a tear." James urged Duke into a canter.

Sarah loaded her pistol and shotgun while she rode. The village looked deserted, but they heard a woman wailing as they walked their horses down the main street.

The *jacales* that hadn't been torn down for firewood still smoldered where they stood. The remains of charred fence posts jutted from the Volunteers' scattered cookfires, but the soldiers themselves had decamped. They had left the gardens in trampled ruins. Gnawed husks of watermelons and broken bottles littered the ground.

They found Juan Duran in the ruins of his field. From the looks of it, scores of horses had grazed on the ripe corn and trampled the stalks.

Juan smiled sadly and said in Spanish, "Sometimes God sends rain, and sometimes hail."

"I'd say the devil sent those boys." Sarah shook her head.

"You can ask for reparations from *El Viejo*," James said.

"General Taylor can't even afford to feed and clothe the volunteers that Washington sends by the boatload, much less make reparations." Sarah looked around at the destruction. "They have the brass to call themselves 'Ringgold's Avengers.' 'The Wabash Invincibles.' 'The Plague of Locusts' is what they are."

"*¿Vamos?*" Juan said.

"Aye," James answered. "The mules await us."

→ ←

The *arrieros*, muleteers, were small, brown, compact, and strong. They were a mix of lineages, like the mules, but not as active. They were content to stand with Sarah outside the fence made of pairs of mesquite posts driven into ground, the space between them filled with mesquite limbs. Inside the corral milled the latest batch of mules and the soldiers trained to be the "catching out" crew. Both the mules and the soldiers were rambunctious, noisy, and irritable. The mules were disgruntled at being deprived of their liberty, and the soldiers at having to deal with the mules. But they were the solution to Zachary Taylor's transport problem, at least until the steamers could navigate the Rio Grande's shoals and marshes this far upriver.

Juan Duran stood in the middle of the flying hooves and flashing teeth and jiggled the noose of his riata to widen it. The meals at Sarah's establishment had put meat back on him and the taut swells of the muscles of his arms gleamed with sweat. He whirled the rope twice overhead and flicked his wrist. The loop settled over the ears of a leggy, dun-colored animal, and slid down his neck. Juan jerked it tight and the mule exploded into a leaping, twisting blur. Juan settled back on his heels, but the mule dragged him anyway, leaving long skid marks.

Swearing, the soldiers closed in and threw their own ropes, missed, tried again until they had enough on him to take Juan's off. Juan stood in the middle of the herd, choosing his next victim. The soldiers hauled his last one into the smaller corral where they snubbed him to a post so James could give him his first feel of a halter and pack saddle.

One of the watching *arrieros* handed Sarah the jug of mescal they were circulating and she took a drink and passed it on.

"The Irish say there are three things that can't be ruled," she said in Spanish. The *arrieros* all leaned closer to hear her over the din in the corral. "A mule, a pig, and a woman."

They laughed and nodded, the *cigarrillos* bobbing in their mouths. She had given them some Virginia tobacco. They had taken it politely and now rolled pinches of it into their cornhusk wrappers.

"Moor-fee, he's Irish?" one of them asked.

"You betcha."

"He doesn't look it."

That was true. James Murphy's short, slender body, black hair, and tanned skin blended with the Mexicans around him.

Sarah scrutinized the mules, looking for the ones she would buy for her own use. She would need them. The army's Pioneer Corps had scouted the road to Camargo, Taylor's next target, and reported that wagons could not travel it. "What kind of benighted people," Twiggs had fumed, "can't be bothered to build and repair roads for wheeled traffic?"

Sarah assessed the *arrieros* too, deciding which ones she would hire. After three months in Matamoros she knew most of them. Their wives worked for her, cooking or sewing or washing. A couple of their sisters did work of another sort, but they seemed to accept that with a pragmatism that bordered on fatalism. She knew them to be honest, polite, good-humored, and hardy.

For their part, the Mexicans could barely conceal their amazement at Sarah's capacity for mescal. They watched her with sideways glances, nonchalant, but pleased to be in her company. Everyone knew the red-haired beauty by sight now. The mule drivers were probably already rehearsing the stories they would tell their children and their children's children.

One man leaned close, the mescal and tobacco mixed on his breath. "I hope you *yanquis* beat Arista," he said. "The army is our greatest curse."

"At least now they are killing Americans," another added. "And not so many of us."

They followed Sarah to the small corral where she walked among the tethered mules. From a prudent distance she studied their bones and the muscling over their loins and hindquarters, the soundness of their hooves. She pointed to a tall, heavy animal, but Juan shook his finger side to side in the gesture that meant "no."

"You should choose the small ones," he said.

"Why?"

"It is difficult to load a tall mule."

Sarah took her time selecting the three she needed, glancing at Juan for the brief nod that meant approval.

When she finished she mounted the mare and headed for home. She smiled to herself at the prospect of walking with Cruz and the other Mexican women to the river, stripping naked in the late afternoon sunshine, and washing off the day's dust and sweat in the cool water. If the soldiers wanted to watch from a distance, let them.

→←

Cruz and the maids hurried in and out of the house, carrying kettles and bread trays, bedding and sacks of clothing and stowing them in the big wicker hampers on the five mules. Sarah laid her wall tent out flat in the garden, rolled it around the poles, and tied it alongside the pack saddle. Her folded canvas cot rode on the other side.

The saddle consisted of a coarsely woven pad stuffed with hay. The four pieces of wood were crossed like a sawhorse, two at the front and two at the back of the frame. They were riveted at the crossing to make two forks that projected above the pad, providing a convenient hitching place for a lariat or a hat. The hampers hung on iron hooks along the sides.

James knew the Second Dragoons were preparing to move out and he should be forming up with them. Instead he followed Cruz back and forth, taking the heavier things from her hands. He was so distracted he strayed too near Jake, who grabbed his forage cap in his teeth and flipped it over his head.

James retrieved it and took Cruz in his arms. "I wish you could go with us."

As Sarah passed she smacked him lightly on the side of the head to knock some sense into him. "She isn't riding a hundred miles in her condition."

"*Mi cielo*," Cruz said. "I will be well."

"Those boats are dangerous. Too few pilots know the channel. Wood is scarce or green. You could run aground and be beset by Arista's men. Or Comanches."

"The women say the river is higher than it's ever been. They say it's a sign from God that he blesses us."

"Stay close to Captain Bragg and the men of the Third Artillery. Make sure you board the boat they're on."

"*Sí.*"

"I hear the bugle," Sarah said. "You'd best go, James."

James grabbed Bertha by the arm. "Mrs. Skinner, you and Nancy look out for her on the boat."

"Yes. Yes."

As he rode off, he turned to blow Cruz kisses and she waved until he was out of sight. Sarah's *arrieros* lashed the loads down and her little train of five animals stood ready to go. Cruz held out a piece of deerhorn strung on a leather thong.

Sarah took it and turned it over in her hand. "What's this?"

"Hang it on Jake's harness until you can mount it on a piece of iron and fasten it there forever. It repels *mal ojo*, the evil eye."

"You might need this more than I do."

"Everyone says he's far away." Cruz could not bring herself to say Antonio Águila's name aloud. "He and his men are stealing and killing beyond Camargo."

Sarah knew that, but anxious thoughts gnawed at her anyway. She turned to the *arrieros*. "Boys, remember what I told you. Keep the mules here until they get restless, then walk them around until the army's train is ready to go. Don't get mixed up in that disorder."

Sarah tied the bulging leather satchels onto her big Spanish saddle and the blanket roll across the back. She put the shotgun in the boot and hung her iron skillet on the other side. Then she and Cruz rode to where the pack trains were forming.

They heard the ruckus before they saw it.

Mules that were being packed by the soldiers distended their bellies and humped their backs. Then they shifted and sidled away while the men chased them. Those that had become tired of waiting bolted, braying and kicking until they scattered the goods. Others lay down and tried to roll over onto their badly packed loads. The ones with tent poles ran at trees, hooking the poles on the trunks and ripping them off.

Soldiers screamed obscenities and threw things. In their frustration they put the mules' ears between their teeth and bit down, and usually got bitten in return. Twiggs strode through the melee in a passion. He realized that shouting at his own men was a waste of time. They were too inept for a berating to improve. The Mexicans were another matter. They knew what they were doing, but they seemed to think they had the rest of the week to do it. They had set out the baggage in rows, arranging and rearranging the packets with infuriating languor.

As a mule was led up next to its load, a man put a leather blind on him. Then he held him while another selected a package, put it on one side of the mule where a third *arriero* held it. A second package, selected for size and weight was placed on the other side and the cargo then tied with a rope. Finally the men passed a broad strap over it to bind it all.

Twiggs stalked over to hustle them along and James hurried after him to translate.

"My God, Duran . . ." Twiggs lumbered so close he looked as though he meant to knock Juan's big *sombrero* off first, then bowl him over. "Can't you speed things up? At this rate, you'll be here until sundown."

Juan took off his hat and held it in front of the leather apron that covered him from neck to knees. It looked as though he were using it as a shield, but when he spoke his voice was firm.

James translated. "He says no one interferes with him and his men unless they want to do the packing themselves."

Twiggs threw up his hands and whirled around, almost knocking James over. "They can follow later then. We're moving out."

He marched off, leaving an expanding blue tailwind of oaths behind him.

The Second Dragoons pulled out singing "Green Grows the Laurel," the song the Irish among them had made popular. Sam Walker's company of Texans and several units of volunteers followed them. Their dust had long since settled before Juan and his men were ready. Sarah's five mules and three *arrieros* appeared as though on cue.

Cruz stood on a crate to kiss Sarah's cheek. Tears glistened in her dark eyes. "I will miss you."

"You'll have a leisurely voyage, my daughter, and we'll see each other before long." Sarah mounted Alice Ann. She hated waiting. And she wasn't partial to good-byes either.

With shrill whistles and cries of *"mula, mula,"* the hundreds of mules and their drivers started moving.

Juan winked at Sarah as he went by. "I am very happy to be out of the army," he confided. "The mules are much easier to bear than Mexican officers. More intelligent, and more reasonable."

For the rest of the day Sarah could hear him singing.

→ ←

Cruz was putting the last of her things into a trunk when the priest entered without knocking. Cruz tried to run, but Águila slipped in behind him and grabbed her.

He was dressed as a poor farmer, barefoot, with short white trousers and shirt, a conical straw hat, and a meek expression, even while his grip choked her. The priest looked unctuous in his faded cassock. His cheeks were smooth and pink, his hands folded across a portly little belly. But Cruz recognized him. She knew he rode with Águila's men and was as bloodthirsty as the worst of them.

Cruz wanted to cry with relief when she saw the young American corporal appear in the doorway. "Help me."

"You're to accompany your husband, ma'm. Orders of General Worth." The soldier turned to go.

"But he is Antonio Águila. He is not . . ."

Águila put his hand over her mouth, still managing to look injured and aggrieved and harmless. He twisted her arm behind her back until the pain was too intense to speak anyway.

"Women are ever the deceivers." The priest spoke English well.

"Águila is a hundred miles from here." His smile was ingratiating, an acknowledgment of men's sad victimization by the duplicitous daughters of Eve. "This wanton left two babes to go awhoring. And she would deny this latest one his father, the honest farmer you see before you."

"Makes no never-mind to me how you Meskins sort out your domestic squabbles." Looking bored, the corporal left.

Cruz struggled, screaming into the hard, callused hand that mashed her lip against her teeth until she tasted blood.

War Is Like Sausages

HIGH, CRAGGY MOUNTAINS RIMMED THE VALLEY FOR
a hundred miles. They cut off the August rains that drenched
the country around Matamoros. From where James stood, choking
in the powdery dust that undulated along the desert floor and
swirled around him like an ocean, they looked cool and inviting. If
a breeze blew into the valley from them, the thorny chaparral
snagged it before it reached this ankle-deep sandpit they called
a road.

This was a country inhabited by crosses, dozens of them, lined up
by the road like soldiers in an entirely different army. They marked
where people had died, hardly ever of natural causes. Some of them
bore crudely lettered pleas for the prayers of passersby.

James shook his wooden canteen, then poured the last of the contents into his wide-brimmed hat. Duke dipped his nose in delicately.
Around them soldiers fell to their knees in the dry watercourse and
dug in the hot sand with their bayonets. Most were too exhausted to
speak, but a few swore steadily when no moisture seeped into the
holes they had made.

Duke drank as much as he could reach and backed away. James
made a vee of the brim, tilted his chin up, and drained the last few
drops onto his lips. As soon as he let his head lie back on his shoulders to drink, he knew he'd erred. He had to keep his personal axis
in line with the earth's core if he intended to stay upright.

The sun flared like an overstoked kiln. He heard a babble of Spanish. He knew the speakers were the ghosts of those who had died here and who inhabited the shallow graves under the crosses. He wondered how he would get along in their company. Well enough, he thought.

The men and horses, the rocks and the thorny snarl of chaparral, canted one way, then another. They began to shimmy. His bones melted about the same time the sun blinked out, flinging him head-first into darkness. He didn't feel Duke nudge his side or nibble his hair as he lay sprawled in the sand. He didn't hear the footfalls of the horses and men who staggered past him.

When he became aware of heat searing his face and hands and soaking into his chest through his shirt, he thought, I've died and gone to hell.

He felt death lift him and he hung limp in its arms, content to be snatched from hell with no effort on his part. But the divine force jostled and pulled at him until he felt twisted inside his skin, like when he awoke at night tangled in his blankets. He thrashed feebly, trying to sort himself out. Death forced him upright and arranged his arms and legs in positions that were neither restful nor fitting for a corpse. James suspected that the dazzling glare that burned its way through his closed lids and replaced the tranquil darkness wasn't heaven.

"Let's get on with it, Murphy."

"Leave me dead, Western." James swayed in the saddle where Sarah had hoisted him. He tried to raise an arm to shield his eyes from the relentless sun, but it had turned to lead. "I was content to be dead."

"Take the reins." She pressed them into his hands. He fell forward against Duke's neck and she reached up and pulled him erect by the back of his shirt. "Time's marching, me boyo." She swung up onto the mare.

"Time can march without me."

"And when your daughter asks for her pa, shall I bring her here to see your bleached donkey-Irish bones?"

"Going to be a son."

"It's going to be whatever God sends."

"Is that why y've been bloodhounding me these three days? To see that I don't shirk me fatherly duties by dyin'?"

"It ain't because you're so pretty." She sliced a flat green section from the ten-foot-high mass of cacti lining the road. She scraped the thorns off with her knife, handed it to James, then cut another for herself.

They broke open the rubbery pads and sucked on them, drawing what bitter moisture they could from them. They rode in silence. Finally James dismounted and walked alongside Duke, whose legs had begun to tremble. As he set one foot doggedly in front of the other, all he could see was the sand pouring in over the tops of his worn boots.

Sarah looked around her. "Looks more like a rout than an advance to me."

Sam Walker's Rangers rode at the front. Both they and their tough ponies had experienced more Mexican summers than the regulars, and their wide hats shaded more of their personal real estate than the regulation forage caps. Several of them chewed on cactus as they rode. Others kept buckshot in their mouths to coax saliva.

The faded blue line of dragoons followed them, with Sarah and James toward the rear. Behind them the column of infantry straggled out for miles. The weaker men and the sick ones and a number of horses, too, littered the line of march. The pack train lagged so far back it would not reach camp until long after nightfall again tonight. The men unloading the supplies and equipment would mix them up until no one could find anything in the dark. The soldiers would have to sleep on the ground, with no food, or at best cold beans and dubious salt pork.

Ahead, a man slid from his saddle. His head and shoulders bounced when they hit the ground. The stirrup held his left foot and the horse stopped, muzzle drooping, wheezing like a bellows, while he hung there. The other men continued on by, some swearing at him when they had to detour around him. By the time Sarah reached him, he had commenced convulsing. A thin froth formed in the corners of his mouth and he clutched at the hot sand. Sarah stopped to unhook his foot and prop him in the scrap of shade his horse provided.

"Hurry along, Western," James called. "They've found water."

The pond had shriveled to a fetid sink of mud and decay, but the men splashed into it, raising a cloud of mosquitoes, gnats, and stinging flies. Officers and men of the ranks alike shoved each other aside to fill their canteens and water their mounts.

Sarah returned with her canteen of muddy soup and put her scarf over it to strain it. James joined her.

" 'Twould be a bloody shame if we died here, wouldn't it, Western?"

"War is like sausages." When she flexed her cracked lips to grin at him, they began to bleed. "Hope for the best, but be prepared for the worst."

➞➔

The steamer squatted low in the river that flowed sluggishly past Camargo. James stood on shore, his hands in his pockets, and surveyed the chipped and faded paint on the brightwork, the broken paddle on the wheel, the scabrous condition of the hull. A Mexican, his white cotton trousers soaked in sweat, struggled past under the huge chest he carried.

"Have you seen a *paisana*, a countrywoman, so high?" James asked in Spanish. He held his hand at nose level.

"*No, Señor.*"

James continued to elbow through the throng swarming up and down the planks connecting the steamer to the shore. He asked the same question in Spanish and English and Gaelic. He had met every steamer in the past week, and as usual when volunteers arrived they created chaos around them. They pushed past the local men hired as stevedores, shoving them into the water if they didn't get out of the way. Once ashore, they milled about, shouting and drinking and interfering with the purposeful.

James fell in step with a soldier as he stepped off the gangplank. From his green shirt James guessed he was one of the Jasper Greens, volunteers from Georgia, most of them Irish. "Did a Mexican woman sail with you?"

"Nay, naught of graisers aboord." He grinned. "Na doubt she found another to suit her fancy." He snapped his head around when a loud chorus of imprecations erupted from the steamer.

A fight had broken out on the upper deck between the Jasper Greens and the brown-shirted Kenesaw Rangers. The soldier snatched a length of firewood, dashed back up the plank, and vanished into the windmilling mass of arms and legs. The Rangers were unarmed, but the Greens pulled knives, bayonets, pistols, and clubs from their belts and boots, their pockets and shirts and hat bands. The melee surged around the boiler deck and up and down the gangways.

A burial detail of Ringgold's Avengers marched past, and their commander, an old colonel, led them aboard to separate the combatants. The Greens' captain rounded on him.

"Damn you!" He brandished his saber. "Measure swords with me, sir."

The two of them hacked at each other until a Green pulled his pistol and fired. The colonel dropped to the deck and his Avengers lowered bayonets and charged. One of them ran the captain through the mouth. The Greens intensified their own assault.

James stayed until officers restored order and details carried the dead and wounded away. Then he went to the horse pickets for solace. He put his arms around Duke's neck, laid his face against his sleek hide, and breathed the fragrance of the spice bush he used to rub him down. Muttering, Duke swung his head around, trying to rub his velvety muzzle against James's back.

"Murphy, we're on the scout for a *fandango*." Major Beall looked down from the back of his crane-colored horse. His red bulb of a nose glowed brightly, indicating that the man known as Old Brilliant had already been celebrating. Six or eight soldiers from Company B pulled up behind him. "There's booze to be had in the volunteers' camp, don't you know." Old Brilliant winked. "The mutinous hounds jettisoned the vittles from the packs and loaded the mules with it, figuring the government would ship them more food on the steamers."

" 'Course," one of the others added, "the gummint ain't sending them shit."

But James was more preoccupied with the army's transportation of people. Fear roiled in his gut at the thought of Cruz's boat sinking, the water closing over her head. If the Rio Grande's meanders were straightened, it would stretch four hundred miles from

Matamoros to here. What if her steamer had exploded or been attacked?

"She'll come traipsin' along soon, Irish," Old Brilliant said.

"Aye, so she will." James shook his head to scatter the fear that she wouldn't. "Duke was just after saying he could use a taste of whiskey."

18

Barnosing the Fandango

NANCY SKINNER SAT ON JAKE'S HAUNCHES SO AS NOT
to crowd Sarah's bustle when the two of them rode through
the volunteers' camp, Sarah sidesaddle, Nancy astride. Sarah had
primed and loaded her pistol. Anything could happen here, and she
planned to be ready.

Twelve thousand men, and several thousand horses, oxen, and
mules and a week of rain had turned the irregulars' bivouac into a
vast and noisome swamp. The flimsy muslin tents stood in straight
lines, but bones and offal and feces lay in fly-covered heaps. Lattice-
ribbed dogs served as the only garbage detail. The mules and horses
wandered about, crunching spiders, ants, tarantulas, and centipedes
under their hooves.

The sun had set, but the air hung thick and stifling. The volunteers sat listlessly in front of their tents. Many of them still wore
civilian clothes. Sarah stopped at a group holding their cards as
though they had become attached to their hands through constant
contact. They all had the look of glazed mania common to those
who drank to excess.

"Have you seen any of the Second, regular army?"

"The bangtail boys?" The man spit and the gap formerly occupied
by his front teeth made the stream of tobacco a formidable one. His
tanned face and felted beard reminded Sarah of dried owl scat. "I

reckon I seen 'em." He went back to studying his cards as though he might learn something useful from them.

"Where are they?" Sarah was in no mood for a rustic's cheek.

"What'll ye gi' me for the information?"

"I'll give you something if you keep me waiting."

"I ain't worried none."

Sarah kneed Jake forward to get a better angle of sight. The man must have thought she was leaving because before he could collect his wits and duck, Sarah drew her pistol from the saddle holster, cocked it, aimed casually at his head, and pulled the trigger. The report brought an alertness to the cardplayers' faces and a snap to their spines that they lacked on the parade ground. The man's pile of a hat flew off and he scrambled to retrieve it while his friends laughed.

"Best not rile the Great Western, Nate," one of them advised. "They say she wrings fellers' necks like they was so many pullets."

"Ya jack-whore!" Nate clutched the barrel of his musket like a club and half rose in an attempt to menace. But when Sarah leaned down from the saddle, as though offering him a shot at her chin, he seemed disinclined to take it.

She smiled at the others. It was an artless, cockles-warming grin of irresistible, green-eyed affection. "Can any of you brave and feckless fellows tell me where the dragoons might be?"

"They said they was goin' to a *fandango* at the old Cantú place, ma'm."

"Can't." Someone else giggled. "Cantú."

"I'm much obliged." Sarah nodded cordially and kicked Jake into motion.

"Will we go there tonight?" But Nancy already knew the answer.

"Can't put off the evils of life, child. They only return in better health and vigor, refreshed by the delay." She primed and reloaded as she rode and she returned her pistol to its holster.

The Cantú family's former holdings lay three miles upriver from Camargo, and though darkness gathered around her, Sarah headed there. Chaparral and rattlesnakes had reclaimed the corn and cotton fields, but the old house, built of caliche blocks cut from the land itself, still stood.

Lemon-yellow lantern light spilled from the windows. A group of men and women stood around a monte bank laid out on a poncho. They were enrapt by the game, and the light and shadows gave them a bony and sinister look. An Indian woman had laid out loaves of sweet bread on the board counter of a makeshift stall. Laughter and singing and guitar music floated out of the windows on the light. As Sarah approached she recognized the song. The dragoons were caterwauling their way through "The Girl I Left Behind Me." But where were their horses?

"Do you see that, Western?" Nancy peered around Sarah's back.

"I do." Sarah stared at the dark forms sliding around the corner, heading for the rear of the house.

"Mexican irregulars," Nancy whispered.

Sarah rode Jake into the opening that once had framed a massive door. The air inside felt hot enough to bake bread. In the center of the large room a dragoon was trying to teach a giggling young woman to waltz to his comrades' two-four-time lament for the much-missed girl who was left behind. The dragoon chorus and their horses stood against the far wall. A door nearby probably led to an inner room. Sarah suspected that room was where the furtive shadows outside had headed.

She couldn't tell if the dragoons were leaning on their horses or vice versa, but not even the four-legged troopers looked capable of standing alone. James put a bottle between Duke's teeth and up-ended it. Duke's throat muscles humped in caterpillar motions as the liquid went down. When Duke finished he produced a noise that sounded very like a belch.

Sarah pulled her pistol from her belt and brandished it as she rode through the festivities. The dragoons left off singing and shouted greetings in English and Spanish. The Mexicans laughed at the latest antics of the Americans. Someone in the crowd shouted "Bienvenido, Western."

"Let's go, boys." She tried to maneuver Jake around behind them and herd them outside, but she was too late.

When the first Mexican irregular came through the inner door, Sarah shot him. He fell back onto the man behind him whose gun went off and shattered a lantern, throwing that end of the room into darkness. The shots jolted the dragoons into action. Shouting orders and suggestions and oaths they put boots into stirrups, though not always the correct boot or the correct stirrup. They hopped around, trying to mount as their horses circled and collided and whinnied. Once aboard and more or less vertical, though not always facing forward, they drew their pistols and sabers. Yodeling the Texans' eerie war cry, they bolted for the door. The party-goers scattered for cover. More bullets ricocheted off the walls. Sarah could hear Beall shouting, "Brilliant! Damned brilliant!" And his men urging him on with "Go it, Bottlenose" and "Fire away, Old Demijohn."

Nancy leaned from Jake's back, grabbed a pottery pitcher from a high shelf, and shattered it on the skull of the first irregular to blunder within reach. Sarah laid about her with the butt of her pistol while Jake backed, kicking and biting, toward the door.

The dragoons retreated in disorder, laughing uproariously in the bright moonlight as bullets whined around them. When they'd gotten out of range and could see that the attackers weren't following, they reined in to savor the moment.

"That's the way to barnose a *fandango*," James shouted.

They all agreed that it was the best *fandango* they had ever attended.

Then James stared at Nancy. He realized that if she was here, Cruz should be too. Suddenly he looked stone cold sober. "Where is she?"

"Another steamer arrived while you and Duke were on a bender." Sarah tried not to sound accusatory. It was just a man's nature to be faithful until it counted, then make a shamble of things.

"Where is she?"

Nancy hesitated. "When I went to help her pack, a neighbor said she had left."

"Left?"

"She went away with a priest and another man."

"What other man?"

"He was dressed like a farmer. The priest said he was her husband."

"No." James suddenly looked completely sober. "No, he's not her husband."

➜ ⭠

In spite of the late hour James found the usual crowd of officers lounging in front of Zachary Taylor's tattered and mildewed wall tent. Taylor himself sat crosslegged on a blanket on the ground.

Sarah and Nancy stood behind James, in the shadows beyond the reach of the lantern's light.

"The general looks grum as a bear," Nancy whispered.

"He has cause to," Sarah answered.

James heard the words, but they held no meaning for him. He paced, crushing his forage cap in his rigid fingers. He wanted to shout at the officers to stop nattering and let him speak. He wanted to throw himself at the general's feet and beg him to restore Cruz to him. He refrained not out of pride, but because he knew such unsoldierly conduct would only infuriate Taylor. Instead he listened for a break in the bitter discussion Taylor was having with the colonel in charge of the Texas Rifles.

"I did my best to dissuade them from leaving, General, but their six-month term of enlistment has elapsed and nothing will induce them to stay."

"We have fed, clothed, and transported six hundred men without getting a moment's service from them." Taylor's scowl etched deeper channels in the leathery hide of his face.

"There's nothing to be done about it. According to the act passed by Congress, volunteers are entitled to return home at the end of six months."

"I know the law, Colonel."

James couldn't bear it any longer. He stepped into the light and touched the brim of his cap in a crisp salute. "Private Murphy, beggin' your pardon, sir."

The colonel rounded on him in indignation, but Taylor held up a hand to calm him.

"What is it, son?" He squinted at James in the flickering light.

"Sir, someone has kidnapped my wife from our house in Matamoros."

"Enlisted men aren't allowed to marry."

"I love her as my wife, sir." He didn't mention that she carried his child. The army frowned on offspring even more than wives. "I was told one of our own soldiers led the felons to her and let them take her."

"One of our soldiers involved in kidnapping? I doubt it."

George Lincoln cleared his throat. "General Worth mentioned it in his report, sir."

"Did he?"

"Yes, sir. A peasant claimed that his woman had been lured into, uh, impropriety."

"You mean whoredom," Taylor broke in. "Why can't you West Pointers call a thing by its name?"

"He said she left him and their three children. A priest attested to the truth of his account. Worth gave them permission to retrieve her." Lincoln looked distraught. "I didn't know she was Cruz."

Cruz, a whore, to be retrieved like a piece of stolen baggage. James felt the heat rising from his neck. "He's not her husband. He's Antonio Águila. He means to harm her."

James heard the murmuring among the officers. All this fuss over a Mexican trollop. He forced himself to stand at attention, dark blue eyes staring straight into Taylor's pale ones. Taylor looked sadly at James. "We are trying our best to kill people, and you want to save one. I commend you, son, but what would you have us do? Send a detachment out to comb several thousand square miles, among a hostile populace, to search for one woman?"

James hesitated. He hadn't thought about what he wanted Taylor to do. He hadn't thought about anything except getting Cruz back. "Allow me to look for her, sir."

"We're a hundred and thirty miles from where she was taken. If her abductor is that Águila fellow, he's proven himself capable of eluding Walker's Rangers, who are the best trackers in the business." Taylor gave a small wave of his hand, a regretful signal that the interview had ended. "Try to sleep, Private Murphy. In the morning we can post a dispatch to Matamoros, asking if there's been any word of Águila's whereabouts."

"Thank you, sir." James saluted, turned smartly, and marched into the night that pooled deep and still and indifferent under the ebony trees.

Sarah and Nancy joined him. "What will you do now?" Sarah asked.

"Obey *El Viejo*'s orders."

"Look me in the eye and tell me that."

James turned his head and she studied him in the moonlight. His blue eyes were remote, calm. They gave no hint of his yearning to lift his face to the cold moon and howl out his grief and rage. "I can do nothing to find her tonight," he said.

"You always were the smoothest liar I ever knew, Murphy." Sarah shook her head. "First light tomorrow, Juan and I'll start the search. Muleteers travel the country. Some of them must know where Águila is."

"Thank you, Western." James tipped his hat to Sarah and Nancy. "I bid ye good night, ladies. May God keep ye in His care." He walked into the shadows, certain that Sarah would be watching him. When he was out of her sight, he doubled back.

He broke into a trot and arrived at Worth's tent as he was giving instructions to his servants and orderlies for the next day's duties. James strode up to him, cocked his fist, and drove it into his nose. Worth's scream of pain and the crunch and collapse of cartilage under James's knuckles satisfied him for only a moment. The blow knocked Worth down and James leaped on top of him. Blood flowed from Worth's nose onto James's hands when he ripped open the colonel's collar and grabbed his throat. The two men rolled and thrashed and bucked. Worth's face turned pink, then red, as James pressed his thumbs into his windpipe.

Three orderlies grabbed whatever part of James they could lay hands on and lifted him off the ground. They could only raise him the length of his arms because James wasn't letting go. One of the black servants knelt warily and pried his fingers off Worth's neck. The orderlies sat on him until the guards came and marched him away.

They shoved him through the guardhouse door with such force he flew across the single room and bounced off the far wall. He landed in a heap on top of the men sprawled there. They stirred and grumbled—volunteers, most of them. They were filthy and un-shaven, and the room reeked, among other odors, of their vomit.

"Wha'd'ya do, Mick?" one asked.

"I tried to murder Worth," James said. "And by Christ and the Vir-gin Mary I'll keep trying till I succeed."

The cheer that went up could be heard as far as the horse pickets and the ground where the cannons dozed under their tarpaulins.

19

Metaphysic Wit

>━━━━◀◆▶━◀━○━◀▶━━━━<

SARAH SAT ON A BLANKET IN FRONT OF THE TENT SHE had pitched just beyond Camargo's grand plaza. She was trying to take advantage of any stray breeze that might ripple the August heat, before the nightly dew made everything feel like the skin of the frogs that lurched past. Camargo seethed with a plague of frogs that would impress Moses and the children of Egypt.

"Sweet potatoes, *Señora*, and eggs. Cheap." The child lowered the big basket from its perch on her shoulder. Her shift hung in such tatters it exposed her thin ribs.

Sarah peered into the basket, checking the quality as best she could in the darkness. "How much?"

"Fie *centavos*, one potato. Fie *centavos*, one egg. Hokay?"

"Okay." Sarah knew five cents was high, but she pulled the coins from her pouch. Supplies of any sort were almost impossible to find here. Sarah spent a good deal of her time on the mare and leading Jake, searching the countryside for food for the officers of her mess. And while she was at it, she always asked about Cruz and Águila.

Sarah had first met the girl in Matamoros. She recognized many of those who came to her tent selling their wares. The army had acquired a second mob of camp followers, this one composed of the people who were supposed to be its enemies. The children were learning English especially fast.

"*Mi mamá* say to tell you she ask everywhere. No one knows where is *Señor* Águila or the woman you seek."

"Tell her I thank her kindly." But Sarah wondered if that was the truth. Águila had pillaged this area recently. He seemed to be following the army, or maybe he was taunting her. She wouldn't put it past him.

"*Buenas noches, Señora* Way-stern," the girl said.

"*Buenas noches.*" Sarah automatically added Cruz's nightly wish in Spanish. "Dream with the angels."

"*Gracias, Señora.*" The child waded away through the frogs, her small bare feet sending them outward in high, frantic leaps.

Sarah took another drink from the jug of mescal. The abandoned buildings that surrounded the plaza made her more melancholy than the frogs and the mosquitoes did. Sounds echoed off them, and the hollow reverberations intensified the feeling that impoverished, disconsolate ghosts loitered about the place. Decades ago some ambitious dreamer had laid out the plaza in monumental proportions, but the river's flood a month ago had completed the job of destroying whatever grand future he had planned. It had damaged all the buildings, half washing away many of them. That disaster—and Águila and his irregulars—had reduced the population by half. The remnants lived in flimsy *jacales* with their molting chickens and their stick-thin goats.

Sarah could hear Juan and the other muleteers conversing softly in Spanish nearby. They lay on their cotton blankets in front of the homely pile of adobe bricks the people of Camargo referred to as the cathedral. The red points of their *cigarrillos* glowed in the darkness. Their mules, hundreds of them, stood tethered wherever there was room.

In the center of the plaza the tents of the Seventh Infantry shone pale in the moonlight. The shadowy forms of soldiers moved about, taking care of chores and visits before the bugle blew "Tattoo." Someone was singing, maybe to drown out the mournful roll of a distant drum accompanying another body to the boggy cemetery. In this heat the dead couldn't lie above ground long. In the morning the surgeons would find more corpses among the volunteers laid low with fevers and dysentery. And the drums would start again. The soldiers had dubbed Camargo a yawning graveyard. It seemed a fitting enough name.

Sarah lit a little cigar from the embers she kept in an earthen bowl, and stared out at the plaza as the aromatic smoke dissipated the mosquitoes. Her gaze came unfocused, her thoughts cut adrift from the meanders and detours in her life that had brought her here. She wondered how she could possibly have come to this godforsaken, demigogue-ridden, death-besotted country. Losing the two men she had loved could be expected. Men died in war, often in large numbers. But how had she managed to lose Cruz?

Sarah had known disappointment, and terror and grief and loss, but she had never felt the gut-sucking agony of abject despair before now. She had always been able to get what she wanted, or had managed to make do without it. For once she felt helpless and dreadfully lonely.

"Good evening, Mrs. Borginnis." George Lincoln waved a long, knobby hand through the mosquitoes. His tall white gelding, Gator, walked behind him. Lincoln picked up Gator's right front leg and showed Sarah the shredded edge of the hoof. "I was wondering if you might know of a supply of horseshoes. I ordered them weeks ago, but none have arrived."

Sarah shook her head. "I'll ask Juan, but the *arrieros* don't bother much with them."

Lincoln sat next to her on the blanket and his horse stood patiently, ears pricked forward. "Actually, General Taylor sent me to ask if you have eggs to sell."

"I could spare him some." She handed him the jug of mescal and he took a drink. She looked around the plaza, quiet now, but for the restless stamping of the mules and an occasional bray. "What we have here, Captain, is a reversal of the loaves and fishes." She gestured at the tiny beacons of the muleteers' *cigarrillos*. "Each day this place fills with mules and their cargoes, and the goods are never sufficient to satisfy all these soldierly bellies." A centipede scuttled past and she crushed it under her boot sole.

"General Taylor says you've cornered most of the comestibles in the market."

Sarah lit the last Matamoros cigar from her own and handed it to

Lincoln. "I pay in coin," she said. "The army hands poor folk worthless chits. And Águila gives them nothing but grief, with the blessings of his government."

"General Taylor says you've cornered all the coin too. You and Cruz and her monte game." Lincoln fell abruptly silent. "It grieved me to hear of the abduction of your friend, Sarah," he said after a pause. "If I had known what was happening, I could have saved her."

"Well, even the innocents have a way of bumbling into wars, don't they? And you know how it is with war."

"I do."

They both sat silent, sharing the numbing comfort of the mescal and thinking of friends dead and gone.

"Yet war brought *Señora* Cruz to you," Lincoln said finally.

"You could say, Captain, that since the hem of my skirt last dusted my father's doorstep, war has brought me everything I hold dear."

Lincoln didn't have a response to that. War had taken him away from what he held most dear. "I sometimes wonder what would impel a woman to endure military life."

"A man's usually at the foot of it."

Sarah thought back to the arrival of the dry-goods drummer, Jack Borginnis, in Grinder's Stand, Tennessee, with his nick-tailed horse and his cart containing a few items for sale. He was the first man to pay attention to her as anything but an oddity, a handsome oddity, but an oddity nonetheless. And she was an old woman then, almost twenty, and desperate. He was on his way to Missouri, he said, to work his ailing uncle's farm. She hitched a ride. She never went back.

Much as Sarah loved Jack, she had to admit that he wasn't any better at farming than he was at selling. Then he heard the army was enlisting men at Jefferson barracks. As it turned out, he was very good at soldiering.

"Remember when you signed us up, Captain, him as a private and me as a laundress? And you fresh from the academy and green as clover?"

"I do." George Lincoln remembered vividly the way the bustle of the army camp stopped, the noise and shouting silenced as she rode through that day. No one had ever seen anyone like her.

He had stood open-mouthed with the rest, stunned by the grandeur of her. The most amazing aspect about Sarah, he had observed over the years, was that she seemed unaware of her effect on men. In time, the more perspicacious of them adopted her own matter-of-fact attitude about her size and beauty, although even the most level-headed might find themselves staring like a raw recruit at times.

Sarah broke Lincoln's reverie. "I would've left Grinder's Stand anyways," she said. "I was a freak in that little hamlet, don't you know. People came from neighboring valleys just to 'view the elephant.' That narrow cove, all ringed in with peaks, it pinched my soul like a tight pair of shoes." Sarah let several moments pass without saying anything. That was one of the reasons she liked George Lincoln so much. He didn't feel obliged to fill silences with noise. "The army, though, it fits me just fine."

Lincoln leaned back on one elbow and crossed his legs. Sarah had pushed her sleeves up in the close heat, and from where he sat he could see the pale column of her right arm. He had a sudden memory of those arms, sliced by sawgrass, covered with blood, carrying men from the swamp around Lake Okeechobee. She was a trollop by some folks' definition, or at least a procuress—but she did that as she did everything, with such exuberance she made it seem natural and right.

She couldn't read and she couldn't sign her name, yet she made her way very well in an indifferent world. George Lincoln wanted to tell her how much he admired her, but he knew that would only embarrass her, and he didn't have much experience speaking to women about personal subjects. What would his wife think, he wondered, if she knew in what esteem he held Sarah?

" 'He knew what's what.' " He recited it more to himself than to her. " 'And that's as high as metaphysic wit can fly.' "

"Did you make that up?"

"A man named Samuel Butler did."

She didn't ask why he said it. Lincoln was always quoting something. And if she had asked, he wouldn't have told her that the poem made him think of her.

"I worry about Murphy," Sarah said. "Cruz was his rudder in this tempest." She glanced at Lincoln. "Murphy says there's no mistaking the real thing where love's concerned. He says it has a kick like a mule. Have you ever experienced that?"

By the light of Lincoln's cigar Sarah saw his neck and jaw turn so red she thought his tall collar might burst into flames.

"Excuse my forwardness, Captain."

"No, no. It's quite all right. I can answer yes. The dear wife who waits at home, though she's small as a minute and fragile as a rose petal, has that effect on me. The very thought of her, in fact, gives my heart a jolt." He turned and looked her square in the face, his eyes a deep shade of melancholy. "She takes my breath clean away."

Sarah opened her mouth to try to give him some comfort, when Juan Duran approached. He spoke in Spanish but Sarah and Lincoln both understood him.

"*Señora* Way-stern, I have news."

"What news?"

"Moor-fee escaped."

"How?"

"Someone smuggled tequila to the prisoners."

"That wouldn't have been you, would it?"

His broad white teeth flashed in a grin. "When they were well fortified, they decided to help James escape so he could complete his promise to finish General Worth. The flood had already damaged the rear wall, so they ran at it and hit it hard enough to knock it out. The roof fell in too, but since God looks after fools and drunks, they all escaped unharmed."

"How would you know unless you were there?"

The grin turned sly and he shrugged. "The guards are looking for them now."

"Did Murphy take Duke?"

"Certainly."

"They won't catch him then."

All for Love,
and a Little for the Bottle

THE CAVERNOUS INTERIOR OF MONTERREY'S CATHE-
dral smelled of incense. The damp stone walls cooled it, as
though August's ferocious heat hadn't extended into the middle of
September. Most of the nave was shrouded in a smoky twilight except where the sun's rays streamed through the stained glass windows and painted mosaics of colored light on the flagstone floor.

El Sastre, the Tailor, and his horde of *Americanos* were on the march
and headed here. The huge altar blazed with candlelight. More than
the usual number of people had stopped to light a candle and pray
that the coming war would spare them. James held his small taper to
one of the hundreds burning in tiers in front of it. Their glow illuminated the ornate carvings and paintings that decorated it. When the
wick caught fire, James tilted it so wax dripped onto the hardened
mounds of it that covered the platform. He centered the candle in
the soft puddle and swiveled it to set it firmly.

He knelt on the stone floor and bowed his head. People came,
women mostly, by ones or twos. They lit candles, prayed, and glanced
curiously at the ragged stranger. James wore straw sandals and dirty
white cotton trousers. His face was tanned the color of saddle
leather by the sun and a black beard covered the lower half of it. His
shaggy black hair hung over the collar of a white tunic of the sort
farmers wore. For all that, the women sensed that he wasn't one of
theirs. They finished their devotions, crossed themselves, and left.

Still he remained with head bowed, eyes closed, as motionless as the ranks of wooden saints staring from their niches in the walls.

Finally James crossed himself and stood stiffly. He rubbed his sore knees, then walked slowly down the center aisle through the somber gloom. He opened the small door set within the huge one, ducked through it, and emerged, blinking, into the glare and noise of the plaza. For a few seconds the aroma of incense clung to him, like a fleeting reassurance that God had noticed him. He pulled the straw hat low and kept his head down. He had no wish for the authorities to recognize him as an American and hang him for a spy.

A pair of matched grays pulled a black-cauled carriage, like some spindly, wheeled beetle, across the square at a brisk trot. As it hustled past, James glimpsed pale, patrician faces inside. He knew a lumbering cart or two of household goods lagged somewhere behind it, with the family's servants chivvying the donkeys along. Monterrey's upper classes were fleeing, but the impoverished lower orders had nowhere to go. They went about their business with only a little more than the usual urgency. Scores of soldiers in their bright blue and scarlet uniforms gave the only real indication that war was imminent. That and the barricades they and Monterrey's citizens were erecting in the main streets.

Duke tossed his head and whickered.

"I'm hungry too," James murmured to him. Before he untied the reins he opened the soft leather pouch hanging by a cord around his neck. "Look you here." He held it up so Duke could see it was empty. "I spent my next-to-the-last *centavo* on corn for you yesterday afternoon. The last one bought a candle for Cruz just now. And would ya be begrudging her that, you ungrateful wretch, as kindly as she's treated you?"

He draped the reins over Duke's back, and the horse plodded after him through the welter of charcoal and firewood sellers and water vendors. He stopped by a woman sitting on a cotton blanket so old the stripes had faded to shadows. The neat patches on her skirt and blouse reminded him of Cruz's handiwork and tears stung his eyes. She patted out a tortilla and laid it to bake on the flat rock over a small charcoal fire. The odor of beans rising from her pot made James's stomach inquire loudly if breakfast would be arriving soon.

She had the sharp nose, flared nostrils, backswept brow, and wide, chiseled mouth of an Indian. She looked fifty, but James knew she was probably no more than thirty. He squatted in front of her.

"*Buenos días, Señora.*"

"*Buenos días.*" When she looked up at James, he knew she knew he had no money.

His Spanish had been good before he deserted. Now he spoke almost without an accent. "I have hunger enough to devour an ox," he said conversationally.

Amusement flickered in the woman's eyes, half-covered by heavy lids. "An ox would not fit inside my pot."

James made an inventory of possessions he might trade for a tortilla wrapped around a spoonful of beans and chiles. He had nothing but Duke and the scant clothes on his back, and pride would not allow him to beg for charity.

"*Bueno pues*—well, then." He smiled cheerfully at her. "If you have no ox, I shall be on my way."

"Wait." She handed him a tortilla, still warm.

He held it open across his palms while she ladled beans into the center of it.

"Thank you, and may God bless you, *Señora.*" He folded three sides over the beans and, still sitting back on his haunches, elbows resting on his spread knees, he took a bite from the open end. He licked the thick juice as it ran down his forearm. He gave the second half of it to Duke.

"*¿Gringo?*" she asked.

"*¿Gringo?*" James gave her a quizzical look.

She began to sing. " '*Gringos da lado.*' " Though the words were an approximation, he recognized the tune: "Green Grows the Laurel."

"Irish," he said.

"It's not possible." She glanced at his black hair, then with her chin she pointed behind him. "That is a *colorado*, a red, an Irish."

James looked over his shoulder. "John Riley!"

"Jamie, lad, you look sorrier than a pile of shit in a mud puddle."

John Riley had added even more girth to his big frame. His ruddy face had grown rounder. He held his shoulder piece casually, the butt resting on the ground. His hand, red and thick as a small ham, made the big British .75-caliber flintlock look considerably smaller. His russet thatch of hair was neatly cropped.

He held his black leather shako under his free arm. The pompom matched the crimson collar, cuffs, and turnbacks on his dark blue coat. The image of an exploding bomb had been embroidered on each side of his high collar. The two dozen brass buttons lined up on his broad wedge of a chest were stamped with the bomb design. His white canvas summer trousers were immaculately clean and pressed. But what James noticed were the gold bars on each side of his collar.

"You're a captain, John?"

"Aye." Riley started to say something else, but was drowned out by a company of mounted lancers clattering by and scattering people in front of them.

Riley took James by the arm and led him to a small adobe shop on a side street. The table hardly spanned the bottoms of the two bottles of *pulque* the proprietor set in front of them.

"What's brought you to this pretty pass, Jamie? Had you a falling-out with your sweetheart?"

"Águila took her. With Worth's blessings."

"Ah well, that would be Worth, wouldn't it? He has no use for us Irish. Nor for any man that won't lick clean the soles of his boots."

"I've searched for her for a month. I've slept in ditches and abandoned buildings. I've sold my uniform, my boots, saddle, tack, musket, everything, to buy food and information."

"And what did you learn?"

James gave a bitter chuckle. "I learned the truth of what the Tiger used to say. Don't believe anything a Mexican tells you. They all reported that Águila was in the next village or in the mountains just ahead."

"He could have been. He's a slippery one, he is."

"Have you seen him?"

"Nay, but I hear reports, fanciful fables, really."

"I thought he might come here, to help stand off Taylor's army."

"Águila?" Riley laughed. "Not unless there's promise of plunder."

"Then I'll keep looking."

"The best way is to let him find you. Join us. We're sure to run into him."

"Join the Mexican army?"

"Nay, lad, the French army." Riley wiped the edge of the table with a kerchief and propped his elbows precariously there. "Say what Twiggs will about the veracity of greasers, they deliver what they promise. Immediate promotion to officer . . ." He tapped the captain's bars. "And fifty-seven dollars a month, instead of, now what did we privates earn? Seven dollars?" He leaned forward with a sly smile. "Listen to this: they've put me in charge of training the artillery crews. That's rich, ain't it? All Captain Ringgold's good instruction is benefiting his enemies."

"Captain Ringgold was killed at Palo Alto."

"And it's sorry I am to hear it. I've fancied the chance to match his flying artillery with me own."

"My mates are with Taylor."

"A lot of them are here. The Mexicans are after calling us the San Patricios, the Saint Patricks. Seamus Hooligan, ever the fool, still speaks fondly of you. Still fancies himself Captain Wattle."

James laughed for the first time in more than a month. He remembered the reference: "Did you ever hear of Captain Wattle? He was all for love and a little for the bottle."

Riley took a thoughtful drink of *pulque*. "And what did America do for you? It's not your country. It makes little of your religion. It treats you like a dog. It let them take your woman because she wasn't worth anything to it." He crossed his arms over his chest and leaned back, a sure sign he was about to get political.

"Theirs is a war of unwarranted aggression and greed, and you know it. The United States plans to throw this country open for settlement by its own. The officers intend to use Mexican dead to further their ambitions. Each one sees himself as a future general or senator or even, God help us, the president. And the volunteers . . ." He snorted. "The volunteers think only of plunder and rape." He let James ponder that a few moments before he leaned forward and added, "Besides, if they catch you, they'll hang you for a deserter."

The *pulque* sent warm tendrils of peace snaking outward from the pit of James's stomach until it tingled in his fingers and toes. He analyzed the prospects of finding Águila and Cruz while he himself was penniless and a stranger in this land. He realized that if he was going to leave Monterrey, he would have to do it quickly. The Americans would arrive any day—any hour, for that matter.

He thought about the rugged mountains that ringed the city on three sides and the stout fortifications and artillery emplacements that guarded its approaches. He remembered the barricaded streets and armed citizens setting up sniper positions on the rooftops. He thought of the thousands of Mexican soldiers he had seen since he arrived two days ago. They outnumbered Taylor's army two to one. And the lancers, no matter what the Americans might say, were as brave and skillful as any dragoon.

"The Yanks will have a hard time taking this city."

Riley grinned. "They're asses to try. They should point their feet northeast and not stop till they cross the Nueces. If they're too stupid to do that, what passes is in God's hands."

"And Duke?"

"As a mounted artilleryman you can keep him under you, lad."

James finished the last of the warm liquid in the bottle, by now unaware that it smelled like an old boot. His thoughts had started to swirl, gently, languidly. He didn't try to separate out how he would feel when he watched his former comrades charging across the broad plain to the east of Monterrey. He didn't think about lifting a musket to his shoulder, aiming at them, and pulling the trigger.

"I'm your man," he said.

Each Bullet
Has Got Its Commission

S
ARAH HAD GROWN UP IN FORESTED MOUNTAINS, BUT she had never seen such peaks as these. They loomed jagged and abrupt and colored the dark blue of cannon smoke against the steely, predawn sky. As barriers to the army's passage, though, she judged them superfluous. For a hundred miles before them God had seen fit to create a wilderness of trees and brush and cacti, all bristling with thorns as long as her fingers. He had tossed house-sized boulders about and gouged stony chasms hundreds of feet deep into the landscape. He had neglected to supply any water, except for the black brew festering in shallow ponds.

"Shoulders to it, boys. Bring on that team!" General Twiggs shouted.

Fifty soldiers trotted back and got a handhold. Those who couldn't reach the wagon pushed on the backs of the men in front of them. The wagon contained the blacksmith's forge, and it weighed even more than the loads of powder and lead shot.

The mules strained until their eyes bulged. Their neck muscles tautened like ship's stays in a gale, their hindquarters quivered. The rig crept upward a couple of wagon lengths, sending rocks rattling downslope. Then it slowed, though the mules continued to lean against the harnesses, their sides heaving. Saliva hung in strings from their lips. Finally they began to back, and the wheels and the men's boots started a grinding slide. The ropes holding the forge in place creaked.

"Great God, men," Twiggs bellowed, "which way are you going? That's not the route up the hill."

Laughing, more soldiers ran to help. Sarah pushed into the sweaty press, taking a position between a meaty Baltimore barber and a beet-faced farmer from Vermont. They all heaved and joked and shouted insults to the mules. The wagon inched forward. When it reached the top of the ridge, the troops cheered, then re-formed into their column. The rub of wooden brake shoes against wheel rims sent up a chorus of shrieks as the wagons bumbled and lurched downhill.

"Doesn't it just sound like a passel of boar cats with their nuts in a vise?" Sarah checked her own brakes and the log drag she'd rigged for the perilous descent. Then she climbed up to the high seat.

Nancy slid over to vacate the driver's position. Nancy's mother and sisters and four sick soldiers rode among the goods in the bed of Sarah's latest vehicle, a light wagon called an ambulance that was much the worse for hard wear. Snipers had fired at the column from rocky defiles along the way, so Twiggs had ordered the dependents to travel in the center of the column.

Sarah gave Nancy an admiring glance as she took the jerkline from her. "Aren't you becoming the perfect gee-hawer, though?"

The child had been working harder than usual, probably in an attempt to make up for the loss of Cruz. Sarah had told her more than once that she wasn't responsible for Cruz's kidnapping, but she doubted that Nancy believed her. Sarah herself still expected to see Cruz, dressed in Murphy's old trousers and shirt and wide-brimmed hat, carrying the musket, and riding Sarah's mare Alice Ann. Now and then she thought she heard Cruz and James singing together as they often did, in Spanish usually, though Murphy had been teaching her an old Gaelic lullaby for the baby.

Tears blurred the high blue peaks and the mulberry-colored clouds heaped up behind them. Sarah wiped her eyes on her sleeve.

"Village ahead." The word came back, passed along from company to company. The bantering stopped.

"Proceed as usual," Twiggs roared. "Captain Walker, you and your men scout the lay of the land."

The low stone houses sat among fig, peach, and pomegranate trees. As the column approached, Sarah saw that no smoke rose from breakfast fires. Dogs howled in a way that sent chills down her spine.

When they reached the outskirts, the dragoons moved in to ride stirrup to stirrup, four abreast. The men of the infantry closed ranks, marching in close order down the dusty main street in the rose-colored haze of early morning. With their muskets' muzzles pointed outward, the bayonet blades formed a savage wall. They reminded Sarah of the old tale of dragon's teeth and the soldiers that sprang from them. Even the skeletal dogs stopped barking and tottered around corners, tails between their legs. The village seemed to be holding its breath, and Sarah could imagine its inhabitants hidden inside, and peering at her through the cracks in the shutters.

The place was silent except for the jangle of hardware and tack, the heavy, rhythmic tramp of boots and hooves, and the rumble of artillery carriages echoing off the line of houses that shared a single front wall. The soldiers moved as one creature, strong, deliberate, and deadly. Sarah drove along in the middle of them, the hair stirring on the nape of her neck.

An ancient woman sat on a piece of blanket in her dooryard. She was grinding a handful of corn in her stone *metate*. She didn't look up and Sarah wondered if she was deaf. Bullet holes pocked the limestone of the wall behind her, and the rusty brown smear there was probably blood.

"Looks like Águila or someone of his calling paid a visit." Sarah pulled out of the line of march and into a weed-grown area between two houses. She took a basket out from under the seat and climbed down. "Watch the rig," she said to Nancy.

She joked with the four ailing men in the wagon bed and made sure they had water in their canteens. Then she walked back and squatted next to the woman while the companies continued to tramp past in a choking cloud of dust. She knew the Spanish words she needed to ask the questions. She had asked them a hundred times and more. She worried, though, that she wouldn't understand the answers.

"Good morning," she said.

The woman gave a small start and swung her head around. The

milk-colored irises of her eyes looked like mother-of-pearl buttons. Sarah put a gentle hand on her arm and she pulled back.

"I have nothing," the woman said. "The devils stole it all."

"Who robbed you?"

"The cursed sons of whores."

"Was one of them Antonio Águila?"

The old woman spat, as though to defile at least his name, since she couldn't touch the man himself.

"Do you know where he went?"

She finished grinding the handful of corn on her stone. The basket next to her was empty but for a few stray kernels. "I don't know," she said.

"Did he have a woman named Cruz with him?"

"I don't know."

Sarah took a small flask of rum from the basket, uncorked it, and put it in the woman's hand. "For the soul's thirst," she said.

The woman sniffed it and a smile flickered across her face like a bat across a gaunt winter moon, though her eyes continued to stare opaquely.

"And to feed your belly." Sarah gave her a small sack of cornmeal and another of beans. She kept them handy for situations like this, though the need always outstripped her supply. Sarah stood up. "May God care for you."

But the woman stared into her own sad night, concentrating on the tingling journey of the rum as it warmed its way to her stomach. Sarah walked back to the wagon. She glared at the young infantryman who had dallied to talk to Nancy, and he hurried to join his company.

At the noon stop Sarah was arching her back to ease her spine and stretch her legs when she heard a woman's low laugh. She went to the tailgate and surveyed the four soldiers who sat or lay under blankets among her household goods. The one with a raging fever was unconscious, but the other three stared blandly back at her.

"Don't you all look like you swallowed a bug." She narrowed her eyes. "Where is she?"

The one with the broken ankle grinned sheepishly and threw back his blanket. He uncovered a small, plump individual sitting between a barrel of water and several sacks of corn. She had the black braids, coffee-brown skin, assertive nose, and pumpkin-seed-shaped eyes of an Indian. She was bruised and dressed in rags. She wasn't young, maybe twenty-five or six.

"When did she come aboard?

"While you was talking to the old lady in the last village."

"Lordy. They can sniff out a pigeon as surely as a cat can." Sarah rounded on Nancy. "Did you know about this?"

"She can help with the cooking," Nancy said. "Her name is Maria."

"I won't put her out by the side of the road. She may stay until we reach camp."

➤ ⭠

George Lincoln found Sarah's four tents pitched and her operation up and bustling. She always collected her own horde of camp followers wherever she went. Nancy Skinner and the stowaway, Maria, were assembling a vat of beef stew while the other Skinner sisters collected sticks. Local women were dividing up the laundry. *Indios* had already appeared with firewood, charcoal, water, and produce. Juan Duran was cleaning the hooves of the picketed mules.

Sarah and a Mexican blacksmith stood next to her wagon. They had emptied it and levered the back of it onto a log so the rear wheel hung free of the ground. She was tacking wet strips of oxhide to it while he heated the iron tire over his small charcoal forge.

She glanced up at Lincoln. "Greetings, Cap'n." She spoke around the wooden pegs in her mouth and went on hammering. "You look like a man with something on his mind."

"The general insists on entering the city with us tomorrow."

"Well, you know what Old Zach always says."

Lincoln took off his hat, mussed his hair, puffed out his cheeks, and growled, " 'I wish no man to go where I am not willing to lead.' "

Sarah laughed. "That would be Old Zach, all right."

From the west came the boom of artillery pieces. Sarah recognized the voices of Captain Bragg's eight-pounders. They sounded like the thunder that had been growling in the gray clouds overhead. "The Second and Third are on their way?"

Lincoln nodded. "Bragg's drawing fire so Worth can swing around to take the hills to the rear and cut off the Saltillo Road."

"And the Mexicans' route for supplies, reinforcements, and retreat." With a pair of tongs, Sarah helped the smith guide the glowing iron tire onto the rim. While he held it, she knocked it quickly into place with a mallet before it cooled and shrank. "They have their work set out for them."

"Yes, they do." Lincoln coughed as the sharp odor of burning hair rose from the oxhide. "I have a favor to ask, Mrs. Borginnis."

"Glad to oblige."

He held out a small rosewood box with a brass clasp. "If something should befall me, please see that this reaches my wife and my son." Whenever Lincoln spoke of the baby boy he had not seen, his voice softened.

Sarah wiped her hands on her apron and took it from him. "I doubt I'll need to do that."

He succumbed to his lopsided smile and shrugged. " 'What argufies pride and ambition?' " he recited.

> Soon or late death will take us in tow:
> Each bullet has got its commission,
> And when our time's come, we must go.

Sarah smiled. But she knew why he was giving it to her instead of entrusting it to another officer. He had no way of knowing who among them would survive.

She had seen the steep, fortified heights that loomed behind Monterrey. She had seen the citadel and redoubts in front, the breastworks and bastions and the long, open approach easily raked by artillery fire. Chief engineer Joseph Mansfield, a major now, had spent two nights crawling along those bastions, counting their big guns. He said there were thirty-two. She also had heard the reports of the numbers of men gathered to oppose them. Twice as many as Taylor had.

Some of her boys wouldn't leave that city alive. Sarah had learned long ago not to wonder which ones.

22

Kindness Has No Price

JAMES WALKED ALONG THE STACKS OF SKULLS THAT lined the perimeter of the little church on the outskirts of Monterrey. Their shade of old ivory blended with the limestone blocks of the wall. Beams of sunlight from the window played on pyramids and tumbled heaps of them in the middle of the floor. An earthenware vase, four feet high, overflowed with more skulls. Baskets filled with bones hung from cords along the walls. Some of the bones had shreds of clothing clinging to them.

Skulls lined the ledge formed by the opening of the large window. Each had words etched across the forehead. James picked one up, careful not to dislodge the strands of long black hair that still stuck to it. The inscription read, "I am Consuela Lopez: an 'Ave Maria' and 'Paternoster' for God's sake, brother." He put it carefully back and picked up the next one. The lettering made a similar plea. And so did the third.

"Do you search for someone, Irish?"

James turned to see the woman who had given him the tortilla and beans a week before. "I am always searching for someone, *Señora.*"

With a bunch of chicken feathers tied together at the quills, she began dusting the skulls on the window ledge. "You look very handsome."

James adjusted the tall, crimson collar of his dark blue jacket, though it was straight already. The uniform hung with a familiar weight on his body, though the insignia and red trim belonged to another country, another government, another people. The coarse wool rubbed his skin raw, but a new uniform chafed the same in every army. After a few washings the cloth would soften. Laundry brought the Great Western to mind, and he wondered what she was doing and if she was searching for Cruz too.

With airy waves of her feather duster the woman swept away cobwebs from the skulls. She caught the spiders gently, walked to the door, and deposited them outside. "For whom do you search, so far from home?"

"My wife."

"Did she die here in Monterrey?"

"I don't know where she died. Or how. Or where she's buried. Or if she's buried."

"Then how do you know she is dead?" She began piling the scattered skulls back into pyramids like melons in the market, and James helped her.

"A friend told me so this morning, the *colorado* you saw with me that day you gave me the tortilla."

"*Ay, sí*. Captain Riley."

Of course. Everyone would know Riley. He stood out in any crowd here.

"Is he sure she is dead?" she asked.

"He said a priest from a neighboring village told him he saw her body. But the priest wouldn't say where. The child within her is dead too."

And Riley couldn't tell me where the priest has gone, James realized suddenly. Or wouldn't tell me.

"A child!" Tears filled the woman's eyes. "A child. What a pity."

Pity. If there had been any pity under heaven, James thought, Cruz and the baby would be alive.

The woman went to the window and picked up a skull. She held it so James could see the inscription on it. "My husband." She replaced it and took a tiny one. "My child." She held it to her breast and ran a hand over it, as though to caress it, to comfort it, or to polish it like a dutiful housewife.

The third, "The priest of our village," she said. "A good man. A kind man." She laid her fingers on the next one. "This is his woman, only fifteen when she died. He loved her very much, though the Church shook its finger at him for it." She gestured to all of them. "I know them. I know their children or their children's children. I know how each one died, although only God knows how each one lived."

She finished her cleaning and knelt in front of the altar with her head bowed and hands clasped for several long minutes. When she rose, James opened her palm and put some coins in it.

"For the tortilla and the beans only," he said. "The kindness has no price."

She inspected them. "This is too much."

"Use the extra to pay the priests for a novena for the souls of your husband and child."

"God bless you, Irish." She took his hand in both hers. Small and brown, they reminded him of Cruz's. She stared into his eyes. "Of all the evils, death is not the worst."

"Death for me would be a great good, *Señora*."

She arranged her shawl over her head and went out into the sunlight.

James stood motionless for a long time. Then he dropped to sit on the heels of his high black boots. Sharing a beam of sunlight with the skulls on the brick floor, he wrapped his arms around his knees and cried like a child.

→←

George Lincoln walked through the cornfield with the long blue line of men advancing on either side of him. The shoulder-high stalks rustled and swayed as he pushed them aside with his bayonet. Ahead, Zachary Taylor's shako and epaulets and Whitey's ears moved along above the silken tassels. In honor of the occasion Taylor wore his uniform, forsaking his old straw hat for the jaunty white plume.

The standing corn ended just short of the range of the Mexicans' artillery. When Lincoln cleared the last row, he felt exposed and vulnerable but he moved into the open. He stepped over the stalks the

Mexicans had mowed down to provide a clear line of sight for their artillery crews in the citadel and three redoubts. Just before reaching the invisible line that marked the cannon's range and death's threshold, Taylor held up his hand and the men stopped.

They dressed ranks as though on parade, as though no gun emplacements threatened them three-quarters of a mile away across the plain. Taylor's army faced a high stone wall with ditches along its outer side. The night before, Juan Duran had sneaked into the city. He said the three plazas were walled with loopholes and embrasures. Along the streets leading to the plazas, the Mexican army had thrown up barricades that sheltered musketry and cannons.

Lincoln knew that soldiers could convert every house, with their thick limestone walls and flat roofs, into a fort. Taking Monterrey was an impossible task and everyone was eager to get on with it. They strained like hounds at their leashes with the scent of possum in their nostrils.

But first things first, and all in good time. Right now the men of the Third Infantry had orders to take out the battery on the far right. As Lincoln studied it and listened to the jangle of bayonets being seated, he felt those old companions, excitement and dread, lurching around in his vitals. He knew the other men trembled with the same queasy eagerness, the same abiding terror. He knew they tasted tarnished brass in their dry mouths. And, like him, each one felt a part of something powerful and all-encompassing, and each one felt utterly alone. He unclipped the wooden canteen from his belt and took a long drink.

It was madness, this soldiering business. Lincoln knew it and had sense enough to wonder at it. But still he yearned to bare his teeth and laugh like a lunatic, to throw back his head and howl. The Texans beat him to it, of course. A man could count on them being the first to do the howling, and to do it best. They'd learned from the Comanche, after all.

When Taylor's sword fell in the signal to charge, the Texans' whoops oscillated between a warble and a shriek, a cat with its tail in a press and the rasp of fingernails across bumpy slate. They and Jeff Davis's Mississippi Rifles charged out ahead, almost overrunning the skirmishers. Bragg's horses raced with their artillery carriages and caissons careening after them, taking up positions to lay down a covering fire. George Lincoln, screaming and not realizing it, not even hearing it in the din, started running while the Mexicans' six-pound cannonballs hit the ground and bounced past him, as though in a rush to leave town before trouble arrived.

Gouts of smoke bloomed at the walls and spread outward, joined to form the familiar blue haze. Smoke from the American artillery enveloped Lincoln and the others. Lincoln knew he was racing at full speed over the furrowed field, but everything around him slowed. In spite of the din and the acrid swirl of fumes, he saw beads of sweat on the faces of the men on either side of him. He saw the fringe missing from one man's epaulet, like a gap in a tarnished gold smile. He saw the musket balls spatter around him, harmless as raindrops.

Lincoln's long legs got him to the unfinished battery first and they carried him over the low wall of sandbags. He raised his bayonet to run it through anyone who opposed him, but the battery's crew had fled. The whitewashed walls of houses loomed ahead of him and he charged in among them. The street turned abruptly right and into a hail of artillery balls and small-arms fire. Lincoln had the brief fancy that an umbrella would protect him. Then he dodged behind a fence. The men following him took cover wherever they could. From every house, every yard, every rooftop came a hailstorm of bullets.

George shouted, "Where are we?" but no one could tell him. Soldiers fell around him. The sight of Zachary Taylor and his staff approaching on foot didn't surprise him, but it did alarm him. Lincoln ran at a crouch to him.

"General, you expose yourself unduly."

Taylor beckoned to the soldiers with pickaxes and pointed to a door on the other side of the street. "Knock in that door."

"Go it, boys." Lincoln and a squad of men raced across through a shower of balls, as if the Mexicans were hurling bushels of hickory nuts at them. While the enemy reloaded, another group crossed. Then another.

Two men raised their axes, but an elegant-looking fellow in a frock coat appeared with a key. He opened the door and let them into his apothecary shop.

"My name is Doctor San Juan," he said in English. He set out chairs for Taylor and his staff. "General Ampudia has four thousand men in the plaza and two thousand more in the citadel. These houses all share interior walls, of course. Cutting through them in that direction will take you there."

The men set to work on the wall with their axes and crowbars. The limestone blocks were so soft that Lincoln and the others cut through the two-foot thickness by the time the doctor had served a cool glass of limeade and Taylor had drunk it. They burst into one house after another in a shower of dust and rubble. Often they found women and children huddled in corners or wailing in back rooms.

An odd way to fight a war, Lincoln thought, in people's parlors.

→ ←

From the rooftop, James could see the woman in the plaza below. She was taking water to the wounded of both sides. She knelt by an American infantryman, took the black cotton shawl from her head, ripped a piece from it, and used it to bandage the ragged hole in his arm. She tore the rest into strips and moved from man to man with her bandages and small loaves of bread and the water gourd she refilled at the fountain in the center of the plaza. Without the shawl shading her face, James could see she was the woman who had fed him, and who had spoken to him in the church of the skulls. That she would be the same person seemed inevitable to him.

He shouted to her to retreat to safety. A musket cracked and she fell backward. James clenched his fists, willing her to rise, to move, to twitch. The firing was so chaotic he couldn't say if the shot had come from a Mexican piece or an American one. For some reason he wanted desperately to know. A horde of Texans occupied one of the rooftops on the plaza. James had heard them whooping and singing and shouting insults there. He felt sure, though he had no way to prove it, that Bravo Jones had killed her and that he had done it deliberately. He said a prayer for her soul, though he knew she didn't need his help gaining admittance to heaven. Her kindness might have no price, but surely it would have its reward.

She lay there the rest of the day and through the long night while James shivered on the roof with the small cannon. In the morning he found two shovels abandoned by the sappers. Before the shooting began in earnest, he and Riley went into the plaza and carried her to a side street. They dug a shallow grave for her amid the bean plants in a garden, while stray grape and round shot passed overhead.

Chock-Full of the Devil

THOUSANDS OF AMERICAN SOLDIERS LINED THE ROAD leading from Monterrey to Saltillo. The hissing noise they made seemed to have the force and volume of steam from a ship's boiler. James couldn't help but think it would scald him as he rode through it.

James rode Duke at the head of the column and carried the make-shift green flag that identified the former members of the American army. Germans, British, Scots, and some Americans had joined the brigade, but because the Irish predominated the Mexicans called them the San Patricios, the Saint Patricks. Still dressed in the uniforms of the Mexican artillery, they rode past the Americans.

General Taylor had agreed to allow the Mexican troops to with-draw from Monterrey with their muskets, sabers, and six pieces of field artillery. They were marching to San Luis Potosí, where they were to honor a truce of eight weeks while the generals talked. James thought it an odd and foolish concession on the Americans' part. He knew the soldiers would be incensed at seeing their ene-mies, armed, leave the city they had taken at such great cost of life. He certainly would be if he were them. He wasn't prepared for the intensity of their send-off though.

James saw the rock coming from the corner of his eye. He kept his gaze straight ahead, but he leaned slightly back so that it cleared his temple. Just behind him John Riley sat astride the rear left horse in the team pulling the lead artillery carriage. Blood flowed down his cheek from where a stone had hit him.

The men shouted curses and insults too, but neither they nor the rocks bothered James as much as the hissing. The din drowned out the jangle of the hundreds of small iron strips hanging from the elaborately chased bull's hide draped across Duke's hindquarters. James had felt hatred from individuals in his life, but never such a concentrated, universal loathing as this. The Americans' officers were having trouble restraining them from breaking ranks and rushing their former comrades-in-arms.

He was relieved to see the end of the line of soldiers. Then he spotted Sarah's wild, dark red hair above the crowd of civilians beyond them. She had the look of some avenging goddess come to earth to pass judgment. She should have been wearing a white toga and wielding a sword. He half expected her to shout something at him, but she remained silent. He avoided looking at her, but he remembered those deep green eyes very well and he felt them staring at him as he rode by.

➜ ←

While the wagons rumbled past on the road, Sarah stood behind a snarl of Turk's head cactus and greasewood shrubs near the lip of a shallow ravine. She adjusted her skirts and sighed. Two days jouncing on the warped boards of the wagon seat took their toll on a person, inside and out. She was about to return to the line of march when a pale splotch in the scrub below and a glisten of crimson caught her attention. She slid a few feet down the slope for a better look.

She crossed herself. "Jesus God."

A naked body lay sprawled among the rocks.

"What is it, Western?" Nancy stood on the wagon seat and craned to see. Her dusty mother and sisters and the Mexican women and children perched in Sarah's big Mexican cart leaned over the side.

"Never you mind. Put the carbine in the saddle boot, throw that spare canvas over Alice Ann's back, and hitch her to the mesquite there. I'll catch up."

Nancy got down, untied the mare's reins from the tailgate, and looped them around the tree. Then she resumed her seat and cracked the smaller whip that Sarah had had made for her. The rig moved forward with a squealing of axles and the mare whinnied soulfully at being left. Sarah's bettys continued their flirtation with the dragoons assigned as flankers to guard the baggage and the civilians.

Sarah waved her hat and an angular, worried-looking young officer rode over. On each lapel he wore a gold bar that had belonged to his lieutenant, killed in the streets of Monterrey. By rights the dead man should have been buried with the insignia of his rank, but lieutenants were such an expendable commodity there weren't enough bars to go around for their successors.

"Another one?" He dismounted and slid down the slope, sending gravel pelting against Sarah's ankles. They surveyed the body.

Exhausted, ill, and footsore, the infantryman must have fallen behind. A lot of them did. They all knew the danger of it, but some of them hid in the bushes so the flankers wouldn't find them and drive them back into the line of march.

The corpse, eyes staring and cheeks bulging, seemed to be sticking his tongue out at them. Sarah closed the eyelids. She pried open his clenched teeth with the point of her knife, pulled the severed penis and scrotum from his mouth and wrapped them in her handkerchief. He hadn't stiffened much yet, and Sarah judged he'd been there no more than half an hour.

She recognized the shape of the dark purple welt around his throat. Some *guerrilla's* lasso had left it there. From the way his skin hung in shreds, the irregulars must have dragged him through the cactus. They had slashed his belly open and his viscera gleamed inside. They had carved two words in the flesh of his chest. They looked as though they had been embroidered in red thread.

"What do they say, Lieutenant?"

" '*Las mujeres.*' "

"The women." Sarah nodded. "Must be payment for the Rackensackers' spree on Christmas day."

"When they . . ." The lieutenant hesitated. "When they violated all those women at Agua Nuevo ranch?"

"I would imagine."

She put an open hand to her hat brim and made a sweeping survey of the countryside. Ripples of white clover washed around the mesquite and juniper flowing up into the green hills that in turn merged into lilac mountains crowned with billows of white clouds. To the north gleamed the whitewashed stone walls of the rancho where they had taken the noon meal. Except for the vultures wheeling overhead, all was still. She saw no sign of the pack of knaves who'd done this.

She gripped the man's ankles and lifted his lower half. "How many today?" she asked.

"This is the third. The poor stupid devils." The dragoon gathered the wrists together and he and Sarah carried him, slung between them like an oxskin of *pulque*, back up the slope.

They opened out the piece of old wagon cover that Nancy had left draped over the mare's back and they stretched him out on it. Sarah laid the package of his severed parts between his legs and wrapped the canvas around him. She folded it neatly and trussed it with the roll of twine slung from her belt.

They were arranging him on the back of the dragoon's horse when Juan Duran galloped up and pulled his lathered little donkey to a sliding stop.

"Los pendejos han volado como tantos conejos."

The dragoon looked at Sarah. "What's he saying?"

Sarah considered the literal translation—"The pubic hairs have flown like so many rabbits"—but decided this was no time to add embarrassment to the lieutenant's problems. "The muleteers have taken to their heels again."

The young trooper looked uncertain. Sarah figured he would rather chase the *guerrillas* than either guard the women or go after the muleteers, but the main body of the army was a mile or more ahead and he couldn't leave this column of civilians defenseless.

"I'm acquainted with the muleteers," Sarah said. "We'll bring them back. Send reinforcements when you can. Dan'll find us." She nodded to the tall Texan slouched under a hat that threw more shade than a lady's parasol. Touching the outer edge of the brim with two fingers in salute almost required Dan to straighten his elbow.

"I can't let you go alone, ma'm." Under his crust of snuff-pale dust the dragoon looked so punctilious that Sarah had to smile at him as she mounted the mare and seated the carbine more firmly in its case.

"Then you'd druther tell Old Zach that you saved a laundress and lost his mule train?"

He hesitated, remembering Rough and Ready's tirades on the subject of supply lines. "No, ma'm" he said finally.

"I thought not. Besides, I'm not alone. Juan is coming with me." Her airy salute ended in a wave as she and Juan rode away.

The cool December day shimmered in glorious azure, amethyst, amber, emerald, and gold. Sarah hummed to herself, happy to leave behind her entourage and the bettys' bickering and complaints that hung over her wagons like a cloud of mosquitoes whining in English, Spanish, German, and some local Indian dialect that Sarah hadn't identified yet. She rode with Juan through a tumble of foothills and toward a ragged defile like a razor slash in the abrupt base of the mountain.

Sarah regarded it dubiously. "The *arrieros* hightailed it through there?"

"Of course not."

"I was afraid of that." This was an ideal spot for an ambuscade. The muleteers would have chosen the long trail to the pass between this peak and the next one, rather than risk an attack by the *guerrillas* who were picking off the soldiers. "I suppose you mean to take this shortcut and meet them on the other side."

"*Sí.*" He flashed her a smile crammed with wide, white teeth, and cheerful malice. Like most of his people, he despised Águila and his marauders. Unlike most of his people, he didn't mind annoying them. Snatching the pack train from their clutches would surely annoy them.

Sarah stood in the stirrups and peered up into the dark cleft. It was so narrow they would have to ride single file.

"Let's have a go at it then." She crossed herself reflexively, settled into the saddle, cocked her pistol, and urged her mare up through the loaf-sized chunks of granite around the entrance.

They spoke in low tones, but their mounts' hooves rang on the rocky ground like hammers on an anvil. The noise bounced back and forth across the passage. The ribbon of sky narrowed to a thread overhead. They scanned the cliff face on both sides, looking for snipers, and when distant shots echoed among the rocks they both jumped.

"Whoever it is, they aren't firing at us," Sarah said.

They rode toward the point of bright daylight that widened

ahead. They halted their mounts at the opening and looked up at a cave in the canyon wall ahead of them. The screams from it echoed against the far wall. Mixed with cries and pleas of women and children were the yells and whoops of men gone mad. A company of soldiers from the regular army clustered outside the entrance. Sarah and Juan dismounted and climbed up to them, leading their mounts.

The sergeant in charge of the guard cupped his hands around his mouth and shouted into the dark opening. "You men come out and give yourselves up as prisoners."

"Go to hell," someone shouted.

"We'll clean y'all out if'n you innerfere with us," added another voice.

At a gesture from the sergeant his men took cover behind rocks and leveled their muskets at the opening. Sarah and Juan ducked behind boulders too.

"File out now or we fire on you."

A brutish-looking creature with eyes like lead musket balls emerged, blinking in the glare. His domed head sloped straight to his shoulders. His face slanted forward into a great hairy wedge of a chin. He held up a bloody blade as long as his forearm in one hand and a dozen dripping scalps in the other.

"H'yar, you regulars! I'm Bill Stamps, I am. We don't muss with you, we don't. We're takin' the hair of the yella bellies as killed our mate, Archy."

He leaped and whirled in a wild sort of war dance. Then he stood stock still and began to sob.

The mob of them, more than a hundred irregulars of the Arkansas Cavalry, filed into the sunlight. Blood had soaked their uniforms. They shouted curses and threats at the regulars, even as the soldiers disarmed them, took the bloody scalps from them, and tied their hands behind them.

Sarah, Juan, and the sergeant tied bandanas over their noses and mouths and walked into the cave. Groans and sobs and the cries of children filled it. At least twenty Mexicans, all civilians, lay dead or dying in bright pools of blood. Most of them had been scalped. Someone had fastened a rough crucifix of sticks to a rock and hung a scalp on it.

The survivors assumed these Americans had come to finish the job and they started screaming again. They clung to Sarah's legs and and the sergeant's and sobbed for mercy.

"We have to take the prisoners back to headquarters, but as soon as we catch up with our squadron we'll come back with surgeons." The sergeant disentangled himself and hurried toward the cave's entrance.

Sarah bent down and unclasped the hands of the child hanging on to her. She lifted her gently and carried her outside away from the carnage.

"We've got to find General Taylor's mule train," Sarah said.

"They're safe," the sergeant answered. "We saw them arriving at Encantada as we were leaving."

She looked at Juan and he nodded. "Then we'll stay here awhile and do what we can."

→ ←

They rode back the way they came with the child sitting in front of Sarah. She had said nothing since Sarah carried her out of the cave, but another survivor pointed out the bodies of the girl's mother and father. She also said that the child's name was Esperanza. When the soldiers returned, Sarah had left coins with them for their burial and a novena.

They had almost reached the end of the defile when a rider clattered down the slope toward them, sending rocks bounding downhill and skittering across the trail. Sarah and Juan drew their pieces and leveled them.

"Don't shoot, Miz Western." He took his hat off so she could see him clearly.

"Well, if it ain't the elusive Moses."

Sarah took in the man's mat of tight curls, wiry as tarnished iron shavings. He wore greasy leather trousers and vest and a white shirt patched from the inside, Mexican style. His skin was such a deep brown that a cast of aubergine glowed just underneath and surfaced in his lips. He smiled at her, all saucer-eyed foolishness.

"I's shorely glad to see you, Miz Western."

"Don't play the field nigger with me, Moses." She offered him a drink from her canteen. He was powerfully built, but he did look worn out and used up and he had one less finger than when Sarah had last seen him. "You ran away from Lieutenant Blake back at Fort Texas. Joined Águila's pack, didn't you, and now you're sorry you threw in with them. Lie down with dogs and you get up with fleas."

"No, ma'm, I didn't. Águila and his men absconded with me."

"Now you're flat-out lying."

"Cross my heart and kiss a Bible, I ain't, Miz Western, ma'm."

"Yes, you are, but no matter. The lieutenant, your master, was killed at Monterrey. He has no kin to claim you."

"I's shorely sorry to hear of the young massa's demise."

"I'll bet you are." She stared him in the eyes and he fidgeted. "What do you want of me?"

Moses opened his eyes wider and started to launch into whatever story he had rehearsed, but Sarah held up an admonitory finger. He gave a slight smile and a shake of his head. His eyes returned to a normal width. His voice lost its broad accent and childlike inflection.

"The Mex'cans all say you be fair. You treat people right."

"You knew your master was killed, didn't you?"

"Yes, ma'm."

"Do you want to work for me?"

"Yes, ma'm."

"I need a bouncer and a barber."

"I don't know how to cut hair, Miz Western."

"You're Negro." She smiled mischievously at him. "You must know how."

"If you needs a barber, I can learn barbering."

He urged his stout little creole pony in the line between Sarah and Juan.

"You stole that horse from Águila, didn't you? And you're afraid he'll catch you."

"Yes, ma'm."

"And you seduced one of his women too, I'll wager."

"One of them did take a shine to me."

"While you're feeling so truthful, there's a question I've been wanting to ask you for years."

"What's that, Miz Western?"

"You were with Wild Cat and Alligator and their boys at the Battle of Okeechobee, weren't you?"

But that was more truth than Moses was ready for. A look of wary cunning crossed his face faster than a hummingbird's flight. It was one thing to be a runaway slave. It was another to be a black man who had killed white men.

"No, ma'm. I surely wasn't."

"Moses, you're so chock-full of the devil it's a wonder your hair don't catch fire."

Whiskey Before Breakfast

GENERAL SANTA ANNA'S LIBERATING ARMY OF THE
North lacked only elephants and acrobats to resemble a circus more than an engine of war. Caparisoned horses and ranks of
soldiers in scarlet and azure uniforms and nodding white plumes
filled San Luis Potosí's main plaza. More troops jammed the boule-
vards leading to it. Acres of bright bunting strung from roof to roof
overhead gave the plaza the look of a circus tent. Women dressed in
their finest clothes crowded the railings of the balconies and waved
the red, green, and black–striped flags of Mexico. The general's
band played a waltz.

"The greasers and we Irish are alike, ain't we?" John Riley had to
shout to be heard over the trumpets and tubas and drums. "We both
celebrate death."

James nodded.

"A kiss for luck, Irish."

One of the beauties on the balcony put a silk rose to her lips and
tossed it. James caught it with a flourish and sent back a smile that
could make flowers grow even in this February chill. He tucked the
wire stem into his hat brim.

James stood with the other members of the San Patricio Artillery
Company under their big new standard of emerald silk. The flag had
brought tears to his eyes when he first held it, soft and clinging and
radiant in his hands. He had run his fingers over the shamrock and

harp, neatly embroidered in silver and gold thread by the novitiates of the local convent. He marveled still that foreigners would take such care with the colors of his country. Now the banner rippled in the wind as though it were a graceful creature whose muscles flexed under the skin of silk.

"I reckon we'll be playing Old Harry with the Yanks, won't we, darlin'?" John Riley shouted louder to be heard above the mules and the trumpets, the sergeants and the women. "With such a fine army and all."

"Maybe."

"And it's ever the pessimist ye are, Jamie lad."

"Look there, Jack." James nodded at the line of mules loaded with cages containing Santa Anna's prized gamecocks. Behind them stretched the general's private baggage train. "How many of us d'ye think those cocks will feed when there's no beef to be had?"

"The general likes his creature comforts."

"He's long on luxuries and short on necessities, if you ask me."

The band launched into "Adiós," and the music reverberated off the buildings around the plaza. The soldiers formed up their ranks and files.

"*Adiós*, Ireesh. May God accompany you." The women on the balcony overhead waved their handkerchiefs at James and Jack.

"May God go with you too." James touched the brim of his tall black hat with the tips of his fingers. May He go with us all, he thought.

He faced the men and horses and the ranks of gleaming cannons behind him. Duke stood patiently in the lead position of the big cannon's carriage.

"Prepare to mount," he shouted. He put his foot in Duke's stirrup. "Mount."

The rattle of hardware and the clatter of hooves started the old happy cadence to thumping in his chest. Santa Anna had positioned his big guns first, and John Riley's company of eighty foreign artillerists rode at the head of it. The field pieces were clumsy and cast of iron. Each weighed over a ton and required six horses to pull its carriage, but they made a momentous rumble as the San Patricios moved out under their big green flag.

The army's finest troop of cavalry followed, their horses prancing in time to the music. Behind them came Santa Anna, standing in his gilt phaeton drawn by eight matched mules, almost invisible under the red and gold leather skirts that draped them. Wide epaulets and ribbons, medals and crimson silk sashes weighted down the general's staff, but they looked as plain as deacons compared with their commander. Behind Santa Anna's chariot flocked the young women who accompanied him everywhere.

Santa Anna's indifference to supplies for his army bothered James. He knew the fierce terrain the army would be crossing. He and Duke had staggered across the same desert in his search for Cruz. He had sweltered during the days and shivered through the nights and almost died of thirst before he came to a village with a meager little pond. Conscripts composed most of the infantry, *mestizo* peons and Indians forced into service. How long would they last in a freezing rain in the mountains with no shelter and little to eat?

Riley reined his horse over to ride next to James. "That latest recruit, Dolan, says most of Taylor's regular forces have been transferred to the gulf coast to join Winfield Scott. *El Sastre* is left with nothin' but volunteers—Rackensackers and Illinois suckers and Baltimore oystermen."

"The dunderheads in Washington can't abide competence in a man. Sure and they are trying to ruin Old Rough and Ready," James said.

"And they're succeeding at it. We outnumber the Yanks four to one."

"Americans are too rash to take odds into account."

"I'm after hoping they don't surrender before we kill a chance of them."

"Old Zach doesn't surrender, Jack."

Nor would he advance with such a scanty supply train as this one. James thought of Zachary Taylor in his frayed straw *sombrero* and stained frock coat, no nattier than a feed sack. He remembered him slouched in the saddle with a stout leg draped around Whitey's pommel. He felt a rush of affection for the old man, and he tried to imagine Santa Anna riding in Taylor's ancient blue Jersey wagon.

→ ←

The day had barely dawned and his patients hadn't begun to arrive yet, but already the surgeon looked harried. He stood in the middle of the church's nave and inspected the surgical implements laid out next to the trestles and boards that would serve as an operating table. A cauldron of water hung over a fire built on a bed of sand. The orderlies had spread straw on the rest of the floor. Sponges floated in basins of water. Wounded were not a priority at the beginning of a battle and they might not get here for hours, but the doctor was ready.

"The damned teamsters stole the whiskey supply," he said. "We haven't a drop to ease the men's pain."

Sarah looked up from the bandages and tourniquets and opium pills she was packing into a rucksack. "I can send you some, Doctor Hitchcock, though I haven't much."

"What kind of creatures steal from the dying?"

"Rogues always think that nothing can be done but with roguery." Sarah put an arm through the rucksack's straps and settled it onto her back. "I'll return to help when I've seen to everything at the hotel."

The surgeon gave her a wave of his hand and continued pacing about his sad kingdom.

Sarah paused on her way to the abandoned stone monastery she called "The American House" and shaded her eyes with her hand. For several minutes she watched gray-blue smoke drift like the acrid breath of disaster among the rocky hills three miles to the west. Unseen artillery coughed. It had started.

Always in war the waiting was burdensome. Waiting for the litters of torn and mutilated men to appear from the smoke was the worst of all. She had been in battle and she thought it preferable to this. In battle the mind became strangely calm and detached from irrelevancies like life and death. The body functioned without orders. Noise and excitement and confusion left space for fear, but none for dread. Fear was useful. Dread was not.

Sarah dreaded the arrival of the wounded. She would lay out the mangled bodies on the straw as though on display in a market. No smoke would veil them nor bushes screen them from sight. No sand would draw away the rivers of blood. No gunfire would drown out their screams. Sarah dreaded being caged with their collective agony.

Two of Nancy's little sisters raced and roughhoused with a crowd of Mexican children under the fig trees in front of the hotel. The youngest Skinner tottered after them. Sarah wasn't surprised that Esperanza, the girl she had brought with her after the Rackensackers' Christmas massacre, wasn't with the other children. She saw her waiting at the door, ready to shadow her for the rest of the day. If Sarah had to go somewhere, the child attached herself to Nancy. She had yet to speak a word to anybody.

Sarah's Mexican laundresses stood around the fires, warming themselves against the February chill. The water boiling in the laundry kettles would be used to simmer sheets and blankets, rags and cotton bandages. Maria stirred a big kettle of soup. Nancy shoveled loaves of bread from the domed oven in a far corner of the yard. Men would die here in the next few days, but not from starvation.

Juan and Hanibal were building benches along the sides of Sarah's wagon for the wounded. Bertha wore Juan's leather *arriero's* apron mounded over another child-in-the-making as she watched a kettle of lead melt. Sarah took the hem of her own long apron and wiped the glistening mustache of perspiration from Bertha's upper lip.

"Remember what happens if water hits hot lead, Mrs. Skinner."

"Yah, yah."

Sarah called the women of the evening shift the Nightingales. They also were wearing leather aprons that covered most of their charms. They ladled the lead out, poured it into molds, and turned the finished bullets onto trays. They all looked up as Sarah stormed past.

She found several teamsters sitting at a table in the midst of the preparations for turning the restaurant into a hospital annex. They were sufficiently disreputable-looking to represent their profession, which Sarah had found to consist mainly of men with severe deficits in civility and the ability to distinguish between right and wrong.

"Morning, boys."

"Mornin', Western." They did manage not to gawk at her, but that was probably because she'd been known to use the palm of her hand against a man's ears to knock manners into him when he stared rudely. The men who'd received the lesson had heard a ringing in their heads for days.

"You boys looking to eat?"

"Yes, ma'm."

"I reckon you wouldn't say no to a drop of whiskey first, would you?"

"I reckon not."

Sarah brought a bottle and five glasses from the back bar and set them on the table. She poured a drink for herself and upended it. They did the same. She made conversation and helped them finish the bottle. Then she brought another one.

"I figure you boys to have a plentiful supply of whiskey yourselves."

"Nah," said an individual whose beard looked like a fertile pasture for six- and eight-legged livestock. "Barcus is hoarding it till the dustup's over and the soldiers return."

Sarah stood abruptly. "I'll have Maria fry you some eggs. Leave the money with her."

She detoured past the kitchen and picked up her hefty iron skillet. Bullets were too precious to waste on a teamster. She walked outside. "Juan, Hanibal," she shouted. "Hitch the team. We're making a whiskey run."

> ←

The look of pleasure on the doctor's face when she drove up with his missing whiskey satisfied her almost more than the surprise in Barcus's eyes just before she used the frying pan to put him down for a nap. She was humming cheerfully when she returned to the American House. In spite of the cold she raised the small shutters and left the door open to coax the afternoon sunlight into the dank corners of the big room. Behind the bar Moses kept a wary eye on the eight or ten teamsters and cattle drovers playing euchre at two tables near the windows.

Nancy dumped the mail out of a battered leather sack that had arrived on the last mule in a long train of supplies. Nancy was the only one in Sarah's household who could read. She held up a creased and dirty envelope.

"A letter from the captain's missus." She put it into George Lincoln's pigeonhole in the tall desk Sarah had commissioned from a local cabinetmaker. Perfect Bliss had labeled the cubbyholes in an elegant hand with the names of the officers in Sarah's mess, which they referred to as the Spinoza Society. Even before the first delivery of mail had slipped past the official post tent and lodged here, anticipation had made the desk the heart of her establishment. Men congregated there on the rare occasions when mail arrived. When the slots stood empty, their glances strayed to it anyway. Sometimes Sarah would find a man staring fixedly at it, as though word from home would appear if he looked long and hard enough.

Nancy's fine blond hair was growing out, hiding the ragged spikes and hollows left by Moses when he used her to practice the military haircut. Nancy didn't own a mirror and she didn't seem to mind the result. Sarah preferred to see her looking like a boy. The child was fast overtaking twelve. Her breasts would begin to call attention to themselves soon. The heavy arches of her eyebrows, bleached pale as cream, glowed against the dark tan of her skin. They and the large front teeth that kept her from closing her mouth completely gave her a startled, inquisitive look. In spite of her scabby elbows, big feet, and heron's gait, some men gaped at her in a way that made Sarah want to whack them across the ears. They must have divined the beauty she would become.

Sarah smoothed Lincoln's second-best jacket, faded to the color of cannon smoke, and heavy and soft in her hands. Its pattern of stains and wear were as familiar to her as her own old shirtwaist. She had sewn every stitch that held the frayed seams together. She had cut the patches from other uniforms too shredded by thorns to keep their owners from embarrassment. And though she had never told him about it, she had sewn a tiny medal of Saint Christopher into an out-of-the-way seam. In war a man needed all the divine help he could get.

She sat on a chair with the jacket in her lap. She took a length of wool yarn that she had unraveled from old cloth, and threaded it through a needle. The needle was a large one, but it almost disappeared in her big hand.

Sarah liked mending. It was one of the few chores that didn't require brute strength and it could be done sitting down. The simple act of passing the needle in and out always calmed her. The bright sliver of steel caught up the raveled ends, salvaged what would have been lost, and gave it new purpose.

She needed calming. Sharing the noise and terror of the battlefield with the men was far easier than waiting for them here, but Taylor had ordered her to stay behind. His unspoken message was that the odds were so heavy against them the Mexicans would very likely overrun the American positions, and any woman found there would endure worse than death.

"Western." Nancy brought a stool over and set it in front of her. She sat down and leaned forward, earnest and worried. "Ma says whoring is a sin and them as does it will burn in hell for eternity."

"All of eternity?" Sarah looked up, amused. "Or just the first six months' enlistment?"

"Eternal damnation is not a jest."

The girl's chiding tone amused Sarah. She would never point out to Nancy that her mother was no saint, even if she didn't take hard cash from the men she tumbled. Sarah had long ago learned that those with the least qualifications to judge others were usually the first to do it.

"If you let a man into your drawers, he reckons he has the deed to you," she said. "The only way to keep them from imagining they own you is to make them pay rent. Even so, I never accepted money for my favors."

"You hire out women for the officers," Nancy said.

"To the benefit of both parties." Sarah left a loop of yarn, ran the needle through it, pulled it tight, and bit off the end. She pressed the knot smooth with her nail, put the jacket in her lap, and looked down at Nancy. "The trade isn't for every woman, but conjugation is a pleasurable thing, child, and folks will do it, come hell or high water. It's a natural force, like a river or an avalanche. There's no stopping it when the blood's up." She nodded toward the women outside, framed by the doorway, like an animated painting of rustic bliss. "My girls are eating when they would've starved. My boys are catching a little happiness where misery abounds. And they both have someone to hold them through dark and lonely nights. If I go to hell for that, then so be it."

"I shall only give myself to the one I love, provided he loves me, of course."

"That's as it should be." Sarah smiled at her, a little wistfully maybe. "That's what I wish for you."

They both looked up when a man from the Second Indiana Regiment roared through the door, his clothes half torn off and flapping as though he'd been deposited by a whirlwind. He jittered, goggle-eyed and lathered, in the middle of the room, struggling to catch his breath. Sarah tossed aside the mending and stood up. She put her hand on her pistol, expecting to see a troop of Mexican cavalry ride in after him. Instead, more of the Indiana men, looking as used up as the first, crowded through the door.

"Taylor's whipped!" the first one panted. "His army's cut to pieces and the Mexicans are coming this way under a full head of steam."

The teamsters and foragers leaped to their feet, scattering their stools like ninepins. Sarah reached the deserter in three strides. Before he realized the enormity of his blunder, she cocked her fist just to the right of her chest and drove it into the concavity where the wide bridge of his nose dipped to meet the eyebrow that spanned his face from one side to the other. He flew backward into a sprawl on the floor. Sarah stood over him.

"You damned son of a bitch! There ain't Mexicans enough in Mexico to whip Old Zach." She fetched him by the lapels, hauled him up like an empty suit of clothes, and shoved him against the wall. She held him there at the end of her outstretched arm, while his toes barely brushed the neatly swept flagstones of the floor. "You spread that report and I'll beat you to death."

She shook him like a mop, dropped him, and turned to the other volunteers. "You boys go back the way you came, unless you want it noised about that a woman fought your battle for you." She grabbed a tablecloth from under the dinner of a shoe salesman, scattering the earthenware plate and mug, and tied it around her waist. She weathered only a moment's pang at the prospect of losing the linens she had accumulated with a great deal of trouble.

"Juan," she shouted, "Hanibal, bring the wagon with all the sheets, tent poles, rope, and canvas you can rummage. We'll need them for litters. Moses, look after things here. If any other deserters show their faces, you have my permission to shoot them."

She strapped on her knife, arranged her powder horn and cartridge box across her chest. She collected the string of filled water gourds hanging by the door and slung them over her shoulder. A barrel of water already stood lashed down in the wagon bed. She threw the army rucksack packed with cotton gauze and linen bandages over the other shoulder. She waved her pistol at the Indianans, herding them outside.

They clustered in the yard conferring, and she strode past them on her way to the corral of mesquite brush. She untied Jake and strapped the gourds and saddlebags across his rump. With the rucksack on her shoulders she stepped onto a block, hiked up her skirts, and swung a leg across his bare back.

Using just the hackamore, she turned Jake toward the rumble of cannons and the distant blue mist flowing like a river from the narrow defile the Mexicans called La Angostura, the Narrowness. The bettys had told Sarah that the old ones remembered when *angostura* also meant "distress."

That Flying Goose Affair

ONLY ONE ROAD ENTERED THE HIGH CLEFT CALLED LA Angostura. Travel along it was perilous even in times of peace, and these were not peaceful times. A series of deep gullies raked into the high plateau on the west. To the east, parallel ridges extended onto it from the mountains, like the bony hindquarters and tails of antediluvian beasts lined up, their backs turned to the destruction rampaging there.

When Sarah could taste sulfur and hot brass on the cold air, she tied her kerchief over her nose and mouth. She and Jake rode into a shifting front of smoke and dust that closed around them like drifts of dirty wool. Her range of vision narrowed to a smoky hollow around her. The dense haze seemed to muffle and distort the gunfire and shouts, the shriek of shells, the clang of bayonets, and the rumble of artillery carriages.

Sarah heard the familiar whistle, faint but unmistakable in the din. She peered into the smoke, but she couldn't tell from which direction the sound was coming. No sense trying to dodge. A sidestep could take them into its path.

"Steady on, Jake."

Time slowed as the whistle ripped into a shriek. Sarah tensed her legs slightly against Jake's sides, more to reassure him than guide him. He shook his head and continued picking his way among the rocks and craters and hillocks thrown up by the artillery shells. The cannonball formed suddenly out of the smoke and plummeted to the ground nearby. Sarah felt the sting of rock fragments as it shattered a boulder, bounced, and rolled to a stop at Jake's feet. She waited for it to explode, but it lay there, nonchalant.

"Thank the Lord it wasn't canister nor grape, eh, Jake?"

Sarah wanted to hunch over, to shield herself behind Jake's neck and head. Instead, she squared her shoulders, sitting straight and easy on his broad back. Caviling in the presence of death didn't appease it in any way. She kicked Jake's sides and rode him into the worst confusion and carnage she had ever seen, and she had seen plenty.

The cannons stilled for a few minutes while the artillery carriages, caissons, crews, and teams of horses and mules careened over the broken ground to new positions farther forward. A fitful wind shredded the smoke and sent it lazing off to be snared by rocky salients. Sarah rode up a rise and stared around her. She looked for wounded among the dead strewn like bright red and blue flowers in the drab brown landscape. They marked the ebb and surge of the battle as surely as surveyors' stakes.

Sarah could see why lesser men like the Indiana volunteers might panic. Mexicans seemed to be everywhere. Phalanxes of Santa Anna's glittering cavalry charged to the music of their buglers. Bugles blared on both sides, in fact, ordering the men to advance or fall back or regroup. But the fighting went on oblivious to their orders.

If the generals had a plan, Sarah couldn't see it. Soldiers fought with bayonets and pistol butts and fists in every gully and crevice. They rushed up hillsides and backed down again under onslaughts from above.

Jeff Davis's Mississippi Rifles thundered past in their red shirts and wide-brimmed black hats. They screamed the Texans' Comanche war cry that had disturbed Sarah's rest so often while they were perfecting it. The high, warbling caterwaul set the skin to crawling on her arms and under the back of her collar.

Then the familiar calm settled over her, like a warm shawl around her shoulders in a chill wind. She guided Jake down the hill toward the largest collection of bodies. As usual in war, the unthinkable, the unimaginable, the unbearable had become routine. Braxton Bragg's cannons commenced again and acrid blue smoke began filling the valley from the ground up. Sarah passed broken bayonets and muskets, scattered shot bags and cartridge pouches, then corpses tumbled about.

She rode a zigzag course from one scattering of bodies to another. She stopped at each, looking for movement, listening for groans. But they were silent. She laid her fingers on the plump artery in the side of the neck where life usually pulsed near the surface. Jake, with the reins dragging, nosed the blood-soaked dirt in search of a few blades of grass that hadn't been trampled by hooves and boots or blasted by the exploding shells.

These casualties were the men farthest back, stopped earliest in the advance. From the clamminess of their skin she knew they had lain there dead for at least three hours. At the third stop she felt warmth on a young man's skin. When she took his hand, his supple fingers curled easily in hers. With a prayer she felt for the heart's tattoo that marshaled his life's forces, but she could detect nothing. She pulled the small mirror from her pocket and held it in front of his nose and mouth. No vapor formed on the surface. He had died while his fingers gripped hers.

She sighed and stood. She wiped her bloody hands on her skirt and gathered the reins. A groan issued from a heap of solid granite that rose thirty feet from the valley floor. With trembling fingers Sarah untied a gourd from the cluster slung behind the saddle. She clambered up to the crevice that split the rock and peered into it.

"Dear God, son, you're wedged tighter'n a tick."

She lay on her stomach with her shoulders and chest in the opening and caught him by the arms. When she heaved him upward, he screamed, but she kept lifting until she could lay him on the rock. She cradled his head in her arm, uncorked the gourd with her teeth, held it to his lips, and tilted it carefully. Water was too precious to waste. When she judged he'd had enough, she picked him up gently, but she jostled his shattered leg and he screamed again.

She laid him across Jake's broad back and led the mule to where the wounded were to be collected. Sarah knew there would be few vehicles or drivers other than Juan and her own wagon. The U.S.

government still didn't consider transportation of wounded or injured or sick a necessity in this war, as though the soldiers were under orders to stay well and sound.

Sarah rode Jake back at a trot. The musket and cannon fire grew
louder, and Sarah could hear the chime of bayonets and the men's
oaths shouted in English and in Spanish. She heard the cries of the
wounded, too, but after the desolate hush of the rear they were music to her. Only living men could raise a ruckus. The screams of the
injured horses always made her melancholy though. No one would
soothe them or carry them out of harm's path or work to heal them.
Whenever Sarah passed one, she stopped to cut its throat and relieve its suffering.

On a ridge to the left of the fighting, Zachary Taylor sat on
Whitey. He had positioned himself too far forward, as usual, exposing himself to the enemy's bullets. Sarah wanted to shout at him to
use the sense God gave him and move back, but he wouldn't have
heard her, and he wouldn't do it anyway.

An artillery carriage and eight-pounder jolted and bounced at full
speed toward her and she reined Jake to one side. She recognized
Old Firesnorter, one of Braxton Bragg's pieces. Bragg himself galloped after it, waving his sword to direct the cannons that thundered along on either side and slightly to the rear of him, like a
skein of cumbersome geese. Lather flew off the horses and their eyes
popped in their heads.

They had just passed in a great rolling cloud of dust when the
lead animal's hind legs buckled and he collapsed onto his haunches.
The rider kicked out of the stirrups, slid off, and hit the ground running as his mount rolled over and expired. The horse's partner on
the right dragged him a few feet, then reared and stopped and his
teammates collided with him or jumped the traces. The cannon's
carriage tilted precariously to the left, with Bragg shouting orders to
keep it upright. The sweat-drenched crew, powder-stained and
burned, gasped for air.

While the horses heaved in exhaustion and the men untangled
the harnesses and unhitched the dead animal, Bragg waved at Sarah.
"Western!" He had lost his hat and a spume of pale hair rose above
his red-rimmed eyes and teeth startling white in his soot-blackened
face. "We must have your mule."

Sarah didn't argue that she needed Jake to carry the injured. Without the artillery there would be a lot more wounded. She led Jake to the carriage and held him while the men hitched him up. She untied the gourds and saddlebags and slung them over her shoulders with the rucksack. Then she slapped Jake on the rump.

"Do your damnedest, you old reprobate."

He bit her with bruising affection on the elbow and made a grab for her hat before the lead rider mounted him and they started the team racing forward again.

Ignoring the bombs and bullets and the occasional companies of soldiers hurtling past her, Sarah knelt beside the wounded. The soft lead balls expanded when they entered a body and they created gaping holes. She gave the men water and cleaned their wounds as best she could. She tucked in protruding organs, closed up gashes, and applied field dressings of lint to staunch the bleeding. She picked each unconscious man up in her arms, and with the string of gourds clattering at her back she carried him across the harrowed ground to the road where Juan and Hanibal could find them. When wounded men filled the wagon bed, Sarah refilled the gourds from the barrel, took another supply of bandages, and waved Juan on his way.

Sarah allowed herself to be distracted only when Jeff Davis's Mississippians, afoot now, ran past on their way to fill a gap in the American line. With thunder rumbling in the mountains and the wind whipping her blood-soaked dress around her, she climbed a promontory and stood panting at the top. From there she watched them create a shallow, V-shaped angle, the open end facing forward. Fifteen hundred Mexican cavalrymen with flags snapping in the rising wind galloped down the slope toward them. Riggings of bridles, reins, cruppers, martingales, red ferreting, iron bells, and silver spangles enmeshed the horses. Tooled and gilded mantles of bull's hide covered their rumps and hung to their hocks. Each man sat erect, lance in hand. The lancers rode knee to knee, advancing in a line as straight as if it had been laid out by surveyors.

"Dear Lord." The beauty and the thrill and the futility of it shook Sarah to the soles of her boots. Her knees went spongy. Tears welled up and ran down her cheeks, leaving cold tracks.

War was an insane pastime when contemplated from the tedium

of one's own hearth, but from here it was the grandest, most significant of enterprises. Today this valley was the most important place on earth. Sarah would not have wanted to stand anywhere else, except in that long line of Davis's men, waiting for her fate to overrun her on a crimson-and-gold-draped stallion.

The Mississippi Rifles stood still until the lancers seemed about to trample them. Anticipation leached what little moisture remained in Sarah's mouth. She tried to lick her lips and her tongue stuck to them.

Then the Mexican colonel abruptly reined his horse to a walk and his men, confused, did the same. Their precise line wavered, undulated, unraveled. The colonel must have expected the Americans to fire early, forcing them to reload as his men got within lance range. Sarah stared, mesmerized by the rapid and gaudy progress of disaster. By the time the Mexicans' bugle sounded "Charge," they were inside the Mississippians' formation. Davis shouted "Fire!" and his men yodeled their feral, hackles-raising cry.

Flames from the Yager rifles converged on the lancers. Many of them toppled from their saddles, and their horses galloped away, stirrups flapping. Davis's men grabbed the bridles of the mounted animals, threw them back on their haunches, and hacked at their riders with bowie knives. The rest went at each other with bayonets and rifle butts.

Sarah saw Davis stagger, drop to one knee, and put a hand to his shoulder. He struggled to his feet, transferred his sword to his left hand, and rushed back into the melee. Sarah scrambled down the steep slope toward him.

Bragg's batteries raced toward the battle with their usual noise and dust, Jake in the lead and Old Firesnorter's carriage vaulting behind him. The crews brought their rigs to a clattering halt, bullied them into position, and opened fire on the Mexicans who were fleeing. Bodies soon littered the ground and began filling the ravine where the Mexican soldiers had taken refuge.

Sarah dodged among the men hacking at each other until she found Davis, whose opponent was backing him toward a narrow gully. Sarah picked up a broken rifle and swung it as she came, catching the Mexican in the back of the head. He fell and she stepped over him.

"Fine piece of tactics, that flying goose affair," she said.

Davis grinned at her. "I warrant it'll be entered in the history books."

She wrapped his broken shoulder while his men, as though slogging through syrup, chased the remnants of the enemy. Panting, they dragged their rifles after them, the butts of the stocks leaving snake trails in the dirt. The gunners, too, gasped for mouthfuls of the sulfurous air. Drenched in sweat and black with burned powder, they leaned on the wheels for support as the drivers backed the teams into the traces and hitched the carriages. They climbed wearily onto their horses and started off behind Bragg to find a position where they could lob balls into the Mexican troops huddled in the ravines.

Sarah knew how they felt. Her arms hung heavy as howitzer barrels. The muscles under her broad shoulders pained her. She had run out of bandages, so she ripped away the filthiest six inches at the bottom of her petticoat, discarded it, and tore off cleaner strips farther up. She was bandaging a corporal's slashed leg when lightning flashed and thunder roared, bright and loud as a shell exploding nearby. Sarah leaned over the man to protect him from chunks of hail as big as walnuts. They hit her hat, thumped her shoulders, and rattled against the gourds. Even heaven is dancing at this *fandango*, she thought.

She lifted him up and put his arm around her shoulder. With her arm around his waist she helped him cross the broken ground where hail lay in a treacherous layer. By the time Sarah got to the road, the hail had turned to rain. She lifted her face and opened her mouth to catch the cold drops.

She grinned at her companion. "Tastes good, don't it?"

He managed a smile in return.

The Mexican army made three attempts to break through the lines that day. The outnumbered Americans were able to drive them back only because of the artillery. The cannons appeared just where they were needed, and raced off as soon as their work was done there. Sarah spotted Jake from time to time. He was always heaving at the harness, the heavy carriage leaping and flying over rocks, out of gullies, and up slopes.

Sarah and the soldiers staggered glassy-eyed across the morass of mud and rocks, spent ammunition, broken equipment, and bodies. By the time the sun had half slid behind the mountains, the Mexicans began withdrawing. Sarah looked up at the promontory and saw Taylor standing in Whitey's stirrups. He shifted from one foot to the other, as though dancing in celebration. The men around her cheered and she laughed out loud at the sight of him. She did a little heel-and-toe jig step herself before she went back to work.

In the fading light, she searched for the wounded among the abandoned artillery carriages, broken caissons, and ammo boxes. Packing tow blew around her like sooty snow. Vultures spiraled down, lit with a lurch, and swaggered among the bodies. They rose in a thunderclap of wings when Sarah threw rocks at them. As night closed in, wolves began to howl in the ravines, and the furtive figures of civilians ghosted through the deepening blackness. Many of the American dead she found now had been stripped naked. In the distance, where the casualties were mostly Mexican, a woman wailed.

When the light grew so dim that Sarah couldn't see the bodies well enough to avoid stepping on them, she wrapped tow around a broken bayonet and fastened it in place with a length of the coil of baling wire she carried at her waist. She took the flint out of her own kit and struck sparks until the tow caught fire. She heard a groan and the growling of dogs, or maybe wolves. In the fitful flicker of her torch she followed the noise.

"Get along, you damned curs!" She waved the torch at the pack of wolves circling the body. They curled their purple lips back over yellow teeth, but they slunk off after other game.

The Mexican was only a boy by the look of him, a poor Indian lad who before this day had known little more than the rocky fields and shabby festivals of his village. A shell had ripped through blue jacket, skin, and muscle, exposing the glisten of stomach and entrails that the wolves had already begun devouring. He shivered convulsively and she draped her coat over him. He stared at her with sad brown eyes, then he looked at the pistol at her waist, and back up at her.

"I have to save my powder, *amigo*." She crouched and gave him a drink.

His thanks were in his eyes. She took the small wooden crucifix from around her neck and held it to his lips so he could kiss it. She stroked his cold forehead with her hand. Then she pushed the hair out of his eyes to distract him and to hold his head steady while she tenderly cut his throat. Her tears blurred the view of his face, but when the air stopped hissing from his severed windpipe she closed his eyelids with the palm of her hand, and murmured the Lord's Prayer.

She knew it would soon be too dark to work without a lantern. She retrieved her coat, arched her back to relieve the ache, and used the last light of the torch to find the makings for another one. She was assembling it by feel when she heard steps. She froze as they came closer and a darker piece of night solidified and staggered toward her.

"Is that you, Jake?" She squinted into the gloom.

Jake butted her in the chest with the hard plane between his ears. She put a hand out and stroked his wet forehead and nose. Ropes of saliva hung from his sagging lower lip and he tilted drunkenly from one side to the other, but he shoved her again, almost bowling her over. She threw her arms around his lathered, muddy neck, and the two of them leaned on each other for support.

Glancing over his back she saw a chalky smudge on the wall of night. She walked toward it, Jake butting her now and then and nibbling her hat brim. Anxiety became certainty as the smudge took the form of George Lincoln's horse. He whinnied, reared, and struck out at the wolves that circled him and the naked body lying nearby.

Sarah didn't hear her own voice wailing over the roar of grief in her ears. Swinging her musket by the muzzle she waded into the wolves. Since plenty of other carrion was available, they decided that contesting this particular piece was too much trouble. Snarling, they retreated.

She fell to her knees, rolled Lincoln onto his back, and put an ear to his chest, listening for the beat she knew she wouldn't hear. She got her arms around him and hoisted him facedown across Gator's saddle. She draped her old greatcoat over him, then took the reins and mounted Jake. Leading the horse, the hot tears turning cold on her cheeks, she shivered and sobbed all the way back to the wagon.

→←

The campfires of Taylor's army flickered in the wind that swept the high plain known as Buena Vista. It seemed to take away with it whatever scant comfort might have been left among the horrors of the place. With lantern held aloft, Sarah led Jake across the broken ground through the bitter cold and icy mist. She moved from soldier to soldier, looking for signs of life. She found many of them stripped and mutilated by pillagers or torn by wolves or vultures or packs of dogs. The lantern's light illuminated the emotions frozen on their faces when death overtook them. Some were defiant, some pleading, terrified, angry, or astonished. The motionless, contorted bodies reminded her of a grotesque mockery of the tableaux the officers liked to perform in the evenings.

Her skirt grew so heavy it hit against her ankles, clinging to her and tripping her. When she stopped to wring the blood from it, she could hear it splatter into icy puddles. She heard a groan and hurried to the man who stirred and groaned again. She held the canteen to his lips.

"Drink some of this and then we'll take you home."

"My brother. Help him." He reached for the soldier who lay sprawled a few yards away.

"We'll carry him in, too."

"Don't leave him."

"I won't."

She got him onto Jake's back, then went for the other one, who looked no more than fifteen or sixteen. Sarah knew before she reached him that he was dead, but she hoisted him onto her left shoulder as the lantern guttered and went dark.

"Time to give it up, old son." With her arm laid across Jake's neck she walked among the campfires, detouring to pass close to each one for the warmth.

The men huddled together around them under whatever shelter they could find or create. Sarah would have felt sorrier for them, but many of the volunteers had sold their greatcoats for whiskey. They had few tents and blankets. Most of the teamsters hired to haul baggage had bolted when they heard the Mexicans were about to whip Taylor. Juan had brought what food and medical supplies he could on each return trip from the field hospital, but they were running out of everything there too.

Juan was waiting when she arrived. The wagon was almost full of wounded men, many of them screaming or groaning or pleading for water or mercy or their mothers. He helped Sarah add the last one and laid his dead brother next to him. He gave her a quizzical look, and she shrugged.

"Brothers," she said, and he nodded. "This'll be the last trip."

"Thanks be to God." He crossed himself and climbed wearily onto the seat.

"Turn the mules out at the American House and get some sleep yourself. Come back at first light."

He waved a hand at her as he drove away. He had set a sack of corn and a kettle of Maria's soup, still steaming, under Sarah's lean-to of brush. Sarah gave the corn to Jake. She ladled some soup into a mug and sipped it. Then she picked up the kettle and took the last small loaf of bread from the basket.

She found Zachary Taylor pacing in front of his old wall tent, pitched on a ridge overlooking the dark valley.

"Ah, Western." He beckoned her past the swarm of staff and reporting officers and messengers.

"Something to warm you from the inside out, General." She set the kettle and the bread on the ammunition crate that served as his table.

"Thank you, Sarah. You are one of the best troops I have."

"You heard about Captain Lincoln?"

"I did. Such an unforgivable waste." He started pacing again. She had never seen him so furious. "They withdrew my regular troops with the express intent of leaving me undermanned. They counted on the Mexicans defeating me."

Sarah knew who "they" were—the Secretary of War and, according to Taylor, General Winfield Scott and a host of other scheming climbers in Washington City.

"A man gets to be popular in the press, it attracts envy," she said. "Especially when folks are clamoring to make you president when this is over."

"They prefer to see us all perish here rather than thwart their own political ambitions."

"You should stay more to the rear, sir. You don't want to give them the satisfaction of dying."

"Most of my wounded were behind me, and I would never pass them while I'm alive." He held his arm out so she could see the two holes in it. "Those balls were getting excited, though. Look at this." He searched the front of his coat, found another hole, stuck his finger through it, and wiggled it at her. "This one went between my arm and my body and clean through the coat. The second one seems to have exited through a button hole. Fancy that."

"It ain't over, is it, General?"

"Maybe not. We'll see if Santa Anna's boys are up for another *fandango* in the morning."

A soldier approached, hat in hand. "Good evening, General."

"Teddy, have you finished that poem yet?"

"I'm trying to compose a final line for the first stanza, sir."

Sarah looked out over the battlefield and the flickering fires that threw light and shadow across the bodies of men and horses and the wreckage strewn everywhere. "Like bivouacking in hell, ain't it?"

"The bivouac of the dead," Teddy O'Hara murmured.

No one slept much that long night in the bivouac of the dead. When the sun finally rose, Sarah stood on the ridge and looked for the Mexican encampment. There was none. They had gone. Taylor's little army had won. This time.

The Evil They Know

JAMES HAD GIVEN HIS COAT TO AN OLD WOMAN, AND
now the cold drizzle soaked his uniform and set him to shivering. A pale shaving of a moon had just risen over the mountains when the sleeping child started to slip off his back. With her cheek on his shoulder, between his epaulet and collar, her long, deep breaths had been warming his left ear. Her arms hung on his chest, her legs dangled at his sides. But now as she slid down, the rough wool of his jacket rasped her cheek. He didn't want to wake her. Asleep she wouldn't feel the hunger that tormented them all.

He held his arms crossed behind him, gripping his forearms so she could sit on them. They had become numb with the weight of her, but he hiked her back into position as gently as he could and limped on through the darkness. He returned his attention to staying in the roadway and not wandering into the night and the cactus.

He heard the harsh rale with every breath Duke took and he let his shoulder touch the horse's neck, taking comfort in his warmth. Duke whickered and stumbled against him. Then he collected his balance and staggered on under the woman and her three children dozing on his back. James wished he hadn't let them ride Duke, but he couldn't leave them where he found them at sunset, huddled by the road and staring up at him with hopeless eyes.

All around him walked the remnants of Santa Anna's army and the families that had followed it. For the most part they trudged along silently, too weary and dispirited to talk. In the darkness he could see only those closest to him, but he could feel the presence of all of them, a great weight of grief and misery and desperation dragging at him. From the side of the road wounded men called out for mercy and for water. Soldiers, hungry, cold, and footsore, walked over those who had fallen. Women and children wept over the husbands and fathers and brothers unable to go on. The starved and exhausted cavalry mounts and pack animals stumbled at every step.

In the darkness James bumped into the corner of a wagon, abandoned and slewed across the road. He made his way around it and the emaciated draft horses lying dead in the harnesses. His badly made shoes had never fit him, and they rubbed away the skin and soaked his stockings with blood. He rolled his feet from heels to toes trying to keep his full weight off them, but the sharp rocks jabbed through the thin soles anyway. Most of the women and children walked barefoot. He couldn't imagine what they must be suffering.

James heard a commotion behind him. He turned and saw lights approaching. People scattered to the sides of the road as a phalanx of cavalrymen, flaring torches held high, trotted past. They surrounded Santa Anna's chariot, obscuring any view James might have had of the general. The great leader of the Liberating Army of the North whirled past in a choking cloud of dust.

James thought of the old sergeants' tales of Napoleon leaving his troops to starve in Russia's winter. He shifted the sleeping child to the front to relieve his aching muscles. He supported her with one arm and pulled the folded San Patricios' green silk flag from inside his jacket. Holding her against his chest, he draped the flag over her to protect her from the cold wind that cut across the valley from the north.

In the darkness Duke gave a long, shrill, rasping sigh. James turned and saw him collapse and roll onto his side. The woman who had been riding him gathered her children, patting them to make sure they weren't hurt by the fall. James handed her her sleeping daughter. He put his hand on Duke's warm chest, but could feel no heartbeat. He sat in the road, wrapped his arms around Duke's neck, rested his cheek in the coarse mane, and, having no tears left, went to sleep.

→ ←

The quartermaster corps was selling off the effects of the soldiers killed at Buena Vista. Sarah went, feeling like a battlefield thief, to see if she could buy anything useful for her household. Then the auctioneer's assistant led Gator out and the bidding started.

"Seventy-five dollars!" The paltriness of the offer outraged her. She pushed to the front of the crowd. "The tack alone cost that. The horse is built like a Conestoga. He ain't worth a penny less than two hundred and fifty dollars."

"Sold for two-fifty."

Sarah opened the sack hanging from her waist and dumped the contents onto the table. Very few coins were left when she separated out the amount. She took a grip on Gator's hackamore and led him away. She carried with her a satchel of Lincoln's clothes and the spare boots that he had left with her before the battle at Buena Vista, the uniform to be washed, the boots to be polished. When she reached the cemetery, she put the boots backward in the stirrups, then she and Gator walked through the gate. The low limestone walls gave little protection from the winds sweeping down the mountain slopes and across the valley floor. Sarah stamped her feet to warm them. Not many real flowers were available in February, but heaps of bright cloth and paper ones lay on the graves of the American men the Mexican women had loved.

She stood at the foot of Lincoln's grave, just one more in the long rows of mounds and neat wooden crosses. Rain had turned the freshly exposed dirt into mud the color of dried blood. She took off her hat and the mist gathered and sparkled like tiny jewels in her dark red hair.

"They gave you a swell send-off, didn't they, Cap'n?"

The army did know how to put on a funeral. The Second Dragoons and the Texans, Jeff Davis's Mississippi Rifles and the others had stood at parade rest through the long eulogies. Then they came to attention with a loud slap of their palms on the stocks of their long pieces and the rattle of the buckles on their shoulder straps. Bragg's cannons had fired their salute. The smoke had drifted up and headed westward, as though determined to join the fog that wound around the mountains' peaks and snaked into their crevices. Then the drums and fifes had played them back to camp with jolly dance tunes.

"I'm not much at speeches, George, but I wanted to say my own good-bye. I reckon old Sam Butler said it good as anybody. You knew what's what, and you can't fly higher than that. You were a fine man. I'm grateful that my life had you in it even if just for a spell. I'll send Gator here home to your wife and your son, soon as I can arrange it."

She bowed her head and said a prayer for the ease of his soul. Then she stood for a while, staring at the mountains and the walnut trees, the clouds and the graves, setting the place in her memory. The site was a beautiful one, but she thought of the young wife and the child who would never be able to visit his grave. She wondered, briefly, where her bones would lie. Then she shook her head. The place didn't matter as long as she was buried with soldiers.

She was about to go when Sam Walker appeared. He led the magnificent horse that the citizens of New Orleans had sent him in thanks for getting through to Fort Brown. He wore the Texans' usual uniform, a weather-beaten buckskin coat, wool vest, unsavory slouch hat, brown duck trousers stuck into his high boots, all accompanied with bowie knife, dirk, a brace of pistols, and a hatchet, as well as his old Hall rifle. The captain's bars looked out of place on the frayed collar of his flannel shirt.

"I'm surely sorry about Captain Lincoln," he said.

"Seems like we leave our dead littering the world like so many empty feed sacks. It ain't right."

"No, it ain't right. He was a good man. Not enough of those in the world."

Sarah smiled down at him, amazed that such an insignificant-looking slice of humanity could hold the absolute loyalty of the lawless band of Texans that formed his company of dragoons. "You returned in time for the *fandango* at Buena Vista."

"Wouldn't have missed it."

"How are things back east?"

"Too many people. Too much brick. Not enough sky." He took a big pistol from the holster at his belt. "This was worth the trip, though."

"Sam Colt's new piece?"

He handed it to her and she hefted it. "It's a beauty, Cap'n." The handle fit well in her hand, but its weight would tire even her in a short time if she tried to hold it there long. "Six cylinders."

"Yep. That was one of the changes I suggested to Mr. Colt. These arrived just before the dustup."

"They're rare as hen's teeth still, aren't they?"

Walker laughed ruefully. "Every general wants to fight the current war with the weapons of the last one. I had to talk up a storm equal to a norther through a field of broom corn to get the army to order these."

"I reckon they operate on the philosophy that the evil they know is better than the one they don't."

Walker nodded ruefully. "I was headed for your place after 'Retreat,' Western. My stomach says it's time to wood up."

"Stew tonight."

He started away, but turned around. "By the way, Bravo Jones made the acquaintance of an artillery ball. Took his head off clean as a whistle. Cut down like a hollyhock in November."

"You don't say."

"Yep. He's stiff as a wedge and twice as cold."

Sarah refrained from saying "Good riddance to bad cess." Speaking ill of the dead did her no good and, worse, it failed to rankle the dead at all.

They parted company, and Sarah left Gator with Hanibal in the abandoned house that served as a stable behind the hotel. Juan was scouring the bed of the wagon with sand, trying to remove the dark blood stain that covered it. Esperanza waited for her by the door. And unless Sarah found something else for her to do, she would dog her steps until bedtime, never saying a word.

"Good afternoon, sweet pea." Sarah took her by the hand and led her to the stable. "Hanibal, let her help you curry the horses."

Hanibal lifted his eyebrows in exasperation, but he gave her a gunnysack and was showing her how to rub down the horses with it when Sarah left them.

The broken blade of an entrenching shovel, worn thin with use, hung on a peg by the back door. She used it to scrape the mud off her boots instead of stamping them on the threshold and alerting the household of her arrival. As she expected, the women and children had gathered in the kitchen to gossip and she could tell by the thinness of the aroma that the stew wasn't ready. Her appearance sent everyone scattering.

She lifted the lid off a pot on the table and peered inside. "Why are there dried toads in here?" All of the kitchen talk was carried on in Spanish.

"A remedy, *Señora* Western." Maria hurried to retrieve it.

"A remedy for what?"

"A woman's monthly pains and noses that bleed."

"I can't have it bruited about that I keep toads in my kitchen." She noticed a white cloth sack sitting on a platter near where the pot had been. It was wet and distended with whatever was inside. "And what is this?"

"You said you wanted a boiled pudding for the officers tonight, so I prepared it." Maria looked anxious. A *yanqui* kitchen still mystified her.

Sarah stooped to look closely at it. "What did you boil the pudding in?"

"A sack that Lara found among the bedclothes to be washed."

Sarah picked it up. "This is the nightcap that Major Bliss was searching for." She sighed. No sense losing her temper, although it did seem as if the bettys stayed awake late at night inventing ways to confound her. "My boys will head here directly after 'Retreat.' Why isn't dinner ready?" Sarah followed the women, hurling questions and orders. "Have you changed the bed linens? Fetch more wood and water. The place needs sweeping."

The drovers and drifters, the reporters, itinerant entertainers, Indians, and traders hardly looked up from their cards as Sarah's Spanish thundered from the kitchen and women hurtled past them, shouting, "*Ya voy, ya voy*—I'm already going, I'm already going."

The entertainers, too, had trailed the army from Corpus Christi. The two jugglers were decorous enough and had never broken any of Sarah's pottery. One of their comrades earned his money eating rocks and scorpions and toads for the amusement of audiences. He spent his money on Maria's cooking, which Sarah said wasn't much of a recommendation. Sarah had forbidden the other one from practicing his art in her establishment. He blew musical renditions on his nether flute, and performed other feats with it, too.

The most desperate-looking of her clientele wore a Mexican blanket over his filthy leather trousers and jacket. Coarse black hair fell in greasy ropes over his bloodshot eyes. He reached out as Nancy passed with a tray of bread and caught her skirt. Before he could reel her in, Sarah materialized, moving much faster than anyone would have supposed. She grabbed the back of his chair and jerked it from under him, dumping him on the floor. Sarah heard a communal hiss as everyone else sucked in their breath and waited for the gunshot that would fell her.

Instead he stood up, the ratted hair on the crown of his head barely reaching Sarah's chin. "That weren't hospitable, Miz Borginnis."

"If you ever touch this child or her sisters or any child of any color anywhere in my knowing, John Glanton, they will not find enough of you strung together to plant." She turned on the others, many of whom looked disappointed that no blood had flowed. "That goes for all of you."

" 'Twas merely a misunderstanding, Western. I meant no insult."

Sarah glared at him until he sat down and picked up his cards.

She went back into the kitchen, where the smell of cilantro and the sound of hands patting tortillas made her think of Cruz. She stirred the stew, blew on a ladle full of it, then sipped it.

"Western." Nancy came in with a folded paper in her hand. "Major Bliss brought this. He said he found it among Captain Lincoln's papers. It has your name on it."

"I'm busy here, squirt." Sarah never would admit she couldn't read, though everyone knew it. "Parse it out for me."

"It don't say much, just something from that Spinoza fellow the captain was always quoting."

"What is it?"

" 'We feel and know that we are eternal.' "

Sarah smiled. "Thank you, Captain," she murmured. She tucked the note into her pocket.

"Señora." Maria lowered her voice so no one would hear her carry tales about the Mexican irregulars. Who knew who was a spy for which side. "A woman told me at the well that Águila is staying at Rancho Incarnación, maybe eight miles south, under El Nariz."

Sarah knew the mountain called El Nariz, the Nose. "When did she see him there?" She had ridden great distances before in search of Cruz, only to find that Águila had long since flown.

"Yesterday."

"Did she say if he had a woman with him, about this tall? And a baby?"

Maria shrugged. "He has many women with him."

Sarah put the cord of her old pistol around her neck and stuck it into her belt. She draped the cartridge belt and powder horn across her chest.

"Are you going to tell the general?" Nancy asked.

"No." Sarah took her hat and coat from the peg and put them on. "He'll send soldiers. If Águila has her, he'll kill her rather than give her up." Sarah couldn't say how she knew that, she just did. "If anyone asks, tell them I'm scouting for beef and brandy. That's all they care to know anyway."

Hanibal saddled Alice Ann for her and she set out along the rocky path the Mexicans dignified by calling a road. The mountains, draped in heavier fog now, hunched up around her. This was such a vast country. So many places to hide, to be lost, to rot and never be found. So many vultures to pick off the defining flesh and leave the anonymous bones. As Sarah rode, she wondered what Cruz's bones looked like. Would she know, somehow, that they belonged to her friend? She imagined them as being delicate and a mellow antique ivory color, a fitting case for Cruz's very old, very wise soul.

The ranch sat by itself, a cluster of low whitewashed buildings under ancient almond trees at the base of a lopsided peak that did resemble the nose of some lounging colossus. Sarah rode past a murky water tank and the cattle yard, where a few mangy steers under their coatrack horns stood with bony rumps to the sharp wind. She took off her hat so the sentry on the flat roof could see her red hair twined in its high bun. She waved her large white kerchief at him and rode on, ignoring his shouts to halt.

She dismounted and strode toward the two abbreviated creatures standing on either side of the door. Their knives and pistols, lariats and rifles looked enough to weigh them down. They were dark and scarred and threatening enough, for all their small size. Sarah stared into the hooded eyes of the more ferocious one. She braced herself for a tussle or at least an argument, but they moved aside, confining their displeasure to unsheathed glares.

Sarah filled the doorway, the pale winter sunlight spilling around her, and blinked to adjust to the gloom. Antonio Águila wore leather trousers laced up the sides with the legs flared over his boots and the white cotton trousers showing between the lacings. A wool *serape* covered him from shoulders to groin and Sarah couldn't tell if he carried a weapon under it or not. Most likely he did.

He sat, legs sprawled, and smoking a *cigarrillo*, in a huge high-backed chair piled with torn and faded velvet pillows, relics of the former owner. The owner had taken his five daughters, Maria had said, and fled before Taylor's advancing army. Sarah assumed that the three women sitting on a bench were not the daughters of the hacienda. Several more peered at her from the inner doorway.

A big rooster strutted at the end of the cord that tethered him to the leg of Águila's chair. He looked sleek and well-fed with a black ring around his right eye. His green and red-brown plumage glittered iridescent in the sunbeam coming through the small, high window. His long tail feathers arced behind him and one gold feather brushed the floor. Sarah assumed he had won Águila a lot of money to be treated so well.

"*Señora Grande.*" Águila held up a dark brown bottle. From the unfocused look in his eyes Sarah guessed it held *aguardiente*. His Spanish was slurred, but Sarah understood it well enough. "How kind of you to grace us with a visit."

Sarah had rehearsed as she rode. She knew the vocabulary of trade in Spanish, but she had never bargained for a life before. At least Águila looked as though whatever the bottle held had mellowed him. But she knew he was most dangerous and unpredictable in this condition. She would have preferred the old raging scoundrel to this unctuous, duplicitous devil.

"I came to offer you a good price for Mrs. Murphy. *Rescate.* Ransom."

"Mrs. Murphy?" Águila feigned confusion.

"Cruz."

"I would be happy to take your money, *Grande*, but the whore died expelling the Irish dog's bastard." He waved the bottle airily. "The brat entered the world dead and unbaptized. It was God's judgment on the mother."

"I don't believe you."

"Your disbelief will not return them from hell." His smile was evil wrapped in a *serape*. He glanced over her shoulder toward the two men stationed at each side of the door.

Sarah whirled and gave them her look, part mother, part mayhem. They hesitated, which was the most she had hoped for. She strode past them, her heart thumping so loudly she thought they would hear it and think fear, rather than fury, caused it. She had expected this from the man who killed civilians and looted villages. Águila's decision to lay up here, just a few miles from the American encampment, was the measure of his audacity. Sarah wondered if he had done it partly to taunt her. Maybe that was why he hadn't had her killed. You can't rankle a dead enemy, she thought.

"*El Sastre*, the Tailor, is beaten, you know," Águila shouted happily after her.

"Not that he's aware of," she muttered.

She wondered if she should have come with soldiers and taken the *rancho*. And found Cruz murdered. She untied the horse and mounted. She scanned the surrounding hills and motts of trees for a place to hide and watch for Águila's departure, but half a dozen mounted men rode around the corner of the main house and followed her almost to the outskirts of Saltillo. She knew that when she went back, the *rancho* would be empty but for the lizards that sunned on its walls and the doves that cooed under the eaves.

→ ←

Águila crossed the weed-grown courtyard to the storeroom at the far corner of it. He opened the heavy mesquite-wood door and peered into the gloom. A single ray of light from a loophole in the outer wall lay in a golden ribbon across piles of corn still in the husks. Cruz lay against one of them, her wrists and ankles tied tightly. A rag had been stuffed into her mouth and held in place with a bandana knotted at the back of her head. A rat skittered over her legs and disappeared into the corn, from which issued the rustling of more of his kind.

Águila untied her hands and removed the rag that gagged her.

"Where is she?" she asked.

"She's well enough."

"Let me keep her with me and I'll do whatever you wish."

"You do whatever I wish anyway."

An old woman hobbled in, the infant balanced on her bony hip.

"Because I possess a kind soul I'll let you hold her. But only for a moment. The men are packing."

Cruz stretched out her arms and the woman placed the baby into them. Cruz bent over her and cradled her close, as if she could prevent Águila from taking her again. With one hand she smoothed the fine hair away from the child's face, and stroked her shoulder and back. She ran her fingers around the tiny earlobe and tickled the little palm. The infant closed her hand around Cruz's finger and held on, her grip strong enough to break a mother's heart.

Águila settled on his heels and studied them through narrowed eyes. He nodded and the woman leaned over to take the baby. Cruz turned away and held the baby so hard against her she whimpered, but the woman pulled on her little arm until Cruz had to let go to keep the child from being hurt.

"Don't worry." Águila's voice mocked concern. "She'll be cared for." He tied Cruz's wrists again and put the rag back in her mouth. "Raúl and Diego will come for you soon."

Cruz sobbed and choked on the gag. The hot tears burned her eyes, stung her cheeks, and soaked into the bandana. She struggled to free herself but she only caused the harsh ropes to cut more deeply into her and she brought corn cascading down on top of her.

At first she had wondered why Águila would bother to have her baby carried from place to place, but she'd come to understand his reason. As long as the child lived, Cruz wouldn't try to kill herself. Cruz knew Águila wanted to keep her alive so he could watch her suffer. Cruz lay back in the rough corn and prayed to God to take her and the baby, then begged forgiveness for the sin of such a request.

The Chickens Are Coming

M AY OF 1847 BROUGHT RAIN, WARM, THOROUGH, and incessant. Sarah was enjoying a few lazy moments of solitude. She lay on her back with her hands behind her head on the down pillow. She wiggled her toes, happily accommodated by the bed she had had built to extra length, and listened to the rain spatter on the roof tiles.

The noise of it muffled the taproom racket and the shouts from the street as people prepared for the feast of Saint Augustine. The rain had almost crooned her into a nap when it ceased abruptly its drumming on the roof, but it continued as a steady roar in her ears, as though it had become a part of her after so many days and nights. Even then she kept some of her attention on the clatter and voices coming from the kitchen and taproom, the guest rooms, women's quarters, and corridors that surrounded the central courtyard.

A man's shouting and a woman's shrill protests rose above the general din of pots and pans and the servants' conversations. Sarah sighed. She got up and hurried across the muddy courtyard, past the stone wall of the well, all grown over with jewel-green ferns, glistening in the slanting rays of the setting sun.

Five or six men dangled like folded jackknives in hammocks slung at the far end of the room. They slept through the commotion. Those playing all-fours, three-up, and monte ignored the altercation in spite of the fact that Sarah's newest employee, Julia, stood naked, her reflection brown and succulent in the big mirror behind the bar. The crowd of officers and merchants wrapped in the fog of cigar smoke over the table of biscuits and sausages watched her in amusement.

Julia was short and shapely and solid. She stood with her feet spread, her arms waving, breasts bobbing, and she screamed in Spanish. The object of her discontent was Lewis Allen, the writer. He must have chased her here from her room at the back of the courtyard. His pomaded black hair stood up in exclamation points around his bald spot. Mud covered his bare feet and he held his trousers up with one hand. His shirt gaped open at the neck. Several of the other women surrounded him, all yelling at him to stop tormenting poor Julia. Red-faced, he turned to Sarah.

"Western, she stole my gold collar button."

"*Mentira*," Julia shrieked. "A lie."

"Where is it, Julia?" With hands on hips Sarah glared down at her.

"No *botón*." Julia opened her palms to show they were empty. She shook her head, sending her thick black hair whipping around her. She poked a finger in each ear and ducked to check her armpits. "No *botón*." With her fingers she spread her labia to give everyone a view, then whirled, bent over, and pulled her cheeks wide. "No *botón*." And with all her caterwauling Sarah knew she wasn't holding it in her mouth.

"*Bruto*," Julia screamed at Allen.

Sarah knew she had to settle this now. She could not have it rumored about that she employed thieves. She wanted to shake the wench until her teeth rattled.

Teeth.

"Open your mouth."

Julia looked up at her, all innocence and noncomprehension.

"Open your mouth."

The girl tried to run, but Sarah grabbed her and pried her mouth open. Nancy brought a lantern and held it up so Sarah could see. The left canine tooth had been filed to a point capable of cutting the thread holding a collar button.

"Well, now I've seen it all." Sarah let go of the woman's mouth but held on to her arm. "Nancy, bring the ipecac. Then collect Julia's things and bring them here."

"No, *Señora* Western." Julia started to cry. "No ipecac."

"She's been putting on airs," Nancy said. "And on Saint Augustine's day they only accept wagers in gold at the genteel tables." She didn't have to tell Sarah that Julia gambled.

"You didn't intend to swallow it, did you." Sarah wasn't asking a question. She shook Julia hard enough to set her breasts bouncing and the thick mantle of her hair to rippling.

Sarah had believed the woman's sad tales of official injustice and the casual cruelty of every man she had ever met. Maybe the tales were true, but some victims were just waiting for the chance to prey on others.

Sarah nodded to Lewis Allen. "We'll have your button shortly."

She marched Julia, still naked, into the courtyard. Nancy poured the ipecac from the old brown bottle. Sarah pressed the sides of Julia's mouth with her thumb and forefinger until the clenched teeth parted slightly. She slid the spoon in, emptied it, and with one big hand held Julia's mouth and nose closed until she had to swallow in order to breathe.

Sarah gave her a bucket, turned her around, and held her by the nape of the neck. She didn't have to wait long before Julia retched. Sarah made her recover the button and rinse it off.

Maria arrived with the frayed basket of Julia's few shabby belongings. Looking at them, and at the shivering woman crouched at her feet, Sarah suddenly wanted to cry. She wanted to enfold her in her arms and weep at the casual brutality that crippled the human spirit. Instead she helped her up and handed her the patched skirt and blouse Julia wore every day.

She turned to Juan. "When you go to Santa Rosa for the corn and beef tomorrow, take her home." Sarah considered the life Julia had led in that village and added, "Or wherever she wants to go between here and there." She slipped three worn silver coins into his hand.

"*Sí*, Western." He knew he was to give them to her when he left her.

"She can sleep in the woodshed tonight."

Staring at the basket of Julia's belongings, Sarah realized that the pallid light of sunset gave it and everything else a pale pink cast, as though the rain had caused the deep crimson of the sky to run. The vesper bell would ring soon. She walked through the smoke and noise of the taproom and out into a plaza that thousands of hands had transformed.

People thronged the gaming tables and the kiosks displaying sweet breads and *pulque*, cactus candies, pottery, carved toys, and masks that now ringed the perimeter. Men had built a cockpit in the center of the plaza, and the serious followers of the cocks already occupied choice places at the low wooden wall. Tall branches formed groves at the corners of the streets, and the roads themselves had become green tunnels of boughs decked with colorful banners. Everything glistened with the recent rain. Drops glittered like diamonds in the light of the setting sun.

"Good evening, *Señora* Western." Saltillo's chief of police tipped his broad-brimmed hat. He was perhaps fifty, stately and serene.

"*Don* Ramón, what a pleasure to see you."

Sarah always befriended the local constabulary when possible, and bribed them if necessary. Saltillo's enforcer of the law was easy to like and impossible to bribe. On his rounds, however, he would stop by her hotel for a small glass of sherry and an English lesson with her. The lessons usually turned into halting discussions of good and evil, love and death, the weather, and American and Mexican politics.

He seemed inclined to start one of those discussions now, but the church bells rang and all activity stopped. The men took off their hats and everyone bowed their heads for a silent minute of prayer. Usually when the second bell released them, they wished each other an amiable good night and drifted home. It was a lovely custom that drove rancor and warfare completely away, if only for a few moments, and Sarah made it a point to participate in it whenever she could. But tonight was the feast of Augustine, patron saint of gambling. No one thought of going home. *Don* Ramón tipped his hat again, smiled the smile that could put a child at ease and set a woman's heart to chattering like castanets, and drifted off into the crowd.

Sarah didn't envy him, especially not tonight. Any festival in Mexico produced a lot of roisterers, but the rowdy American volunteers made *Don* Ramón's job much more difficult.

A flurry of trumpets sounded, as though each musician were trying to finish first. A tall, distinguished old man dressed in brilliantly white pants and shirt and a new straw hat climbed on top of a table. He took the hat off and held it to his chest.

People hushed long enough for him to shout, "Praise Mary most pure, the chickens are coming." Then the crowd parted to let pass the fighting cocks in their open-weave baskets and the men who carried them. A few wore masks as part of the celebration, and assistants held torches high to light the way. Everyone surged after them, calling out the names of their favorites and asking God's blessing on them. Sarah stepped back.

She could see well enough above this crowd, and she didn't relish finding a knife in her side or a noose around her neck. Taylor's bold show at La Angostura had subdued Saltillo's populace, but Sarah sensed the undercurrent of hostility. And lasso-wielding *guerrillas* still roamed the streets at night, ambushing drunken volunteers as they left the *cantinas*.

The cocks' owners uncovered them and paraded them around the pit so the spectators could choose the one they thought would win. Sarah was amused to see that Hanibal had achieved his ambition of being a broker for the bettors. He had wet the rebellious uprising of his hair and combed it back neatly. He wore a clean pair of white trousers, a new shirt, and the solemn air of a village elder.

People crowded around, handing him money and pointing to the cock they had picked. Hanibal nodded at each one and added the coins to his satchel. He would keep the wagered amounts of those who lost and use it to pay the winners. The more generous of his customers might give him a small gratuity. Sarah considered herself an astute businesswoman but she always marveled at how the broker never confused the bets or forgot who had lost, who had won, and how much he owed each one. Sarah made a mental note to give Hanibal more responsibility.

She was about to go back to the American House when a particular cock caught her eye as he strutted around the far side of the ring. His owner wore shabby farmer's clothes and the usual straw hat and a mask carved and painted to look like an affable skull. Sarah moved closer for a better view of the bird. The rooster had a black ring around his right eye and one gold tail feather that hung down below the others.

Águila's got *cojones*, she thought.

The Americans weren't the only ones out for his blood. The local Mexican authorities wanted him too for his depredations among the villages. Sarah backed into the crowd and went off in search of *Don* Ramón and his policemen.

➔ ←

Sarah and Juan were saddling by lantern light in front of the stable when William Worth rode up. The usual gaggle of aides, adjutants, and servants trailed after him.

Worth looked as though he wanted to ask Sarah where she was going at this hour, but dared not risk having a woman tell him, in front of his inferiors, to mind his own business. Sarah had done it before, and she looked likely to now. "Quite a to-do in the plaza tonight," he said instead.

"Some shootin' and shoutin', General," Sarah said. "*Don* Ramón arrested Antonio Águila and threw him into the *calabozo*, with the help of a few hundred of Saltillo's riled citizens." She grinned into the mare's side as she tightened the girth. Saltillo's *calabozo* was not a place she would want to spend five minutes. She glanced up at Worth. In spite of the coating of dust from the road, he sat his horse as though posing for a military monument. "Did you just come from Monterrey?" she asked.

"I did."

"How's the general?"

"Well enough. General Taylor seems content to let Scott take over the campaign in the south and wait out the war in comfort in the north."

Worth's disapproval of that plan wasn't lost on Sarah. She mounted the mare and gave him a perfunctory salute. "Tell Nancy to warm you some grub. She'll know where the good brandy is. The linens are clean in the room on the southwest corner."

She and Juan headed at a cautious trot down the moonlit road toward Rancho Incarnación. With pistols drawn and the lantern held high, they searched every corner of the deserted buildings. Sarah hadn't dared believe that Águila's people would have returned to this place, but she couldn't resist hoping. In the adobe shed where the animal feed was stored, the constant dampness had caused the low heap of corn to sprout. The spindly white shoots all leaned toward the single high, narrow window, as though trying to escape their prison.

Sarah found a soiled cloth lying in a corner. She held the lantern close to it. "Looks like a baby's."

In the bare yard outside the main house, Sarah and Juan stared at the confusion of tracks—horses, mules, men, cattle, and dogs— going and coming. The light of the full moon filled the hollow prints with molten silver. They looked ghostly, as though their makers still hovered, an invisible mob, over them.

"Can you trail them to their next hidey-hole, Juan?"

He shrugged.

"You've got some Indian in you," Sarah said. "You're supposed to be able to follow tracks."

"Need Comanche for that."

"They're never around when you want them, are they?"

Juan gave a wry chuckle.

They led the horses through the main house and into the courtyard, where they tethered them to a twisted mesquite tree. They wrapped up in their saddle blankets and lay against the wall. The moon shone in their faces for only a short while before it set behind the mountains and they went to sleep.

At first light they fed and watered the horses and rode back to Saltillo. Sarah stopped at the hotel, saw that Nancy and Maria had everything under control, then went on to the city jail. She carried a handkerchief soaked in vinegar in case she could talk to Águila only in his cell. She didn't expect him to tell her where Cruz was, but maybe he would inadvertently give her useful information.

She had wrapped her ankles in vinegar-soaked rags to discourage the vermin from hopping aboard there, and she held her skirts up so that no lice or fleas could stow away in the hems. From the rooms along the dark corridor beyond *Don* Ramón's tiny office, she heard drunken shouting and an Indian singing mournfully in a tongue that was not Spanish.

"*Señora* Western." Don Ramón bowed as gallantly as the cramped quarters would allow. "To what do we owe the honor of your visit?"

"I want to talk to Antonio Águila."

"Alas, *Señora*, he is not here."

"Where in hell is he?" Blood rushed to Sarah's face and pounded in her ears.

"Your General Worth came last night and freed him."

"Freed him!"

"Sí. He had a letter of permission from the mayor."

"Why in God's green creation would he do that?"

Don Ramón lifted his shoulders and held out his hands, palms up, the gesture of a man who had long ago given up trying to understand people's stupidity. "How do you say *reclutar?*"

"Recruit."

"General Worth recruit Águila as a spy."

"A spy?" Sarah couldn't believe her ears.

"Yes. The general offered him *clemencia* . . ."

"Clemency?" Sarah felt like a parrot, too stunned to do more than repeat what Don Ramón said.

"*Sí.* Clemency and money and uniforms for him and all his *poblachos,* his rabble. He went, of course. If he stay here, we garrote him for his crimes." *Don* Ramón put a hand to his throat and pretended to squeeze.

Sarah wanted to ask *Don* Ramón how he could have let Águila walk out of the jail, but she knew the answer. Whatever an American general wanted, he got. "Where were they going?"

"To join General Scott in Puebla."

Sarah walked out into the busy morning with rage tolling like a bell in her ears. She wished James had killed Worth when he had the chance. And she imagined James wished so, too. If James were still alive.

Traitorous Dogs

T HE SILVER RIBBON OF THE CHURUBUSCO RIVER
looped in graceful falls from the copper-colored mountains.
It leveled out in the valley, threading together the marshes and
dikes, ditches and tender green cornfields. The scene would have
been a peaceful one except that blue-jacketed men seethed across it.
Cannonballs sang as they ripped paths through the tall corn. Canister and grape shot raked the crossroads. Dead and dying lay heaped
together along the causeway leading across the swamps and the
low-lying fields to the walled church and convent of Churubusco,
aptly named for the Aztec word meaning "place of the war god."

James didn't have time to remember the long, sad road that had
led here after the rout at Buena Vista. All he thought about was that
the corporal had set the keg of powder near the cannon in the em-
brasure twenty yards from his own. He shouted that it was too close
to the red heat of the eight-pounder's barrel, but no one could hear
him over the crash of artillery around them. He had just started
toward the cannon when the powder ignited. Flames washed over
the corporal, Captain Santiago O'Leary, two other crewmen, and
General Anaya. The general ran with the others, their clothes flaring like torches, and leaped into the mud of the irrigation ditch.
The fire engulfed the last box of grape shot and it exploded, launch-
ing fragments in all directions.

Seamus appeared at the top of the breastwork and slid down into the snug emplacement where James's cannon crouched. He put his mouth to James's ear and shouted, "No more shot left, lad, and Worth's men have taken the bridgehead. The dragoons are close at their arse. General Anaya says to withdraw to the monastery." He waved the rest of the crew after him and took off running toward the gate in the wall on the hill above them.

James hesitated until he saw men leaving their guns all along the fieldwork. He took an iron spike used to swivel the cannon's carriage wheels and, with a maul, pounded it into the vent, disabling it so the Americans couldn't fire it. Then he took off after Seamus.

Mangled artillery horses and mules blocked the road and filled the ditches. Even over the deafening roar of cannon and musketry and the screams of terrified animals and the shouts of men, James thought he could hear the galloping hooves of the dragoons' mounts growing louder behind him. Bullets whistled around him, but exhaustion had replaced fear with detachment, as though leaden death had nothing to do with him.

Ahead of him, Seamus grabbed his thigh and pitched forward. James hoisted him onto his shoulder and kept going. By force of will he made his weary legs move faster, his heart pump blood, his lungs draw in each painful breath. With Seamus's legs and arms bumping his chest and back he veered off the road and pelted through the broken cornstalks, laboring up the slope, and leaping the bodies that littered his path.

He crowded through the big gate with the last of the San Patricios and into the milling confusion of men and animals inside. He set Seamus down. The big oak door slammed behind them with a comforting thud. James leaned against the wall, gasping for air in the smoky heat of the yard while his heart tried to hammer its way out of his chest.

The rough stone felt reassuringly solid against his shoulder. The wall encircling the two hundred acres of the church's grounds was twelve feet high and built of limestone blocks as big as ammunition caissons. It snaked along the dips and rises in the terrain for a mile or more in diameter.

"Look lively, Jamie me darlin'." The patched toes of John Riley's boots poked over the edge of the wall's catwalk, at about eye level. "They're close enough to sniff your breeches."

Riley leaned down, held out his burned and filthy hand and hauled James up to stand next to him on the wooden banquette. Then he and James pulled Seamus up. On either side of them, two lines of men, one kneeling and the other standing over them, fired intermittently through the double rows of loopholes. Riley kicked over an empty ammunition box for Seamus to sit on. Seamus made himself as comfortable as he could at one of the lower loopholes, though the red stain was spreading across the torn shirt tied around his thigh.

"They brought a wagonload of ammunition," Riley said. "All of it the wrong caliber for any muskets but our own dear sweethearts." He patted the stock of his Shaw caplock, then tossed James and Seamus three boxes of paper cartridges.

"God himself knows we're the ones to have it." James tried to chuckle, but it snagged in his parched throat. He knew the punishment for desertion. Death by hanging awaited him and the other San Patricios if the Americans overran this place. We shall die fighting here, he thought, or dancing on a gallows tree.

James glanced over at Riley, who grinned in return. Soot and gunpowder caked Riley's face and so did dried blood from the burns left by the cannon's glowing iron. James knew he looked as bad. He had almost expected the heat from the eight-pounder to sear the flesh away from his bones, and set the grease in him to sizzling. In comparison, the August temperature on the other side of the sandbag wall of the emplacement would have felt like autumn.

James felt August now, though. When he wiped the sweat from his eyes, the coarse powder grated across his scorched skin. He leaned to one side and peered through the loophole, framing his abandoned cannon in the circular opening. It looked as though it were waiting to greet the attackers. James half expected to see it wag the wooden trail of its carriage, like a dog's tail.

While he watched, soldiers poured over the breastwork and around the Mexican artillery emplacements and streamed up the hill toward them.

"*Aguántense, muchachos.* Hold yourselves." General Anaya was still covered with mud from the irrigation ditch and his face and arm were badly scorched, but his clipped Castilian lisp was unaffected.

James eased his finger off the trigger and wiped his sweaty palms on his trousers. His pulse thrummed an erratic counter to the steady beat of the American drums. He watched the blue wave sweep closer until he could distinguish the hairs in the soldiers' mustaches. He was about to turn to see if Anaya had fallen asleep, when the general's sudden shout startled him.

"¡Tiren!"

James squeezed the trigger, relishing the power, savoring the way the curve of the metal pressed against the crook of his finger. The roar of his musket blended with those around and above him, deafening him again, leaving him dizzy and elated. Through the loophole he saw men drop out of sight in the corn as though pulled under by some invisible creature of the depths. The advance faltered. He and the others cheered until their parched voices gave out.

"The First?" James asked while he and Riley reloaded.

"They would be carrying the First Division's colors, now, wouldn't they?"

"Worth's men."

Riley glanced a grin at him. "P'rhaps they're Worth-less."

"I would give my life, Jack, to have Worth in my sights."

"You may be after having the opportunity, Jamie lad."

James rammed the bullet down the barrel and fired, then loaded and fired again. Around him men shouted and fell, hit by American sharpshooters perched on the nearby heights. Braxton Bragg's artillerists managed to heave their howitzers through the swamps to within range of the walls. The high arc of their trajectory rained shot from above. Exploding fragments tore through the churchyard. For the next two hours the world consisted of heat, noise, blood, and death.

As the sun beat down James passed beyond the yearning for coolness. His throat felt as though it were lined with metal shavings and his mouth with sulfur and ashes, but he could no longer remember how water tasted. He thought he would never hear anything again except the thunder of cannons and musketry and the screams of dying men, but he could think of nothing he wanted to hear. Except silence.

The sun, a blur through the smoke, had slid halfway to the horizon when the Mexican fire slowed and thinned. James knew their ammunition was giving out. With a triumphant shout the Americans raced across the open ground and braced their ladders against the wall. The defenders threw the first few back, the men leaping to safety as they fell, but soon they were clambering over the parapet.

"To the church," Riley cried.

The green silk flag streamed behind him as he leaped off the banquette. With the San Patricios behind him, he dodged into the roiling mass of men and carts and animals. Already Americans were dropping from the top of the wall to the banquette, then onto the heaps of bodies that littered the ground underneath. The tinny music of bayonets rang as they closed hand to hand with the Mexicans.

James stopped to rip down the white flag of surrender that a Mexican sergeant was raising. He wadded it up and carried it with him so no one else could use it. The remaining San Patricios and a few thousand Mexicans sprinted toward the huge cross-shaped church whose graduated tiers of flat roofs rose on a hill behind the monastery. With its high central dome, ornate arches, curved buttresses, and domed turrets, it looked like the palace of some Eastern pasha. The men jostled through the tall door and barred it behind them as the first Americans hit it.

The Mexicans and the San Patricios ran across the cool nave, up the stairs, and through a maze of dark, narrow passages and stairways. The steady thud of a battering ram and the sound of splintering wood reverberated behind them as they climbed the ladder to the first roof. They ran out in time to see one of the Mexicans there drape his white shirt over the muzzle of his musket, raise it high, and walk toward the edge with it. Riley swiveled, sighted on him, and fired. The man pitched forward into emptiness, the shirt fluttering down after him.

"We do not surrender," Riley screamed. "¡No entregamos!"

Men dropped to lie still or to moan and writhe as the Americans crouched in the darkness of the passageway and fired out into the light. The Mexicans threw down their empty muskets and scattered to the end of the roof where they knelt with their hands up. The San Patricios lay behind the heaps of bodies, some still alive and screaming, and kept on firing. They knew there would be no parole or mercy for them if they were captured.

A few Americans fanned out from the door, scuttling at a crouch along the wall supporting the next roof, taking cover behind the tall

stone braces that jutted out from it. James could see that soon he
and the rest would be trapped here, their backs to the precipice, and
he had just fired his last ball. He threw down his musket and ran
along the façade to a fifteen-foot-tall buttress. It was stepped at the
bottom, then rose straight up to support the tower over the main
door at the end of the apse, the short arm of the church's cruciform
shape. James started up it, hugging the rough stone surface and finding foot- and fingerholds in the crevices between the blocks. Bullets
whined past and he felt some of them ruffle his hair.

He hauled himself onto the flat top of the buttress and looked out
over the sea of American soldiers, rank after rank, surrounding the
building's outer walls. James stood against the sulfur-colored sky,
with wisps of smoke swirling around him, insubstantial as a ghost,
and prayed that one of the sharpshooters below would take aim at
his heart. For once they wouldn't or couldn't accommodate him, and
he could hear voices speaking English at the other end of the bridge
from the apse's second, narrower roof.

James knew that taking his own life was a sin God wouldn't for-
give, but to allow himself to be captured would be merely another
form of suicide. The Americans would kill him. He knew that. He
doubted they would even wait for the formality of a hanging.

He closed his eyes and rejoiced in the faint breeze that cooled his
face. He felt happy and weightless, as if when he stepped off the
wall he would float out over the war and away. He prayed that Cruz
waited for him in the other world, though he doubted he would find
her where he was going.

He crossed himself, raised his arms as if to embrace oblivion, and
stepped forward. He was surprised and disappointed when something grabbed his belt and jerked him backward. He turned, trying
to wrench away from the hand that held him. He turned to see the
predacious angles, scars, and pits of Antonio Águila's face. He froze
for an instant, stunned by Águila's green uniform jacket and the
colonel's insignia on his collar. The man's voice set him into motion,
though. He understood the Spanish well enough.

"You will not die so easily, dog."

James yanked at the heavy silver Angostura Cross of Honor,
breaking the chain that held it around his neck. In the same motion
he smashed it into Águila's face, opening a cut that sliced through

his brow, starting a flow of blood into his eyes. The two of them grappled at the edge of the wall. James didn't bother to break away from Águila's hold. Instead he used all his strength to drag him over the edge with him. He almost succeeded, but more hands hauled the two of them to safety.

"We finally got you, you traitorous son of a bitch." The lieutenant was a volunteer, a member of Worth's First Division. He yanked James's wrists behind his back and tied them there so tightly his fingers began to tingle, then went numb.

Making jokes about throwing him over the edge, they hauled him across the apse roof and through the broken stained glass window in the third-story wall and down a passage to the ladder. As he started down it, the man above him put the sole of his boot on James's head and shoved. James plummeted to the bottom while the Americans laughed.

They added him to the rest of the surviving San Patricios, Seamus included, and marched the group of them, several hundred in all, past bodies heaped like leaves in a windrow around the church walls.

General Anaya marched just in front of the San Patricios. When he saw Águila and his bandits dressed in the round felt hats, red scarves, and green jackets the Americans had given them, he broke from the rest of the prisoners to stand face to face with him.

"¡Perros pérfidos!" he shouted. Traitorous dogs! He had more to say, and he was still saying it when an American prodded him back into line with his blood-crusted bayonet.

As James marched past the Bengal Tiger, the creativity and breadth of Twiggs's stock of Anglo-Saxon expletives made him almost nostalgic. This wasn't the first time Twiggs had cursed him, but it was the most thorough and personal.

The American officers, in fact, had all they could do to restrain their men. The troops lined the path and screamed invectives as the San Patricios marched past with their slack-head drums keeping the beat. James felt warm sputum hit his face. More of it rolled down the front of his coat. He made no sign that he even knew it was there. He looked straight ahead, focused on a quiet place, a place with clear running water, green fields, and Cruz. He only noticed when a soldier lunged at him with his bayonet because he had a sudden brief hope that the man would kill him and make an end to the misery. But an officer stepped in front of the man and pushed him back. James wanted to protest, but he would not stoop to asking for the favor of death. He certainly would not beg for life.

As James passed Worth, he turned his head for the first time. He stared straight into Worth's eyes, hard as flint. Worth looked through him. He obviously had no idea who James was. James broke ranks and leaped at him. With his hands tied behind him, he couldn't have done much. Maybe he intended to clamp his teeth onto Worth's throat. Before he got close enough to inflict any damage, though, six or eight pairs of hands threw him to the ground.

"You son of a bitch," James screamed. "You murdering son of a bitch."

All in a Lather

>━¦━◀▶━◆━◯━◆━◀▶━¦━◀

SEPTEMBER'S COOL NIGHT AIR LINGERED IN THE SEC-
ond courtyard of the sprawling collection of adobe buildings
known as the American House. The sun hadn't risen, but its first
light flowed as thin and silken and full of promise as aged champagne across the flat roofs of Saltillo. It had yet to seep down the
east-facing adobe walls and into the weedy square ringed by
kitchen, stables, the farrier's shop, and servants' quarters.

Sarah's rooster had finished his heartfelt challenges to the other
feathered pretenders in the neighborhood. He had flapped about in
the dust to discomfit his mites, and he had run each quill and pinion
through his beak, coaxing oil out to the tips of them. Now that he
considered himself irresistible, he was chasing the hens and hopping
aboard each one in turn. His ladies complained that they would
rather peck at the maggots and beetles in the piles of horse manure
not yet shoveled up.

Sarah lay back in the warm, sudsy water that filled the big horse
trough near the stable. She drew in a lungful of aromatic smoke
from the slender cigar Jeff Davis had given her the night before and
softly sang one of Jack Borginnis's favorite songs. The thought of
him singing it made her want to smile and to cry.

When weary I are
I smokes my cigar:

And when the smoke rises
up into my eyeses,
I thinks of my true loves,
And oh, how I sighses.

She had pinned her wild hair up in a careless pile on the top of her head. She rested the nape of her neck on the edge of the trough and listened to the muted rattle of Maria's pots in the kitchen on the other side of the courtyard. Sarah loved this hour of the morning, when the world drowsed and the light crept in hushed as though reluctant to wake it. At this hour the day's perplexities hadn't reached a simmer yet, much less a boil.

Sarah drifted into a warm, soggy reverie that Maria's scream of *"¡Ay, Dios!"* interrupted. Maria said *"¡Ay, Dios!"* often, though not in a tone quite this frantic. Then Sarah noticed that the voices and early morning racket from the adobe houses on the nearby streets should have been louder by now.

Nancy and her sisters, billowing cotton skirts and wild yellow hair, came flying into the yard from the kitchen.

"Los brutos have caught Concepción and Zenaida at the market." Nancy passed the trough and went directly to Sarah's old horse pistol hanging from a peg on the wall. "They say they shall brand them as *yanqui* spies and whores."

"Damned banditti." Sarah rose, sending a surge of water over the sides. "My chemise, Caroline." She climbed out dripping onto the straw mat by the trough.

"They say they'll cut them into pieces and feed them to the crows." Caroline, the second eldest Skinner, handed Sarah the knee-length cotton shift, with capped sleeves and a narrow frill of lace at the square neckline. Sarah threw it on over her head and tugged it down her glistening body. The water soaked through the flimsy cloth until it clung like a membrane, alternately revealing and concealing her magnificent hills and hollows. Sarah considered dispensing with clothes altogether, but decided a distraction was called for, not a riot.

Nancy tried to hand her the pistol, but she waved it away. "It'll just slow me down." She grabbed her riding crop and put the rawhide loop at the butt end of the handle over her hand so it dangled from her wrist. She knew Juan had left with the mule train for Monterrey that morning. "Nancy, find Moses and send him on along. And roust my boys." Hardly a minute had passed when she took a canteen from the wall and the bar of soap from the trough's rim, hiked her shift up to midthigh, and set out at a run for the square.

"Even Colonel Davis?" Nancy called after her.

"Especially Colonel Davis."

Jeff Davis had smuggled in a couple of bottles of brandy, contrary to the orders of the new commander, General Wool. Sarah missed the Tiger, mercurial as Colonel Twiggs was. Davis and his brandy had annoyed Sarah by putting her operation at risk with the military authorities. He annoyed her even more as the brandy went down, by boasting about his tactical brilliance at the Battle of Buena Vista. To hear him tell it, he and his Mississippi Rifles and their wedge formation had won the day. He would be feeling the brandy's effects this morning, but Sarah didn't care. She might need every gun hand available.

When she could hear Concepción and Zenaida's pleas for mercy in the square, she poured water into her palms and worked up a lather with the soap as she ran. She dabbed the foam around her mouth and dropped the soap and the canteen onto a window ledge as she passed it.

The market people had vanished except for the riffraff who specialized in annoying the honest folk. They watched from a safe distance as the irregulars pushed Zenaida and Concepción to their knees in front of the fire they had built in the center of the square. One of them ripped away the front of Zenaida's blouse while another pulled an iron rod from the coals. The letters "U.S." glowed on the end of it, red as the dawn sky. Zenaida screamed and struggled.

Fury formed heavy as an ax head in Sarah's stomach when she saw the brand. She threw back her head and let out the Texans' high, eerie cry. The ululation buzzed like bees in the bones of her face. It made her unstoppable, all claws and menace and brimstone. The call echoed among the shuttered buildings on the side streets. Startled doves and swallows rose from their roosts among the eaves in a drumroll of wings. For several blocks outward from the square, dogs howled in chorus with her and parrots set up a ruckus in the mahogany trees.

The men stood silent, though, a crowd of open mouths, bushy

black mustaches, and battered brown faces. They were the same faces Sarah had seen skulking about town for months. They were the rogues who had terrorized the populace and attacked roistering American volunteers as they left the *cantinas* and the *fandangos*.

Still screaming like a banshee, she jogged straight toward them through the heaps of beans and corn and tomatoes. The soap lather dripped from her chin. The pace caused her breasts to test the structural integrity of the flimsy cotton shift. Her long legs easily cleared the tethered chickens and trussed pigs laid out in the dust. She kicked pumpkins out of her way and they tumbled outward, as though desperate to escape her wrath.

She thought one of the scoundrels would surely gather his wits soon enough to kill her, but she didn't know of a better or more soul-satisfying plan on such short notice. Every man of them certainly had the wherewithal to stop her, what with the knives in their boots and machetes, pistols, and lariats at their belts. No one moved, though. They stood as though transfixed by the sight of her under the wet chemise.

"*¡La rabia!*" someone shouted.

Even the dread of rabies couldn't divert the men's attention from the satiny muscles of her thighs sliding and bunching beneath the wet shift as she ran.

She charged into them, lashing out around her with the riding crop. She would have preferred to shoot the rogue wielding the branding iron, but she'd learned to avoid the Mexican legal system whenever possible. The whistle and crack of the rawhide strips against his face and shoulders and his yelps of pain were almost satisfaction enough, though. In Mexico, as in most other places, humiliation was usually worse for a man than death anyway.

She handed the crop to Concepción who took up where she had left off, adding a freshet of observations on the men's lineage as she worked. Sarah grabbed the muzzle of the rifle a dazed irregular foolishly pointed at her and twisted it hard, wrenching his arms in their sockets. She yanked it from his grasp and swung it by the barrel, grinning when the heavy oak stock connected with the skulls under the wide-brimmed hats. The men still able to do so took to their heels, but Sarah figured they wouldn't run far. They'd circle like vultures, looking for a way to take her.

She helped Zenaida up, supporting her as she sagged, quaking and sobbing. She and Concepción each took an arm and hustled Zenaida past the blank adobe façades and locked doors and shutters. The local folk had left the streets deserted and even the dogs skulked away as they approached. Sarah wondered if men with muskets were sighting down on them from the flat rooftops.

She was relieved to see Moses and her boarders rounding a corner. The officers were still tucking in their shirts and priming their pistols. Moses held his carbine loosely, and it swung forward and back as he trotted along. He took Zenaida from Sarah and supported her with one arm.

He murmured to Sarah so the officers wouldn't hear him being familiar with her. "Miz Sarah, you look ready to take scalps and beat their owners about the ears with 'em." He chuckled. "And leave 'em grinning for all of it."

"Things are about as sour as three-day milk here, Moses," she said. "So be on the trigger."

"They only get worse with each American victory." Colonel Davis's stubbly cheek still bore the imprint of the blanket's coarse weave. His eyes were limned in red. "The Mexicans are shabby losers, and that's a fact."

"Well, they shan't harm my people." Sarah almost smiled to see Concepción sprint for the hotel door.

Concepción had spunk to spare, but Sarah didn't blame her for fleeing to the refuge of the American House. She herself wanted to bar the door behind her, but she didn't. No one would make a prisoner of her in her own establishment.

She expected the folk of her household to be in an uproar, and they didn't disappoint her. The Mexican women huddled at the far end of the big ornate bar. Hanibal, Lewis Allen, and Nancy stood behind the bar, between the women and the door. They had laid out on the polished mahogany counter every knife and gun, club, powder horn, and bullet pouch they could find.

"Looks like you're ready to fight the Battle of Buena Vista all over again."

Nancy let out a gust of Spanish oaths and curses that she had probably learned from Concepción.

"With reinforcements on the way to the square," Lewis Allen nodded at Davis and the others, "I thought I might be of more use here."

"The show is over," Sarah said. "Get to work, all of you. These gentlemen are hungry. And there're linens to change and wash, boots to polish, wood and water to haul."

Sarah began setting upright the tables, chairs, and stools they had overturned to form a makeshift barricade in front of the bar.

Jeff Davis helped her, maybe to make amends for his behavior the night before. Sarah could think of no other reason for his sudden willingness to engage in physical labor. Like most of the Southerners Sarah had met, Davis held that a gentleman never did anything a slave could do.

"I would rather fight a thousand lancers dripping crimson, brass, and tinsel folderol," he said, "than a dozen rascals dressed like ragpickers and indistinguishable from the populace."

Sarah thought of Concepción, Zenaida, Maria, Juan, and the others who had thrown in with the Americans. "Imagine what it must be like, Colonel, to have your own people warring against you."

"Mexico's incessant uprisings against her own government bespeak a weak and morally destitute people."

"Is Colonel Davis here?" A private, a leather courier's pouch at his side and his face pale with a coating of snuff-colored dust, stood in the doorway. He held out a piece of paper.

Jeff Davis took it from him and unfolded it. When he finished reading it, he whooped. "It's from Perfect Bliss, so I must translate his elocutionary acrobatics. In essence he says that Scott took Churubusco and is marching on the capital."

"That is good news." Sarah signaled for Maria to take the messenger to the kitchen by way of the wash basin, then feed him.

"There's more," Davis went on. "They finally ran those Irish curs to ground there."

"The San Patricios?"

"Aye. They have stood trial and are sentenced to be hung."

The other officers let out three huzzahs.

"How many?" Sarah asked.

"Nigh unto three hundred. Bliss says they fought like badgers, but will finally receive the judgment due them."

Sarah left Davis and the others gloating while they waited for their corn bread and eggs. She crossed the yard to the kitchen. The private stood by the fire, shoveling beans off a wooden plate with a tortilla.

"Is the grub to your liking, Coburn?"

Coburn smiled up at her and nodded, his mouth full.

"Do you by chance know if an Irishman named Murphy was captured?"

The soldier swallowed. "Mebbe."

"James Murphy, the one with the black gelding smarter than any two colonels."

"Oh yes, Duke. I remember him." The messenger went back to shoveling beans. "Murphy'll swing with the rest of 'em," he said with his mouth full. "Don't know what happened to Duke."

"When's the execution?"

"When the capital falls, which c'd be any day now."

Sarah closed her eyes in a brief prayer for James's soul. She was about to give Maria her day's instructions when Coburn spoke again.

"Colonel Harney is in charge of the execution, ma'm."

Sarah paled. "William Selby Harney?"

"Yes, ma'm."

"Lord help them," she murmured.

"The colonel's a right hard hater, and that's a fact."

A right hard hater didn't cover Harney by half. Sarah knew him from the Florida campaign. The knowledge was common there that he raped Seminole women, then hanged them from the moss-covered limb of a live oak in the morning. He had beaten a slave woman to death in St. Louis, then fled to escape being hanged by outraged citizens. Sarah knew he had also embezzled funds from his own mess. Worse, he was incompetent and mendacious.

He would have something special planned for the San Patricios' execution. Sarah was sure of that. She was glad she wouldn't be there to see it.

An Ear for an Ear

SARAH HIRED LOCAL MEN SHE KNEW AND TRUSTED TO strip the American House and load the wagons. They were an honest bunch, and good-humored, but they took careful note of every warming pan and pickle crock, the nutmeg grater, sadirons, and coffee grinder. They made sly jokes about the size of Sarah's bedstead and the passion it could contain as they heaved the mighty piece onto the wagon bed. Now, in the flickering candlelight, Sarah's room looked incomplete and forlorn without it standing solid and imposing as an outcrop of granite in the corner.

Sarah blew out the candle and set its holder on her upended traveling trunk, the only furniture left. She sat on the big feather mattress laid on the bare slate floor, and took off her shoes. She put her yellow artillery cap next to the candle, but she was too tired to wrestle with her red silk dress, the various petticoats, the bustle, chemise, and corset. She stretched out on top of the covers and lay on her back, staring into the darkness while plans and details tumbled over each other in her head.

In her years with the army she had packed more times than she could count. Each move was more arduous and complicated than the last as she accumulated goods and chattel and added members to her household. This one was the worst. As the war ground on, the number of women who depended on her grew, not to mention their children and parents, their siblings and orphaned nieces and nephews. She couldn't take them all with her to Monterrey, but whom could she leave behind to the vengeful mobs roaming the town? She thought she could hear their pleas in the sigh of the wind among the mahogany trees outside. "*Socoro, Señora, por Dios, socoro.* Help, *Señora,* for God's sake, help."

The local watchman cried midnight through the streets, his high voice hollow in the tunnel formed by the adobe walls of the houses. Sarah lay awake a long time after that, thinking and planning the move. She was finally sliding gratefully headfirst into sleep's lazy eddy when she heard a tap at the shutter. She jerked awake, her heart racing, ears straining in the darkness. Another tap echoed faintly in the empty room.

Sarah took her pistol from beside the mattress and held it in one hand as she silently unbarred the door. She pushed it ajar and peered out into the moonlit courtyard.

"Way-stern." The call was soft, the voice familiar.

Sarah shaded her eyes against the full moon's glare and searched the murky shadows under the eaves. "Cruz?"

"*Sí.*" A small shade detached itself from the darkness near the window.

"Oh, glory! Thanks be to God!" Sarah hurried to meet Cruz. She stooped and put her arms around her and wept silently into the musty folds of the thin *serape* covering Cruz's head and shoulders. So many had died, and now the dearest of the dead had returned. Sarah was too happy to notice Cruz flinch when her hand brushed the side of her head.

"Do not hurt the baby, Way-stern." Cruz could hardly draw breath in Sarah's embrace, much less speak.

"The baby's alive too?" Sarah took the bundle of filthy rags from Cruz. She held the child up so the moonlight shone on her face. "Boy or girl?"

"Girl. Her name is Paz."

"Well, she's a dazzler, she is. She must be almost a year old."

"Ten months."

Sarah held the child in one arm and put the other around Cruz's shoulders. She felt so frail and thin, Sarah was afraid of breaking her. Cruz shivered in the chilly wind and the baby whimpered. So many questions jostled for answers that Sarah could only think to ask an inane one. "How did you know this was my window?"

"Your *pantalones rojos*." Cruz nodded to the long red drawers hanging to dry on a peg next to the shutters.

"Washed them for the winter." Sarah draped them around Cruz's shoulders to warm her.

Cruz turned and beckoned and an old woman hobbled out into the moonlight. A tattered shawl shrouded her and her upper body bent at the waist as though trying to make headway into a gale. "She does not speak or hear." Cruz made signs to her with her hands and the old woman nodded.

"Marta was afraid you would be angry with her," Cruz said. "She says everyone is afraid of you, because you are so strong and wild and you shoot people."

"I haven't shot anyone lately." Sarah held the door while Marta crept in at her own pace. "Why would I be angry with her?"

"She's Águila's great-aunt, but she says he's a devil and cursed by God."

"We're of a mind then."

"She brought me food and took care of the baby. Águila wouldn't let me keep my daughter with me."

"So that's why you didn't escape."

"He also kept me chained."

"For an entire year?"

"*Sí.*" Cruz lifted the frayed hem of her skirt and held her ankle out in the moonlight.

Sarah felt the hard, satiny scars left by the iron manacle. It had worn the flesh from the bones, and Sarah could easily enclose the ankle with her fingers. "I reckon he's someone I shall shoot soon as I get him in my sights."

Sarah left them in her room and took the candle to the kitchen to light it with an ember. When she returned she found the three of them asleep, huddled together on one half of the big mattress. She laid a blanket over them and blew out the candle. She lay gingerly down next to them and put a protective arm across them. Tears slanted across her cheeks and soaked into the down-filled feed sack that served as a pillow.

Cruz had come home.

→←

With a great shrieking of axles the three teamsters were jockeying Sarah's two big oxcarts into position and shouting imprecations at the carmen who were finishing up the loading. Maria, her hair loose from its braid and flying about her round face, hustled breakfast to the remnants of Sarah's dispossessed boarders. The forlorn-looking officers sat at a wide board laid across two kegs in the echoing emptiness of what Sarah referred to as the *Sala*, the Hall.

The old woman, Marta, was crouching in the corner and Cruz had just finished nursing the baby when Sarah returned with a basket of warm tortillas, a pot of beans and chiles, and her entire staff trailing behind her. Nancy and her sisters dodged around her and threw themselves at Cruz. Exclaiming about the child's blinding beauty and charm, they passed her from one to the other.

Sarah knelt on the mattress and reached out to push away the filthy shawl that still shrouded Cruz's head. "We can throw this rag away, Cruz. I brought you a new one." But when she tugged at it, it stuck. Cruz cried out and put her hands up to hold it in place. "What is it?" Sarah moved Cruz's hands and gently peeled away the rough cloth. "Oh Lord, child."

Cruz's head had been crudely shaved, leaving cuts and patches of dark stubble on her skull. Worse than that, blood crusted where her ears had been.

"Did Águila do this?" Sarah's hands shook with rage.

"No. When Águila went off with the Americans, he sold me to other men, men as evil as he. They got drunk and said they would take vengeance on all the *yanqui* whores, and they would start with me. When their bottles of *pulque* were empty, they went off to steal good whiskey. They said they were going to steal it from you, so I knew you were in Saltillo. Marta helped my daughter and me escape and find you."

Nancy returned with warm water and soft cloths and began cleaning the wounds. "They look to be putrefying, Western."

Sarah turned to Concepción and said, in Spanish, "The doctor hasn't come down from the priest's room yet. Go up and tell him he must vacate now, and ask him for the use of his salve and maggots."

Concepción looked dubious, but she went. The women called the

room at the back of the house the priest's room because they insisted that the noisy ghost of a priest still inhabited it. Also, the doctor's habit of keeping tobacco tins full of rotting meat and dung
around for the breeding of his blowfly larvae made the air there less
than palatable.

"A group of men attacked Zenaida and Concepción yesterday,"
Sarah said. "The leader of the pack was a malodorous slab of a devil
with two front teeth missing and his pinky bobbed." She held up her
hand with the little finger folded down.

"They call him *El Mofeta,* the Skunk," Cruz said.

"He's the one who did this?"

"*Sí.*"

"We'll find him." Sarah waved her hand at the women crowding
the narrow doorway and spilling out into the courtyard. "What are
you all gaping at? Get your possibles into the wagons if you're going
with us."

With curious glances over their shoulders, they drifted to the servants' quarters to collect the last of their belongings.

"James was captured at Churubusco," Sarah said.

"Santa Anna captured him?"

"No, the Americans."

"The Americans?"

"He joined the Mexican army."

"He wouldn't. He was no traitor."

Sarah shrugged. "He had his reasons."

"Águila told me he'd been killed, running away from battle."

"No, James fought gallantly, and that's a fact. He just fought for
the wrong side." Sarah took the baby in her arms and rocked her.
She saw James in the child's mouth and dark blue eyes. "Americans
don't take kindly to deserters, Cruz. General Scott intends to hang
the lot of them for treason."

"God save him!" Cruz crossed herself and tears welled up in her eyes.

Maria returned, panting, with the tin box. Sarah gave the baby to
Nancy. Then she pried off the perforated lid and picked out the
wriggling inhabitants, one by one. She deposited them gently in the
bloody holes where Cruz's ears had been so they could eat the putrefaction and clean the wounds. She smeared salve on the smaller cuts.

"We're headed for Monterrey today. General Taylor is in camp there with a small number of men. The folks in Washington City must've figured if he won any more battles, he'd get elected president when this is over, so they decided to rein him in." Sarah wound a clean cotton bandage around Cruz's head and tied it in place. "The troops have been leaving Saltillo to join General Scott in the south and it's too dangerous here for my girls. I figure we'll do better with Old Rough and Ready. He's more soldier than the rest of them put together anyway."

"There are many bandits on the road, Western. Evil men, and desperate ones. May God grant you a safe journey."

"You're going with us." Sarah held up a hand to stop Cruz's objection. "There's nothing you can do for James. It's a hard thing to say, but he may be dead already."

"I would be indebted for the loan of a mule or horse, maybe a broken-down one you can't use."

"Mexico City is two weeks' hard ride from here. And through hostile territory."

"I'm going there."

"What of the child?"

"Moor-fee will see her, if I'm not too late."

Sarah sighed. If you want to make God laugh, she thought, just tell him your plans.

"We can catch up with the Texans," she said. "They just left, and they travel faster'n anybody."

"*¡Los tejanos!*" Cruz shuddered and hesitated. Then, "Okay."

"Nancy, can you and Moses and Juan and Hanibal get this crowd on the road?"

"Surely, Western. Everything's stowed."

Outside, the din of packing rose to a crescendo of shouts and threats and oaths, barking, braying, cackling, squealing, and squawking. But the thumps and crashes were what caught Sarah's attention.

She rolled her eyes as though appealing to heaven. "Ben Franklin was a hundred percent correct when he said a few moves are equal to a fire."

Maria appeared with baskets of food as though she'd known from the start that Sarah and Cruz would head south. Before she led Águila's old aunt off to load her onto the last wagon, she whispered to Sarah. Sarah nodded.

"Hanibal," she roared through the window toward the stable, "saddle Jake and the mare."

Sarah rifled her traveling trunk for a spare shirtwaist and stockings, knife, flint, flea powder, cornmeal, and beef jerky, all of which she stuffed into her saddlebags. She cradled the bottom of her bustle, feeling the weight of the coins she had sewn inside it for emergencies. Nancy's sisters found a big basket with a handle and lid that had held magnums of champagne. They lined it with a soft wool shawl. Cruz laid the sleeping baby in it, closed the lid, and carried it outside. Two sturdy men hauled Sarah's trunk to the wagon and stowed it with the rest of her household goods.

Hanibal led Jake and the mare into the courtyard. Sarah threw her saddlebags across Jake's back and tied a pair of rolled blankets and hammocks across it. Nancy helped Cruz tie the baby's hamper on one side in front of the mare's saddle and balanced it with the basket of food on the other. Cruz hoisted her skirts and swung up into the saddle. She followed Sarah, who rode Jake.

They passed by the caravan, almost formed now, though its component parts kept climbing down to run off to chase a chicken or look for some forgotten item. The women had arranged themselves on top of the big bedstead. They reached through the tall palings that made the big two-wheeled carts resemble birdcages and clutched the hands of friends and relatives who walked alongside. Moses maneuvered the drivers and their mules and oxen into line and made sure the buckets dangling from the axles were filled with grease. Nancy strode among the wagons, her white-blond hair barely topping the big wheels, and harangued the women in Spanish.

Sarah wrapped herself in a cotton blanket, slumped in the saddle to disguise her height, and pulled her wide hat low. Then she and Cruz set out for the Monterrey road. As they neared the straggle of disintegrating mud and stick huts that marked the rooster-infested outskirts of Saltillo, Sarah turned to Cruz. "Maria told me where to find the men who hurt you." Sarah pulled her hat further down. "I reckon you would like to settle this score."

Cruz nodded.

"The local authorities would no doubt inconvenience you over the murder of even a scavenging vulture like him. But being an

American might give me some advantage. For the sake of little Paz there, might I have permission to act in your behalf?"

Cruz gave a reluctant nod, and Sarah touched two fingers to her hat brim in salute. She yanked the reins right at a small chapel and kicked Jake in the ribs. He lunged forward and careened down the narrow alley, sending dogs and chickens in all directions. She pulled him up abruptly in front of a hovel with a faded sign that optimistically read "La Gloria." The house backed up against a wall, offering no rear exit.

Sarah spun Jake around and backed him up. As usual, he seemed to know what she wanted. He rocked forward onto his front legs, letting fly with his rear ones. One blow splintered the assembly of mesquite sticks that served as a door and another tore a wider hole where the door frame had been. Then she reined Jake back around.

Ignoring the screams and curses of the occupants, Sarah stood in the stirrups and caught hold of one of the poles that formed the eaves. She pushed upward, ripping away the rotted straw rope that had lashed it in place. She heaved it sideways, letting light in through the roof and showering everyone inside with straw and dirt and insects. She rode Jake into the clatter of falling *pulque* jugs and cries of *"La Grande," "La Colorada,"* and *"La Rabiosa,"* the rabid one. Jake occupied most of the small room, and in his fidgeting knocked over the single table and four stools.

Six men and two women crowded against the back wall. *El Mofeta,* the Skunk, was wriggling out a tiny side window. Keeping her pistol trained on the others, Sarah side-walked Jake a few steps and grabbed the man by the sag in his trousers just above where the greasy leather cupped around his bony buttocks. She hauled him out of the window and flung him into his companions like a ball into a set of skittles.

"You." She leveled her pistol at a squat, long-armed individual she recognized from the square the day before. "Cut off his ears." She gestured at the Skunk. "The rest of you hold him."

No one moved to hold the Skunk or to cut off his ears. Sarah leveled her pistol at the squat one and fired, the report deafening in the tiny room. He clapped his hand to his newly notched ear. Blood seeped through his fingers, ran down his neck, and soaked into his dingy cotton shirt.

"Lively now," Sarah said. *"Apúrense."*

The others rushed to hold the struggling Skunk while his bleeding henchman hacked off his ears with a machete. Sarah leaned down from Jake and received them into her kerchief. She backed Jake outside and handed Cruz the folded cloth. They rode away at a brisk clip toward the city of Mexico.

Sarah sang one of James's old rhymes, full volume, as she went.

> *Me father was hung for sheep-stealing,*
> *Me mother was burnt for a witch,*
> *Me sister's a bawdy-house keeper,*
> *And I'm a son of a bitch.*

There Goes a Brave, Jolly Lad

ARAH AND CRUZ RODE SEVERAL WAGON-LENGTHS BE-
hind the company of Texans. Their smell was one reason. The
other was that the men were given to shooting at the wildlife,
whooping without warning, and alarming the baby. One of their
party, a hirsute individual named Bill, rode with Sarah and Cruz,
though. He looked like a grizzly on horseback. He was huge, with
at least two feet of felted hair and beard sticking out from under his
big hat. Paz sat in the saddle in front of him, and he held one furry
arm around her. He had been entertaining her with stories of en-
counters with the Comanches, told partly in English, partly in Spanish, partly in sign language, and partly in Comanche. He added
buffalo roars, wolf howls, panther screams, hawk keening, and simu-
lated gunfire for effect. The child was enchanted.

Some of the Texans approximated respectability in red flannel
shirts and cotton duck trousers. But many of them wore leather
chaps and buckskin coats japanned with grease and the blood of
battles fought and game killed over the past decade or so. The long
fringe on them swayed with the motion of their mounts. They had
stuck feathers into the bands of their slouch hats. They had decked
themselves with Indian beads, hairpipe necklaces, bear-claw necklaces, and hawk bells.

All of them had tucked the bottoms of their trousers into their
high boots. Dirks and hunting knives stuck up from their boot tops.

Bowie knives rode sheathed on their belts. They carried rifles and Colt revolvers stuck into their coat pockets, belts, and saddle holsters or tied to the pommels of their saddles. They were official U.S. volunteer troops, but they wore no insignia of rank and they carried no baggage, not even a spare shirt, and certainly nothing so extravagant as clean socks. They had not, in fact, taken off their boots or spurs since leaving Saltillo ten days before. That was probably a blessing.

They gave Sarah the unshakable feeling she had thrown in with a band of landlocked pirates.

She saw the bell tower and the low, whitewashed houses ahead and rolled her eyes at Cruz. As was their custom, the boys spurred their mounts, screamed their Comanche war cry, and entered the village at a gallop. Some of them stood on the backs of their horses. Others threw one leg over their saddle to ride backward. The rest chased the chickens. They hung off their horses with one foot in the stirrup and the toes of the other hooked on the pommel, grabbed the poultry by the necks, and whirled them around their heads.

Usually when they reached the plaza they circled it at full tilt doing their acrobatics while their captain demanded to see the mayor and requisitioned supplies for the next leg of the trip. Now they were almost to Mexico City, so they roared on through. On the other side of town they slid to a stop in a storm of dust and gravel. They turned and waited for their captain, the one holding Paz.

"We part company here, ma'm." He handed the baby to Cruz.

He paused and the Texans moved closer, their big horses fidgeting and snorting from their run. The men's oddly attentive looks made Sarah uneasy. Being the focus of the Texans' attention was not generally a desirable situation.

Bill fished through his mostly empty saddlebag and brought out a flat, rectangular box. He cleared his throat and Sarah was astonished to see tears overflow his lower eyelids and flee for cover into the thicket of his beard. "The boys want you to have these." He thrust the box at her. "Fer what you did at Buena Vista, saving the wounded and nursing them and all. They're Sam's."

Sarah opened the lid. Inside lay two revolvers nested barrel to butt.

She understood then the captain's tears. Sam Walker, the man responsible for the army ordering these guns, had died in a skirmish in an out-of-the-way village called Huamantla. His men had wept then and she wasn't surprised that they were weeping now. Engraved on the cylinder was the figure of a horseman, Walker without a doubt, galloping full-tilt, pistol leveled at a Comanche war party.

"Lordy, they're beauties, and rare as hen's teeth."

"Yep."

"These put Mister Colt back in business, I hear."

"Yep." So much chatter obviously made the captain uncomfortable, and the prospect of her saying "thanks" ruffled him thoroughly. He headed her off by pointing to the dirt road that meandered away through the cornfields. "I believe you'll find the Irish in Mixcoac."

"We're beholden to you, Bill."

He touched the brim of his hat with two fingers. Sarah put the pistols in her saddlebag. She and Cruz set out, riding into the growing darkness. Side by side, Jake and the sorrel mare picked their way at a fast walk down the middle of the road. Their hooves rang like metal on the rocks.

Cruz handed Paz to Sarah then dozed, slumped in the saddle. In the distance, a few lights glowed, offering the possibility of food and a roof where they could hang their hammocks. Sarah was staring so hard at the lights she didn't notice the figure standing by the side of the road until the mare did her skittish two-step and jerked Cruz awake.

The Indian backed away, poised to flee into the cover of the underbrush and night. He looked no bigger than a child. His head was thrust forward, his back bowed under the wood he carried there. He must have stayed late on the mountain cutting a few more sticks to add to the top of the towering bundle.

"*Buenas noches, Señor,*" Cruz called out.

"*Buenas noches.*" The man took off his hat, crushed it into the bony concavity of his chest, and bowed his head.

Cruz spoke to him in a language that wasn't Spanish, and he responded in a low voice. She turned to Sarah.

"He says everyone knows about the San Patricios. He says they're great heroes. Everyone thinks so."

"Everyone except the Yanks."

"He says Mixcoac is just ahead."

Cruz called down on the man's head God's blessing and that of the Virgin and all the saints. Then they rode on toward the pale dots that blinked out as the hour grew later. Only one still burned when, dusty, thirsty, hungry, and weary, they clomped down the village's single street. The hoofbeats echoed against the shuttered windows and crumbling adobe walls. A regiment of dogs started barking and the baby whimpered in her sleep. Laughter and a golden wedge of light spilled from a half-opened door, and Sarah and Cruz stopped there. Sarah handed the baby to Cruz, dismounted and stretched, aching everywhere.

She pushed the door open and blinked in the feeble glare of a few smelly lanterns with wicks so short they seemed to burn by sheer will. Sarah had seen scores of *pulquerias* like this one—soot-shellacked adobe walls decorated with gaudy crucifixes and portraits of the saints, hard-packed dirt floor, and a few small tables hardly sturdy enough to support the elbows of the men who sat around them on wobbly stools. This one had an unusual feature, though. A snarl of coppery red hair bobbed among the dark heads at the far table.

"Seamus! Seamus Hooligan."

Seamus's Mexican companions collected half a dozen empty bottles from the tabletop and moved away, watching Sarah from the corners of their eyes all the while. Sarah pulled up a keg and sat across from him. When she leaned over the table, it disappeared under her breasts.

"So tell me, man, where are the others?"

"Others?" Seamus had trouble enough focusing on her face, much less on what she was saying.

"The Irish deserters. Scott gave you a reprieve, did he?"

"Wistern?" His brogue always thickened when he was drunk.

"You Irish booby." She dealt him a glancing clout across the ear with the flat of her hand. "Did you think I was Queen Victoria?"

He hardly seemed to notice. He stared fixedly at her breasts, reached out, and laid a hand on one. "Would ye care fer a tumble, lass?"

"You always did have peat for brains." She whacked him across

the other ear, hard enough to cross his eyes and lay his head perpendicular to his thick neck.

The blow seemed to help him relocate his wits. He shook his
head to clear the ringing from his skull. "No reprieve, Wistern. Harney intinds to hang thim in the marnin'. The gallows've been a-
buildin' all day."

"Then what are you doing here?"

"They lost me induction papers." When Seamus laughed he
sounded like a cat being throttled. "They cannot convict me of de-
sarting an army I nivver joined, now, can they?" He pondered for a
moment, dredging up a pertinent bit of flotsam from the murky
sludge of his thoughts. "They'll not be hangin' Riley nayther."

"He's the worst of them. Of course they'll hang him."

"Nay. He desarted before war was declared and the courts-martial
aquitted him."

"I never . . ."

"He wishes he were dead, though. This marnin' Colonel Twiggs
found the biggest, meanest muleteer in Mexico to be givin' Riley his
fifty lashes. His back looks like a possum that a regiment of dragoons and the supply train trampled. And they branded him twice
wi' the desarter's mark. The first D was burned upside down." Seamus leered cheerfully. "A mistake, I'm sure. So they had to ask him
to turn the other cheek. Smelled like a first-rate barbecue, he did."

"Take me to where the prisoners are being held."

Seamus looked as though he'd rather refuse. Obviously the Mexicans had been buying *pulque* for this particular Irish hero. But even
drunk he knew better than to try to thwart Sarah. He stood with a
gusty sigh of grief for spirits yet untasted, jammed his hat down until his big ears bent out under the brim, tugged his shabby linen
weskit over his burl of a stomach, and trudged outside.

➔ ←

Four or five lanterns hung on the scabrous walls of the guardroom.
Their light twined languidly with the cigar smoke and illuminated
an oddly decorous game of euchre in progress around a blanket on
the slate floor. From the cell along the hall beyond the door came a
doleful Irish lament.

Get six jolly fellows to carry me,
And let them be good and drunk,
When they carry me along in my coffin
Then they will let me fall with a bump.

Let them all start cursing and swearing,
Like men that are going to go mad,
Just tip a glass over my coffin
Saying, "There goes a brave, jolly lad."

"You've had her long enough, Davis." The guard glared across the cards at a moonfaced hulk with a gold ring in his ear. The shaggy brown hair draped over his unbuttoned collar gave him the appearance of a bison. Both men and the three others sitting crosslegged around the blanket wore the unkempt beards and navy blue tunics of Colonel William Selby Harney's dragoons.

"She's sleeping." Davis glanced down at Paz, her dark head visible above the brawny cradle of his left arm, her heels resting in the palm of his hand.

"It's my turn." The first guard looked to Sarah as arbiter.

"Give her over, Davis," Sarah said. "You're dealing anyway."

As Sarah watched the transfer she considered again attempting to help James Murphy escape. Again she rejected the idea. To do that would separate her forever from the army and her livelihood. It would exile her from the life and the men she loved. Besides, James had committed treason. He had killed his comrades in arms. She would not aid a traitor, not even this one. Not even for Cruz's sake. And Cruz had not asked it of her.

The guards were so distracted by Paz, Sarah was inexorably emptying their pockets of their pay. She glanced toward the long, dark hall. At the end of it a sentry nodded at the door to a small, windowless room where the guards usually slept when off duty. Sarah had paid them to let James and Cruz use it, instead of saying goodbye in the cell James shared with twenty-eight other men. Sarah had brought the child from that room only an hour ago so they could have time alone together.

Sarah picked up the five cards Davis threw onto the blanket in front of her and studied them. Paz woke up and started to cry. Sarah glanced over the top of her cards at the men, all five of them now, who were cooing at the child, singing to her, and chucking her under the chin to cheer her. Sarah had already won back the bribe she paid for the use of the guardroom for Cruz and James. Now her nostrils twitched in anticipation of garnishing their next month's salaries as well, but her wide mouth and green eyes gave no hint of how much she relished the prospect.

➤ ←

Cruz and James lay entwined on top of an old saddle blanket thrown over a straw-stuffed pallet the guards used for naps. The room was dark as tar, and silent. When Cruz rose on her elbows to search for James's mouth with her own, her bare shoulders lifted the rough blanket that covered them and released the scent of love. Then she lay across him, her head cradled in the hollow of his neck and shoulder. He wrapped his arms around her and she felt herself sink into him until she could not have told in the darkness where her skin ended and his began. She felt as though her blood coursed through him and his pulsed in her.

James put his lips to her ear and said softly, "I have already lived in hell, thinking ne'er to see you again on this earth, lass. I thank God for the chance to kiss you and bid you farewell."

Cruz wanted to say that she would rather curse God than thank Him. She wanted to point out that neither of them was faring well, but she could not shatter with harsh words the fragile tenderness that was their only comfort. "I wish He would make the night last a hundred years."

"Our span is but a blink of an eye," he said. "We shall not be separated long."

"The time without you will last an eternity." Tears scalded her cheeks and dropped like live embers on his chest. "I cannot bear it."

"I shall wait for you on the other side. We'll be together again. I promise."

He held her more tightly, trying to contain her grief, or at least absorb it into his own. He stroked her hair, damp with his tears, and ran his hand up and down her back to soothe her.

The door opened a crack and lantern light seeped around the

edge of it. "Cruz." Sarah held Paz on her wide hip, and carried the lantern in her free hand. "It's time."

"No!" Cruz wrapped her arms tightly around James's neck.

"The sun will rise soon. The guards only let me fetch you because I pulled trump on the last hand." Sarah had left them nothing more to wager. Davis's gold earring lay in her pocket.

James sat up with Cruz's arms still around his neck, and he reached for her clothes. He brushed her lips with his own, lightly and lingeringly, then he unwound her arms and pressed her skirt and blouse and shawl into her hands. While James pulled on his Mexican uniform, Cruz dressed as though in a trance, her fingers trembling, her eyes stunned.

Sarah handed Paz to James. He kissed the top of her head and her tiny hands. He held her to him until Sarah gently took her. She gave her to Cruz so she would have a life to think about as well as a death. Cruz still had the glazed stare of someone in shock and Sarah had to guide her toward the door and the long dark hall beyond.

Outside Sarah untied Jake's reins. She knew about grief. She knew what few people did, that neutral talk could be kinder than overt sympathy. "We'd best get started if we're to make Tula by nightfall."

"I will stay here."

"No."

"Sí."

"Did you ever see a man die by hanging?"

Cruz shook her head.

"To see a stranger go that-a-way is bad enough. To watch your beloved, well, it'll haunt you all your days. He'd not want you there." Sarah had to shout the last at Cruz's back. She sighed at the persistent tragedy that dogged humanity and strode after her. "Cruz." Sarah took her arm. "This is no place for your little one. Come away."

But Cruz shook off her hand and joined the crowd of Mexicans climbing the high rocky rise on top of which the gallows stood, black and skeletal against deep-pink clouds scattered like rose petals along the horizon of the dawn sky.

Death's bones. The gallows always reminded Sarah of that. She heard the roll of drums like the growl of a hungry predator. The hair stirred on her arms. Her stomach shifted anxiously.

Lord, she thought. Let it be quick.

But knowing William Selby Harney, she had a feeling it wouldn't be. She led Jake back to the building where the prisoners were being rousted and formed up. She knew just which guard to ask a favor of. Private Davis could be talked into anything.

→ ←

The prisoners filed down the hall where the morning light was creeping in under the outside door. James stopped at the other cell and grabbed the bars.

"John Riley."

Riley stood slowly and shuffled over, unable to straighten up for the lashes that had flayed the skin from his back. He wore the iron collar with the six-inch spikes that would adorn him for the next six months. His head had been shaved. The two "D's" on his cheek were red and raw and charred black around the edges. He moved his mouth as little as possible when he spoke.

"Aye, Jamie lad."

"Why did you tell me she was dead?"

"We couldn't have you breaking ranks to traipse about the countryside looking for her, now, could we?"

"You unconscionable dog." James tried to wrench the bars free to get at him and the guards grabbed him. "You son of a bitch," he shouted as they chicken-winged him away. "May you rot in hell for a thousand years, John Riley. And may rats gnaw at your heart."

Colonel Darlin'

T HE GALLOWS THAT LOOKED SO SPINDLY FROM A DIS-
tance expanded and solidified as Sarah approached it. The
soldiers had built it of oak. It stood eighty feet long and fifteen feet
high, a long beam supported by four uprights. Cruz bought tortillas,
rice, and beans from a toothless old woman, one of dozens of vendors selling their wares to the onlookers who had gathered since the
soldiers started building the gallows. She gave two to Sarah, who
took them with her and walked up the hill to the sturdy framework.
She stood under it, resisting the urge to bow her head under its im-
placable weight.

She narrowed her eyes against the glare of the rising sun and
looked up at the thirty nooses hanging in a soldierly rank from the
crosspiece. The chill wind teased strands of hair from the coil on
Sarah's head and set the nooses to swaying. The ropes were the
same as those she had seen in the marketplaces, pale maguey fiber,
neatly twisted, exuding an aroma of smoke and dust. These were
thicker than the usual, though, each one stout enough to dangle
P. T. Barnum's famous elephant. Harney's men had taken no chances
that the timbers would crack under the weight of thirty bodies,
or that the ropes would break.

From here, Sarah could see two miles across the valley to the
steeples and walls of the capital, the city of Mexico. On a precipi-
tous hill two hundred feet above the marsh behind the city towered

the massive fortress and military college known as Chapultepec. Its
enclosing wall encompassed an area three-quarters of a mile long
and a quarter of a mile wide.

The Mexicans' flag still floated over it, but the Americans had begun their attack. Sarah could hear the growl of artillery and the distant pop of small-arms fire like corn kernels bursting in hot coals.
Puffs of pearl gray smoke bloomed on the hillside around the
citadel. They gathered and thickened, like coupling wraiths.

A number of Irish prisoners had avoided the death sentence because, like John Riley, they had deserted before the war started.
Harney had ordered them to dig the graves of the men who would
die today. Several of them had the letter D burned into their cheeks.
Some of them wore the spiked iron collars. The sound of them
singing as they worked deepened Sarah's melancholy. She walked
back to where Cruz stood with a group of women who looked like a
flock of grieving crows in their black shawls. On the ground at her
mother's feet Paz played with a small *burro* carved of pecan wood.

"*Las lloronas.* The weepers." Cruz put a hand on each one's arm as
she introduced her to Sarah. She didn't have to tell her that each of
them loved a man about to die. Sarah stood with her arms folded
across her waist in the midst of the collective despair and desperate
hope and let it wash over her.

The throng grew as a detail from a rifle regiment and the generals
and their staffs formed up with a clear view of the proceedings.
Sarah thought Harney looked quite satisfied with himself for such a
despicable rogue. He wore his dress uniform, badly laundered and
rumpled. The black arc of his plumed hat sat over his ears like the
keel and hull of an upturned boat. His hair poked red and brittle
from under it.

The rattle of harness hardware and the creak of wooden axles announced the arrival of the prisoners. People jostled for a better view,
but Sarah could see over their heads. Each driver rode the lead mule
in his team. Two blue-eyed redheads in Mexican uniforms sat on a
board laid across the rear end of the first wagon. Fourteen more
teams followed with their cargoes, two men to a wagon. Harney
had ordered the brass buttons ripped off their uniforms, leaving
them drab and shabby-looking. The prisoners' ankles were tied and
their wrists lashed behind them, but the Irish among them joked

with the soldiers as they passed by. One leaned over the side when he reached Harney, who sat on his horse as though posing for a monumental sculpture.

Sarah recognized O'Leary. He had belonged to the Second Dragoons since they were formed to fight the Florida war. O'Leary would have something to say. He always did.

"Colonel, oh Colonel darlin', will ye grant a favor to a Florida man, one of the old Second?"

"What's that?" Harney had given his hat to his orderly, who was snapping his bandana at it to scatter the dust. The morning sun ignited the tips of the colonel's red curls.

"I know ye have a kind heart, Colonel. Please take me pipe from out me pocket and light it by your elegant hair, Colonel."

With an oath, Harney spurred his horse forward and smashed the prisoner in the mouth with the iron hilt of his sword.

O'Leary spat and two teeth rattled onto the boards of the empty wagon bed. "Bad luck to ye," he said cheerfully. "Ye've spoilt me smoking entirely. I shan't be able to hold a pipe in me mouth for the rest of me life."

"You'll not be inconvenienced for long, Mick," a soldier called back.

"And how's yer fair rib, Yank?" he called back. "Kiss her for me and tell her I enjoyed the use of her whilst you were away."

When Sarah spotted her mule toward the end of the long procession, she took Cruz by the arm and pushed to the front of the press. "I talked the guard into hitchin' up Jake," she said. "I figured James'd fancy a familiar face to keep him company, ugly as the face may be."

As the wagon drew close Cruz walked alongside amid the Americans' catcalls and the Irishmen's retorts. She held Paz up, but she wasn't tall enough, so Sarah took the child and lifted her. James leaned out as far as he could and managed to kiss Paz on the forehead. Sarah gave her back to Cruz.

"I love you more than life," James called softly to Cruz in Spanish.

While the guards were waving Cruz away from the wagon, Sarah noticed the Mexican driver beckoning with a sideways shift of his dark eyes. She ambled to where he lounged in Jake's saddle. He glanced at the off mule. Sarah ran a hand casually down the animal's neck and found the thong hidden under the harness. She slipped James's heavy silver crucifix from under the hame and lifted the thong over the animal's head and ears. Sarah smiled in thanks, and one corner of the driver's mouth hitched in acknowledgment under the cover of his drooping mustache.

With her fingertips she traced the ornate chasing, rubbed smooth and satiny by James's hands. Much luck this has brought him, she thought, though he once had told her that if it gave him nothing except Cruz, that was luck enough for any one man. She handed it to Cruz, who held it up so James could see it. She touched it to her lips, then put the thong over her head. She clutched the cross in one hand, and balanced Paz on her hip with the other arm.

The teamsters kicked their saddle mules' sides with their heels and chivvied them into position, all the while shouting their appeals for patience and succor as though the saints were profoundly hard of hearing. The Mexican driver of the fifteenth wagon backed and advanced his rig until he had aligned his single passenger's head directly under the last noose. He was so intent on the task he jumped when Harney rode up behind him and bellowed.

"I count only twenty-nine men here."

The driver stared hard at him, as though he could read the meaning of the colonel's gibberish in his bulging eyes and the flecks of froth lodged in the corners of his mouth. Harney raised his voice until his red face turned purple, his usual solution when someone didn't speak his language. "Where's the last prisoner, you ignorant heathen?"

The Mexican shrugged and looked around for help. An aide scurried alongside the colonel's big gray.

"He's in the hospital, sir. He lost both legs and won't last long."

"Bring the damned son of a bitch out. My order is to hang thirty and by God I'll do it."

Harney charged off toward the hospital tent and the onlookers clustered around the food vendors and monte dealers while they waited. Harney returned fifteen minutes later with the dying man laid out in a wagon. A hum of outrage and astonishment buzzed through the crowd as soldiers lifted him onto the board across the rear of the last wagon and propped him up with sacks of grain.

"Oh, Colonel, ye old bricktop," sang out O'Leary. "How kind ye are to let the lad dance on air, now that he has lost his legs."

The condemned men laughed.

"*Qué barbaridad,*" Cruz muttered.

One of the women spoke rapidly and the others nodded and hummed in agreement.

"What'd she say?" Sarah asked.

"She says the Irish are true patriots and should be treated as prisoners of war, not criminals."

"Not in this army. And I'll wager that reptile Harney's been awake all night cogitating on how to make this as ugly as possible." But Harney had plans that surprised even her.

He gestured for the drivers to drop the nooses over the men's heads. He walked his horse to the center of the gallows, stood in the stirrups, and shouted so the condemned men on each end could hear him. "You shall remain here until the American flag is raised over Chapultepec castle, at which time you shall be hung until dead."

"If we don't swing until yer dirty old flag flies from the castle," called out one of them, "we will live to eat the goose that fattens on the grass that grows on yer own grave."

Harney scowled, but if he intended to search out the rascal and punish him, he thought better of it. This lot would all claim to have said it and the mockery would spread.

Five priests, their vestments fluttering in the morning wind, stepped forward to perform mass and hear the condemned men's confessions. Muttering about popery, Harney dismounted, dropped into the camp chair his aide set up for him, and called to his black servant to bring him a jar of whiskey and a tin of oysters for breakfast. He settled back and trained his telescope on Chapultepec castle, solid and formidable against a deep blue sky. Blue coats swarmed through the thick stand of trees carpeting the slope to the castle.

Sarah passed her battered spyglass from hand to hand, and each woman in turn scanned the roofs and ramparts of the citadel. The artillery barrage stopped at seven-thirty and gunners lowered the muzzles to cut across the tops of the encircling wall where the defenders stood. At eight o'clock all American firing stopped, but by then the dust and the smoke from the guns swaddled the crest of the hill. The sun's light appeared like butterfly wings through rips in the undulating chrysalis of it. It gilded what little was visible of the fort, angles where two walls met and poked through the haze, swatches of tiled eaves, green spikes of cypress trees.

The crowd hushed, listening, as did Sarah, for more gunfire under the frantic ringing in their ears. The silence from the hill meant the Americans were about to attack. The women crowded around the one with the telescope, looking for massed blue coats. Sarah wondered who had volunteered for the Forlorn Hope, the squad of men who would storm that formidable rampart.

"There are children inside." Cruz lowered the glass and gave it to the woman next to her.

"Children?"

"Cadets at the military academy. Twelve years old, maybe thirteen."

"General Bravo could send them out under a white flag."

Cruz shrugged. "The boys will not surrender."

Sarah took the spyglass and gave an ongoing account that Cruz repeated in Spanish. Men charged up the hill and scaled the outer wall and dropped from sight. The women waited, silent and motionless, eyes on Sarah. Then the first troopers emerged from the cypress marsh. They scrambled up the steep muddy slope to the castle. The news of it rippled outward. When the Americans began to fall under a winnowing fire, the murmuring rose to a hushed cheer.

The Irish gave three cheers for Old Bravo, the Mexican commander. Sarah herself began to wish that the city would stand and the prisoners be spared. Soon though, a couple hundred Americans made it up the slope and huddled at the base of the wall that soared fifty feet above them. They waited there under the slanting sheet of small-arms fire from above until the scaling ladders arrived, scuttling up like so many centipedes. Sharpshooters kept the defenders' heads down and men swarmed over the walls.

By nine-thirty the Mexican flag sank slowly toward the roof. The women around Sarah groaned. The flag disappeared and that of Johnston's Voltiguers rose in its place above the east walls. The prisoners let out a cheer that rolled across the valley. Sarah heard Harney mutter that they soon would not have breath for cheering. And what they could be cheering about was more than Sarah could guess.

Harney vaulted out of his chair, sending it toppling behind him. He mounted his gray and stood in the stirrups again.

"Every man of you, get on your feet."

The prisoners struggled to obey and keep their balance with their wrists tied behind them and their ankles hobbled. Harney raised his sword, held it for a breathless moment, and let it drop. The drummer gave a sharp rap to his drum. The mounted drivers kicked their heels into the lead mules' sides. The wagons leaped forward with a rattle of loose sideboards and a shriek of sandy axles. Sarah pulled Cruz to her, pushing her face into her chest and wrapping her arms around her head so she couldn't see. Cruz struggled briefly, then went limp, her body shaking with sobs.

The women began to wail. The prisoners kicked wildly. Their bodies swung in wide arcs, hitting against each other. Then they quieted, only swaying gently. All except James. He continued to kick, his eyes bulging.

"Dear Lord in heaven. They botched it." Sarah put herself between Cruz and the gallows and pushed her toward the other women who closed in around her. Sarah could hear her wailing, though, as if in a nightmare from which there were no waking.

Before the guards could stop her, Sarah ran to James, wrapped her arms around his legs, and pulled, using her weight to strangle him. He stopped struggling, but it seemed to take an eternity. When his legs dangled at last without moving, she continued to hold on to them, as though in a farewell embrace. The women walked among the bodies to claim those they loved and take them away for burial. Cruz gave Paz to a new friend in the crowd, then she joined Sarah. The two of them stood with their arms around each other and James, his legs still warm and supple, as though he would drop to the ground, laugh, kiss them both, and make a joke.

→←

Sarah picked up the last cadet and laid his body at the end of the neat row of them, all dressed in their gray uniforms. The six boys had leaped from the wall that seemed to sweep into the clouds above Sarah, though the clouds were the remnant of artillery and small-arms smoke. The boys' high collars framed faces so young and innocent they might have been only sleeping. She wondered who would carry word of their deaths to their mothers. She wished she could comfort them.

Beyond the wall Sarah could hear screams and the clash of bayonets. The Americans were continuing the slaughter, chasing their prey through the castle's corridors. Sarah knew they were taking revenge for the battle at Molino del Rey, when the Mexicans bayoneted American wounded, but she dreaded what she would find when she went inside.

Cruz said at least fifty more boys had stayed in there. The cadet whose legs Sarah was straightening still clutched the Mexican flag to his chest. She put a hand on his small cold ones, bowed her head, and prayed for all their souls.

Washington Crossing the Great Western

>—I—‹•›—•—O—•—‹•›—I—‹

JUNE OF 1848 HAD JUST ARRIVED, BUT EVEN NOW AT close to midnight the air simmered like mid-July. Sarah stood against the adobe wall of the gaming room, enjoying the coolness of the plaster through her perspiration-soaked shirtwaist. As solid as the wall was, she could hear the uproar in the barroom beyond and she could feel vibrations from the celebration in full career there.

The Mexican senate had ratified the Treaty of Guadalupe Hidalgo two weeks earlier. Word had just arrived that the volunteers would be mustered out soon. Sarah could hear them shouting toast after toast to the end of the war and their own imminent freedom. They had another reason to celebrate. A New Jersey carpenter had discovered gold while hammering together a sluice for a miller named Sutter in California. Many of the irregulars who hadn't deserted already planned to leave for the west as soon as they received their discharge papers.

In this dim oven of a room, though, the soldiers of the regular army were more interested in the damp cards in their hands. Their enlistments didn't end with the cessation of hostilities. The treaty meant that they probably wouldn't be shot at in an official capacity, but it would change little else in their lives.

The ghostly blue layer of cigar smoke hung almost motionless here, undisturbed by the great sweaty jostle in the barroom next door. It absorbed and muted the buttery light from the overhead lanterns. Sarah stood in a fog of it so dense the clusters of officers and favored civilians hunched over faro games and hands of whist seemed to float in it like islands. They grew more indistinct with distance, until in the far corners they dissolved into wavery shadows.

Sarah strolled to the center of the room where Cruz worked her monte bank. As always, men stood three deep around the table. At Cruz's game no one sprawled with boots splayed or elbows draped over the backs of chairs that teetered precariously on the rear two legs. They didn't even chew tobacco, much less spit amber sluices of it into the earthenware pots Sarah provided, or, more likely, onto the floor around them. Cruz never scolded or lectured those whose money she so graciously won. A look was enough, an upslanting glance of sad dark eyes from behind thick, black lashes, a suggestion of mild surprise. An assurance that she understood the man hadn't meant to act that way and would desist immediately.

The way Cruz managed the cards and the men attached to them was ever a pleasure to watch, and Sarah paused a moment, sighting between the spectators. Cruz had tied back her shiny black hair with a yellow ribbon at the nape of her neck, but springy tendrils danced motionlessly alongside her face. Her expression was as serene as always, but her eyes were remote, the light in them as dimmed by grief as the lantern light was by cigar smoke.

Sarah's eyebrows bunched in worry. She figured that love had its price, and the greater the love the higher the price. Cruz was paying dearly indeed. Sarah understood the feeling and she despaired that she could do nothing to ease her friend's grief.

Cruz talked. She smiled. She even laughed on occasion. But Sarah knew she had emigrated to sorrow's far country and she wouldn't be returning anytime soon. She had left in her stead a lovely, efficient facsimile. Only Paz could lure her back for brief visits.

Sarah knew about loss. She still expected to see Jack Borginnis or Will Kelly lounging in the kitchen. At times she thought she heard Jack's laugh, loud and carefree, in the hubbub of the bar. She missed George Lincoln sitting at one of the gaming tables, his long legs jutting out. And she missed James Murphy.

She looked around at the gamblers. The sight of them always cheered her, and not just because her cut of the money they left behind had accumulated far beyond the capacity of her bustle. A well-run game of cards bestowed on its participants a certain grace and dignity as well as wile and luck. While studying his cards even a ninny could appear thoughtful and manly.

Usually the talk stayed subdued here, the laughter confined to an occasional chuckle, but tonight the players had to raise their voices to be heard over the din next door. The crystal explosion of glass there caught Sarah's attention. She hurried into the heat and noise of the barroom where Moses and his hired crew of hulking mule-teers barely kept the party from sliding pell-mell into riot.

The three black musicians, elbows pumping, were doing their best to be heard. One rasped the back of a knife blade along the jawbone of a cow. The cricket rhythm joined the fiddler's melody that rose and receded, darting like a hungry mosquito through the crowd. The only one who mattered, though, was the small, coffee-dark man pounding out the beat on a small drum. The volunteers had commandeered all the women who weren't ferrying the drinks or food. When they exhausted the supply of female partners, they paired off with each other. The thud of their boots stomping through a reel caused the ceiling lanterns to sway and bottles to rattle on the tables. By this time of night, any dance was a reel.

Men elbowed each other at the long bar and Sarah's two bar-tenders rushed from one end of it to another to keep them supplied. The jingle of coins falling into the iron box bolted under the counter was sweeter music to Sarah than any fiddle. She surveyed the trestle table that at the beginning of the evening had sagged un-der platters of fried oysters, roast beef, corn bread, and vats of beans. Now wreckage strewed it, as though an army had marched across it, looting and pillaging as it went. Wine puddled on the boards and grease stained them. Crumbs, lumps of pudding, and chicken carcasses littered the floor.

This would be a profitable night, no two ways about it. Sarah thought about the trapdoor in the floor under her bedstead and the small trunk that hunkered patiently there. It was so heavy with the gold pieces inside that a pair of strong men had to strain to lift it.

The hay-rick hair and green-clad shoulders of an Indiana Volun-teer rose above the press like a swimmer surfacing in a turbulent pool. He balanced precariously on a stool and raised his glass.

"Hurrah for the United States and for home."

The men answered with huzzahs.

"Boys," he announced, "I think I'll bag me a smoked Yankee to take home." He raised his flintlock pistol in both hands and aimed it at Moses, who was separating two gladiators in a far corner. "That'll leave one less uppity nigger in the world."

Sarah covered the ground between her and him in three strides and wrenched the gun upward. When it went off, the report could hardly be heard above the jawbone and fiddle and drum, the shouting, and the stomp of feet. The bullet buried itself in the latticework of the ceiling, dislodging a shower of dust.

Dangling the miscreant by the back of the collar, she marched him on tiptoe to the open door. Still holding him with one hand, she raised her skirts of pale green lawn daintily with the other. She set the sole of her new leather dancing pump in the hollow above his wool-clad nates and impelled him into the street. He sprawled face first in front of a pair of high black boots, polished until they reflected the moon. Looming over the boots was a dour-looking individual in a collar so tall and starched he would have drowned in his own salivary juices had he tried to expectorate over it.

"Good evening, Colonel Washington." Sarah nodded to him.

"Well past evening, I would say, Mrs. Borginnis." Washington glanced around her to the revelers cavorting beyond the open door. "Army regulations prohibit the American House from purveying spiritous drink."

"That was Saltillo, Colonel. This is Monterrey."

"The regulations apply equally to all jurisdictions."

"I'll see to it, Colonel."

"The Good Book forbids drunkenness and fornication out of the bounds of most holy matrimony, Mrs. Borginnis."

"I'll bear it in mind, sir."

She touched two fingers to the small brim of her yellow artillery cap and watched him shuffle off into the night. He was headed, no doubt, for the small house he rented for a few *pistoles*, and the sad-eyed Indian woman and infant who shared it with him. No preacher had married Washington and the woman to Sarah's knowledge, but the infant, even at three months of age, bore a striking resemblance to him.

⇥⇤

Like the men of Braxton Bragg's artillery company, the countryside itself was putting on a splendid show, as though celebrating the end of war and the departure of the army. A sapphire sky shimmered over the army's encampment in the vast grove of ancient walnut, orange, and pomegranate trees outside of Monterrey. Birds as brightly colored as jewels fluttered and preened and sang in the green canopy overhead. Clouds of yellow acacia blossoms perfumed the clear air. A cool breeze dispelled some of the July heat.

Nancy Skinner had helped Bragg's men prepare for this day. She had scrubbed and mended their uniforms. She had buffed the cannons with them until here in the shade the brass barrels glowed soft as old honey. She had watched them paint the ammunition limbers red, white, and blue. She had helped them curry their horses until their coats shone like satin. She had polished buttons and oiled the leather of the teams' harnesses.

The men had maneuvered the artillery carriages into line and now stood next to their horses, ready to mount and move out. With banners undulating and plumes stirring in the wind and uniforms newly washed and starched, they were, in Nancy's opinion, as handsome a lot as had ever assembled or ever would. She loved every one of them and she knew she would likely never see them again.

She wore an old pair of uniform trousers taken in to fit her, though the trousers were none too long for her stork's legs. She had on a red flannel shirt and the yellow cap of the Third Artillery. She stood at rigid attention just beyond the gaggle of reviewing officers. The bugle sounded "To Horse" and the men swung onto their saddles amid a jangle of hardware and a creak of leather. At the next signal the soldiers mounted on the lead draft animals spurred them forward. The mules and horses leaned into their harnesses and the heavy carriages rolled forward with a loud rumble.

Nancy bit her lower lip to keep it from trembling. Whenever the Third Artillery left camp she had ridden on the cannon of the first carriage. She was their good luck charm, they said. Now she could only watch them pass and she thought her heart would surely break.

As the column reached the reviewing officers, Bragg and his men raised the fingers of their right hands to the brims of their hats in unison. They held the salute several seconds after they passed, until they came abreast of Nancy. Bragg turned his head just enough in her direction for her to see him smile and wink.

When the company moved out into full sun, the glare off the cannons hurt Nancy's eyes and she squinted under the shade of her hand. She intended to watch them until they vanished into the shadows of the mountains, but the last carriage had barely gone by when she heard her mother's high voice calling her. Her path blurred by tears, she skirted the tumult of the infantry and the dragoons hurrying to form up. She walked among the huge wagons and draft animals of the baggage train and through the storm of the teamsters' blasphemy as they heaved grain sacks and crates into the wagon beds.

"Where you been, girl?" Bertha slapped her, her hand leaving a red blotch on Nancy's tanned cheek. "Lazin' with those men instead of helping your mother. We're almost ready to leave."

Bertha grabbed her arm and towed her, stumbling to keep up, to a small cart hitched to a *burro* whose dejected look indicated he could foresee hard times ahead. Bertha's new mate, Newt, had piled the cart precariously high with shovels and picks, coils of rope, basins, and a small mountain of rough-sawn boards scavenged from Sudsville's abandoned shacks. A wooden barrow liberated from the stables capped it all. Newt had lashed the barrow down with the local maguey rope and it looked like a manure-crusted turtle perched up there.

Newt was one of the Indiana Volunteers who had bolted at the Battle of Buena Vista. In his thirty-some years he had settled into a short-legged, long-bodied, kettle-bellied individual with hair the color and texture of old lard and a view of his adenoids through the space his front teeth should have occupied. He was using a rock to hammer a sprung spoke back into the rim, but he was doing it without unloading the cart. The cargo shivered and shifted with each blow. Nancy's sisters stood in a row, watching from a safe distance.

Nancy could foresee disaster in his method, but she wasn't surprised. Disaster followed Newt as fleas dogged a hound. She had known his like often enough, unprepared and untidy, a man whose means would never meet his ends, a man for whom misfortune always lurked in wait like a roguish cat ready to pounce and toy with him.

Nancy squatted by a heap of broken and worn belongings scattered in the dirt next to the cart. She picked up a hand spike carved with the crossed cannons, the insignia on the artillerymen's shako badges. Bragg's men had given it to her as a keepsake.

"Leave that trash be." Bertha knocked it out of her hand. "We ain't got room fer it and Newt says he'll buy us new things when we get to the goldfields."

"I notice Newt didn't leave none of his own trash behind." Nancy was relieved to see Sarah sauntering along on her magnificent new roan and leading Jake and Alice Ann. Sarah could usually remedy Bertha's everyday quandaries, though no one could successfully advise her on men, the cause of most of her calamities.

Sarah arrived in time to put a hand out and keep a stack of boards from sliding off the cart and onto Newt's head. She heaved them back into place.

"I should've let 'em fall, Newt." She winked at Nancy. "Might've knocked some sense into you."

"I got sense enough, and ambition too." Newt threw the hammer onto the load, where it smashed Bertha's only china plate. "Not like some fellas as is content to draw an enlisted man's pittance and chew on the officers' dust and stare up their horses' bungholes."

"I couldn't have stated the charms of army life more eloquently myself." Sarah handed the mare's reins to Nancy. She could see from the way the cart was overloaded that the girls would have to walk to California. In any case, it likely wouldn't reach the border before it broke down completely. "I'm giving you Alice Ann for luck, Nan. You already know her crotchets."

"Thank you, Western." Nancy's eyes lit up and her mouth curved into a grin, startlingly white in her tanned face.

She gave the reins to her younger sister, took a running start and leaped, scrambling onto the horse's back. Sarah lifted each of her sisters up, three to sit behind her and the latest baby, Margaret, in front. The younger three perched with their short, stout legs pointed almost straight out.

"I reckon you'll see the elephant out in California."

"I reckon." Nancy bit her lower lip to keep it from trembling.

Sarah wanted to cry, too. She would miss them as much as if they were her own children. She wanted to remind Nancy that the army was heading for California, too, with orders to protect the thousands of gold-hungry emigrants from Indian attacks. But the country was vast and travel uncertain and there wasn't any guarantee they'd see each other again.

She knew that tearful good-byes only made the parting harder, but the sight of them with their pitifully few belongings started an ache in her chest. They would have to cross deserts and mountains where too many mischances waited to befall them. Sarah knew the goldfields lay to the north and she had a sudden image of Newt-the-feckless delaying until winter caught them in the Sierras. She saw Nancy and her sisters frozen under blowing snow in some high pass, like that unfortunate Donner party. She shook her head to clear out the thought.

Newt didn't qualify as a bad man, except when he could afford liquor, which was blessedly infrequent. But he wasn't what Sarah would call a bright light. He always arrived a day late and a dollar short. Even now he was starting out weeks after the rest of the gold-struck volunteers had packed up and headed into the setting sun.

Sarah watched the *burro* lean into his harness. The little caravan creaked and strained and shuddered and finally lurched with a loud clatter into motion. Newt and Bertha walked alongside.

Sarah leaned down from her own horse and hugged each of the girls while Alice Ann fidgeted. Then Nancy reached out to put her arms as far around Jake's neck as she could. He turned and rubbed his cheek against her shoulder. Nancy settled herself back in the saddle. She flipped the reins and the mare started after the cart. She didn't look back, although the other girls turned and waved. Jake sent a long, mournful bray after her.

"Widow Borginnis, I've been looking for you."

That can't be to my good, Sarah thought. She recognized Colonel Washington's tone. It was the one he adopted when about to indulge in the pleasure of delivering bad news. If he had had good news he would have sent a subordinate to tell her and not dust up his boots himself.

"How can I be of service, Colonel?"

"You cannot. Not in any official capacity." His round face, pug

nose, and bushy side whiskers above his high collar always reminded Sarah of a peevish groundhog peering from a weed-grown
burrow.

"What do you mean?"

"A new order has come down." Washington took a folded paper
from the front of his jacket and waved it. "No one may travel in the
army's train unless employed by the United States goverment or
connected with it through marriage." He could barely contain his
satisfaction. "You could return to drawing rations as a laundress, I
suppose."

"That isn't my line of work these days."

"I know what your line of work is, Widow Borginnis." Washington's cheeks turned pink. "A woman has no place in business for herself. It flies in the face of nature."

You're a fly in the face of nature, she thought. What she said was,
"Old Zach wouldn't concoct an order like that."

"General Taylor has returned to the States and the frivolous acco-
lades of an adoring public. The fools are yapping about elevating
the old rube to the presidency."

"All right then, Colonel. I'll marry the whole squadron and you
thrown in, but what I go along." She reined the big roan around and
rode off into the hurry and scurry of the infantry and dragoons' departure preparations.

A Modest Proposal

THE DISTANT ROLL OF DRUMS RUMBLED UNDER THE cacophony of wailing children, barking dogs, and shouting women. Sitting sidesaddle Sarah urged her big roan into a trot through the welter of dependents swirling around the motley collection of vehicles in the civilians' wagon park. She had put on her purple velvet riding costume for her wedding, though she had no idea yet who would serve as groom.

She wouldn't have chosen this method of staying with the army, but Colonel Washington gave her no choice. The alternative, a civilian existence, was unthinkable. She wasn't the sort to fret about problems she could remedy, and once she decided on a scheme she wasted no time implementing it. An added appeal of her plan was that it would embarrass Colonel Washington as well as thwart him.

The troops wore crisp, broad-brimmed hats of black felt, bright red flannel shirts, and trousers of brown canvas so new they still smelled of the pine crates in which they'd arrived. They had whitened their belts with pipe clay and burnished their weapons. Their new silk ensigns undulated in the breeze.

Sergeants shouted orders and the long ranks of soldiers began closing into formation. The bugle would blow "To Horse" soon. Sarah kicked the roan's side and cantered to the front of the troops. She hiked up her skirts as far as the garters that held her stockings above the knees. Her legs seemed to go on forever. They were shapelier than the most creative of the men had imagined, and they all had tried to imagine them at one time or another. She rode at a walk along the front rank.

"Who wants a wife with fifteen thousand dollars and the longest legs in Mexico?" Sarah's brilliant smile included every one of them. But boasting about what one would do with a woman like Sarah was one thing. Fulfilling those fancies was quite another. "Come, my beauties, don't speak all at once. Who's the lucky man?"

The silence lengthened. If Sarah's future with the army hadn't been at stake, she would have been amused by their chagrin.

Finally someone spoke from the middle of the formation. "I have no objection to making you my wife if there is a clergyman here to tie the knot."

Sarah recognized the voice of Davis. Of course. The perpetual volunteer. He had made corporal at last through attrition and persistence.

"Bring your blankets to my tent tonight," she called to him. "And I will teach you to tie a knot that will satisfy you."

As laughter rippled through the ranks, Sarah nodded regally to Colonel Washington. The colonel's face had turned crimson as a new poppy, but since there was no regulation to cover this maneuver he could only stare at her, mouth slightly ajar. She flicked the reins and cantered past the precise lines of men while they cheered her.

When the last rank became a wall of red-clad backs, she progressed into the din of oaths and skull-rattling whip cracks as the muleteers and teamsters jostled their animals into line. The mules had their own opinions. They had been recently purchased, newly trained, and none too well at that. The cattle milled and lowed, their long horns clashing like saber blades while the drovers whistled and shouted and circled them to keep them from straying.

Behind them, any remnant of order surrendered to chaos. Hundreds of women and children were preparing to set out in everything from a leather-upholstered phaeton with a fringed canvas top to the hulking, obstreperous Mexican carts. Some families planned to walk to California pushing wooden barrows. The higher-born Mexican women reined their skittish mounts in tight circles to keep them from bolting. Colonel Washington's edict be damned, they intended to follow their *gringos*. The collective pulse of urgency and excitement thrummed in Sarah's bones.

Sarah tensed when she approached the poorest of the local women. She had heard the stories of reprisals against those who had worked for the Americans. As she expected they would, some of them clung to her skirts. Others knelt in her path, their hands clasped in supplication, their dark, desperate eyes imploring her to let them come with her. Some held up infants and called out to her, in the name of God and the Blessed Virgin, to take the children if she couldn't add their mothers to her household. At the fringes waited a silent crowd of those who knew the futility of pleading for mercy. They were Indians mostly, young and old, waiting to swarm over the abandoned campsite and scavenge every discarded item, no matter how worn out or broken. This was the part of breaking camp that Sarah always dreaded.

The splendor of her new wagon cheered her a little. She had selected the seasoned lumber herself so it wouldn't dry out, shrink up, and come apart on the trail. She had ordered hubs and axles that were large in proportion to the wheels. She had insisted on a wagon bed so tightly caulked it would float across streams. The canvas cover was the heaviest she could obtain. Best of all, Moses had painted it a brilliant lemon yellow with blue wheels. And he had added a scene around the sides, an adobe village and church, gardens and fields and a river with trees along it. She admired it as she tied the roan to the wagon gate alongside the gray she had taken from Antonio Águila's henchman so long ago.

The other two vehicles were the lumbering Chihuahua oxcarts. Their maker had fashioned the ten-inch-thick disks of the wheels from a tree trunk five feet in diameter. Mahogany saplings formed the axles and great slabs of oak their beds. Still, they looked about to founder under the load of women and children spilling through the tall slats of the sides. Cruz stood on the left rear hub of the last one. She was counting heads.

"Demasiado," she said sternly. "Too many."

A wail of pleas and recriminations rose from the wagon, but Cruz was adamant. Only Sarah knew what pain the sum of the wagon's humanity and its consequences gave her. Stoically, Cruz pointed to the stowaway friends and relatives of Sarah's staff. They clambered down, trudged a short distance, and turned to watch.

Cruz sighed and climbed up onto the driver's seat where Sarah sat with the silent child Esperanza, who held Paz. Cruz's thick, loose curls had grown long enough to cover most of the scars where her ears had been.

"Will the *coronel* allow us to go with the army?" she asked.

"Corporal Davis has been breveted to the rank of husband." Sarah winked at her. "We're on the rolls again."

Cruz shrugged. "At least he's an armful."

"He'll do." Sarah gave a sigh herself. The best she could say about Davis was that he would be tractable, but he had solved her dilemma and she would be as good as her word.

The phaeton with the fringed top pulled alongside the wagon and the captain's wife leaned from inside it. "Mrs. Murphy," she said.

"Yes, ma'm." Cruz regarded her uneasily. Officers' wives rarely went out of their way to be sociable to Sarah or Cruz.

"I want to tell you how sorry I am about the loss of your husband." She reached as far as she could across the distance between them and laid the tips of her fingers on Cruz's hand. "He is at home with God now. And you have the little one and your memories of him to comfort you."

"Thank you." Cruz's voice was hardly audible, but she touched the fingers with her own. The tenuous connection lingered for several heartbeats before the woman drew her hand away. She put the fingertips to her lips, then held them up in a sort of salute to a gallant soldier's widow before the phaeton drove off.

Cruz drew farther back under her shawl, wrapped the ends around her, and held it there with her arms tightly crossed. Sarah saw a shudder pass over her. A person could rally against malice, but there were few defenses when ambuscaded by kindness.

"She meant well." Sarah handed her a bandana.

"I know." Cruz wiped her eyes with it. "But memories are knives that stab the heart."

Sarah wanted to tell her that time would heal her heart as surely as it healed torn flesh, but the words sounded hollow to her before she even said them. Time had hardly blunted the hurt her own memories inflicted.

Sarah saw a tear leave a shiny track down Cruz's cheek. She must have a thousand memories of James, any one of which could make her weep, but she was probably remembering when James and Duke rode so proudly in the ranks of the dragoons. Cruz would cry silently for miles. She had done it before as they rode long hours on the wagon, wiping her eyes and nose with the corner of her shawl.

"The spare mules is seen to, Western." Moses stood with Concepción, who had decided to stay with him and take her chances. Moses had only recently discovered his talents as a painter, and he was in great demand for portraits and church murals. He was held in such regard as an artist that Sarah figured Concepción would be safe, even if she was a *yanqueda*, a woman who had collaborated with Americans.

"Are you certain you don't hanker to view the elephant?"

"I've seen enough elephant for one man. And taken a bite out of his ear." Moses grinned. "Look out for the Comanch. They's thicker'n head lice on a Rackensacker where y'all is headed. And the Apach too."

"Come with us. California's free territory. No one will hinder you."

Moses looked skeptical about that, but he said only, "Folks here is making a fuss over my dabblings." He glanced at the painting that decorated the wagon. "I think I'll become a gentleman artist."

"God keep you then."

"And you, Miz Sarah." He took off his hat and gave an eloquent bow. "Keep your Colts close to hand and your hair attached to your head."

"I'll do that."

Moses knew better than to bid her good-bye. People didn't say that in the army. Bad luck, maybe.

Sarah sighed. She would miss him and Juan Duran too. Juan and Hanibal had headed north for Santa Fe with a pack train of mules. In her memory Sarah could still hear their cajoling cries of *"Mula, mula, mula"* as they set out.

"Western." Lewis Leonidas Allen hurried toward her.

"Howdy, scribbler."

"I wanted to say good-bye."

"Where you off to?"

"I'm going to write my novel. You'll be hearing my name one of these days."

"I've no doubt of it."

"Well, I made your name famous enough, didn't I?"

"You told a pack of flattering lies, scribbler, but there was no help for it. You can't threaten a writer. They haven't the sense God gave a flea."

The bugles sounded "To Horse." The multitude of people and animals sprawled across the mesa shivered and agitated as though a stroke of electricity had jolted it. Even Jake jigged on his big flat hooves and leaned into his padded leather collar, ready to charge flat out to California.

The dragoons began singing the first of a few hundred verses of "Happy Jack." The dark-eyed townswomen who loved them flanked their soldiers like brilliantly uniformed outriders on their caparisoned horses. Farther out, hundreds of poorer women from the surrounding villages followed on gaunt Indian ponies and *burros* or on foot. The provost guard would have its work cut out for it to drive them all back, per Colonel Washington's orders.

Sarah cracked the big whip and the wagon started forward. She joined in the dragoons' chorus. She waved at Moses, who gave her a crisp salute in return. Then she stared ahead, so she wouldn't see the poorest of the poor swarm over the campsite, scrabbling for ruined shoes, broken pots, scraps of cloth. So she wouldn't see them collecting the fallen kernels of grain from the livestock.

➔ ←

Once the littered walnut grove that had sheltered them receded from sight, Sarah cheered up. She loved being on the move, bivouacking each night in a different place but under the same canopy of stars. She relished visiting with the women, swapping lies with the men and watching them wolf down her chicken and dumplings and pot liquor. Death and war had fallen away behind her, and the freedom of the trail lay ahead. The possibilities were endless, and the surprises would keep life interesting. Even the thought of Corporal Davis invading her tent at night like a slow-moving bison couldn't mute her joy.

The column stretched for three miles along a road that meandered through vineyards and neat fields of corn and barley and sugarcane. Groves of fig and pear trees shaded it. It passed white-walled haciendas and neat villages. Each time the Americans stopped to rest or ford a river, children gathered to sell watermelons and jugs of delicious wine pressed from the local grapes. Even Cruz brightened and joined Sarah in the choruses of some of the countless songs she knew. Behind them in the wagon Esperanza played with Paz, though they conducted their play without words.

At dusk they topped a rise and saw a village gleaming white among fruit trees in the valley below. A lovely little church with its simple bell tower sat like a jewel on the plaza. Buzzards spun lazily overhead.

Sarah began to anticipate a hot meal with her boys. Then she saw the men ahead bunching up, the delay passing down the line until Sarah and the others at the rear had to halt and wait. The troops didn't stop in the village, but the column inched forward as each company slowed to look at something. By the time Sarah neared the outskirts, night had almost fallen but enough light remained to see what it was.

At first Sarah thought the men were staring at a pile of trash. Then she saw the captain's wife lean from her phaeton ahead and retch.

"Dear Jesus God." Sarah crossed herself. Cruz gave a little cry, drew her shawl across her face, and turned away. Sarah held her bandana over her nose and mouth.

The women's bodies lay in a heap. They were naked and mutilated, obviously tortured before their throats were slit. Flies swarmed over them. Dogs trotted back and forth at a distance, waiting for the intruders to leave so they could return to feed. As Sarah's caravan passed the corpses, the women in the two Chihuahua carts stared in silence through the tall bars of the sides.

"Yanquedas," breathed Cruz.

Sarah gagged up bile. She took a mouthful of water from the canteen, swirled it around her teeth, and spit it into the dust of the road. "This is the work of Águila or someone as bad." She passed the canteen to Cruz. "There's no dearth of the bad ones, is there?"

Cruz shook her head.

"Sometimes I wonder if there's a limit to what the human spirit can endure," Sarah murmured. "Heap up too much grief and a soul must collapse like an overloaded mule."

"They say that God does not burden us with more than we can bear." Cruz smiled sadly. "That must be true because my sorrow is surely unendurable, yet I am still here."

They passed through the silent village. Sarah could see no one in the narrow streets, nor any lights through the cracks in the shutters. She lowered her voice, as though at a funeral. "The forlorn hope," she said.

"What?"

Sarah searched her Spanish vocabulary. *"Esperanza desesperada,* the hopeless hope."

Cruz gave her a quizzical look.

"The men who charged up that hill through enemy fire at Chapultepec and scaled the walls, such an assault will likely get you killed. That's why they call it a forlorn hope. All those soldiers volunteered for it." Sarah struggled to say why the words were important to her, what they meant to her own life, that she and the rest of humanity were all nonvolunteers for a mission of forlorn hope, but she couldn't explain it even to herself. Instead she murmured, "Captain Lincoln used to say, 'If all men were just, there would be no need of courage.'"

The men continued marching in the darkness, putting miles between them and the horror of the place. When they finally reached a camping site, under peach trees near a river, Sarah and the women erected her four tents. Some of the women had made assignations during the trip and they disappeared into the night to find their soldiers. The others laid out their blankets in the extra tent or in the carts. They ate the provisions they had brought with them or bought along the road. Sarah had given them fine-toothed combs and could hear them murmuring as they searched each other's heads for lice. She wondered what they were talking about. What did one talk about when one had become a fugitive in one's own land?

Davis arrived after the work was done, but in time for cold smoked ham, roasted sweet potatoes, and corn bread, all cooked the day before and packed for such a need. He had bathed and put on a clean uniform. His hair always looked as though a small, shaggy animal had expired on his head. Tonight it seemed that the creature had drowned in a vat of axle grease. He had used a generous quantity of the stuff to slick it close to his big head. He exuded the perfume of whiskey and had a glazed and happy look in his fog-gray eyes. The boys of Company E must have helped him celebrate the coming consummation of his nonexistent nuptials.

Sarah was glad enough to see him, actually. A tussle with him would be uncomplicated by cogitations and emotions, since Davis seemed unfamiliar with both. She had seen so much death in the last months, the life-giving act of physical union would be a nostrum for the sadness. Maybe Davis would do something useful in spite of himself and start a child. Sarah hoped so. She never stopped wishing for a child of her own.

The officers didn't tarry over their meal discussing Spinoza and Plutarch and von Clausewitz as they usually did. Braxton Bragg saluted Sarah and winked at her when he left. Sarah put Maria in charge of cleaning up and went to her tent. Davis was pacing in front of it. She gave him a playful shove inside. He was at least as tall as she and he seemed to fill the tent from one side to the other. He looked terrified that he would stumble over his own immense feet and smash something and be scolded.

She felt a rush of affection for him. She knew that coupling without love was a fleeting pleasure at best, but fleeting pleasure was still pleasure, and she'd had little enough of that.

"Davis, you old hound, they say you're hung like a donkey. Shed your clothes and show me what you've got."

→ ←

She rose while the sky was still soot-black. She stepped over Davis, who was snoring on the dirt floor of the tent like a bison being strangled. He had finished his work quickly the night before, rolled over, and fallen into a deafening sleep. Sarah had finally planted her feet in the small of his broad back and shoved him over the side of the camp bed. He landed like a sack of shot and didn't wake up. Nor did he stop snoring. Sarah slept with tow in her ears and the pillow over her head.

She blew up the embers in the cookfire and moved quietly about the campsite, putting the kettle of water on for coffee and setting dried peaches to soak for cobbler. She liked being the first one up. She liked the tranquillity, the promise. She liked hearing the horses whiffle and stamp in the darkness of the pickets nearby. She liked hearing the song of the mockingbird, undisturbed by bugles and shouts and the general morning rattle. She liked to watch pale gray tendrils of smoke from the fire climb like vines toward heaven.

The women began drifting back before "Reveille," before sunup and certain discovery by Colonel Washington. Dawn brought the colonel, though. Sarah saw him coming and motioned for the women to hide in her wagon under the loose canvas that would later cover the cargo.

"Good day, Widow Borginnis."

"I'm Mrs. Davis now, Colonel."

The colonel grunted. He had observed all the amenities he intended to. "I understand you have brought your tarts with you."

"We'll have peach cobbler this morning, sir, but no tarts."

"I'm not in the mood for your impudence." He walked to the Chihuahua carts and peered in. Then he went to the wagon and threw back the cover, exposing the women crouched under it. He motioned for them to get out and they did.

"They're my employees, Colonel. My bettys."

"You're allowed three servants."

Sarah wanted to remind him that he had five for his personal use, but she refrained. "Where are the others to go?"

"That's not my concern, nor yours either."

"And where are your woman and babe, Colonel?" she said softly.

"I don't know what you mean." He turned on his heel and stalked off, calling back over his shoulder, "Don't let me find them with you when we camp tonight."

"You shan't find them," she muttered when he was too far away to hear her.

Sarah turned to the women. "Maria, Cruz, Zenaida, and the children can stay with me. The rest of you hide under the river bank. I'll come back for you when the soldiers have left."

The colonel would likely be too busy on the march today to check on her. As for tonight, she'd either find a way to avoid discovery, or she'd wear him down. She was willing to play this game until he tired of it. Every one of the officers of her mess knew their secrets were safe with her, and she was privy to plenty of them. But, hell, she'd threaten to expose Washington's peccadilloes if need be, though she didn't think it would come to that. Bullies could always be bullied. It was what they understood.

Marching with Pigeon Toes

I
N THE PARCHED OCTOBER AIR OF NORTHERN MEXICO
the wagons' planks dried, shrank, and came apart. The curved
sections of wheels pulled loose from each other. Metal tires wore
through or slipped off, spokes worked free of the rims. When the
soldiers halted to put their vehicles back together, Colonel Washington rode up and down the line cursing them and the fate that had
consigned him here. He swore that they would all perish in Chihuahua among the molting chickens and the hairless dogs.

The men trudged past the fluted columns of the petaya cactus
towering fifty feet over them. They passed the saguaro cacti that littered the landscape like candelabras left by a feckless gang of titans
after a particularly riotous feast. Tiny owls peered down at them
from their holes twenty-five feet up in the saguaros.

By late September Colonel Washington's column had advanced
into the state of Chihuahua. It had broadened to ten horses wide as
men veered to the sides in an effort to escape the dust raised by
those ahead. The procession snaked across the high, wind-scoured
tableland like a sand sculpture come reluctantly to life.

No one wanted to talk and swallow the blowing dust, so the train
was silent except for a rattle of sabers and harnesses, a great creak-
ing and grinding of sand in all its parts, and the rhythmic chuffing of
the exhausted animals. Chihuahua's snuff-brown earth coated men,
women, children, and horses, cattle, freight wagons, and mule

trains. It saturated the soldiers' once-red shirts, the women's pat-
terned ginghams, and the occasional silk parasol. Dust clung to eyebrows and lined nostrils. It stung eyes and grated under knees and
elbows. It filled shoes and crept into every crevice of Sarah's cargo.
She thought it would surely smother them all before the end of
the day.

Sarah shifted on the wagon seat to ease the ache in her tailbone.
The cushion she used to soften the hard boards had long since flattened until it served no more purpose than one of Captain Lincoln's
flimsy copies of the Baltimore newspaper, *The Register*. She ran a dry
tongue across her lips even though she knew it would add more dust
to what lined her mouth and throat. Her hat already rode just above
her eyebrows, but she pulled the brim lower and squinted through
the narrow slit between it and the bandana tied across her nose and
mouth.

Not that she needed to look at the scenery. The view of Jake's and
Buck's hindquarters hadn't changed in the last two months, of
course, but in the past week neither had the scenery beyond it. Each
white-walled hacienda sat as distant and remote among the smoke
trees and acacias and the tall spindly cacti as the last one. Each village contained the same crumbling chapel and town hall, the trampled
cockpit and shabby dance hall, all fronting the same dusty, weed-
grown plaza. Every low-roofed house seemed to be flowing, slow
as glass, back into the hard-packed earth from which it had been
formed.

The dragoons in the lead halted, and the horses shirred up behind
them. The infantrymen scattered into the spiny brush along the
road and began flailing with their broad-brimmed felt hats to rid
themselves of some of the dust, but it settled back over them as soon
as they stopped. Sarah stood on the wagon seat and looked for
Cruz. She finally saw her and the roan emerge from the ambient fog
of Chihuahua soil. Paz rode asleep and strapped into a seat made
from a converted pack-mule hamper tied behind Cruz's right leg.

As Cruz drew alongside Sarah she said, "Sacramento."

"Do tell." Sarah held the wagon's lines out to her and stood up.
She tensed and released her muscles, trying to unknot them. Cruz
handed the sleeping child over and Sarah put her to bed in the

box under the wagon seat. Then Cruz slid from the roan's back onto the seat. Sarah stepped across the saddle and settled into her place, the worn leather still warm from Cruz's occupancy.

"Time to bid Corporal Davis a fond adieu," she said.

"*Dele un besito y una bota*. Give him a little kiss and a boot." She grinned, happier than Sarah had seen her in the months since they buried James. She had little patience with Davis. She'd been pleased to hear that at the Mexican town of Sacramento his regiment would break off and head north to Santa Fe with Colonel Washington and half the army. The rest of the command, under Major Graham, known to his men as Old Pigeon Toes, would continue on to California.

Sarah found Davis standing stolidly in the high wind of Old Pigeon Toes's wrath. He and the major stood next to the left front wheel of the sprung water wagon Davis had been driving for a teamster laid low by too much whiskey. The spokes had sprung from the cracked rim and splayed out like the ribs of a broken umbrella. The wagon attached to the wheel had pitched down on that side as though making obeisance to the ascendancy of the terrain.

"Damn it, Davis," Graham shouted. "If you'd deserted to the Mex army we could've won the war a year earlier."

"I didn't see the hole, sir."

"You were asleep, goddammit."

"Well, sir, not exactly."

"Not exactly! How can you be not exactly asleep?"

That confused Davis. He shuffled his foot and reached a long, black-edged fingernail under his brittle hair to tug the gold ring in his ear. Sarah had won it from him in the card game outside James Murphy's cell the morning of the hanging, but she had returned it to him as a sort of wedding present. Davis looked slantwise at Sarah now, his bloodhound's eyes appealing to her to extricate him from his difficulties, as she had done the entire trip.

"Morning, Major." Sarah touched her hat brim with long fingers. She graced Pigeon Toes with a radiant combination of even white teeth and green eyes. "I have a spare rim in the wagon somewhere. Pliny'll have it fixed before the troops clear the river."

"See that he does." Graham stomped off in a cloud of dust and cigar smoke, each of his boots pointed inward as though determined to head the other one off like a *vaquero* cutting a horse from the *remuda*. "I'll miss you, Western," he called over his shoulder, "but I'll be devilish glad to see the heels of your man heading north."

As Sarah and the wheelwright, Pliny, set to work, Davis remembered urgent business in the vicinity of the whiskey sellers' wagons and the cardsharps' tables already in place under canvas awnings. Sarah and Pliny wrestled the rim onto the wheel while the sun hammered at them. Davis arrived as they were finishing. He squatted in the wavery rag of shade thrown by his horse.

"That offside looks loose," he pointed out helpfully. "You sure you heated it enough?"

Pliny was a short, powerful individual with skin as dark as anthracite and a dark temper to match. He heaved a clod of dirt at him. Davis fended it off with a look of honest aggrievement on his round face. Sarah didn't even glance at him. He was one of those men who thought their advice was as useful as their actual labor. Discussing their error with them only resulted in aggravation.

Sarah had watched a lot of soldiers ford rivers in the past ten years, and she had repaired a lot of wagon wheels. She knew how much time each took. She and Pliny had just finished when the last horse and rider clambered up the far bank and the bugle sounded "Advance." The teamsters of Colonel Washington's baggage train started their teams forward to the crossing.

Davis climbed onto the wagon seat, took up the reins, and tipped his hat to Sarah. Gallantry to women had been beaten into him by his father and was now as reflexive as scratching an itch. It had fooled a few women into thinking Davis was a gentleman, though Sarah had known better for years.

"I reckon beef stew and a pan o' that there yeller bread would slide down easy tonight, Western."

"Then you'll have to fix it yourself, Davis." She reached up, grabbed his filthy belt where it crossed in the middle of his chest, and pulled him down so she could stamp a sisterly kiss on his cheek. "We part company here. May God keep you, for you aren't up to the job your own self."

He stared at her, mouth slightly ajar as usual. "But Colonel Washington's orders . . ."

"The colonel won't miss me. And Old Pigeon Toes won't mind if I tag along with him." Sarah had given Major Graham enough bottles of brandy to ensure his friendship. It was worth the expense to be shut of Corporal Davis. And Graham's command would be much pleasanter than Washington's. "Besides, I have a notion to wet my fetlocks in the Pacific."

"It's October now," he said. "Winter could catch you in those California mountains like it did the Donner people. Who do you think will make the best stew?" He paused to consider. "Major Graham, now, he's put on some meat, especially in the hams."

Sarah laughed, surprised to find that Davis harbored a spark of wit in the cold ashes of his intellect. "I'll take my chances."

Davis studied on that, but could think of no persuasion equal to the lure of gold and the Pacific Ocean. Sarah waved cheerfully as he sat there ruminating. The gesture could have been a wave of good-bye or a shooing motion.

She led the roan back to where Cruz was forcing a bottle of vinegar down the throat of the black-and-white spotted milk cow to wash some of the alkali dust from her plumbing. The cow wasn't happy about it. Cruz watched from around the cow's nose until Davis had driven off, as though she wanted to be sure he was truly leaving.

She shook her head. "I don't understand why you tolerated his lazy ways."

"Trying to change any man is more trouble than it's worth, and a fruitless endeavor in any case. You just heat yourself to a rolling boil that produces no vittles."

➜ ➜

Sarah climbed onto a flat boulder and put a sun-browned hand to her hat brim to extend its shade farther into the sun's glare. The heat of the granite seeped through her worn boot soles and threadbare wool stockings as she watched the last of the army wagons rock along the sloping trail between the cliff's edge and the sheer face of the mountain wall.

"Dear Lord," she called back to Cruz, who drove the wagon, "Jeremy's slicing it thin, though."

She knew the young teamster driving the rig was tired. She was too. They all were. People made mistakes when they were tired. She shouted at him to pull his team farther from the edge, though she doubted he could hear her over the clatter of the metal tires over the rocks and the rumble of the barrels of salted beef knocking against each other in the bed of the wagon.

The offside rear tire rolled up a slanted stone, tilting the wagon toward the empty blue sky that lapped at the edge of the trail. The barrels shifted, pulled downward by gravity. The wagon canted steeply. Sarah leaped from the boulder and started to run, but she knew she would arrive too late.

The wagon hung poised there, as though to give the driver a chance to rectify his error. Then the rim of the trail crumbled like dry biscuit under the wheels and the rig slid slowly into the breach. The driver tried to scramble up the slope of the seat to leap to safety, but the lines of the reins looped around his leg. He was still clawing at them when the wagon went over the side. Sarah watched the wagon and team spiral down through the emptiness as gracefully as a swan on the wing, if a swan had sixteen mules' legs churning air.

Sarah closed her eyes, but couldn't shut out the driver's cry that rose in pitch as he and his rig dwindled to a toy, then shattered on the rocks. She crossed herself and said a prayer for his soul. She added one for his mother, who she knew waited for him in a paling plank farmhouse in Indiana with sunflowers and hollyhocks around the door. She knew it because Jeremy had read Sarah a letter that had arrived from her just before they left Monterrey.

Sarah wished she could write to the woman and tell her that her son had spoken often of home, and that he had been a good soldier and a brave one. She wanted to console the woman whom she could imagine standing in that doorway among hollyhocks as tall as she was and looking down the road, hoping to see her boy silhouetted by the setting sun.

She heard her own wagon rattle up behind her. She climbed onto the seat and took the reins from Cruz, who crossed herself and said a prayer for the unfortunate Jeremy, then looked at her intently.

"You look pale, Western."

"Am I?" Sarah realized that for the first time in her memory she had a steely shard of pain wedged between her eyes. The world had developed an unsteadiness and a blur.

Cruz grabbed the back of Sarah's shirtwaist to keep her from falling face first onto the wagon tongue as she pitched forward in a faint.

"¡Ay, Dios!" Cruz looked for help among the women in the cart behind her, but Sarah opened her eyes and swayed, panting, on the seat. "Are you sick, Western?"

"I'll be right as rain." Sarah regained her seat, though she kept a hand on the brake for support. She winked at Cruz. "I reckon this morning's fatback bacon exceeded the age of retirement and is not sitting well in service."

→ ←

The downhill pitch on the other side of the pass was the steepest Sarah had ever seen. It looked close enough to perpendicular to suit any government inspector Sarah had ever met. From the top of it Sarah could see an unsettling collection of sharp curves and sheer dropoffs, outcrops, and holes. The soldiers had cleared debris from avalanches, but rocks remained, along with barrels and crates and sacks fallen from the wagons that had gone ahead of her.

If hell has a chute to it, Sarah thought, then surely we have found it.

"Dear Lord," she said out loud, "deliver us safely and I'll never ask another favor of You." She looked back at the soldiers detailed to hold the ropes tied to the wagonhound. She crossed herself quickly, snapped the whip above the rear mules' high rumps, then stuck it in its cylindrical holder. "Go 'long, Jake. Move on, Buck." With the jerkline wrapped around her forearm, she hauled back on the brake with both hands.

The wagon tipped abruptly downward and she braced her feet against the dashboard to keep from sliding out. She struggled to stay aboard as the rig picked up speed. Each wild bounce sharpened the pain behind her eyes and stirred up the bacon lying uneasily in her stomach. Her skin burned as though coals smoldered under it.

In its mad descent the wagon hauled the soldiers in a headlong race behind it. The heels of their boots dug furrows in the dirt. As the wagon swayed and leaped over the rocks the load in the bed crashed about in its webbing. The lashing held, but a kettle worked free of it and soared over the side. It landed with a clatter and bounced several times. Sarah risked a look over her shoulder to see where it came to rest amid the general clutter so she could retrieve it. The problem would be distinguishing her kettle from the selection of them along the trail. Two soldiers had been assigned to run in front of the team to snatch lost obstacles from under the mules' hooves. It wasn't an assignment for which anyone volunteered.

The wagon careened on two wheels around the last bend, and Sarah saw Zenaida and the other women pelting downhill with their skirts up around their waists. Maria had sat down and was sliding on her broad rump. They should have been at the bottom by now.

Sarah half stood and waved her arm at the steep cliffs that rose on either side. "Maria," she shouted. "¡Al lado! To the side!"

The women screamed when they saw her. They scrambled for the slopes, pulling themselves up by the tough stems of the creosote bushes. The wagon passed so close to Zenaida that a jagged edge of the wheel's iron rim caught the hem of her skirt. Fortunately the cloth had worn so thin it tore away easily.

Then Sarah saw an overturned wagon at the bottom and the soldiers swarming over it, trying to free the oxen tangled in their harnesses. She reined left where she could see a few inches more clearance. Jake and Buck swerved, but the wheels locked with those of the other wagon. With a shriek of dry wood rubbing against more of the same, Sarah's rig dragged the other one a team-length. As the whole assemblage came to a crashing halt, Jake tried to jump the other wagon tongue, and ended straddling it and snarled in the welter of lines. Sarah leaped down from the seat to straighten them out.

The pain in her head exploded, blinding her. Her knees turned to sand and she groped for something to steady herself. Buck swiveled suddenly, knocking her into the whiffletree, the swinging bar hanging low on its chain behind the mules. She fell forward and heard a crack somewhere below her knee. She thought, briefly and ruefully, that it probably wasn't the whiffletree breaking before she toppled against Jake's sweaty haunch and slid down it. The last sensations she registered were the familiar smell of him and the coarse, wet hair of his hide rubbing across her cheek.

Make My Bed in Hell

>—⧓—⟨⬦⟩—⬦—⊖—⬦—⟨⬦⟩—⧓—⟨

THE CORPORAL HAD TAKEN HIS HAT OFF, BUT HIS YEL-
low hair still lay flat down to the circular indention left by its
crown. As he talked to Cruz the corporal worked the sides of the
felt brim into tighter rolls. Then he bent the back into a more ex-
treme upward curve and folded the front further under.

"Can't find the drivers of Western's two carts anywhere, ma'm.
Looks like they've absconded with her grubstake." He studied a fat
lizard crawling along the crumbling wall of the abandoned ranch
house. "Wish we could do more for you, ma'm."

"*Gracias.*" Cruz watched two soldiers stand on barrels to put the
last armfuls of brush onto the arbor they had built over Sarah's wall
tent. Four more carried the cot inside with Sarah unconscious on it
and set her down gently. Her left leg was splinted and wrapped.
"We will be ho-kay, Corporal." Cruz had taken a fancy to the word
"okay." It formed like a bubble between her rounded lips, expelled
with a small gust of breath and ending in a smile, even though she
didn't have much to smile about.

"Major Graham says he don't like to abandon members of the fair
gender in the wilderness this-a-way, but we got our orders. And
since the Great Western ain't accompanied by Corporal Davis no
more, she ain't officially part of the army."

The corporal moved aside so another soldier could lower a keg of
water from his shoulder and set it among the crates of horseshoe

nails, gunpowder, and other gifts left by the men who had come to pay their respects. Cruz nodded thanks to him and he touched two fingers to his brim and hurried off.

Cruz turned back to the corporal. "Tell the major we'll follow soon, when Western is well enough to travel."

But she glanced toward the line of mountains as jagged as shark's teeth against the yellowing western sky and fear prowled the dark hollows around her heart. The scouts said that on the other side of them the deep gorges and vertical cliffs stretched for hundreds of miles. The army's route wound through them. But the army had its surveyors and engineers and its pioneer corps to repair roads or clear them, to locate drinking water and bridge rivers. Even if Western's fever abated, her leg would take time to heal. How could Cruz get the household across that barrier without Western's strength and skill?

"We'll be traveling at night on account of this infernal heat." The corporal jammed his hat down over his ears, where it crouched like a high-hipped cat poised to pounce on the prominence of his nose. "My company will be the last to move out. If you think of anything else I can do you for, send word."

"I will."

He started off, then turned back and held out a wooden box. "For you or the Western, whoever's driving into the sun."

Cruz reached inside and took out a flimsy contraption of twill tape straps and two disks of bottle-green glass set into holes in a leather band. "What are they?"

"Sun goggles." He looked sad at parting with them. "Western'll know how to put them on."

"Thank you."

He spurred his bay into a trot when the distant bugles signaled "To Horse." Cruz could imagine the urgent stir and the creak of leather and jangle of metal passing down the long lines as the men moved forward. A longing for James shook her until she trembled with it. A sense of grief and loss washed over her.

"Have a care!" Sarah cried from inside the tent. "Don't drop that!" The last was a shout, louder than Sarah's earlier ravings. Cruz went inside to check on her. The tent, even this late in the afternoon and with the sides rolled up, felt as though someone had left a furnace door ajar.

Sarah's eyes were opened wide, but her stare wasn't fixed on anything Cruz could identify. She moaned and thrashed, rolling from side to side and rocking the cot. Cruz lay across her, trying to hold her still, but it was like staying aboard a fractious horse. She could feel the dry heat through Sarah's shift and her own thin blouse. When Sarah finally quieted, Cruz tipped the water jug dangling in its rope net from the ridge pole and wet a rag. She folded it and laid it on Sarah's forehead.

"*¡Sin verguenzas!* Shameless ones!" A crash followed Maria's scream, then high-pitched laughter and quarreling and shouts of triumph.

Cruz ran outside and saw Maria standing in the puddle of shade from a stunted mesquite tree. The other women swarmed over the wagons. They had cut the lashing with Sarah's butcher knife and were stuffing goods into sacks. Three of them had heaved Sarah's big trunk over the side. They were rifling the contents, pausing only to tug at a particular dress that all three wanted. They ignored Esperanza, who threw rocks at them. The sound of ripping silk followed Cruz back into the tent.

She grabbed Sarah's shotgun, primed and loaded it. When she ran back outside, Maria saw her and ducked behind the tree, though it supplied little cover. Her scream warned the women, who scrambled over the tailgate, dragging their loot behind them and keeping the wagons between themselves and Cruz. Cruz fired anyway, the shot rattling against the sideboards. While she reloaded, the bolder ones threw the sacks onto Sarah's draft mules and the two horses and leaped aboard. The rest scattered on foot like quail into the dense growth of greasewood and sage. One of them tried to mount Jake, but he launched her into the crotch of a stunted mesquite tree. While she screamed and extricated herself from the thorns on the trunk, he began delicately separating mesquite berries from their branches.

"*¡Malditas!*" Cruz knew she had little chance of hitting the women, but she fired again, the shot spraying out across the brittlebush and broom sage, rattling like gravel among their dry branches. "*¡Hijas del diablo!*"

She watched them grow smaller as they set course for the army's flanks. Sarah had risked her own position to shelter and protect them and this was how they repaid her. Before long, though, Buck came galloping back riderless. In the tent Sarah began to sing.

Buckskin moccasin, towheaded Bill
Once went a-courtin' up Jingleberry Hill . . .

Maria ambled over to stand next to Cruz. The two looked like sisters, as though the Creator had experimented with a heavier and a lighter version. Maria shaded her eyes with a pudgy hand.

"*Pues,*" she said with a sigh of resignation. "*¿Qué hacemos?* What do we do?"

"*No sé,*" Cruz answered. I don't know.

> →←

Behind the mountains to the west, the sky glowed like fire opal along the horizon. Cruz sat naked in the shallow water at the river's edge and splashed water over Paz, washing the day's dust off her. She felt feverish and worried that she was getting whatever had laid Sarah low. A spell of vertigo tilted the world sharply and she reached down to steady herself on the sandy bottom.

She looked up and saw a woman standing in the river, the water plastering her white dress to her thighs. Her hair fell in wet tangles down her back. When she turned around, Cruz saw that her face was featureless as a platter. Cruz crossed herself, but her legs refused to lift her and carry her and Paz away.

Though she had no mouth the woman wailed. She combed the water with twisted fingers and long metallic fingernails that glinted in the sunlight. Was this *La Llorona,* the Crying Woman, or a creation of the fever that harried her?

Seduced by a rich man and abandoned, *La Llorona* had drowned her children rather than give them to him when he demanded them. God refused to let her into heaven until she could retrieve their souls, and so she dragged the rivers for them. If she could not find them, she would steal other children to take their place. For fear of her, mothers did not let their little ones play near rivers.

The look on Cruz's face must have frightened Paz because she started to cry. Her voice brought Cruz's will back to her. She scooped the child up and splashed from the river, holding her under one arm. She grabbed her clothes and the shotgun as she went past them. She stopped at the top of the embankment, her heart thumping, and looked back at the river. It flowed slow and green and empty of specters. With shaking hands Cruz put on her blouse and skirt and straw sandals.

Halfway to the crumbling hacienda walls and the nearby tent, four men rode up and blocked her path. The sun's rays and years of accumulated grime had turned their faces dark as any Apache's. The high boots, leather chaps, wool trousers, flannel shirts, and Mexican blankets they wore were all the same dirty shade of brown. The wide brims of their hats hid their eyes, but Cruz knew that if she could see them she would find no pity in them.

She recognized the leader of the pack. The bundle of scalps hanging from his saddle horn formed a thick fringe of long black hair that obscured his knee. When he left the army, John Glanton must have turned to bounty hunting for the Mexican government. The authorities were offering fifty *pesos* reward for each Apache or Comanche scalp turned in. Whether the scalps belonged to men, women, or children made no difference to the government and certainly not to Glanton, Cruz was sure of that.

These scalps might have belonged to Apaches or Comanches, or they could have been taken from the local populace. No one could have told the difference.

"G'd evening, ma'm." Glanton touched the brim of his hat with the tips of two fingers. He gave her a scummy smile.

Cruz set Paz down and pulled her by the arm until she stood behind her skirts. As she stared silently up at him, she could feel the child's arms clasped around her knees, bunching up her skirt in back.

"Sorry to hear the Great Western is feeling poorly."

"We have nothing left to steal."

Glanton pushed his hat up on his forehead and studied her with those narrow, icy eyes. His mouth curved in a smile but his eyes would have none of it. Cruz had little doubt that he intended to rape her with her child looking on, and then pass her to his men. She tried to think of something she could say that would dissuade him from doing it.

"I have something for you." His smile did the impossible and grew even more evil. Cruz feared she would faint. Glanton detached a scalp from the bundle of them and held it up. "I b'lieve you knew this gentleman. Went by the name of Águila. He weren't exactly Apach, but he was mean as one."

He tossed it to her, and she stepped back so it would fall short. She stared at it, aware that it was a generous present on Glanton's part. He could've turned it in with the rest and received the bounty money.

"Apach are thick and furious in these parts," he said. "You'd best have a care." He touched his fingers to his hat again and spurred his horse into a trot. The others wheeled and followed him. "Give Western my regards," he called back over his shoulder.

Cruz's knees wobbled and she almost fell. Stunned by the vagaries of fortune, she picked Paz up and walked unsteadily back to the tent. She found Esperanza standing guard outside as usual, and Maria pacing.

Maria's battered and patched wooden statue of San Antonio looked as though it had seen quantities of abuse of the sort she was giving it now. She held it in both hands and shook it so hard her breasts, hips, and buttocks quivered as if experiencing a very localized tremor. Tendrils of hair worked loose from the thick braid bisecting her back as far as where her waist would have been if she had had one.

She held the statue up until the broken tip of its nose almost touched hers. "Look here, Baldhead," she said in Spanish. "If you don't cure La Grande, it won't go well with you."

Cruz sat on the seat of the wagon parked in the shade of a lightning-blasted quince tree, the remnant of an ancient orchard. "Maria," she called. "Déjalo. Leave it."

But she watched intently as Maria carried the statue, dangling from the long cord tied around its leg, to the dried-up well of the abandoned hacienda where they had stopped for the night. They had pitched the tent inside the walls, although they weren't in condition to keep out Apache raiders.

"He finds lost articles," Maria called back to her. "He helps lovers."

"Western isn't a lost lover."

"He grants petitions." She jigged him on the end of the line once more for good measure. "I have a petition for him."

Cruz didn't argue. She was grateful for the shade and for the rest. After three days of waiting for Sarah's fever to break, she and Maria had enlisted the aid of passing *arrieros* to lift her into the wagon and lay her on top of the mattress there. Cruz had wet down the canvas cover to cool the air underneath. Then she had hitched the mules and set out while Sarah raved.

For two days she had wrestled Jake for control of the jerkline. She felt as though she hadn't the strength to lift her arms from their resting place on her knees. She couldn't help but hope that the old ploy of beating cooperation out of Saint Anthony worked.

They needed a miracle. Two *curanderos* from the town near where the army left them had argued and sweated over Sarah. Both of them wanted, Cruz supposed, to claim credit for curing such a large and prestigious patient. One had claimed that *mal ojo*, evil eye, had brought on the illness. The other was sure that *espanto*, severe fright, had stolen her spirit. The first healer had passed an egg over her, making the sign of the cross with it from her head to her feet. Then he had buried it under her cot. The other had spread her arms to form the shape of a cross and had swept her with a bundle of seepweed and saltbush branches while he recited the Apostles' Creed.

Cruz was dubious about both diagnoses. *Mal ojo* usually affected babies or the weak and Sarah was neither. As for *espanto*, Cruz had never known anything to frighten Sarah. Cruz herself had burned a black candle to dispel evil. She and Maria had tried poultices and compresses and every remedy they knew. None had broken Sarah's fever.

Cruz dreaded another day of her and Maria lifting Sarah's unconscious body so bedsores wouldn't form. The covers were stained and filthy, and tomorrow she would wash them in the river.

"What's to eat?"

Cruz jumped at the sound of Sarah's voice, clear and calm. Sarah sat up on the cot. Her pale face glistened with perspiration. Sweat had soaked her shift and the rumpled coverlet under her.

"I will heat some chicken broth for you."

"Broth, my bounteous butt. I could eat a steer's hindquarters, hooves and tail and all."

"You must start with broth."

"Only if a haunch of beef is dog-paddling in it." Sarah stared at the mesquite splints and the bandages on her leg. "What's this?"

"It broke."

"Broke?"

"Sí. When Buck pushed you into the whiffletree." Cruz handed her her faded calico dress, rescued from an ocatillo cactus where it had floated free during the women's flight. She had mended the thorn holes in it.

"Have we crossed the river yet?"

"No." Cruz helped her stand and balance on one leg while she pulled the sweat-soaked shift over her head.

Sarah swayed and sat abruptly on the cot, almost pulling Cruz down with her. She lay on her back and listened. The only sounds were Maria's threats and the shrill of cicadas.

"Varsal quiet, ain't it?"

"They've gone to California."

"How long gone?"

"Seven days. We've been traveling for three days ourselves."

"Then we're only four days behind. We'd best shake a leg." Sarah looked ruefully at her own leg and patted the gritty rag bandages. She winced at the pain that shot up her thigh. "Looks like Doc Turner's work."

"Sí."

"The boys can prop me in the wagon bed and we can still catch 'em."

"The drivers, those thieves, ran away, may they roast slowly on a spit in hell. They stole your trunk full of money. And the *sin verguenzas*, the shameless ones, left with what they could carry off." Cruz could not help but feel responsible for all of it. "I shot at them, but they would not stop."

"They did what they had to do. We all do what we have to do." Sarah thought ruefully of her two months as Mrs. Davis. "We're better off without them. Fewer mouths to feed." Sarah waved her hand to dispel any notions of guilt. "Don't fret, little sister. I started with nothing, so startin' again with it ain't no great difficulty." She thought a moment. "Did they take my bustle?"

"No."

"Then we got bit of a stake left."

Sarah pulled herself up again and, holding the dress in her hand, hopped naked to the door of the tent. She clung to the pole there and looked out across the dusty valley to the mountains in the west.

"We aren't three days closer to those peaks."

"We're following the range north. We can find a doctor in El Paso del Norte, on the Rio Bravo, what the *yanquis* call the Rio Grande." Cruz wanted to point out that two women, a thirteen-year-old-girl, a two-year-old, and an invalid could not cross those mountains and the long deep gorges that gashed the arid earth for a hundred miles beyond them. But she knew that Sarah knew it already. So she waited silently while Sarah stood with her splinted leg held out.

Light from the setting sun colored the line of mountains a pale lavender. It ignited the undersides of the clouds to a gold as brilliant as an angel's halo, darkening to a golden peach, then violet shot through with threads of light. Sarah stared at the mountains as though she could see the long tail of dust curling over a thousand men on the march.

"Have you ever lived apart from the soldiers?" Cruz finally asked softly.

"Not since I became Jack Borginnis's bride, thirteen years gone."

Maria turned at the sound of Sarah's voice. "*¡Ay, Dios!*" she shrieked. She hauled Saint Anthony from the well where she had dangled him by one ankle. As she trotted toward them she covered him with kisses and endearments. "I told you the little saint would fix her."

Sarah looked at the two mules munching the brittle grass. She studied the dusty, battered wagon that was her home and her estate. She swiveled for one last view of the mountains and the vast, silent emptiness that had swallowed her boys, her livelihood, her joy.

"How far you do think El Paso del Norte is?" she asked.

"The *arrieros* said maybe three hundred miles."

"It'll be a tough pull upcountry."

"*Sí.*"

Still looking at the western mountains Sarah recited softly to

herself in English. Cruz recognized the psalm, though. She had
heard Sarah say it every night before she went to bed.

> *If I ascend up into heaven, thou art there:*
> *If I make my bed in hell, behold, thou art there.*
> *If I take the wings of the morning, and dwell in*
> *   the uttermost parts of the sea;*
> *Even there shall thy hand lead me.*
> *And thy right hand shall hold me.*

None of them spoke while they watched night leech the color
from the clouds and fade the day's light. Without the sun to heat it,
the air was already turning chill. The nights would grow colder as
they went north.

"North to El Paso it is, then," Sarah said finally. "We'll fill every
container with water. And we'll have to soak the wagon wheels and
lay up grass for the animals."

"*Sí.*"

"Have we still a supply of alum, cream of tartar, lemons, horse
shoes and nails, powder and shot?"

"*Sí.* And cornmeal and bacon. The whores couldn't wear them so
they left them."

"The more fools they." Sarah studied the heat shimmering above
the savannah of grass and oaks. Beyond it lay a desert that stretched
to the northern horizon and the river the Mexicans called "Bravo"—
"Wild"—and the Americans called "Grande," "Big."

A Wily Old Owl

‍➤━◆▶━◉━◀◆━◆━➤

EVEN THOUGH NOVEMBER HAD COME, THE SUN throbbed in the sky. It sent waves of heat across the bare plain like storm surges against an unprotected shore. The mules shambled hock-deep through sand hot enough to roast eggs. Their heads hung low. Flies squabbled over the alkali sores on their eyes and mouths. Cruz rode the roan. Maria played with Paz under the wagon's canvas cover. On the wagon seat, Sarah ran the back of her knife blade in a syncopated beat across the jawbone of a mule. The road was littered with those percussion instruments and the skeletons that had supported them in life.

She had hiked the skirts of her old calico high on her thighs to let any stray breeze circulate underneath them. She wore her green glass goggles, but even so she closed her eyes against the glare. She was enjoying the cricket song on the jawbone, experimenting with the rhythms and the vibration of it, when Jake brayed and stopped abruptly. Ears forward, body rigid as a spaniel on point, he stared northeast at the spiny ridge rising like a coyote's hackles from the snuff-colored expanse.

Sarah rested the shotgun across her thighs and patted the pistols in their holsters on either side of the pommel. Two mules and riders popped up at the top of the ridge to be briefly silhouetted against the bright morning sky before they slid down the slope in a shower of sand. They had reached the flat and were tearing toward the wagon when eight more mounted figures appeared and flowed down after them.

"Indians," Sarah said.

"*Ay, Dios.*" Cruz crossed herself. "What if they take my child?"

"No one's gonna do that."

"*¿Qué pasa?*" Maria poked her head through the round opening in the front of the canvas cover where a cord gathered it and pulled it taut across the arch of the bows.

"Indians."

"Apaches?" Fear put a quaver in Maria's voice. "Or Comanches?"

"Does it make a difference?"

"Comanches maybe will talk. Apaches only kill." Cruz squinted in an effort to see the pursuers. "They ride like Comanches."

"I reckon you've had experience with them both."

"*Sí.*"

Maria must have decided one was as bad as the other. "*Indios bravos. ¡Ay, Dios!*" she keened. "*Ay, Dios mio.*"

Paz began to cry too.

"Pull the coverlet over you and keep the little one quiet, Maria."

Maria muttered a prayer as she drew back into the wagon's interior.

Sarah bent her left leg, though it pained her to do it. She pulled her hem down to cover the bruises still visible a month after the break. She reached around to pat the bustle under her skirt. It was reassuringly heavy with the silver coins she had sewn inside it. She wondered if the coins would mean anything to Comanches. It wasn't as though they shopped at the sutler's store.

She took off her Mexican hat and shook her welter of red hair until it stood out around her face like flames. Might as well be scalped for a sheep as a lamb, she thought.

One of the Comanches' quarries waved his hat as he thundered toward them. "Western!" he shouted.

"Juan." Sarah put a hand up to shade the glasses and looked into the morning sun.

"Juan Duran?" Cruz asked.

"Juan is coming?" Maria stuck her head out the opening again. "That shameless good-for-nothing?"

"Appears so. Him and Hanibal." She watched them approach.

"Lucky for them the Comanch're leading spare horses or he would be mess for the buzzards by now. They must've figured to wear him down."

At the mention of Hanibal's name, Esperanza poked her head from the canvas opening next to Maria's. Juan and Hanibal reined their lathered mules into a skid that carried them past the wagon. Juan wheeled and began loading his flintlock pistol. Hanibal slid off his mount's rump and scrambled over the wagon's tailgate. He reappeared with a shovel brandished like a club. Esperanza smiled shyly at him, and he grinned in return.

"Good to see your ugly viz, Juan."

"*Igualmente, Señora* Western," he panted.

"And you, Hanibal."

"*Buenos días, Señora.*"

The Indians sent up a spray of gravel and dust and settled into a slow lope around the wagon, counting heads, and assessing the mule and horse supply. Juan kept the muzzle of his pistol trained on them. The Indians had added an odd assortment of clothing to their breechclouts and leggings. One wore a calico sunbonnet, another a top hat. Three had on vests and one a satin claw-hammer coat, a fifth a blue roundabout jacket. They seemed equally at ease with the arid, unforgiving country and the unlikely combination of apparel.

Their spare horses were loaded high with loot—kettles and axes, a large mirror, a life preserver, a cask. No wonder they hadn't caught Juan and Hanibal.

A burly individual, with short legs and a stomach that overhung his scanty breechclout, separated from the rest. His only other clothing besides moccasins and a bear claw on a thong was a dusty silk plug hat, a woman's pearl necklace, and a pair of purple suede gaiters laced on his thick forearms. He rode close enough to reach out for a lock of Sarah's hair. She leveled the Colt at the juncture where the bridge of his lumpy nose met his thick eyebrows. Apparently unconcerned, he continued to advance. She lowered the pistol until the muzzle pointed at the large rosette beaded onto the front of his stroud-cloth breechclout.

She stared at him, her own green eyes hidden behind the green of the goggles that gave her the look of an oversized, hungry insect. She clicked the hammer loudly. "Juan, explain to him the meaning of half-cock. Tell him that half-cock shall have a second definition if he touches me or anyone or anything of mine."

Juan obliged in Spanish and Comanche and pantomime. Plug-hat glowered as he backed his pony away. The biggest of the lot came forward then. He had a face as round as a platter and wide shoulders as solid as an ox yoke. His bow, arrow quiver, and ancient Brown Bess musket rode slung across a back plenty broad enough to accommodate them all.

"He says his name is Spotted Wolf," Juan reported. "He says he's a good friend to all Goddamns."

"Goddamns?"

Juan shrugged. "They hear *yanquis* say it so much, they call them that."

Spotted Wolf gestured at the pistols. "Pop, pop, pop, pop, pop?"

"Pop, pop, pop, pop, pop, pop," Sarah said. "It's a six-shooter, son."

Spotted Wolf extended his hand, beaming in friendship. Sarah took it, knowing what was coming. Smiling convivially he went to work on it. His hand felt like saddle leather laced with steel rods, but she commenced to squeeze back. She fixed her glassy, emerald-green stare on him and didn't flinch though she thought he would grind her bones to meal before he finished. Pain shot up her arm and tingled in her elbow, but she continued to squeeze his hand as though it were another sodden wool uniform to wring out. She compressed his palm and rubbed the bones against each other until they creaked.

For the better part of a minute they sat there until the raiders began to mutter among themselves. Spotted Wolf's eyes flicked a look at them, cold and quick as summer lightning above the quarter moon of his smile.

"They're betting," Juan said. "And you're favored. Because of your hair they think the fire spirit helps you and that no man can beat you."

Spotted Wolf laughed finally, and released her hand.

"He says he likes your pistols very much."

"He can admire them all he wants, so long as he does it at a distance." Sarah wanted to rub the pain out of her hand and the feeling back into it, but she took the jerkline up, as though to be on her way. "Ask him how far to El Paso del Norte."

"He says four days, maybe five."

From the corner of her eye Sarah saw a wiry man, holding a fringed blue silk parasol over his head, drift toward the back of the wagon. He reached into the opening in the canvas cover and lifted the coverlet. Maria screamed. He grabbed her wrist and held her, ignoring her struggles.

"He says he'll give you two ponies for this fine woman."

"No deal."

With her eyes still on them, Sarah reached under the seat until she felt a small roll of calico and several bandanas. She added them to a braid of tobacco and a loaf of sugar wrapped in brown paper. She beckoned to the old man, shriveled and wizened, who sat his pony at the rear of the group. He wore a filthy white vest. A monocle dangled among the beads and bear claws of his stringy neck. When he rode forward, a flicker of a smile played across his thin lips. It was part pleasure at being recognized as the real leader here, and part amusement at the flame-haired, goggle-eyed woman whose breasts would have been at a level to smother him if they had both been afoot. Comanches appreciated the wonders of nature, and this one seemed to appreciate Sarah.

"*Jefe*, I reckon you're the man to distribute these presents to your warriors." She held them out to him. "My name is the Great Western."

Before Juan could translate, the old man pointed to his bony chest and answered in English. "Old Owl." He gave her a kingly nod. "You, me damn good friends. I trade damn good pony for horse." He pointed his lance to the emaciated, hard-mouthed beast that Sarah had found at a water tank and had been saving to eat when the salt-bacon gave out. One of the men rode forward with a sprightly, fat little paint on a lead, a horse with a sage's eyes and a felon's curl to his lip.

Sarah pretended to study the matter, but she looked sideways at Old Owl. Old Owl stared, solemn as his namesake, politely into the space next to her left shoulder. She waited long enough to let him think she might take his offer.

"I thank you, *jefe*, but I've a powerful fondness for that little jade," she said at last. "She once saved my life, don't you see. Rode me through a whirlwind and out the other side, which is why she looks used up. Couldn't part with her, tempting as your generous offer is."

Old Owl allowed himself a second twitch of his lips and a twinkle in his eye, and she felt twice graced by it. He obviously wasn't one to give away his intentions by a careless tic or twinkle. He was letting her into his thoughts. He was acknowledging that he knew she was on to his ruse. That she knew he would have taken her horse in trade, then waited for his own shrewd paint to escape and catch up with him. It probably had worked for him before.

He raised his lance to his men, wheeled his high-hipped and sullen mustang, and rode away. The rest followed, talking heatedly among themselves while the blue parasol cast longing looks over his shoulder in Maria's direction.

"What're they arguing about, Juan?" A knot formed in Sarah's chest. She imagined them debating the pros and cons of turning around and finishing what they had begun, leaving her and the rest for the buzzards. They must have been pillaging wagon trains to have acquired the clothes and trinkets they wore and the goods they carried.

"They're arguing about where to camp tonight," Juan said. "And which of our villages to raid tomorrow."

→ ←

Sarah, Juan, and Hanibal waded into the marsh in line one after the other until Sarah, who was first, stood waist-deep in the water. Their feet sank in silt that sucked at them with each step. They had tied bandanas across their noses and mouths, but all three of them gagged on the alkali stench. In silence they hacked with their machetes at the tough grass growing there. The three of them passed their bundles back to Esperanza, who piled them on the driest spot she could find.

When they had amassed a heap almost as tall as Esperanza, they waded out and started tying bunches of grass together with strands of it that Juan rolled between his callused brown fingers and his thigh.

"How'd you happen to be in this country?" Sarah asked while they worked.

"We met a mule train on the road," Juan said. "The *arrieros* said they had seen you. They said you were ill with fever, but your companions were coming north anyway. They helped lift you into the wagon."

"Why'd you leave your own train to come looking for me?"

"It's a long story." He looked sheepish.

"I've got time."

"Hanibal and I joined that troupe of entertainers."

"Not the same gaggle of mountebanks who've dogged the army since Corpus Christi?"

"*Sí.*"

"That fumbling pair of jugglers, the bearded woman, the fellow who eats rocks and scorpions, Harry the Human Hairpin, and the one who extinguishes candles and imitates the shelling of Fort Brown with his farts?"

"*Sí.* Except Martha, the bearded one. She married a soldier."

Hanibal brought their two mules and held them while Sarah and Juan tied the grass onto their backs, piling it so high the animals almost disappeared under it.

Sarah took the alum from her knapsack. She mixed it in water to make a paste, then rubbed it on the ugly sores the alkali dust had opened on the mules' nostrils.

"So how were you planning to earn your keep?" she asked Juan. "Swallow fire? Belch a rendition of 'La Cucaracha' while Hanibal dances to it?"

"They were going to California."

"The Windmill and the Hairpin intend to prospect for gold?"

"*Sí.*"

"Well, if that don't beat all." Sarah followed Juan and Hanibal and the mules back to the wagon.

She was amused to see Esperanza move up cautiously to walk alongside Hanibal. The boy was the only being to light a spark in her eyes.

"Boats full of *yanqui* gold seekers are steaming up the Rio Bravo as far as Matamoros. They are outfitting there and traveling across northern Mexico in search of a shorter route. *Arrieros* coming from El Paso del Norte say they saw hundreds of them. They say all the *gringos* in the United States are in wagons heading for California."

"So you caught the fever."

"Fever?"

"Gold fever."

"Maybe."

"How'd you end up in a dead heat with Old Owl's flock?"

"Hanibal and I were headed for a village to buy some pack mules for the journey and heard about you. Then the Comanche came upon us. We decided that as long as we were headed this way, we would find you and see how you were faring."

Sarah knew Juan well enough to realize he was tweaking her. "Can't say as I'm impressed with your Camino Real, the Royal Road. Wouldn't serve as a cart track even in the mountains where I come from."

"North of San Bartolomé the country is called *El Despoblado*, the Depopulated."

"I figure those crosses we been passing mark the graves of travelers."

"*Sí.*"

"It's kindly of folk to remember the dead that way. And by the numbers of them, I'd say there are a lot of dead to remember."

"The crosses aren't so much for the dead as for the living." Cruz put a spoonful of cream of tartar into the canteen and shook it.

Sarah took a drink but the alkali taste still made her stomach churn. "How so?"

"Without the blessing of the Church their unhappy spirits would stay here. More and more of them would accumulate until a great quantity of evil would wait to seize travelers."

"Then I reckon we only have to concern ourselves with the evils of this world." Sarah grinned.

Juan and Hanibal settled themselves on the wagon seat, and Sarah mounted the roan. As she set out at a walk beside Jake, the word *"despoblado"* repeated in her head. A place where people could not or would not live hadn't much to recommend it. But she thought about what her grandmother used to say: "A merry heart doeth good like a medicine, but a broken spirit drieth the bones."

She took up the sprightly beat of a reel with her knife on the jaw-bone again.

The Elephant's Scat

❯━┃━◄❯━•━⊖━•━❰►━┃━◄

SARAH, CRUZ, AND JUAN STARED AT THE FARMER sprawled chest-down in the sun-blasted, wind-scoured field. His arms were flung outward, his fingers dug into the dry soil as though embracing the earth. Disgruntled vultures spiraled overhead. The body, stripped of the shirt and trousers he had been wearing, had begun to swell in the heat, giving the dark skin a taut, shiny appearance.

Juan kicked a broken arrow that lay among the dried stubble. "Apaches."

Sarah walked closer to see better through the brown cornstalks and shriveled bean vines. The narrow swath of trampled plants behind him marked his attempt to reach the scant refuge of the cactus-topped mud wall that encircled his mesquite pole shack, leaning to leeward in the distance.

"Hasn't been dead long," she said. "The crows haven't taken his eyes yet." She turned in a circle, searching the flat, noncommittal horizon for signs of the raiders who had riddled the man with arrows, then, apparently ever frugal with their resources in this penurious land, had retrieved them.

The arrows and his scalp weren't all they had retrieved.

"Why do you suppose they did him that way?" Sarah studied his arms and back, flayed to the glistening bones and black with a shifting crust of flies.

"They use the sinews of the arms to tie the steel points onto their arrows," Juan said. "They make bow strings of the ones in the back."

"They've pretty thoroughly used up the poor fellow, haven't they?" Sarah limped to the wagon for the shovels whose blades had worn thin as foolscap from digging the wagon wheels out of two hundred miles of mud and sand. "We'll bury him and say a prayer. Then we'll get supplies in the village."

When they had thrown the last heap of dirt onto the mound, pounded the cross of sticks into the stubborn soil, prayed, and crossed themselves, they moved on. As the wagon rattled through the silent streets and the horses' hoofbeats echoed against the walls, dogs skulked around the corners and crows rose screaming from the eaves.

"Where'd they go, Juan?"

He shrugged. "Into the mountains. Hiding from the Apaches."

Sarah rode Hanibal's mule under the portico of the long, low communal building and looked in at the door. She breathed in the must and heat and dust emanating from the dark interior. As the gelding fidgeted, the noise of his hoofbeats bounced around the empty room. "Reckon they have stores anywhere?"

"What they didn't take with them the *indios* stole." Juan said it as though he were discussing a plague of locusts or corn borers or a particularly dry season.

As they continued north the land became drier and more barren. They found other solitary villages, but the few people who remained were too frightened of Apache attacks to harvest what remained of their crops. Then the meager fields and pitiful huts became fewer and farther apart until two days passed without their seeing any. It seemed that even the poorest Mexicans desperate to escape the violent currents of revolution and official corruption had accepted the impossibility of sustaining life here.

Toward late afternoon the little caravan plodded across a tawny, treeless plain that wavered in the heat like thin custard on a platter held in an unsteady hand. Maria sat next to Juan on the high seat. Paz and Esperanza napped in the wagon bed, and Cruz and Sarah rode flank. When the first gust of a hot breeze fingered Sarah's hair, she turned to see a dark band expanding on the southern horizon.

"Juan," she shouted, "bring the team into the wind and unhitch them."

He leaned out to look beyond the big canvas cover. "*¡Carajo!*" He jumped from the seat onto the whiffletree and from there he leaped onto Jake's rump. He slid into place on the mule's back and yanked his halter around. The wagon slewed so suddenly to the left that Maria almost fell off.

"Are you crazy?" she screamed. "Do you want to kill me, *pendejo?*"

"I have often considered it, my daughter." He unhitched the team and led them behind the wagon.

"Thanks be to God for the rain." Maria tugged the wooden crucifix from the tight cleft between her breasts where the low neck of her blouse constricted them, and kissed the cross.

"That's not rain." Sarah shooed her toward the rear of the wagon. When Maria didn't climb aboard fast enough, Sarah made a circle of her arms under her backside and boosted her up, dumping her unceremoniously inside.

While Juan tied grain sacks over the mules' eyes, Sarah grabbed spare rope from the back of the wagon and several blankets and cotton duck coverlets. She pulled the lacings of the wagon cover as tight as they would go and tied them off. The gathers of the canvas were too bulky to close completely and the opening, big enough for a five-gallon whiskey jug to slide through lengthwise, looked like a yawning chasm to her. Hanibal began stuffing grain sacks into the opening from the inside.

Sarah and Juan threw the blankets over the animals' backs and lashed them in place with the ropes. While they worked, the bright sun turned to a sudden amber twilight. A roaring filled the air as the wall of sand and gravel swept toward them. Gusts whipped Sarah's skirts around her legs. The first grains stung like fowling shot as she followed Juan through the front opening and tied it closed after her. She and Juan scrambled over the others in the dark, pushing goods to the sides to make room and to insulate them from the sand. But it soon began to seep in everywhere. Before long, the wind began driving it through the cloth.

They lay side by side under the last of the blankets while the wind roared outside and shook the wagon like an angry bear. Through the noise they could hear Jake's aggrieved braying. Paz started to cry and Sarah sang so she herself wouldn't have to listen to Jake.

> *Miss Ella is a gallus nag,*
> *Miss Ella she is neat;*
> *Her eyes look like a saffron bag,*
> *And, Lord, what awful feet.*

Sarah grabbed each of Paz's feet by the toes and shook them.

> *I saw Miss Ella on the Platte,*
> *Where she got alkalied;*
> *Her jackass he was rolling fat*
> *And straddle she would ride.*

Sarah lost all sense of how long they lay there before the roaring faded, to be replaced with a silence as deafening in its own way. Maria, Cruz, Paz, Esperanza, and Hanibal fell asleep. Juan lifted the blanket, heavy with a heap of sand, and moved carefully to the rear so as not to jostle them. Sarah took the last earthen jug with water sloshing in it and followed him.

They climbed out into a cold night gaudy with stars and a country washed in molten silver light from a gibbous moon. The tranquillity made Sarah think she might have dreamed the storm, were it not for the grit inside her clothes and in her mouth and eyes and nose. Jake sneezed loudly.

Shivering with the cold she poured the water into a bucket and held it for the animals to drink, starting with Jake.

"The last of it?" Juan asked.

"There's a mouthful for the baby."

"We have to keep moving then. There's supposed to be a spring not too far from here." Juan searched the heavens for the Big Dipper and the North Star trailing the handle of it pointing toward the north. He shook his head sadly. "This is a country abandoned by God."

"He abandons no one," Sarah said. "But sometimes folk abandon Him."

Sarah pulled the covers off the mules. Jake's had slipped or been blown off by the wind and she could feel raw flesh and the sticky warmth of blood where the sand had scoured away the hair and skin. He shuddered when she touched him. The harness would be torture for him.

Jake nuzzled her hair and whiffled in her ear before his muzzle drooped earthward again. She put an arm over his withers and laid her head against his neck on the undamaged side. She leaned against him, knowing he would support her weight for the instant she gave in to her exhaustion, or for the rest of the night if need be.

As the sun drove back the night's chills, the plain shimmered to the perimeter of the mountains whose bases shimmied in the heat. After the animals rested, Sarah, Juan, and Hanibal unloaded the wagon and shoveled out the sand that filled its bottom. They abandoned everything but necessary tools and hardware and lumber to repair the wagon, the few blankets that hadn't been shredded in the storm, casks for water, and a keg of cornmeal and one of hardtack.

The storm had obliterated the trail that hadn't been more than a track anyway. They left Paz playing with her doll in the wagon, but everyone else trudged through ankle-deep sand. Juan and Sarah walked beside the team.

As the hours passed, their tongues swelled until they could no longer close their cracked lips. Maria and Cruz staggered forward as if each step took more effort than they could manage. Sarah kept looking back at them, ready to catch them if they fell. But her own tongue felt wrapped in hot wool and the desert jigged mischievously around her.

"Why is a dead duck like a dead doctor?" she called out.

"I do not care," Maria said.

"Because they're both done quacking." Then she had to explain the English.

Water shimmered on the horizon, glinting in the sun. The wavery black shapes of men and horses danced above it. Far ahead, the tiny silhouettes of buzzards circled on the high currents of warm air. Sarah remembered the Comanche, as at ease in this unforgiving wilderness as she was in the barroom of her hotel. No wonder they include a trickster in their tales, she thought. They travel the desert

and the desert is a trickster. It freezes you at night, then heats you to
a simmer when the sun rises. It deprives you of water, then lures you
with a sea of it always out of reach.

They were forced to stop at intervals that came closer together
and lasted longer. Finally Juan's mule's legs folded under him and he
collapsed. He twitched as if to knock flies off his hide, then became
still. Jake swung his head around to study him.

While Juan unhitched the body from the traces and put Hanibal's
mule in his place, Sarah slit the dead animal's throat and caught the
blood in a bucket. She passed it to Cruz, who wrinkled her nose but
took a sip.

Maria backed away, holding her first and last finger up with the
middle two folded down as though to dispel the evil eye. "No, by
the saints. I will not drink blood like some worshipper of the devil."

"Suit yourself." Sarah took the bucket from Juan. The blood was
warm and sticky and salty and only made her thirstier, but at least it
wet her lips. "No sense butchering him, is there?"

Juan shook his head.

"I figured not."

Neither of them said aloud what they both were thinking: thirst
would kill them before hunger would.

"Still, my grandmother always said, 'Waste not, want not.' " She
cut some of the meat from him in strips anyway and draped them
over the wagon sides to cure.

They traveled far enough for the distant buzzards to grow to the
size of crows when Jake and his new harnessmate came suddenly
alert. Their nostrils flared and quivered. Jake threw his head up and
brayed. His joy was so evident and so human that tears filled Sarah's
eyes at the sight of it.

"They smell water. Thank you, Lord." She made the sign of the
cross. "Try to hold them till I get aboard, Juan. No tellin' what we'll
find ahead."

Juan jumped onto Jake's back while Sarah grabbed Paz from inside the wagon and handed her to Cruz. "We'll come back for you,"
she said. Then she clambered into the seat, but she stood, bracing
her feet and trying not to damage her tailbone. The mules leaped
forward and galloped across the waste with the nearly empty wagon
bouncing behind.

With knees flexed Sarah moved as best she could with the wagon, and she searched for the patch of trees that meant a pond, or the green strip that embraced a river's sinuous course. She imagined splashing into the cool water, falling facedown in it and letting it soak into her clothes, her pores. No trees appeared, though, only the buzzards and the shimmering rock and sand, the bristle of cactus and creosote bushes and the lavender shadows of distant mountains.

They didn't see the river's gorge until just before the two mules went over the edge of it. The river lay in a narrow cleft at the bottom of a steep slope. The animals slid down the high bank on their haunches, the wagon flying behind them.

As they approached the river, narrow here, shallow and slow-running, the stench of rotting flesh hit them like the flat of a hand. In a thunder of wings, crows and buzzards lifted in a blanket from the bloated corpses of oxen, cattle, horses, dogs, and mules lining the banks or lying in the water. Jake tried to stop at the water's edge but the other mule strained forward, dragging him into it. The wheels sank in the sand and the wagon came to an abrupt halt. Sarah fell backward, hitting her hip against the side and wrenching her back.

She climbed painfully down into the thick brown brew, ripe with the smell of death. She felt the bottom sludge seep in through the holes in her boot soles. Knee-deep in the water, she tried to help Juan drag the mule out before he drank too much, but they couldn't move him. Gagging from the smell, they unhitched the two animals. Jake came away with Sarah, but, oblivious to their efforts, the other mule went on drinking in great gulps. Sarah bent her knees, wedged her shoulder under his neck, and heaved his head upward while Juan hauled his hackamore and together they got him to shore. He collapsed there, and they could see he wouldn't rise to his feet again.

"Damn!" Sarah held her kerchief over her nose and mouth as she surveyed the carnage along the river. The enormity of the effects of the gold-rushers hit her. The wreckage of wagons and abandoned possessions littered the country as far as she could see on both sides of the river and in both directions to the east and the west. Sand in the dead animals' eyes gave them an eerie glitter. "Looks like we found the elephant's scat, at any rate."

Juan squatted wearily, his back to the river. "The dead have tainted the water for miles."

"It's all we've got." Sarah walked the low bank looking for the tell-tale crust of salts. "It isn't too badly alkalied. Those animals drank themselves to death."

She waded back out, pulled two buckets from the wagon, and stretched her skirt over one. Juan filled the second one and poured the brown liquid through the cloth. Sarah added half the contents of the last jar of cream of tartar in an attempt to sweeten the water. Jake looked dubious, but he drank, slurping noisily.

"I suppose this is the Rio Bravo," Sarah said. "Which way do you suppose lies El Paso del Norte?"

Juan shrugged, but pointed west with his chin.

Sarah nodded at the wagon standing next to the carcass of an ox mounded above the water like an air-filled bladder. "We'll take parts from these wagons and make repairs. Let Buck and Jake blow. Rest up ourselves. And we'll have to soak the wheels in this cesspool."

But even as she said it, she imagined the stench of death permeating the wood of the wagon, rolling along with them. Never leaving them.

39

Amazing Grace

S ARAH'S LITTLE CARAVAN HAD TO LEAVE THE RIVER
when it deepened and passed through a rock cleft too narrow
for the wagon. From there the canyon rose steeply in a series of
shelves, and they were forced to follow the bluff above the river.
From time to time Juan or Sarah found places where they could
scramble down and haul water back, but mostly they had to look at
the verdant ribbon from a distance.

The wagon creaked as though each individual board and bolt
would pull apart from its neighbor and all would land in a heap in
the sand. The sandstorm had scoured off the tranquil scene Moses
had painted on the sides. The tatters of the cover, abraded to the
finest chintz by wind and sun and blowing sand, fluttered against
the arced ribs of the bows. The hills were low and rolling, but Buck
and Jake were so badly winded they could barely move the wagon
forward.

Even here on the Mexican side of the river, debris littered the
trail, the possessions of the gold-seekers Juan had talked about, the
ones who had taken steamers to Brownsville, then had struck out
across northern Mexico. Maria, who claimed to be unable to walk
another step and had begged to ride, found the strength to leap
from the tailgate again. She trotted off among the stranded wagons
and bedsteads and iron stoves, the log chains and millstones, the

discarded books and trunks and the bedding and clothing that flapped in the wind.

"Lord help us." Sarah walked with Cruz beside the mules, and she pulled the jerkline to halt them. They didn't require persuasion. They stood with knees quaking and heads low. "What's she after now?"

Cruz shrugged. She herself wore a brand-new frock of blue dimity, still bearing the creases from the abandoned trunk where it had nestled neatly folded along with two dozen white linen shirts and starched collars. Juan wore one of the shirts, the tails of which covered the holes in the seat of his trousers. He was on the scout for a new pair of trousers.

Cruz glanced at Sarah's threadbare dress that would have shown more of Sarah if she weren't wearing a faded army tunic over it.

"Maybe you could find new clothes, too." Cruz nodded at the hundred square miles of emporium spread out around them.

"Other women's dresses are no more'n *pingajos* for me."

Cruz smiled at *pingajo*, the word for a cloth patch.

Sarah handed Cruz the jerkline. "I will shop for a new pair of shoes, though." She pointed her chin at a big Kentucky wagon with its sturdy cover still in place and four oxen dead in the traces. "We can take the canvas too. Salome's veils spanned her better'n our old awning would."

She walked to the Kentucky and ran her hand along its sides, dislodging the flakes of blue paint still left on it after its long journey. It was the only one she'd seen in better shape than her own, but Jake and Buck couldn't haul it, even emptied. She saw that someone had sawed off sections from the top boards along the sides, leaving rectangular gaps. She didn't have to look far to find the three graves they marked.

She climbed onto the back step and looked inside at the trunks and barrels stacked around the sides, the oaken sideboard and rocking chair, an apron hanging from a nail in the middle wagon bow. It was quiet as a funeral parlor, and as dimly lit, but with an air of expectancy, as though the occupants had only stepped out and would be returning soon.

She lifted a quilt leaning against the side of the wagon and stared at the portrait laid down in oils underneath it. The pair wore clothes of an earlier time. Maybe they were the parents of the present owners, or grandparents. They looked stern, as though displeased with their predicament. The hair stirred on her arms as she stared into those accusing eyes.

She dropped the quilt, but she could still feel the eyes. She felt no better than one of the human vultures who skulked across the battlefield while the smoke still drifted over it and stole from the dead and the dying. At best she was like the impoverished Mexicans who overran the army's old campsites to scavenge even the dropped grains of feed. Well, one does what one must. This wasn't the first time she had thought that.

She lifted the feather ticking and sorted through the wooden boxes on which it rested until she found the one containing footwear, also never used by the look of them. She held a boot to her foot, against the sole of one of the shoes she had sewn from the dead mule's hide. The miles of rocky ground between here and the mule's flayed corpse had worn out several pair. These had holes in them and so did the pieces of leather she had put inside.

The new ones were men's and they would fit her well enough. She found three pair of women's leather shoes that looked like Maria's, Eperanza's, and Cruz's sizes and a child's pair for Paz. She picked up a miniature rocking chair that she thought would please Paz.

She climbed down with the shoes and the chair in her arms. She picked a handful of sulfur-yellow flowers from the rabbit brush growing next to the wagon wheel and took them to the graves. The small mound over one of them no doubt roofed the remains of the child for whom the shoes and the chair were meant.

"I hope you all don't mind my taking these things," she said to the occupants of the grave. "You had a daughter yourself, so I reckon you loved children. I wish your little one and Paz could've played together."

Even if Sarah could have read the inscription written in charcoal on the board driven into the ground at the head of it, her tears would have blurred it. She laid the flowers on the raw earth and murmured a prayer that blended with the buzzing of the flies on the dead oxen.

She called to Juan and together they pulled the cover off the wagon, exposing the contents as though laying bare the personal lives of their owners. From somewhere in the jumble of goods came the random notes of a pianoforte and Maria singing.

"At least she can't heft that into the wagon."

Juan rolled his eyes, indicating he wasn't so sure of that, and picked up his end of the bulky roll of canvas.

They arrived in time to see Maria toting a large oval mirror with an ornate walnut frame of carved grapevines and stags. She stowed it in the back of the wagon, but as soon as she headed out to scout for more goods Cruz heaved it over the side. It landed with a shattering of glass. This was a routine they had settled into for the last ten miles. Maria didn't seem to notice that Cruz discarded each treasure she salvaged from the gold-rushers' abandoned belongings.

Sarah glanced at her own fractured face reflected in the shards of the mirror. The sun had blistered her skin and raised sores on her mouth. The linings of her eyes and her nostrils were red and raw and burned even when she closed them. She pushed the tangled tendrils of hair under her hat, then she laid her palm on her own cheek as though to soothe an unhappy child.

"I would frighten the very devil himself."

"We all would." Cruz put an arm around her waist, and Sarah encircled her shoulders, pulling her close. They stood side by side staring at the splinters of themselves.

"When we reach El Paso we'll pretty ourselves up," Sarah said.

"Sí."

They started off again with Paz riding on Jake's back, but the new canvas proved too heavy for Buck. He slowed until he barely moved, raising each hoof as though everything from the knees down had turned to lead. He stopped finally and swayed forward, then back, then from one side to the other. His legs folded under him and he settled onto the sand, looking as peaceful as if he intended to take a nap. A trickle of blood flowed from his crusted nostril. Jake lowered his head and butted it against Buck's neck trying to get him to his feet. Then he set up a mournful braying echoed by Paz's wails.

"Carry what you can," Sarah said. "We're forming a walking committee." She filled the powder flask and shot bag hanging from her belt. She slung her shotgun across her back and settled the leather strap between her breasts. She poured the last of the corn into a satchel, put the cord over her head so it hung at her left hip behind her Colt.

"We cannot leave the wagon." Maria clung to a spoke as though it were a raft in a raging torrent.

"Stay with it, if that suits you." Then she noticed the look of terror and grief on Maria's face and gentled her tone. "We can't be far from the settlements at the Pass."

Juan took Maria's arm and, as though coaxing a child, led her to where Sarah and the others waited. When they had salvaged what they could, and loaded a few sacks onto Jake's back, Sarah turned to look at her rig before she slogged away through the sand.

Cruz saw the look. "*Es lástima*," she said. "It's a pity."

"No pity about it, little sister." Sarah slowed her stride so the others could keep up. She reached behind her to pat the bustle's bulge at the small of her back. "When I left home I'd've been pleased to own the few coins I have here." She grinned, the smile a mockery of humor in her dirt-crusted, sun-blistered, and wind-battered face. "You got your monte box in that sack?"

Cruz smiled back. "*Sí.*"

"Don't you suppose there'll be sheep to shear when we reach El Paso?"

"Of course."

"And men are such a predictable bundle of itches." Sarah had not shared her favors for money, but she would if she had to. "There's one commodity they will always pay for. And thank you for the privilege." She thought of her mother's saying, "You do what you must," and wondered what she would think of this interpretation of it.

➤ ⬸

As they neared El Paso del Norte the greenery along the river became thick and lush. From the trail on the bluff they could see mountains hazy in the distance with slim poplars and broad cottonwoods gracing the valley like dancers in the foreground. The broad plain was patched with fields and dotted with scattered ranches and cattle tanks. The line of green where the Rio Bravo

meandered marked the new border between the United States and
Mexico, and redefined it with each whimsical new curve in its bed as
it ate away at one bank and deposited silt on the other.

Far below the trail along the bluff, the Rio Bravo divided at the
end of an island that was ten miles wide and stretched twenty miles,
almost to El Paso del Norte and the pass through the mountains on
the other side of it. Silver ribbons of irrigation ditches wove a glit-
tery net among the island's green fields, rampant gardens, and orchards. The small adobe houses of the farmers nestled behind their
walls in the shade of fruit trees.

Sarah and the others skirted the rim of the canyon wall for a few
miles before they found a way down to the river. Their new shoes
had been fashioned for city streets, and by the time they slid down
the rocky path to the valley floor the thin leather and the fine stitch-
ing fell apart. They walked barefoot and merry past the encampments of other travelers and the hooded wagons parked and tranquil,
as though grazing. They hurried through the soft grass under the
towering cottonwoods and alders and into the water. Sarah didn't
stop to shed her clothes. She waded out until it reached her chest,
then she scooped handfuls of it into her mouth.

When she felt cooled to the bone and filled to bursting she threw
her head back, raised her arms toward the ceiling of deep green
leaves and laughed. *"Gracias a Dios,"* she shouted.

On her way back to shore she twirled with her hands in the water,
sending sprays over the others. They returned the gesture and
laughed and chased each other through the shallows. Thoroughly
soaked, they lay on their backs in the grass and stared up at the
leaves rustling in the breeze. Even Esperanza, who had contrived
to lie next to Hanibal, smiled for the first time since Sarah had
found her.

"What's that?" Sarah raised herself on her elbows and turned her
head toward the singing, just audible over the shrill of the cicadas.

The others listened.

"It's 'Amazing Grace.'" Sarah hummed along. "But they aren't
singing it in English."

She followed the music past companies of people clustered around
the cookfires. A small group stood apart from the others, and as
Sarah walked toward them she could see they were gathered at three

freshly dug graves. When she got close enough to make out their features, she knew why no one from the other encampments had joined them to pay respects to their dead. No matter how low white people might sink in the social order, they would always find some-one on whom they could look down.

"Who are they?" Cruz whispered.

"Cherokee by the looks of them."

Sarah remembered them from her childhood in east Tennessee. She remembered hearing some of her neighbors bragging about how they had raided a Cherokee settlement at night and burned the cabins. "Drove the red niggers out," they had said. "And good rid-dance." But the Cherokee she had known had always been better neighbors than those who advocated eradicating them like rats in the corncribs. They'd been hardworking and generous, with soft voices and rare but lovely smiles.

These Cherokee stood quietly while a tall, slightly stooped man with short black hair read from the Bible in their own tongue as the bodies were lowered.

When the service ended, Sarah said, "I wanted to tell you how sorry I am for your loss."

"It was God's will." The man's English was quite good, with a Carolina accent.

"What took them?

"Cholera."

"Is it bad then?"

"Yes." He nodded politely, his dark eyes taking in the tattered condition of her and her companions. "Our provisions are poor, but we'd be pleased to have you join us in breaking bread."

"We thank you kindly. We've had a hard haul ourselves." Sarah knew they would never accept money for the meal. But as she and the others sat down she schemed the most diplomatic way to leave one of her few coins with them.

✦✦

Sarah could recognize trouble from a distance, and the three men gathered at the board gate of the irrigation ditch fit the description. They were filthy and solid as water casks. The creases in their faces had not been formed by a lifetime of smiling.

Each as broad as a skinned mule, Sarah thought, and nigh onto as ugly.

They seemed as out of place in the neat field as a cockroach in a teacup. The owner of the field looked like a child next to their furry height and bulk. He clutched his straw hat in front of him in supplication. Its brim covered his chest from the high, narrow arch of his nose to the crotch of his ragged cotton trousers. He stood low enough to the ground to find shelter under the men's chins.

The spire rising from the nearby grove of cottonwoods belonged to the settlement of Socorro del Sur, which meant he was probably a Piro, a descendant of the tribe that accepted Catholicism two hundred years earlier. When the Pueblo peoples to the north had had enough of Spanish demands in 1680 and rose in bloody retaliation, the Piro had fled here. They'd been in the area ever since, still stubbornly faithful to the Spaniards' God. The farmer had skin the color of weathered cedar and the craggy cheek planes belonging to the folk who watched the first Spanish soldiers clatter across the desert on their alarmingly large beasts. In his sad eyes remained the recognition that his ancestors' worst fears about the pale, hairy men had proven true. Across the small field, his wife and children stood at the opening of the spiny fence of ocatillo cactus around their house.

Sarah knew that the nearest officials with any authority were eight miles away in El Paso del Norte. And she had seen enough of this particular stampede of *gringos* to know that an appeal to authority would have little effect anyway, especially on an island in the middle of a river marking an international border between two unfriendly countries. The Rio Grande itself had no use for authority. It altered its channel frequently, confounding those who would use it as a perimeter for sovereignty.

"You fellows needing something?" Sarah reined Jake in and rested her elbow on the pommel. Juan and the others stopped well behind her and watched warily.

"Fixin' to water our stock." The tallest one nodded toward a knot of slat-sided cows munching on the last of the Indian's third corn crop.

"These sluices are regulated by the government." Sarah kept her tone reasonable, though anger warmed her cheeks. "If you take his allotment, he won't have water for his fields."

"That there's the dirty little greaser's problem, ain't it?" He turned away from her and waved a grimy hand to the man nearest the gate. "Open the son of a bitch."

"En nombre de Dios, Señores." The farmer moved to stop him, and the third one caught his arm and flung him, as though clearing a fallen tree limb from a trail. The Mexican fell over his mattock, twisting his ankle on the way down.

Sarah slid off Jake's back and stepped lightly over the hillocks of hand-hoed bottomland. She moved faster than any of the three expected. She grabbed the leader by the loose shoulder of his big coat and jerked him around. When his nose came into range, she cocked her fist and hit it so hard the cartilage made a grinding crunch that satisfied her deep down. He flew backward, landing on the seat of his pants in a soft, round keepsake left by one of his cows. She knew that slamming the palm of her hand against the front of his nose would have caused him more pain and her less, but a closed fist did more damage to a man's morale.

"Damnation!" Blood filled his nostrils and gave the word a damped, bubbling sound.

The others backed away as she stalked toward them, sucking her aching knuckles. She knew they wouldn't fight her. She had met men who would have raped her if they could, especially when in a pack such as this. She'd known some who had no qualms about hitting women too timid to retaliate. But she had never met one willing to engage in fisticuffs with a female, even one of her altitude and muscle. The whole notion was too outlandish and fraught with threat to a man's dignity.

She kept her tone almost cordial, always more unnerving than bravado. "If you are any part of a gentleman, you will quit this fellow's property." Then she lowered her voice, until they would have to pay attention to hear her. Oddly enough, they did, leaning slightly forward as though she were a stiff breeze. "And if you are a fool, you will persist in annoying him."

The injured party's friends helped him to his feet. They picked up his hat and brushed the manure from the seat of his trousers with it until he snatched it from them in a fury.

"Reckon I'll settle you one dark night." He looked as menacing as he could, given that he had to breathe through his mouth as well as talk through it and he had to cant his head back to meet her gaze. "I shall open your gullet from ear to ear whilst you sleep."

"The blade of vengeance cuts two ways." She glanced at the handle of her meat cleaver projecting from the oversized sheath snugged against the skirt of her saddle. She raised her eyebrows mockingly and twitched her wide, sensuous mouth in a grin before she turned her back on them. She knew Juan would empty the shotgun into them before they could pull their own pieces, but she felt certain they wouldn't try to shoot her. They were mean as tan-yard dogs, and no doubt of it, but not vicious. She'd seen enough of the vicious ones to know the difference. She figured she'd see a lot more of those before much time had passed.

" 'Sufficient unto the day is the evil thereof,' " she murmured while they rounded up their cows and trampled as wide a swath as possible through the corn on their way out.

"*Gracias, Señora.*" The farmer bowed, graceful as a grandee, and put his hat back on, sending his dark face into deep shadow.

"*Por nada.*" Then she added, also in Spanish, "Have you horses or cattle to sell?"

The farmer shook his head, disoriented by the fact that a *yanqui* could speak Spanish. "*Apaches los robaron todos.*" He made an elaborate apology for the discourtesy of allowing the Apaches to steal his cattle, leaving him none to sell her. Then he invited her to eat at his table, to sleep by his hearth, to drink from his well for as long as she and her friends and generations of her unborn children desired. When Cruz and the others approached, Sarah introduced them.

"Ramón here has offered us shelter," she added. "Seems he and his family usually sleep with relatives in the village there." She nodded toward the huddle of houses and the chapel among the trees. "On account of the Apaches being so rapacious. But he figures we'll keep them at bay." She winked at Cruz. "It's no wonder the black robes converted them so easily," she added in English. "If they think I can scare away Apaches, they're a gullible bunch, aren't they?"

Cruz shrugged. She believed it, too, everybody did, but she didn't say so. "Gullible?"

"*Crédulo.* Like the men who'll soon be leaving their worldly assets at your monte game."

The bell in the church tower began to ring, and people left the outlying houses to converge on the village plaza. The women carried flowers. The children waved flags made of bright cloths tied to sticks. Ramón's wife approached draping a black shawl over her head. Each of their three children carried their own small flags and flowers, as well as skulls molded of sugar, with black seed pods marking the eye holes. One of the skulls sported a small straw hat and clenched an unlit cigarette jauntily in its teeth.

"Is this the first of November?" Sarah asked. "*¿El Día de los Muertos?*"

"*Sí.*"

"We're in time for the party then." No one could celebrate death the way the Mexicans did. But then, she thought, who would want to? "And we can say a few words of thanks to God for bringing us through the desert."

"The priest will make a *Te Deum* and a Mass of Intercession too," Ramón said.

"For relief from the Apaches?"

"Against the cholera." Ramón set off for the village with Sarah alongside and the rest trailing behind. "The *gringos* bring it with them. It prowls the country like a starving wolf."

Mother Goose

>———I———<♦>———⊖———<♦>———I———<

"**G**OOD LORD ALMIGHTY!" SARAH WORE HER OLD
calico dress, but she crossed one leg over Jake's saddle
anyway, as she had seen Zachary Taylor do hundreds of times.

Under the star-bright sky the gold-rushers' encampment seethed
and quivered a couple of miles southeast of the American settlement
across the river from the Mexican town of El Paso del Norte. It reminded her of a huge anthill her horse had kicked once while following Taylor's troops through a Florida savannah of longleaf pine
and saw palmettos.

Each caravan of travelers had circled its wagons and gathered inside to cook and visit, to mend gear, hang out wash, and air out the
barrels of flour. Almost everyone tossed their debris and garbage
outside the ring. And they had trampled under foot and hoof every
blade of grass for miles around. Even now, at night, Sarah could hear
the syncopation of axes at work on the cottonwoods along the river.

Sarah rested her elbow on her thigh and surveyed the welter of
wagons, tents, tarps, and sagebrush lean-tos illuminated by the
campfires. The firelight outlined the profiles of men, women, and
children, but night erased the colors that gave individuality to their
clothes. Shadows filled the hollows of their faces, making them look
strangely alike.

Sarah spoke over her shoulder to Cruz, who shared Jake's broad
back with her. "I do believe every sly-eyed opportunist from east of the

Mississippi could hardly delay to button his trousers, he being in such a lather to reach the easy pickings in this mob." She said it in English, her Spanish, as good as it was, proving inadequate for the occasion.

"Easy pickings." Cruz rolled the words around in her mouth. She liked them. She poked Sarah in the ribs, above and to the left of her bustle. "Will we find easy pickings here, Western?"

"You can stake the *hacienda* on it, little sister."

They passed makeshift corrals of cattle and oxen and the picketed horses and mules, then entered the noisy haze of smoke from the creosote bush, sage, and greasewood burning in the cookfires. The valley teemed with humanity, much of it in motion, as though the bewitchment of gold declined to let them rest even at day's end. The few children in camp darted about like lizards. Shouts and song and the quarrels of dogs and cats mingled with fiddles and flutes. Somewhere in the throng a banjo scuffled with a melodeon. The melodeon was losing.

They heard laughter, too, a lot of it, from travelers who had arrived barefoot and blistered, ailing and hungry, and who knew they faced more months of peril in the wilderness ahead. People who had watched their oxen sicken and die, who had had to abandon everything they owned in the wind-scoured wastes between the Pecos River and here. For Sarah the frantic gaiety had a familiar tone. It reminded her of the mood of soldiers on the eve of a battle.

As they passed campsites, they heard English, of course, in a variety of accents. They also heard German and Spanish, French, and Indian dialects from both north and south of the Rio Grande. Some tongues they couldn't identify at all.

"Beats the Tower of Babel, doesn't it?"

"The Tower of Babel?" Cruz asked.

"I'll explain it later."

Then Cruz heard Gaelic. She stiffened and looked around until she spotted the men sitting at a small fire near a collection of handcarts. For the most part they wore flat wool caps and patched linsey-woolsey shirts, vests of coarse homespun, checked wool trousers, and brogans. Cruz slid off Jake's back.

"*Spalpeens,* by the look of them." She smiled up at Sarah. "Potato diggers, mowers, reapers. Like my James. Maybe they knew him in the old country."

"They won't understand Spanish, you know." Sarah feared they would bring on the sadness again for Cruz. It was never far off anyway. A scrap of song, the creak of saddles as men settled into them, the call of a bugle—they all could start the memories. Sarah saw the tears glittering in Cruz's eyes at just the sound of their talk. "They probably don't even speak English."

"James taught me some words in his language."

"You still remember them?"

"I remember everything about him," she said softly. "I remember everything he ever said to me."

"I'll be over yonder then, taking the measure of the half-shark, half-alligator, half-weasel breed."

"The gamblers?"

"Exactly."

"I'll see you there." She moved off among the wagons toward the fire.

Sarah watched Cruz walk into the fire's light and greet the men in Gaelic. They all stood, snatched off their wool caps, crushed them to their ragged flannel shirts, and answered with a courtesy that approximated reverence. They had the look of men confronted unexpectedly by an angel in the road, and unsure of the protocol. Cruz took a bundle of her hand-rolled cigarettes from the drawstring bag at her waist and distributed them. When Sarah could see a ring of glowing dots surrounding her, she left, satisfied that no harm would come to her. She went in search of the gamblers.

They were easy to find. The click of their cards sounded like a field of autumn crickets. The games went on by candle and torch, lantern and rushlight, in tents or on blankets laid out in the open. Other men clustered at the tailgates of the whiskey sellers' wagons. The talk here was louder, harder, the laughter spiny, fortified and honed by the whiskey sellers' wares. Horses, mules, dogs, and the occasional pig wandered about. The heaps of refuse made a Rackensackers' bivouac look like a model of tidiness. As Sarah rode among them, she started a wave of whoops and catcalls and propositions rolling along with her. She ignored them all.

She could detect in their faces every possible mix of race and nationality—American, German and Mexican, Indian and African, Scandinavians with eyes like sea ice. Skin hues ranged from parchment-pale to the ebony tinged with copper of an African and Indian union. She saw the occasional frock coat unbuttoned to show a satin waistcoat a-dangle with a gold watch chain; but most men wore flannel shirts and canvas trousers. More than a few sported feathers and bear claws, hawk bells, fringes and patches, rags and menace. Dirt, grease, and old blood lacquered their leather breeches and hunting coats to a black patina. They bristled with knives, hatchets, pistols, bludgeons, even swords, usually army issue. Sarah suspected that the frock coats' owners had stilettos or pepperbox pistols stuck in the tops of their high boots. This was a place where anything could happen and probably would before long.

Even their animals had a dissolute look to them, as though the cows would have no compunctions about consorting with a mule or a horse. Jake laid back his ears at the sight of them. Sarah leaned forward to rub the base of his ears and tug them affectionately.

"Such a hotchpot of deadbeats, desperadoes, and Salt River roarers as I ever hope to see," she confided in him. "Decency must sink to her knees and plead for mercy in their company." He shook his head and snorted in agreement.

As she passed a wagon, she didn't have to be able to read to know that the blue letters on its side spelled "U.S. Army." Parked next to it was one of the government's traveling forges. Sarah smiled. The owner wasn't around, but Sarah would have wagered the last silver peso in her bustle that he wore the blue trousers of his old army uniform, and that stripes of dark blue on the sleeves of his faded tunic marked where he had torn off his sergeant's insignia. She would even have bet that a sparse, short fringe of the threads that had held the chevrons in place still outlined where they had been.

The chaos that surrounded her and pressed in on her made her uneasy. She felt a stab of longing for the army, for its order and pride, the sense of duty. She did not want to live among people who lacked an overarching code of honor, whose only goal in life was to enrich themselves.

She was distracted from her thoughts by a young woman walking away from her, striding through the confusion of men and animals. Against the November night's chill she wore a castoff army jacket that reached halfway to her knees. Her pale hair rippled past a waist that Sarah's hands could almost have spanned and rode the sway of her slender haunches. She carried a small cloth satchel whose shoulder strap let it ride at her hip. As she glided barefoot past a blaze of cottonwood logs, the firelight behind her threadbare skirt silhouetted the scissoring of a lithe pair of legs. With each stride the thin calico swirled and clung to her hips, thighs, calves, and ankles. Heads turned and conversations stilled as she passed. Even without seeing her face, Sarah could tell she was young.

She doesn't belong here, Sarah thought.

She wasn't surprised when a shaggy individual in a raccoon hat, greasy shotgun chaps, and a dirt-colored flannel shirt caught her arm. She tried to free herself, but he yanked her to him. She turned away to avoid the bristly kiss he'd intended for her mouth and it scraped her earlobe. He shook her so hard the strap broke on her satchel. She held on to it with one hand and dug in her heels as he hauled her toward a nearby wagon.

"Reckon we'd best hamper the man, Jake."

But Jake was ahead of her. With a bray he lunged forward, scattering the knot of hounds quarreling over a bone. He snatched the man's hat and tossed it out of the way. Then he sank his teeth through the flannel shirt and into his shoulder until they scraped against the bone. The man screamed. He reached for the pistol stuck into the front of his *chaparerros*, but Sarah kicked it out of his hand, damaging his fingers in the process. She caught the young woman's arm between elbow and shoulder and swung her, one-handed, behind her on Jake's back.

"Hold tight." Sarah didn't know why Jake was so riled, but she did know he hadn't finished yet.

The girl twined her arms around Sarah's waist. Jake released his grip on the miscreant's shoulder and Sarah kicked his sides to urge him into what he liked to consider a canter. On the way past he dropped his head, folded up in the middle, and kicked with his hind legs. He drove his hooves into the man's stomach, doubled him over, and sent him flying into the fire. His friends pulled him out and pounded out the flames, but Jake was well out of earshot before he had sucked in enough wind to swear.

"Thank you, Western."

Sarah turned around at the sound of Nancy Skinner's voice. "Dear Lord, child, is it really you?"

She pulled Jake to a stop and the two of them dismounted. When she put her arms around Nancy, the fragile bones felt like so much kindling. She buried her cheek in the silkiness of her hair and relished the pressure of her thin arms around her. Then she leaned back and looked at her.

Nancy's small mouth still could not encompass her white, even teeth, and so her lips stayed slightly parted as if in constant wonder, her jaw pushed forward as though she were tasting the world. Her eyes shimmered like candlelight through pale blue silk. The old army tunic still bore the insignia of the Third Artillery. It couldn't hide the fact that her breasts were larger than Sarah would have expected in one so thin. The child had become a woman. She must be fifteen years old at least.

"I thought never to see you again, Western," Nancy said. "I reckoned we might die here, my sisters and I."

"Why were you trucking with this riffraff?"

"They're the ones with money." She held up the satchel. Sarah could see the familiar angles of a deck of cards and a monte box under the cloth. "They belonged to a gambler who's dealing out cards in hell now most like, but I figure the devil supplies the deck there. So I took 'em to make my way with 'em."

"Did your mother send you here?" The thought made Sarah furious. By the light of a campfire she could see the violet hollows of hunger around Nancy's eyes. She would give Bertha such a tongue-lashing when she saw her.

"The Asiatic cholera took her, and her man too."

"I'm so sorry, child." Sarah held her close again.

When they backed to arm's length, Nancy stared into Sarah's face and alarm was plain in her eyes. She could see that Sarah looked ill. She had watched more folk than her mother die of cholera. They would be healthy in the morning, screaming in pain and writhing with convulsions by afternoon, dead by nightfall.

"You look peaked yourself." She laid her hand on Sarah's cheek to see if her skin felt hot.

"It's only a touch of fever. It tries to overrun me from time to time." Sarah looked around. "Where are the sprats?"

Nancy pointed toward a train of Conestogas. Sarah led Jake first to the Irishmen's fire, though, and stood in the shadows, savoring the joy on Cruz's face when she saw Nancy. Then the three of them headed for the circled wagons. Sarah didn't notice the Irishman who stood in the shadows and, with a look of longing, watched Cruz go.

Sarah could see that a woman had come along with this train. Inside the ring of wagons two ladder-backed chairs and a rocker sat on a braided rag carpet laid out on the bare earth. Tin cups, dishes, and spoons were stacked on a makeshift table of wooden crates. A canvas awning sheltered all of it. One side of the canvas was fastened to the top rim of the wagon's bed, the other tied to two tall poles. Someone had tacked a yellowed print of *The Last Supper* to the side of the wagon. Sarah felt as though she had wandered into someone's parlor after a tornado had blown away the walls and left the contents intact.

The owner of the rocker appeared carrying a bucket of water. She couldn't have been more than thirty-five, but a snowy streak of hair flowed back from her left temple. She had a long face and nose, thin lips, no chin, and a spindly neck. The nose, neck, and high, wide bosom reminded Sarah of a goose.

"Nancy, you were to fetch water. And I told you not to wander," she said. "There're too many of the ungodly out there waiting to tempt the innocent. You set a bad example for the little ones. Joesph is looking for them now."

"Mrs. Bushrod, these here are my old friends, Mrs. Borginnis and Mrs. Murphy."

Mrs. Bushrod surveyed Sarah from bottom to top, then proceeded to assess Cruz. "And where would Mr. Borginnis be, madam?" Apparently Cruz didn't merit that much curiosity.

"Only God and the devil know that, Mrs. Bushrod. I expect the devil sees him on a more reg'lar basis." Sarah smiled at her. "It's kind of you to take in the young ones."

"We've only just arrived ourselves, and found them looking like perfect urchins. We offered to take them with us, but the oldest one insists they will make their own way."

"Cruz and I have known the Skinners awhile. They can come with us."

"They need discipline. They're wild as Indians. And shamefully unchurched."

"Mrs. Murphy and I will see to it."

"Mrs. Murphy is Catholic, I would suppose."

"We both are."

Mrs. Bushrod looked as though she had a great deal more to say on the subject of churching and the evils of Catholicism. And, by the way, if Mr. Borginnis was dead how did his widow intend to make her living? Sarah headed her off.

"I reckon we should round up the little ones before the night gets any older. We have a long way to travel tonight."

Nancy took a turkey-bone whistle from her pocket and blew a shrill blast on it. Her three sisters came at a trot soon after, the latest baby, Margaret, jouncing on ten-year-old Caroline's hip. Sarah held her arms wide.

"Western! Cruz!" The children flung themselves at both of them, running from one to the other to hug them.

Sarah finally managed to gather all of them into her arms. Her family had been returned to her. She didn't intend to lose them again. That she was less than a stone's cast from indigence herself didn't occur to her.

"Look at my puppy." Seven-year-old Fanny held out the smelly, wriggling creature, and Sarah and Cruz both admired her.

"We're going to California." When Caroline put her hands on her hips, she looked very much like her mother. "They let children pan the sweepings from the saloons and the bawdy houses there. They collect thousands of dollars in gold dust that the men drop."

Mrs. Bushrod put her hands over her ears and rolled her eyes. "You see what I mean, Mrs. Borginnis? Shameful talk."

"Come along, girls." Sarah lifted Caroline, Fanny, and little Diana onto Jake's back. Fanny held the puppy, who immediately fell asleep.

Cruz took off her shawl, folded it diagonally, and knotted it into a sling. Sarah put the opening over her head and arranged the knot in the middle of her chest while Cruz settled Margaret in it so she rode against Sarah's back. She, too, was soon asleep.

"Where will you be staying?" Mrs. Bushrod folded her arms across her bosom, as though to keep the contents of her shirtwaist from prying eyes.

"With a family in Socorro."

"Mexicans?"

"Yes, ma'm."

"You be careful they don't steal from you. They're all thieves, I hear."

Sarah looked down at her, sad that the woman's charity had such foolish limits to it. " 'Judge not, that ye be not judged,' Mrs. Bushrod," she said softly. "And Mrs. Murphy and I thank you for looking out for the girls."

"Weren't no trouble."

Cruz led Jake away, followed by Nancy and Sarah, who planned to make sure no one intent on trouble followed them from camp. Nancy didn't look back.

"Nancy calls Mrs. Bushrod 'Mother Goose,' " Fanny said when the light of the woman's cookfire had faded behind them.

"You should've thanked her, Nancy," Sarah chided.

"She just wanted us as servants."

"It was kindly of her to offer you a place at her board nonetheless. We all have to work for our keep."

"She's glad to be shut of us. Of me anyways. Mr. Goose is always wanting to pray with me so he can lay his paw on my leg. Sometimes he gets so fervent I have to use both hands to remove it. And her saintly son Joseph keeps trying to sneak under the blanket with me. He's all the time brushing up against me."

"What's El Paso like?"

"El Paso del Norte is the town on the Mexican side of the Rio Grande. I haven't been there, but it looks nice. Over here there're just a few herders' huts. Before all these *gringos* arrived hardly anyone lived there, and now everything in the way of supplies has been bought or stolen, eaten or broken."

"We'll find what they've overlooked." Sarah glanced behind her and saw a figure trailing them on foot in the shadows. She cocked her Colt and leveled it at him. "Step out where we can see you."

The man held his hands out to the sides, fingers spread to show they were empty, and moved into the moon's pale light. He said something in Gaelic, and Cruz halted Jake and turned to look at him.

"He's one of the men I spoke with earlier," she said.

"What's he want?" But Sarah already knew. He had the same look in his blue-gray eyes that she had seen in James's when he first saw Cruz. In fact, he looked remarkably like James.

"He says he means no harm," Cruz said, "but only wants to keep us safe."

"Do you want him to dog us to Socorro?" Sarah asked.

Cruz hesitated. "I think so," she said softly.

"What's his name?"

"His name is Rhett."

When she said Rhett, the roll of her tongue on the "r" made it sound like "debt." Good Lord, Sarah thought. Another Irishman to bring ruin down upon us, though he'll probably keep us laughing in the process.

"Rhett Murphy," Cruz added.

"Murphy?" Sarah sighed. "I should've known as much."

Sarah beckoned him to join them. He walked beside Cruz all the way to Socorro del Sur.

The Pass

WITHIN MONTHS, THE BEDRAGGLED SETTLEMENT ON the American side of the Rio Grande swelled with thousands of gold-seekers on their way to California. After surviving the trek across hundreds of miles of Texas desert, all the newcomers lacked were life's necessities. The place had no name yet, though some had begun referring to it as the Pass. It was the jumping-off point, the last opportunity to stock up on information, supplies, and the mischievous brew called Pass Whiskey. To the west lay the notch in the mountains, the gate to the wilderness beyond. People here had the distant stare of pilgrims seeking the promised land. This place didn't qualify.

For Sarah the Pass was gold mine enough. She had spent the winter finding provisions and selling them to travelers. Now, even her sources were exhausted, which was why she was talking to this particular trader.

The man's frayed canvas galluses clung by one button each in their struggle to hold up trousers that sagged around legs remarkably meager for someone of his bulk. He leaned back from his belly as though he were carrying a bass drum in front of him. The trousers dangled so low under it that Sarah wondered if he had managed the journey from St. Louis without them falling around his ankles. She knew that if she ventured behind him she would see more of his terrain than she cared to.

What passed as springtime in other parts made no pretense of being anything but summer's oven here on the Rio Grande. In the April heat the trader had unbuttoned his coat and the upper half of his shirt, neither of which were up to the task of containing his torso anyway. A snarl of black hair spilled out of the opening. It reminded Sarah of a certain captain's wife's tautly stuffed settee. The horsehair always poked out from the saber cut inflicted on it during the officers' anniversary celebration of Andrew Jackson's victory at New Orleans.

The trader hawked a fat oyster from the depths of his chest and spit it, without a care for its trajectory, onto Jake's left hoof. "I'll take that sorry mule off'n your hands."

"Right after the fight," Sarah muttered, distracted by her inspection of the wares he was offering for sale.

She ignored his prairie dog bark of a laugh. The man couldn't distinguish a threat from a jest. She continued her survey of the red-eyed, sunken-sided, fly-infested cows he was touting as prime beef.

"Well, now, because you're a fellow Missourian, Sarah, darlin' . . ."

She glanced up with a look that would've chilled one of Jeff Davis's juleps and he reconsidered his approach.

"Mrs. Borginnis, you won't find better beef here."

She didn't point out what he already knew, that she wouldn't find any other beef here nor within a day's parched ride of here.

"Looks like you neglected to graze them between here and Santa Fe," she said. "If I had a couple sticks I could tap out 'Hail Columbia' on those ribs." She walked among the cows with Nancy close behind her. Margaret and Diana watched owl-eyed from their lofty perch on Jake's back. "I never saw such a muster of pinkeye, foot-rot, gotch ear, red-water, blue tail, and bloat. Not to mention staggers and spangs. Two of those misfortunate creatures would be required to make a shadow."

She primed the back of her throat for her own supply of west Texas phlegm and launched it in an arc that landed it at the very edge of the crudely patched toe of his boot. It wasn't a gesture he would've expected from a beautiful woman, even one six feet tall. He stared at the dusty puddle as though to find some new species swimming in it that eastern academics would insist on naming after him.

"Twenty *pesos* each," he said finally. "Take 'em or leave 'em."

"I'll give you forty-five *pesos* for those three." She knew it was more than they were worth, but the emigrants were willing to pay any price. Food, tobacco, whiskey, they all cost eight times the going rate back east. "Bring them to the back door of my place." She almost smiled at the notion of a door on the tent that sheltered her latest enterprise.

Nancy caught the cheek strap of Jake's hackamore, though he would have followed her into a barn fire. She led him into the roiling current of pack trains and pedestrians, horses, oxen, dogs, and every conceivable form of wheeled vehicle. The traffic surged along the rutted sandpit that passed for a street in the collection of tents and makeshift shelters that presumed to think of itself as a town.

Sarah followed Jake and the girls, not noticing when folk jostled her and stared at her. She looked glumly at the sacks of beans and corn that barely reached the rims of the wicker baskets tied to Jake's sides. The baskets swayed seductively with the wide undulations of his hindquarters. Like an old bawd parading on the Fourth of July, she thought. Like me.

A point of vertigo expanded into a vortex behind her eyes, and she closed them to keep the ground from tilting under her feet and the world from spinning out of control. She put a hand on Jake's hot, dusty rump and steadied herself.

Lord, don't let me fall sick again.

She willed the dizziness back to a manageable case of lightheadedness. But the throbbing in her skull refused to quit and the incessant shouts and the rumble of wheels, the tattoo of hammers and axes and saws intensified it. A cloud of dust from a train of Conestogas swirled around her and she coughed.

" 'I've traveled the mountains all over,' " she sang. The tune was "Old Rosin the Bow," but the gold-rushers had adapted the words.

> And now to the valleys I'll go,
> And live like a pig in the clover
> In sight of huge mountains of snow.

The girls pitched in on the chorus. The music cheered her as it always did. She paused on the bluff above the river and looked wistfully across to the Mexican side, at the fields and gardens of El Paso del Norte with its big houses of the wealthy old families and the

white adobe tenements of the lower classes. The whitewashed spire
of the Church of Our Lady of Guadalupe reminded her of a fairy
castle. She wanted to walk in the shade of the quince and peach and
pear trees and listen to the wind romp among the new leaves. No
one except Cruz and Maria had attempted a garden here, and the
gold-rushers' cattle and draft animals had eaten everything they
planted. The hordes had trampled to dust every other bit of greenery.

El Paso del Norte radiated a fragile tranquillity and shabby gentil-
ity, but it lay in another country, and besides, Sarah knew that the
merchants and farmers had hardly an onion left to sell there. This
no-name hamlet below the Rio Grande ford was where commerce
bumped and churned along as noisy and contentious as a wagonload
of cannonballs.

"Nancy."

"Yes, ma'm."

"Tell Cruz I'm seeing to that sick fellow by the river."

"The one with the Asiatic?"

"Yep."

"Do you want I should come with you?"

"No need. I'll be back shortly." Sarah took a canteen of water, a
small pail of beans, and a packet of tortillas wrapped in sacking from
one of the baskets. "See that Maria and Lara start supper on time.
And tell Hanibal to butcher the lop-eared cow soon as it arrives.
She looks to have a hoof on the threshold of Death's back door
anyway."

"Yes, ma'm."

Sarah waved and smiled reassurance as Nancy looked back over
her shoulder. "Don't fret about the cholera, child. This fever's been
trying to kill me all winter and it hasn't succeeded yet."

Sarah watched the traffic wrap them in its dust before she started
down the trail to the river. Spring rains had swollen it, and the official ford lay farther upstream. The rocky path here was too steep for
wagons and so had been spared the destruction they caused. Nor
had the axes been at work. The river flowed slow and green and
three hundred feet wide. Deep stands of willows along its banks created emerald galleries, cool and shady. Birds sang in their branches.
A gangly heron the color of a blued gun barrel lifted himself labori-
ously off the mud flat, his loose-jointed wings popping like distant

musket fire. His feathers flashed iridescent in the sunlight as he lazed away downriver.

Sarah found the little raft in its hiding place in the grass. She took off her shoes and skirt and shirtwaist, rolled them into her gutta-percha pouch, and set them in the middle of the raft. Dressed in her linen chemise she pushed the raft out of the grass and poled it across, beached it, and dressed again.

She found the herders' tiny hut of gnarled mesquite logs and grass thatch the same as she had left it, but her patient now sat slumped against the front wall, his legs sprawled. He looked dead and she put her hands on the pistols in her belt. She made a complete circle where she stood, searching the buff-colored landscape for signs of Apache.

"The Injuns just left, Miz Borginnis." The man tilted his head back so the sun's ray could warm his face and grinned wanly at her from under the brim of his hat.

"Apach?"

"I reckon. They paid me a social call. They said that seein' as how I wasn't a Mexican they wouldn't kill me. They was right neighborly."

"You're coming back to the hotel with me, Knapp."

"I'm a jug-totin,' slow-thinkin,' flea-crackin' farm boy from North Carolina, ma'm. I can't abide noise and crowding."

"You aren't staying here. They mightn't be in such a convivial mood next time." She slid a stump over to sit on. The herders who had used it as a chair for years had worn its top smooth and slightly concave. "Besides, the first time you saw our little metropolis your comrades pronounced it paradise."

"We had wandered in the desert far longer than Moses, Mrs. Borginnis, and were like to've perished. Hades would have resembled paradise if the devil's wife served us cold beans and warm whiskey."

"You look less like the ragged remnants of an ill-spent life than when last I saw you."

"Your venison broth was a tonic."

"Here's more kitchen physic, then." Sarah set the pail on the ground next to him.

His hands still shook so she scooped beans onto a tortilla and rolled it for him. While he ate, she talked. Farm boy or not, a man sick and alone for a week could benefit from the sound of a human voice, especially a woman's.

"That colonel of yours, he should be stood against a wall and shot for unalloyed stupidity. Leading a hundred men, green as catnip, into a thousand miles of desert with scant supplies and not a notion of how to follow a trail or ford a river."

Knapp, his mouth too full to talk, looked toward heaven.

"You say the good Lord carried you through. Well, the colonel made a rough ride of it, didn't he? Three of you never walked out of that wilderness." Sarah brooded for a few moments. "They will set themselves to it, won't they, the ignorant and the slothful and the vainglorious. They take out across the continent as though to a neighbor's house in the next valley, and when they pitch into trouble they expect everyone else to drop reins and rush to their aid. I never thought to see the like of it. They act like a bunch of schoolboys on holiday."

When he finished eating, she left the canteen for him. "I'll bring the mule for you to ride, Mr. Knapp."

She headed back to the river. She put her outer garments back into the bag and started across. She had almost reached the other side when she saw the soldiers watering their horses at the river. She gave the pole a push that sent the raft into the shallows. She leaped out and splashed ashore, soaking herself on the way. While they stood stunned by the sight of her, she grabbed each of them in turn and gave them a wet hug, lifting the lighter ones off the ground. She shook the lieutenant's hand and hugged him again. He turned a charming shade of pink and straightened his uniform when she finally released him. Two large wet circles darkened the front of his coat where she had pressed against him.

"Lieutenant Henry Chase Whiting, Corps of Topographical Engineers," he said. "We're on a reconnaissance, looking for the best route into the area."

"Is the army behind you, Lieutenant?"

"They should be coming within a few months."

"You are heaven-sent." Sarah kissed him on the cheek. "What units? Third Artillery? Second Dragoons?"

The lieutenant shrugged. "The men who ride the desks haven't passed that information to us."

"No matter. I shall have accommodations waiting for them when they arrive."

As she watched them mount and trot north toward the ford, she began making plans. She would have a talk with Ben Coons this very afternoon. He was the most prosperous merchant in town. He had already announced his intentions to build a blacksmith shop, tavern, and store. He needed a partner who could run a hotel and restaurant, one the officers would find congenial. He needed her.

Her boys would want companionship too. As soon as she had a building instead of a tent, she could hire women to provide it. She began to think about ordering some furniture from Santa Fe.

As she left the river, she sang so loudly the birds took flight from the trees overhead.

Shipwreck and Indigestion

T HREE MEN THREADED THROUGH THE TRAFFIC IN THE
settlement now known by various names, the politest of
which was the Pass. The first two, tall, blond, and covered with
dust, slumped in their big Mexican saddles. They both looked to be
about thirty-four years old. They wore trousers of brown cotton
duck and black slouch hats with the brims turned down all around
to shed rain, in the unlikely event one should occur. One had on a
red flannel shirt open at the neck with a bandana tied there in the
heat of late April. The other wore a loose white cotton tunic like the
local farmers. He was so big, it must have been made especially for
him, to be big enough. The one in red flannel was quick to smile.
The one in white cotton almost never did. Otherwise they looked
remarkably similar.

They carried bowie knives at their belts and Colt pistols in their
saddle holsters and who knew what all up their sleeves and trouser
legs. They were lean and tanned, and in their eyes shimmered the
intense blue of a summer Texas sky. They appeared weary to the
bone, but they had the look of men at home here, of Texans. Their
dust-caked, ladder-ribbed horses seemed to have all they could do
to carry them.

Behind them a mustang, the brick red color of east Texas clay,
minced along as though he had taken a short jaunt through shady
country instead of traversing the five hundred harsh miles between

here and San Antonio. His rider was the color and texture of his buffalo-hide moccasins. He wore a doeskin breechclout that clung desperately to his skinny shanks. A few pitiful eagle feathers protruded from above his skimpy gray braid. A filthy white cotton vest hung from the narrow promontories of his shoulders. Two of him could have occupied the vest comfortably. He observed everything around him without taking his eyes off the space between his pony's notched ears. People stared at him, either in curiosity or hostility, but he didn't seem to notice.

The Texan in the red flannel glanced over his shoulder at the Comanche sitting erect on the bare back of his peevish little cayuse. "What do you suppose would be required to tucker the chief out?" His drawl made it clear that if he was a Texan it was by way of Tennessee.

"The devil, after having tried for the past two months to do just that, is probably asking himself the same question."

"Friend," the red flannel called to a boy pushing a barrow of firewood, "where can a man find a feed bag and a pile of straw?"

"The American House, on the plaza. Ask for the Great Western."

"The one become notorious in the late war?"

"I shouldn't doubt it. Have a care, though. She's about the roughest fighter on the river."

"We shall endeavor not to offend." The red flannel tipped his hat and tossed the boy a nickel. He snagged it from the air with one hand as though it were a fly, bit it, and grinned.

The Texans found the plaza taking shape out of dust and chaos. Like an acorn transforming inevitably into an oak tree, adobe and pine board buildings were rising around the same sort of square found in towns on both sides of the border. Next to the spindly skeletons of Ben Coons's tavern and his blacksmith shop stood the largest of the framed buildings, its pine boards still bright yellow and redolent of resin. It sported a sign reading "American House." It boasted a narrow veranda and a few chairs whose occupants looked as though they had been there so long the hotel had been built around them. They sat balanced on the hind two legs of their chairs. Their feet were propped on the railing and they were intently studying their boots.

The Texans had just dismounted and handed the reins to the

Mexican lad who waited at the stoop when the door flew open with a force that slammed it against the front wall. Several men dashed out and scattered for cover. John Glanton appeared from the dim interior, his small, rail-thin body framed in the doorway. The Texans leaned against a wagon bed and watched.

"You low-lived, chicken-stealing dog." Glanton raised an old muzzle-loading pistol and sighted on an individual trying to pull all his limbs out of sight behind a bale of calico not big enough for the task.

Suddenly Glanton's boots rose a few inches off the threshold. Astonishment replaced the fury in his ferret eyes.

"John has broken so many laws," one of the Texans remarked to the other, "it should not surprise us that he has found a way to violate the law of gravity as well."

Still hovering above the ground, Glanton floated into the sunlight. When he did, the Texans could see that a large woman in a crimson velvet shirtwaist and riding skirt and the yellow cap of the Third Artillery held him suspended by his shirt collar and the crossing of his galluses. Her grip on his suspenders wedged his wool trousers well up into his bony crotch. He swore creatively at her as she cleared the doorway and pitched him into the street as though emptying a bucket of slops.

He landed headfirst and still swearing, but tucked and rolled neatly. He pulled his feet under him and in one flowing motion stood with the gun still in hand. He whirled and leveled it at Sarah. The boy who'd been holding the Texans' horses had already bolted forward with a stirrup and handed it to her. She twirled the leather strap around her head and let it go, the heavy oaken loop at the end pulling it through the air like a locomotive.

"Looks like Goliath has got ahold of little David's sling," the red flannel remarked to the white cotton.

The stirrup hit Glanton's hand and sent the gun flying. Someone made a rush for it, but Sarah drew her Colt and pointed it at him. "Touch that, you possum, and you're giblets." He retreated and she stuck the pistol back into the waist of her skirt. "Mr. Glanton, pick up your piece and take your business elsewhere."

He seemed to ruminate on it. He would have shot her, that was plain, but with her gun put away he could not claim self-defense.

And there were witnesses. He wasn't used to operating with witnesses. He picked up his pistol, turned on his heel, and sloped off. The spectators edged away in the opposite direction, keeping a wary eye on him. When Glanton was in the mood to kill someone, he wasn't particular about who it was. The stable boy retrieved the stirrup and fastened it to the Texan's saddle before leading the horses around back.

Sarah noticed the two men and touched the brim of her yellow cap in salute. "It was time to shoot the puppy."

"I never heard John Glanton referred to as a puppy." The man in the red flannel took his hat off and ran a hand through his wheat-straw hair.

"When trouble starts, I cut the instigator from the herd, mortify him in front of the others. Settles 'em all down."

"Begging your pardon, ma'm—" The red flannel remembered the boy's admonition to treat her with respect, though he would have anyway. "—that could get you killed."

"I don't plan to live forever, but while I'm here I like to keep the fools in my company to a minimum."

"I've never heard John Glanton called a fool either," said the one in the white shirt. "He's a savage son."

"Oh, he's well west of savage," Sarah said. "He's positively meat-axish, he is." She took off her cap and shook her head, letting the gold wisps in her dark red hair catch the sunlight. "But my scalp is the wrong color for a bounty, so I reckon he thinks it not worth his while to take it." She surveyed them from the dusty toes of their boots to the crowns of their hats, taking in the lean muscle, tanned cheeks, straight spines, blue eyes, and yellow hair in between. "You boys brothers?"

"Yes, but of different mothers and fathers." The one in the white shirt gave a courtly bow. "You must be the famous Mrs. Borginnis, the heroine of Fort Brown."

"Don't believe what you read in the newspapers." But she looked pleased. "You have a military air about you yourselves."

"My friend here is John Ford, though we generally call him Rip," the white shirt said. "He was Colonel Jack Hays's adjutant. My name is Robert Neighbors, from San Antone."

"You both look like the tag end of famine."

"We've been scouting a trade road for the past two months." Ford grinned. "We've been blown up and shot down, suffered shipwreck and indigestion."

"My backbone has acquired saddle sores." Neighbors's expression went from noncommittal to doleful.

"You been riding on your back?"

"No, ma'm. My stomach's rubbed it raw."

"Well, come inside. We'll pitch some fodder into the hole." Then she noticed the Indian still astride his pony. "Old Owl, you old rooster." She strode over and held out her hand. He grabbed it and pumped it until her breasts jiggled. He liked the effect so much he solemnly shook it some more. "Hanibal," she bellowed. "Take Mr. Owl to the kitchen and see how much that tough little rind of his will hold." She turned back to the Texans. "I see the fox is running with the hounds."

"We thought that having Old Owl along would dissuade the rest of the brunets from taking potshots at us," said Neighbors.

"Can't say he's worth his weight in alkali dust as a hunter though," John Ford added. "We almost starved."

"That isn't his fault. The rushers have eaten everything that can't move out of the way," Sarah said, "or driven the rest off."

Still talking, she led them into the lobby. It loomed gaunt and echoing and seemed as busy as the street outside. The floorboards creaked underfoot. Servants rushed up and down the stairs and workmen shouted orders at each other. Behind the reservations desk a Mexican on a scaffold used a chewed mesquite twig to smear bright pink pigment onto the loaf-sized breast of his creation, a large woman reclining naked, but for a diaphanous wisp of blue drapery, on a flat rock. From the neck down she was more than amply endowed, although above that she resembled the Madonna.

Ford nudged Neighbors. "You ever seen anything like that?"

"Not since I was weaned."

Shouting orders to the kitchen, Sarah ushered them into the restaurant, lit bright as the day outside. The back wall was only rough-framed and sunlight streamed through the openings, throwing a large grid pattern of light and shade onto the sawdust-covered floor. On the other side of the spindly uprights, carpenters hammered at the cornerposts and beams of a line of rooms and connecting hallway. Sarah seated them at the end of a long table covered with cotton blankets of the sort found in the market in El Paso del Norte across the river.

In a corner a lovely Mexican woman dealt monte while half a dozen small children, two of them towheads and the others dark, played on the floor nearby. The men gathered at her table had the air of worshipers at the altars of both Chance and Beauty. She herself concentrated on the cards. The fact that she had no thought of being desirable made her all the more so.

Neighbors and Ford watched a carpenter walk through on his way to the wall that was going up. He was slender with dark hair and blue-gray eyes, Irish by the look of him. As he passed behind the monte dealer, he touched her hair with the tips of his fingers. She glanced up and the two exchanged the look of people at ease with each other.

One of the children, a dark-haired girl, left the others and ran after him, hugging his legs until he picked her up. He threw her, laughing, into the air, caught her and returned her to earth. He blew her a kiss as she ran back to her mother's monte table.

Sarah saw it too and gave a small smile. Rhett Murphy hadn't brought ruin on them yet, and didn't seem likely to do so. Life was full of surprises.

"I reckon food is the first order of business," she said.

"Yes, ma'm."

Sarah shouted an order in Spanish and a voice responded from the kitchen.

"Supper tonight is chicken and dumplings and will cost you fifty *centavos*, a bed seventy-five," Sarah recited. "A hammock is twenty-five, the floor a dime. We can fetch beer or bourbon from Coons's place. And I have a cache of the local wine and brandy that are excellent, and some *pulque* that'll grow hair on your teeth."

"Have you a room?" Ford asked.

Sarah glanced at the outline of a hotel taking shape on the other side of the uprights. "I will by sundown."

"I trust we shall not have to share it with half the population," Ford said. "In Washington City I was promised the room that Senator Stephen Douglas had just vacated. I found that the room con-

tained seven men in four beds. I told the proprietor that I did not intend to sleep with the entire Democratic party."

"My friend here will also require a candle," Neighbors added. "He
reads the Bible every night as a promise to his mother."

"We have candles." Sarah eyed the monte table and the winnings
piled in front of Cruz. She leaned down so that only Ford and
Neighbors could hear her. "Soon we shall have a pneumatic washtub
for a hot bath. The little journalist there, Lewis Allen, is the one
who wrote all those lies about me in the papers. He and his rubber
tureen went through the siege of Fort Brown with me. He's been losing all afternoon and has just staked it."

Three men rushed in, waving a silver peso. "Western, we must
have the badger."

"They've all been emptied and scrubbed."

"The boys can fill it again."

"I'll have to charge you two dollars for the hire of it. You brought
it back dented the last time."

They rummaged through their clothing and produced a handful
of small Mexican coins, nickels, a pewter collar button, lint, and a
cigar. She nodded and they dumped the booty and the *peso* into the
pouch hanging from her waist.

"Lupe," she called out. "Bring the chamberpot."

"You all are running the old badger-fight dodge?" Ford asked.
"Taking bets on whose dog can kill the badger in the sack and getting some greenhorn to yank it out on a rope?"

"You bet." The man grinned, giving them a view of gums as red as
the wallpaper in a bordello parlor. "The boys are priming the sucker
now, a drummer just in from St. Louis and as full of fizz as a scuttle
of spruce beer in dog days."

Sarah leaned close when she handed them the chamberpot. "See
the little dandy at the monte table there, the one with the stiff
dickie and so much fur about his jowls he looks like he's taking a bite
out of a possum?"

They gave the journalist a slanting look.

"He's always game for a take-in. Only wait until he's lost his
bathing tub."

They left, turning as they went to admire the young woman who brushed past them. They admired her so much they kept walking backward and collided with the wall. Her skirt was short enough to reveal a snug pair of ankles and the beginnings of shapely calves. She had tied the drawstrings of her white blouse so loose the neck of it had fallen off her shoulders and rode low enough to provide an inspirational view. She strode past them with her chin and chest jutted out, giving her an air of defiance and invitation. The cascade of her shiny black hair brushed a bottom as round and taut as a pair of india rubber balls. She looked as though she would bounce if dropped on it.

"If you gentlemen will excuse me, I have to interview a prospective employee." Sarah beckoned the young woman toward the kitchen.

Ford and Neighbors watched them go.

Ford shook his head in wonder. "Taken as a whole, the daughters of Mexico must be the most beautiful examples of their sex in the world."

Neighbors sighed. " 'Beauty is truth, truth beauty, that is all ye know on earth and all ye need to know.' "

"Keats," Ford said. " 'Ode on a Grecian Urn.' " They had passed many hours on the trail playing this game. He took his turn. " 'Beauty is nature's brag and must be shown.' "

"An easy one. John Milton's *Comus*." He had his own favorite lines from the same work. " 'What need a vermeil-tinctured lip for that, love-darting eyes, or tresses like the morn . . .' "

"Good Lord, educated men?" Lewis Allen waved a hand at Cruz indicating that he wanted no more cards dealt him and came over to the table.

"Won't you join us?" Neighbors said. "Western says you're a journalist."

Allen pulled up a chair and dusted the seat before he sat his white linen trousers on it. He put his patent-leather-gaitered feet primly side by side under the table and extended his hand across it. "Lewis Leonidas Allen, formerly of *The Spirit of the Times*."

"Robert Neighbors." Neighbors shook his hand. It was moist and soft.

"John Ford." Ford wanted to ask him if he had lost his bathing tub, but refrained. "Formerly?"

"I'm a novelist now."

"Really?"

"Yes. I'm writing a romance of the west. I'm calling it *Wayworn Wanderer in the Western Wilds*."

"You don't say." Ford got the twinkle in his eye that Neighbors knew well.

"I do say."

"I know a man you should meet then."

Allen took out his memorandum book and pen from the satchel at his side. He uncorked his inkwell, dipped the point, and held it poised to note the information.

"His name is William Wallace. He's the greatest Indian fighter that ever lived. He has a ranch on the Medina River outside of San Antone. He can tell you everything you need to know."

"And then some," Neighbors added.

"I'll surely look him up."

Sarah arrived with their trenchers, each containing half a chicken buried under an avalanche of dumplings and gravy.

"Western, these fine fellows tell me I should look up William Wallace for my research." Allen stood and collected his stove-pipe hat from the peg by the door. "So, I'm off to San Antone. I trust you'll enjoy the use of the pneumatic bathing apparatus."

"Keep your hair on your head, Lewis."

"I shall endeavor to do that."

When he had gone, Sarah turned to Ford and Neighbors. "Would that be Bigfoot Wallace who leads a company of Rangers?"

"The same," Ford said.

"Oh Lord. Sam Walker told me about him." She threw her head back and laughed. "From what I've heard about Bigfoot, he'll pull the scribbler's leg till it's two feet longer than the other one. He'll run him through the chaparral while he's about it till there's not enough left of his clothes to patch a musket ball."

"I suppose that's a possibility." Rip Ford looked as though the possibility had only just occurred to him and Sarah laughed again.

Dream with the Angels

S ARAH CLOSED THE INN'S HEAVY DOOR BEHIND HER
and hugged her old army overcoat to her against the December wind. It seemed much colder here, 175 miles, more or less,
north of El Paso. She paused before stepping into the quiet street off
Socorro's main plaza. She wasn't ready yet for the gaiety in the
plaza, the folk promenading there in dusk's pastel light. She wasn't
in the mood to join the giddy anticipation of the Feast of the Nativ-
ity. Instead, she watched the lavender shadows reach across the
blunt walls of the houses lining the east side of the street.

The weather was too cold to bathe in an irrigation ditch as was
the usual practice, but her skin still tingled from the scrubbing she'd
received. The servants had carried the big wooden tub to her room
with great ceremony. The scalding water had washed the dust off
and with it the disquieting memory of the long pull she and Juan
had made through the arid waste referred to as *Jornada del Muerto*.

Leave it to the Mexicans to grin, unflinching, up into the hairy
nostrils of death and call a thing by its most fitting name, she
thought. *Jornada del Muerto*. Day's Journey of the Dead Man. *Jornada*
also meant a passage through life. The Life's Journey of the Dead
Man. She let her mind follow the notion.

We're all traveling our dead man's journey. We just don't know it.

It wasn't like her to indulge in what she called the sulks. But the
close of a day was an occasion for melancholy anyway. It was a time

to assess what she had or hadn't accomplished since sunrise, to know that eternity had crept a day closer, to lose the light that kept the creatures of darkness and imagination at bay. It was when distractions retired for the night, leaving memories to sadden her. She was a week's journey from Cruz and the Skinner girls, alone near Christmas in a mud-daubed way station on the Santa Fe trail. It affected her.

Her life, she realized, was full to the brim, and empty. She was thirty-three years old and not since Jack Borginnis died almost five years ago had a man looked at her with tenderness in his eyes. With lust, yes. With passion, maybe. With tenderness, certainly not. Love was too puny a word to describe the divine insanity she craved. She wanted a man for whom she would happily do anything, up to and including dying. If she hadn't found him by now she never would— of that she suddenly felt quite certain.

She decided to go to the *cantina* that Juan had eyed as they drove the wagon through Socorro's narrow streets. She would find Juan there, no doubt, and his company, taciturn as it was, would be a comfort. She would take solace at a rickety table with a bottle of the local wine in front of her while the slow current of Spanish flowed over her and riffled around the rocks of occasional laughter.

She found it on a narrow street several blocks away. Except for the faded lettering painted on the front wall, it was indistinguishable from the adobe houses flanking it. She pushed open the door. As in a thousand other such places, the smoke from badly trimmed lantern wicks had darkened the whitewashed walls and the latticework ceiling. A crucifix and pictures of the saints decorated the walls. A mahogany bar, polished by the forearms of generations of barroom philosophers, paralleled the left side of the room. Acrid clouds of tobacco smoke drifted, collided, and mingled overhead.

The talk hushed in a stunned collective intake of breath when she entered, as it always did. But tonight the hum took up quickly again and people returned their attention to the soldier standing in front of a chopping block in the center of the room. A game of *peloncillo* was about to commence. Tables had been moved to the walls to make room for it. Sarah hung her coat on a peg and stood where she could have a side view of the soldier through the crowd and over it.

Juan glanced at her from the other side of the room. He hitched his shoulders in a shrug under the striped wool blanket he wore over his shoulders. He raised one woolly-bear eyebrow, made a little pout with his lower lip, and tilted his square chin toward the *yanqui*. It was an eloquent statement of admiration on his part.

The soldier towered head and shoulders over everyone but Sarah. His hair glowed like corn silk in the lantern light. His trim, curly beard was the color of pale honey. He wore his blue wool uniform trousers tucked into a dragoon's high black boots. His army tunic hung on the back of a chair. The chair was heavy and ornate, with a far more illustrious past than its present. The soldier's gray wool under-shirt was unbuttoned halfway down his broad chest, exposing a golden mat of hair. His sleeves were rolled tight around the hard muscles of his arms.

The master of ceremonies set a small loaf of dark brown sugar, narrow end up, on the block. It had the same structural fortitude as limestone. That and its conical shape made the game difficult. The player had to slice it in one stroke so that at least two ounces were left on one side. The dealer carried a small scale with him to weigh the results.

"*Dos tlakos.*" The dealer held up two fingers. "*Dos.*"

The soldier dug into his pocket, opened his hand, and looked for the *tlakos*, bits of silver worth about a cent and a half each. The clos-est of the spectators crowded nearer to give him advice. They pushed the coins around the rough plateau of his palm with the tips of their fingers and triumphantly retrieved the proper ones. All the while they earnestly explained the monetary system to him, though it was obvious he didn't understand Spanish.

Sarah wanted to walk through the crowd to stand next to him. She wanted to put the tip of her finger on his palm and trace the ge-ography of his heart there. The desire to touch him was so fierce she thought it would stop her own heart. She stood absolutely still and watched him in a world that had, in an instant, changed irrevocably.

The man in charge offered the soldier the old machete that con-testants usually used. He waved it away and drew his saber out of the scabbard hanging from his belt. The rattle of it brought Sarah a rush of nostalgia for mounted charges, the scream of horses, the rumble of cannon carriages, the thunder of artillery, for the valor and the tumult of war.

The prospect of sudden death is what puts the fizz into life, she thought. She assessed the soldier's high-set haunches and the long, powerful legs that so superbly filled his rough wool trousers. Sudden death and one other thing, she decided.

Holding the hilt in both hands the dragoon raised the saber, halting the tip of it an inch below the mesquite beam not far above his head. With muscles steady he stood poised, oblivious to the hush that fell over the room. Sarah held her breath along with everyone else.

When she thought he had gone off wool-gathering, he brought the blade down so fast she almost missed its descent. It sank into the block and half the cone of sugar lay on each side of it. The crowd cheered. He picked up his winnings, the sugar that was worth about six cents, and put it into a feed sack. The dealer laid out another cone and he sliced it as precisely as the first.

He went through fifteen sugar loaves while the celebration around him grew more boisterous. Finally the dealer threw his hands up, palms out, to show he had no more. The soldier took his jacket from the back of the chair, shrugged his bulky shoulders into it, and buttoned it. Sarah watched him, her thoughts churning. He hadn't noticed her. How could she get his attention? What should she say? The usual pleasantries wouldn't do here, she knew that.

He picked up the sack and a bottle of local brandy in one hand and his chair in the other. He carried it effortlessly through the spectators, all of whom wanted to clap him on the back. Sarah would have been content just to watch him the rest of the night. She had known a few men as large, but never one so graceful. He moved like music playing, like a slow waltz.

A guitarist began an agile tune with a two-four beat. The clientele, unaware of the magic set loose in the room, went back to their *pulque* and their games of monte and their analyses of how the world should work but didn't. Juan seemed absorbed in his conversation with a trio of *arrieros*, but Sarah knew he was keeping an eye on her.

Good Lord, he's young, Sarah thought as the soldier approached. He couldn't be more than twenty-five. West of the Mississippi that was an advanced age, which made her ancient at thirty-three. She wanted to move deeper into the shadows, afraid that he would speak to her, terrified that he wouldn't.

Her own anxiety and the shortcomings of physiology blinded her, made her unable to see herself as she was. The fever that had pounced on her repeatedly during the winter and spring had trimmed the weight she had added in Saltillo. Her broad shoulders and the curve of her hips under her dress of sage-colored velvet made her waist seem small. Her hair glowed like a halo of soft fire against the dark wall. After a season indoors, her skin had resumed its pale color, with a sprinkling of freckles across her small nose. To any man with a discerning eye, her strong jaw, emerald green eyes, and full lips bespoke humor and strength and tenderness.

He stopped in front of her, set the chair and the sack down. He graced her with a smile that made it plain a rogue and a knight shared tenancy behind eyes the dark amber of old whiskey. He held out his left hand, palm up, and she laid hers on it, her heart pounding. He put his right hand on her waist and whirled her into a polka. People moved to the edges of the room so the two of them could maneuver. They hopped and dipped and turned until the room began to revolve around them.

When the song ended he led her, laughing, to a table, pushed away a stool with the toe of his boot and replaced it with the chair. He bowed, and with a courtly sweep of his arm invited her to sit. With a nod she hoped looked regal and composed, she started for the chair and was startled when he moved it closer to the table while she was still inches above it. She had seen officers help their wives into chairs but she'd never had the experience herself.

He sat across from her, leaned his forearms on the table with his palms spread on the rough boards, and stared straight into her soul. She laid her left hand over his right one, feeling the warmth of skin and flesh and the ridges of bone. When he covered it with his other one, she could feel his spirit enter her like a warm current. They stared at each other while the guitarist concluded a lengthy ballad with a flourish of ruffles and arpeggios.

Several men had imbibed enough courage to propose a *corrida* with a neighbor's bull before the soldier stood and pulled Sarah gently to her feet. He put on his forage cap, then helped her into her coat. He picked up the bottle and the sack of sugar. They walked out, arm touching arm, into a town asleep under a sky exploding with a celebration of stars.

Sarah tried to clear her head long enough to think. She didn't want to wake the household at the inn, nor face their curiosity. She knew the soldier most likely shared a tent with two or three other men, so she took his hand and led him to the wagon yard behind the inn. Juan had been sleeping there, but she figured he could find other accommodations.

Jake grunted a greeting. He sidled to the end of the line tied to the wheel of Sarah's Studebaker wagon, as though he had spotted a succulent tuft of grass in the trampled dirt behind them. He made a grab for the soldier's hat, but his victim sidestepped and rapped the tender end of his nose with the bottle of brandy. Jake pulled his lips up over his teeth, raised his jaw to the amused moon, and let out an aggrieved bray.

Sarah laughed. "I don't recollect anyone ever dodging that old sinner." She held Jake's hackamore with one hand so he couldn't retaliate and kissed the soldier lightly on the mouth by way of congratulations.

She had to rise a little on her toes to do it. He set the sack and the brandy on the wagon's tool box. When his arm encircled her waist, she understood what it must feel like to swoon. Joy and desire were so acute she shivered with them. Thinking that the cold had affected her, he opened his coat and pulled her into the heat of him and into the aroma of smoke and horses. She dropped her hold on Jake and slid her arms around him, savoring the span of him and the solidity.

She spread her hand wide to touch as much of his back as she could and laid her cheek in the hollow at the base of his neck, entranced by the flutter of his breath across her temple. Beneath the rough linen of his shirt she felt the slide of hard muscle across his shoulder blades. She leaned more against him, unable to trust her legs to hold her up, and knowing he could support her weight with little effort.

He moved his hand to the nape of her neck and up under her hair to the base of her skull. The pressure of his fingers there drew her head back. He kissed her gently, tentatively, as though they had eternity to finish what they had started. She closed her eyes and concentrated on the touch of his lips, his breath mingling with hers.

Still kissing her he unbuttoned her coat, put his hands under her collar, slipped it off her shoulders and arms, and tossed it into the wagon.

He let down the tailgate and loosened the drawstring that held the canvas cover closed. He put an arm around her back and one behind her knees and swept her up, damping her protests with another kiss. He stood on the crate set there as a step and lifted her into the wagon. She knelt in the nest of blankets and looked out. The darkness inside made the circle of starlight framed by the canvas cover seem bright. Through the opening Sarah saw Jake, teeth bared, make another lunge, but the soldier caught his mouth in his hands, clamped it shut, and shoved Jake back on his haunches. Sarah chuckled at the startled look in the mule's eyes.

The soldier climbed in and pulled the tailgate closed behind him. He and Sarah knelt in the nest of blankets and the big bison robe while he kissed her temples, eyes, and mouth, her jaw, chin, neck, and shoulders. Going mostly by touch, they removed each other's clothing.

Jake made one last assault, a kick to the side of the wagon that rattled the hardware. When that received no response, he lowered his mouth over the abandoned brandy bottle with the delicacy of a Beacon Hill socialite. Holding it steady with his lips, he worked the cork loose with his teeth. He upended it and let the contents gurgle down his throat. He picked the sack up by one corner and dumped the contents onto the ground. After he had eaten every grain of sugar, he retired to the end of his picket to sway on his feet, belch, fart, and mutter dire threats at his rival in the wagon.

→ ←

Dawn was still hours away but a rooster was loudly anticipating it when Juan and his new friends, the muleteers, left the *cantina*. The musician decamped with them, his guitar slung upside down on his back. They careened down the dark street, their progress marked by a fanfaronade from the local dogs. They entered the wagon yard and stumbled across the rough ground.

"¡Ay, Dios!" One of the muleteers, his eyes wide, froze in his tracks and crossed himself, twice. "Un fantasma."

"*¿Dónde, amigo?*" Juan looked for the ghost among the wagons that loomed like beached ships around them.

The muleteer pointed a trembling finger at Sarah's Studebaker. In the spectral glow of the moon and stars, an apparition fluttered pale and diaphanous at the tailgate. It billowed in the fitful breeze, collapsed, then swelled again, as though caught on a nail and struggling to free itself.

Juan walked closer, squinting it into focus. By the time he realized it was Sarah's long linen camisole, he no longer needed it as a sign to tell him to seek other lodging. He'd already noticed Jake, ears laid back against his head, glaring at the wagon that rocked with a steadily increasing rhythm on its iron springs. The Studebaker bounced with such vigor, in fact, that Juan crossed himself at the wonder of it.

He grinned. "*El amor.*"

The others stared, awed, at the wagon's gyrations.

"*¡Dios mio!*" the guitarist breathed as the springs' squeals increased in volume and tempo. "*¡Qué barbaridad!*"

Juan beckoned him closer to confer. The musician nodded and tugged the leather strap across his chest so the guitar slid into position there. He strummed the first bars of "Beautiful Golden-Brown Girl," while his companions sucked in the quantities of dung-scented, wagon-yard oxygen their lungs would require to do it justice. They attacked it, singing loud and high and almost on key, and dogs far and near ceased barking and began to bay. Jake abandoned his vigil long enough to swivel one eye at them, then he too pointed his nose at the moon and started to sing.

Sarah and her soldier hardly heard them. This third time they arrived at their destination together in a rolling, thrashing, slippery passion of arms and legs. The sensation that exploded at the base of her belly, that vibrated in her bones, that made her knees tingle was more than physical. She managed to throw her head back and release a long, sighing moan before the exultation set her to laughing and crying all at once.

The soldier shuddered and fell across her, his hair brushing her cheek, his heart thumping in rhythm with hers. They lay that way while the serenaders drew out every word of their song as though their hearts would break were it to come to an end. When the last note finally died away, they lifted their hats in salute and bowed to the silent, motionless wagon.

"*Buenas noches, enamorados,*" Juan shouted. "Dream with the angels," he added in English.

Sarah heard them troop out of the yard, stumbling over picket lines and wagon tongues and singing as they went. When Jake had fallen silent and only the most distant dogs still howled, the soldier lifted himself onto his elbows. He brushed Sarah's lips with his.

"My name is Sergeant Albert Bowman." He spoke with a slight German accent.

"I'm Sarah Borginnis."

"I'm very pleased to make your acquaintance."

Author's Note

The 1850 census taken in Socorro, New Mexico, lists Sarah's household as consisting of Juan Duran, the five Skinner children, two servants, and a boy. The same census lists Albert Bowman as a sergeant born in Denmark, though he later listed his place of birth as Brunswick, Germany. Sarah took Bowman's name and shared the next fifteen years of her life with him.

After Albert's discharge in 1852, he and Sarah ended up in Yuma, Arizona, which didn't become a U.S. territory until 1863. For centuries the ford near the confluence of the Gila and Colorado rivers had been used by native peoples, bandits, conquistadors, missionaries, bounty hunters, trappers, soldiers, traders, and settlers. John Glanton and his gang took Indian scalps in the area and robbed emigrants until natives killed him and his men at the crossing in 1850. That made the government decide to establish a permanent military presence called Camp Yuma.

The commanding officer, Major Samuel Heintzelman, mentioned Sarah often in his journals, and finally decided to board with her. Sarah ran a boardinghouse for the officers again, hiring others to do the cooking and washing. Albert took an interest in prospecting.

In 1854 an officer and his wife tried to take Nancy Skinner to San Diego as a servant. To keep that from happening, Sarah moved her operation across the river into Sonora, Mexico. Heintzelman gave her a tent to use until Albert could construct a new building. It wasn't a very promising site, a salt cedar flat swarming with mosquitoes, lizards, and snakes. But she soon established a going concern. To Heintzelman's consternation, boatloads of officers crossed to drink at her place.

Sarah also began providing an additional service, and Heintzelman, angered by it, referred to her in his journal as a "strumpet." He wrote that he was provoked at her because she "had a peon come to join her and made the woman swim across the river, or rather she stripped all to her petticoats and got astride a balsa and clasped it with her arms whilst an Indian pushed her across." It was good advertising for the latest amenity of her house, and, actually, stripping to one's petticoats in the river must have felt good.

One lieutenant claimed that the heat caused the hens to lay hard-boiled eggs. Kit Carson declared that the general area was "so desolate and god-forsaken that a wolf could not make a living on it." An eastern newspaper described Yuma, then known as Arizona City, as "so hot in the summertime that the wings melt off mosquitoes, and flies die from the excessive heat of the scorching sun. The Indians cover themselves with mud, the Mexicans crawl into their little huts, while the Americans stand in the Colorado River half the day and keep drunk the rest of the time to avoid death from melting."

Nancy Skinner, meanwhile, had more than one suitor among the soldiers. As Heintzelman put it, "She had three more strings to her bow" besides Sergeant Burke, who was, in Heintzelman's opinion, "the best of them." She married Burke on her seventeenth birthday in two big celebrations that Sarah threw, both in the army's camp then across the river at her place. An "Ethiopian Band" played for the dancing, and the entertainment included songs and recitations. A couple of Sarah's female employees helped make up the dance set. Liquor was plentiful and "some rather misbehaved," according to Heintzelman.

Lieutenant Sylvester Mowbry came to Yuma in 1855 after leaving Utah in a rush when he attempted to seduce Brigham Young's daughter-in-law. He took up with a seventeen-year-old Mexican woman who was living with the Great Western. He wrote about Sarah that "Among her other good qualities, she is an admirable 'pimp.' She used to be a splendid-looking woman and had done 'good service,' but is too old for that now."

In 1856, after five years' captivity with the Mojave Indians, Olive Oatman, her chin tattooed, arrived in Yuma and stayed with Sarah. On the way to Tucson, Sarah accompanied Olive to the site of the massacre of her family and helped her bury the bones still scattered there. From Tucson, Sarah and Albert moved to Patagonia, near Fort Buchanan at the head of Sonoita Creek. A boy who lived there at that time described her: "She packed two six-shooters, and they all said she shore could use 'em, that she had killed a couple of men in her time." He remembered Sarah telling him "there was just one thin sheet of sandpaper between Yuma and hell."

The 1860 census listed three people living with Sarah and Albert, a fifteen-year-old Mexican girl named Lucia and her two-year-old daughter, and a fifteen-year-old Indian boy from New Mexico. In 1863 a lieutenant mentions that she had adopted and raised them.

The Civil War required the withdrawal of U.S. troops from the west in 1861, leaving the citizens at the mercy of bandits and Apache. The U.S. Army did maintain a presence at Yuma, and Sarah stayed there, though she sent her women back to Mexico for safety. Two travelers reported visiting the Great Western's house and finding her the sole inhabitant of the town. Earlier, Augustus Knapp, whom Sarah nursed back to health in El Paso, wrote that she was "able to hold her own in all circumstances. She was held in dread by the Mexicans who lived all about there; and as she was usually armed . . . no one ever thought of troubling her." The Indians "seemed to hold her in perfect awe and had a superstition that she was a supernatural being."

Sarah continued running her business throughout the Civil War. Albert was listed as owner or part-owner of dozens of mining claims around Yuma. An 1864 census listed him as single. He and Sarah had apparently separated. In 1866 he had taken up with Mary Jane Bailey, whom he married in 1868. Sarah died at about age fifty-three at Fort Yuma on December 23, 1866. One source said she died from the bite of a tarantula, which seems unlikely unless she was hypersensitive to a specific antigen.

She was buried according to the Catholic rite and with full military honors in the Fort Yuma cemetery. In 1890, when all the bones there were disinterred for removal, hers were said to be the largest. They now rest at the Presidio in San Francisco.

The *Arizona Gazette* reprinted a copy of Sarah's obituary in July of 1867. It said, in part:

> She was familiarly known as the "Heroine of Fort Brown," and was at several battles during the war, caring for the wounded. Blunt and unguarded of speech, she was yet the possessor of a kind heart, and whatever her failings, engendered by wild associations, many will remember with grateful feeling the acts of tenderness bestowed by her on themselves and associates in that inhospitable section . . . Brave and determined almost beyond precedent, she lost no opportunity of doing good which offered itself.

Sarah Bowman really was the Great Western.